A FOLLY OF PRINCES

David, Earl of Carrick, High Steward of Scotland and heir to the throne, rose to his feet, took a pace forward and then halted, his face flushed with wrath, wine and his immediate exertions. It was a remarkable face, beautiful rather than handsome, winsome with a delicacy and regularity of feature that any woman might envy, yet somehow redeemed from any suggestion of weakness by the firm mouth and chin, the keen sparkling eyes and the autocratic carriage of the head. There was nothing of femininity there – nor indeed was the lower part of him, so very patently on display at the moment, lacking in any degree in masculinity; much the reverse, in fact, being at least complementary to the lady's plenitude. At nineteen years old, David Stewart's manhood was not in doubt.

"Jamie Douglas!" The apparition raised a hand to point an accusing finger at the intruder – and suddenly, surprisingly, burst into a cascade of melodious laughter. "Jamie Douglas – only you, in all this realm, I swear, would so behave! Aye, and from only you, by God, would I bear with it! Well – what is it, man? Out with it?"

A Folly of Princes

The second volume of the
House of Stewart trilogy

Nigel Tranter

CORONET BOOKS
Hodder and Stoughton

PRINCIPAL CHARACTERS

In Order of Appearance

SIR JAMES DOUGLAS OF ABERDOUR (JAMIE): Illegitimate eldest son of the Lord of Dalkeith. Knighted at Otterburn.

DAVID STEWART, EARL OF CARRICK: Youthful High Steward of Scotland and heir to the throne. Later Duke of Rothesay.

SIR DAVID LINDSAY OF GLENESK: Brother-in-law of the King. Later 1st Earl of Crawford and Lord High Justiciar.

SIR ALEXANDER STEWART OF BADENOCH: Eldest and illegitimate son and heir of the notorious Earl of Buchan, Wolf of Badenoch.

LADY ISABEL STEWART: Sister of the King. Former Countess of Douglas, now married to Sir John Edmonstone of that Ilk.

LADY ISOBEL DOUGLAS, COUNTESS OF MAR: Countess in her own right. Sister of the late 2nd Earl of Douglas and wife of Sir Malcolm Drummond.

MARY STEWART, LADY DOUGLAS OF ABERDOUR: One of the King's illegitimate sisters. Married to Jamie.

ROBERT III, KING OF SCOTS: Great-grandson of the Bruce.

QUEEN ANNABELLA DRUMMOND: Wife of the King. Sister of Sir Malcolm Drummond.

THOMAS DUNBAR, EARL OF MORAY: Son of one of the King's sisters.

ROBERT STEWART, EARL OF FIFE AND MENTEITH: Next brother of the King, Governor of the Realm. Later Duke of Albany.

HAL GOW, called OF THE WYND: Perth blacksmith and sword-maker.

GEORGE COSPATRICK, 10TH EARL OF DUNBAR AND MARCH: Great noble.

GEORGE DOUGLAS, EARL OF ANGUS: Young noble. Founder of Red Douglas line. Half-brother of late Earl of Douglas.

LADY MARGARET STEWART, COUNTESS OF ANGUS: Mother of above. Countess in her own right.

SIR HENRY PERCY (HOTSPUR): Great English noble and champion. Heir to the Earl of Northumberland. Warden of the Marches.

ARCHIBALD (The Grim), 3RD EARL OF DOUGLAS: The most powerful noble in Scotland. Also Lord of Galloway.

JAMES DOUGLAS, LORD OF DALKEITH: Statesman and wealthy noble. Father of Jamie.

JOHN PLANTAGENET, DUKE OF LANCASTER (JOHN OF GAUNT): A son of Edward III. Uncle of Richard II of England.

MARIOTA DE ATHYN (or MACKAY): Mother of Sir Alexander Stewart of Badenoch. Late mistress of the Earl of Buchan.

LORD JAMES STEWART: Younger son of the King. Later James I.

BISHOP GILBERT GREENLAW OF ABERDEEN: Chancellor of the Realm.

SIR MALCOLM DRUMMOND OF CARGILL AND STOBHALL: The Queen's brother. Husband of the Countess of Mar.

BISHOP WALTER TRAIL OF ST. ANDREWS: Primate.

SIR WILLIAM LINDSAY OF ROSSIE: Fife laird. Kinsman to Lindsay of Glenesk.

SIR JOHN DE RAMORGNIE: Fife laird. Prolocutor-General.

ARCHIBALD, MASTER OF DOUGLAS: Eldest son of Archie the Grim, 3rd Earl.

SIR WILLIAM DOUGLAS OF DRUMLANRIG: Illegitimate son of James, 2nd Earl.

SIR ARCHIBALD DOUGLAS OF CAVERS: Illegitimate son of James, 2nd Earl.

KING RICHARD II: Deposed by Bolingbroke, Henry IV. Possibly an impostor.

DONALD, LORD OF THE ISLES: Great Highland potentate. Son of eldest of King's sisters.

SIR JAMES DOUGLAS, YOUNGER OF DALKEITH: Half-brother of Jamie. Husband of the Princess Elizabeth.

THOMAS STEWART, ARCHDEACON OF ST. ANDREWS: Illegitimate son of Robert II. Brother of Mary.

HENRY IV: Usurping King of England.

MURDOCH STEWART, EARL OF FIFE: Eldest son of Albany.

JOHNNIE DOUGLAS: Illegitimate full brother of Jamie.

DOUGLAS GENEALOGY

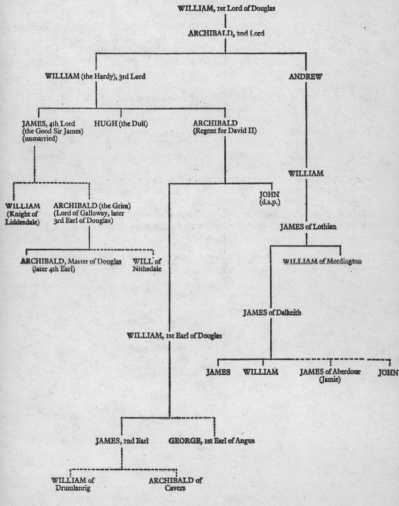

STEWART GENEALOGY

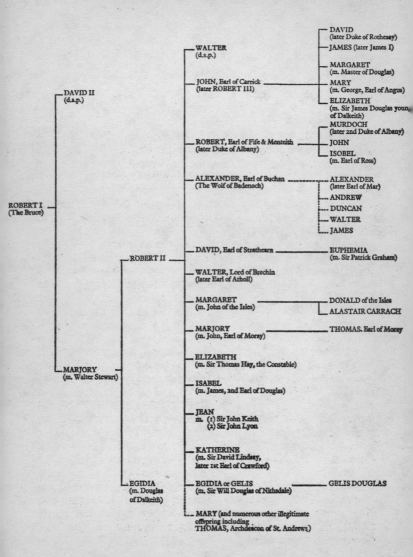

```
ROBERT I ──┬── DAVID II
(The Bruce) │    (d.s.p.)
            │
            └── MARJORY ──── ROBERT II ──┬── WALTER ──┬── DAVID
               (m. Walter              │   (d.s.p.)  │   (later Duke of Rothesay)
                Stewart)               │             ├── JAMES (later James I)
                                       │             │
                                       │             ├── MARGARET
                                       │             │   (m. Master of Douglas)
                                       │   JOHN, Earl of Carrick ── MARY
                                       │   (later ROBERT III)       (m. George, Earl of Angus)
                                       │             │
                                       │             └── ELIZABETH
                                       │                 (m. Sir James Douglas young.
                                       │                  of Dalkeith)
                                       │
                                       │   ROBERT, Earl of Fife & Menteith ──┬── MURDOCH
                                       │   (later Duke of Albany)             │   (later 2nd Duke of Albany)
                                       │                                      ├── JOHN
                                       │                                      └── ISOBEL
                                       │                                          (m. Earl of Ross)
                                       │
                                       │   ALEXANDER, Earl of Buchan ---- ALEXANDER
                                       │   (The Wolf of Badenoch)          (later Earl of Mar)
                                       │                                  --- ANDREW
                                       │                                  --- DUNCAN
                                       │                                  --- WALTER
                                       │                                  --- JAMES
                                       │
                                       │   DAVID, Earl of Strathearn ──── EUPHEMIA
                                       │                                  (m. Sir Patrick Graham)
                                       │
                                       │   WALTER, Lord of Brechin
                                       │   (later Earl of Atholl)
                                       │
                                       │   MARGARET ──┬── DONALD of the Isles
                                       │   (m. John of the Isles) └── ALASTAIR CARRACH
                                       │
                                       │   MARJORY ──── THOMAS, Earl of Moray
                                       │   (m. John, Earl of Moray)
                                       │
                                       │   ELIZABETH
                                       │   (m. Sir Thomas Hay, the Constable)
                                       │
                                       │   ISABEL
                                       │   (m. James, 2nd Earl of Douglas)
                                       │
                                       │   JEAN
                                       │   m. (1) Sir John Keith
                                       │        (2) Sir John Lyon
                                       │
                                       │   KATHERINE
                                       │   (m. Sir David Lindsay,
                                       │    later 1st Earl of Crawford)
                                       │
                                       │   EGIDIA or GELIS ──── GELIS DOUGLAS
            ┌── EGIDIA                 │   (m. Sir Will Douglas of Nithsdale)
            (m. Douglas                │
             of Dalkeith)              └── MARY (and numerous other illegitimate
                                           offspring including
                                           THOMAS, Archdeacon of St. Andrews)
```

I

SAINT JOHNSTOUN OF Perth seethed. Being the nearest town to the Abbey of Scone, where the coronations of the Kings of Scots took place, it was quite accustomed to being overcrowded on occasion. But today's thronging went beyond all experience and report. Not only the walled city itself, on the bank of Tay, but all its environs and surroundings, was so crowded with folk that it seemed that scarcely another could be crammed in; yet still more arrived by every road — and Perth was a great hub of roads and routes from all directions, the first point at which the long estuary of Tay grew sufficiently narrow to be bridged, the gateway to Scotland's North and East. It was claimed that 20,000 people converged on the town that October day of 1396. It was as likely an under- as an over-estimate. No King's coronation had ever drawn such a concourse.

Poor old King Robert was there, to be sure, third of his name — although his true name was John and he had only been crowned as Robert to capitalise on the fame of his mighty greatgrandfather, Robert the Bruce, John being considered an unlucky name for kings; which fame and capital he direly needed. He was installed in the Dominican or Blackfriars monastery, on the northern edge of the walled city, overlooking the wide, green levels of the North Inch, a favourite haunt of the gentle monarch, who himself was something of a monk by inclination. His Court filled the other religious establishments and best houses of the town — these too in much larger numbers than normally troubled to grace the presence of the self-effacing and studious monarch. His brother's, the Governor's Court, of course, was larger, but he had taken over Scone Abbey, three miles to the north, for the occasion, preferring always to keep his stiff distance from the King.

Sir James Douglas of Aberdour pushed and struggled his way through the crush of people in the narrow streets, seeking to preserve his patience and a modicum of good humour. Good humour was indeed all around him, the folk in holiday mood — galling for a young man on urgent business. He had left his horses and small escort behind at the Red Bridge Port, being there assured by the porters that he would by no means get them all through the press short of using the flats of their swords to beat a path — which would be likely to provoke a riot in present circumstances. He was not of an overbearing character but he *was* in a hurry.

Once out of Shoegate and High Street, into Meal Vennel, the going was easier, the crowds less dense; and by the time he was into Blackfriars Wynd there were few people to hamper him. At the north end of the wynd royal guards stood watch at the monastery gates; but Sir James was well known to all such and he was let through without question.

The Blackfriars monastery was a haven of peace compared with the packed city so close by. It was indeed an unlikely place to find within the perimeter of a walled town, open, spacious, with large gardens and orchards all around the conventual buildings, very rural-seeming for its situation, with pleasant paths and arbours, cow-sheds and dairies, stables, beehives let into the walling to supply wax for the chandlery, doocots with their strutting cooing pigeons everywhere. There were people here too, of course, strolling amongst the fruit-trees and rose-bushes, but these were courtiers and their ladies, in couples and small groups, not packed together in noisy, smelly propinquity like the commonality without. Not a few of the ladies especially smiled or raised eyebrows towards the hurrying young man, for he was attractive to the other sex, good-looking in a dark almost sombre way, tall and well-built, with an air of preoccupation that was alleged to intrigue womenfolk. He acknowledged their salutations civilly, with nod or brief word, without pausing in his stride. Only once did he smile, and that to his young sister-in-law, the Lady Elizabeth Stewart, second daughter of the King and wife to his own namesake and half-brother, Sir James Douglas, Younger of Dalkeith — and when twenty-six-year-old Jamie Douglas smiled, his sober, almost stern features were transformed and lightened remarkably. Getting a smile out of this young man was something of a ploy, indeed, at the Scots Court.

Making for the monastery guest-house, which the King had taken over for his own use meantime, the newcomer asked where was the Earl David, and was informed that the prince had gone over to the Gilten Arbour, to ensure that all was in readiness for the comfort of his father. This did not sound like the nineteen-year-old David Stewart, for whom comfort, the King's or any other's, did not normally mean much; but he hurried in the indicated direction nevertheless.

The Gilten Arbour was a summer-house, at the extreme northern edge of the monastery gardens, a rather special summer-house, more of a pavilion perhaps in that it was two storeys high, circular and with a wide balcony above a pillared portico all round, the whole decorated with gold paint, classical figures and signs of the zodiac, the fancy of some former Prior — a sports-lover presumably, for the upper storey was so contrived that it looked over the high town-wall here into the North Inch directly beyond, the hundred-acre riverside parkland which constituted the best disporting-ground and tourney-court in Scotland.

At the arbour door a single large and tough individual stood. He raised a cynical eyebrow at the visitor.

"He is . . . occupied!" he said. "Wearied of waiting. Do not go up, Sir James."

"I must see him. And at once."

"I tell you, he is not to be disturbed. Bide you for a whilie . . ."

"No. Stand aside, Pate. You have done your duty. Let me do mine. This is urgent. I come from the Clan Chattan camp. I am going up. Or would you, or he, prefer that I went to the Governor instead?"

"I warn you, he is drink-taken . . ."

"I never yet knew drink to blunt his wits. And I will risk his temper." The Douglas brushed past the other, and ran up the wooden stairs.

On the balcony, a woman's shoe and a silken bodice, none too clean, was preparation for what was to come. Feminine skirling choked off to breathless laughter, from near at hand, offered further guidance. There were two apartments on this upper floor. At the second, James Douglas rapped sharply on the door, took a deep breath, and stepped inside.

"Fiends of hell! How dare you! How dare you, I say — curse and burn you! God's eyes — get out!" Very strangely, despite the abrupt ferocity of that, the voice that spoke managed

11

to sound almost musical, mellifluous, without thereby lessening the anger.

"I dare for good reason," the other asserted, his own voice more raspingly gravelly than he knew. "And would dare still more, my Lord David, in your service and your royal father's, if need be!"

"Damn you, Jamie . . .!"

The room, simply furnished with a rustic table and benches, row upon row of stored apples on shelving around the walls, was a shambles. Clothing lay scattered, male and female; an upset wine-flagon spilled its contents, like blood, over the wooden floor; a bench was upturned, with a gleaming golden earl's belt flung across it; apples had rolled everywhere. In one far corner, on a spread cloak, a young man was half-rising, bare from the middle downwards, and under him sprawled a wholly naked young woman, notably well-endowed, all pink-and-white lush invitation and challenge, seeking to hold him down.

The two men stared at each other, the younger glaring hotly, the other frowning with a sort of determined concern.

"If the Lady Congalton will excuse me for a few moments," Douglas said stiffly, "I have matters for your privy ear, my lord, which will not wait."

David, Earl of Carrick, High Steward of Scotland and heir to the throne, rose to his feet, took a pace forward and then halted, his face flushed with wrath, wine and his immediate exertions. It was a remarkable face, beautiful rather than handsome, winsome with a delicacy and regularity of feature that any woman might envy, yet somehow redeemed from any suggestion of weakness by the firm mouth and chin, the keen sparkling eyes and the autocratic carriage of the head. There was nothing of femininity there — nor indeed was the lower part of him, so very patently on display at the moment, lacking in any degree in masculinity; much the reverse, in fact, being at least complementary to the lady's plenitude. At nineteen years, David Stewart's manhood was not in doubt.

"Jamie Douglas!" The apparition raised a hand to point an accusing finger at the intruder — and suddenly, surprisingly, burst into a cascade of melodious laughter. "Jamie Douglas — only you, in all this realm, I swear, would so behave! Aye, and from only you, by God, would I bear with it! Well — what is it, man? Out with it?"

"My lord . . ." Jamie glanced from the other's nether parts

to the still recumbent woman — who had now elected to place one small hand over the joining of her legs and the other amidst the opulence of her swelling breasts — neither of which achieved more than an emphasis on what was there.

"Never heed Kirsty," the Earl advised, apparently untroubled by his own state of undress. "She'll bide. Speak up — and stop nodding your head at yonder door. I am not going outside. I am not finished here, as even you can see!"

The intruder shrugged. "As you will. I come from Luncarty, six miles north. The Clan Chattan company is halted there. About thirty-five strong. They will come no further. They have been shadowed for some time, they say, by the Governor's men. They captured one and put him to the question. He revealed that the Governor was waiting, at Scone, requiring word of their progress. At Scone, between them and Perth, here. Sir Alexander Stewart is with them, and fears a trap. He has reason, after all! I tried to persuade him to come on, but he would not . . ."

"A plague on it! He has the King's safe-conduct."

"He requires more than that, my lord. He asks that you yourself come. With the royal guard for escort. Only so will he trust the Governor not to attack them."

"But . . . saints above! My wretched uncle will not assail them. He is a devil, yes, and hates us all. But he would not dare to interfere in this. It is *my* affair, mine and Moray's. With my father's agreement and blessing."

"This I told Sir Alexander. But he is not convinced. The Earl Robert imprisoned him once before, contrary to your word, and mine. He asks why the Governor should lie at Scone when all others are at Perth. If he smells knavery, can you blame him?"

"Curse them all . . . ?"

"To be sure. But curses will not bring Clan Chattan to the North Inch this day! It lacks but a bare two hours until the contest is due to start — so it will be late anyway. Sir Alexander says that he will wait at Luncarty until the hour set for the affrayment. If you, and the escort have not come by then, they turn back for their own Highland fastnesses."

"But, save us — what is Alexander Stewart that Clan Chattan comes and goes at his word? My bastard cousin — what has he to do with it?"

"They appear to trust him. Look on him as guide and protector. Against Southron treachery. In place of his dead

13

father. The Wolf was long their overlord, however savage his rule. These Mackintoshes, Shaws, Macphersons, MacGillivrays and the rest of the Clan Chattan federation, they have taken his eldest son in his place."

"Are other of his oaflike brothers with them?"

"No. Only Sir Alexander. With one Shaw Beg MacFarquhar, who seems to be their champion, and he they call *Mhic Gillebrath Mor*. Not the Mackintosh himself, Captain of Clan Chattan."

"Well, Jamie — we must pleasure them, I suppose. Since my own credit depends on it. If this contest does not take place, now, my name and repute suffers. And my intolerable uncle smiles — if smile he can! Which is no doubt his object in this business — to frighten off these Highlanders and so bring the entire project to naught. To my hurt."

"That same thought came to me, my lord. So — you will come?"

"I will not! I have more to do meantime — as you can see! — than to run to and fro at the beck of the unlamented Wolf of Badenoch's bastard! But I shall send him the royal bodyguard, to comfort his faint heart! You will take it, Jamie — and bring those clansmen to the North Inch, within the hour."

Douglas shook his head. "It will not serve, my lord. I myself suggested as much — but Alexander said no, that the Governor could countermand such escort, dismiss it. You, the heir to the throne, he could not countermand — you in person. So it has to be yourself . . ."

"I tell you it has not, man! Are you deaf? See you — take Moray. He is my cousin, the King's nephew. He will serve. Cousin to your Alexander too. If he will not have *you*."

Again the stern shake of the dark head. "The Earl of Moray has always been against Clan Chattan, in this feuding. He champions the Comyns, who are his own vassals. They would never accept their enemies' protector as escort."

"Damnation — who are they, this Hielant rabble, to refuse this earl and accept that? I'm minded to let my Uncle Robert at them! Teach them a lesson . . ."

"And lose your great contest? And bring your Lieutenancy of the North to an ill start indeed."

"God's sake, Jamie Douglas — you must ever have the rights of it! Ever the last word. Does that bonny aunt of mine, tied to you in wedlock, not find you beyond all bearing?"

14

A brief glimmer of his famous smile flickered across the other's sombre features. "She says so, yes — frequently."

"Aye — and much good it will do her!" The Earl David chuckled, himself again. "See, then — take Lindsay. My Uncle David, of Glenesk. He is here, at this Blackfriars — I saw him but an hour back. My father's good-brother. He will do as well as Moray. Better, for he is older, a seasoned warrior. And he does not love the Governor. Aye, Lindsay will do. Now, of a mercy, man — be off! This lady has been patient — you will agree? If she catches her death of chill, *your* blood her husband will be after! Myself, I was contriving to keep her warm! Eh, Kirsty?"

Douglas bowed stiffly. "I will do what I can, my Lord . . ."

"Do that, Jamie. And haste you. Hasten, both of us. You a-horse and me astride, eh?" As the other left the room to that silvery laughter, he heard the High Steward of Scotland add, "Now, lassie — let us see if we can raise this issue to its former heights, blackest Douglas or none . . .!"

* * *

The hard-riding company pounded northwards, parallel with Tay again, five-score strong, under no less than three proud banners, the royal Lion Rampant of Scotland, the red chevron on white of the earldom of Carrick, and the blue-and-white fess chequey on red of Lindsay — signs and symbols enough, surely to prevent anyone seeking to interfere with their passage, even in this ungoverned and ill-used kingdom. Jamie Douglas, leading the way, was now flanked by two somewhat older men, both dressed a deal more splendidly than he — Sir David Lindsay, Lord of Glenesk and Sheriff of Angus on his right, and John Stewart of Dundonald, Captain of the King's Body-guard, on his left. Both, oddly enough, were brothers-in-law, of a sort, of himself and of each other, for Lindsay was married to the King's lawful sister Katherine, John the Red was that sister's illegitimate brother by the former monarch, and Jamie's wife was the King's illegitimate sister Mary. King Robert the Second, the Bruce's grandson, had made up for his lack of prowess on the field or in the council-chamber by his prowess in the bed-chamber or anywhere else convenient, with fourteen legitimate children and innumerable otherwise. His grandson David but followed in the family tradition — although he had wits far in advance of his grandsire's.

Sir David Lindsay was none too pleased at being dragged away on this unsuitable and unnecessary errand at his nephew's second-hand command. He was a vigorous, stocky and powerful man in his early forties, the most renowned tourneyer in two kingdoms, lord of two-thirds of the county of Angus, as well as Strathnairn in the North, a proud man in his own right and considering himself of better blood than any Stewart, cousin and heir to the chief of his name, Sir James Lindsay of Crawford and Luffness, Lord High Justiciar. Adding injury to insult, he had been grievously wounded six years before, at the deplorable Battle of Glasclune, by one of the disreputable brothers of the man he was being sent to escort, all bastards of his late brother-in-law the Earl of Buchan and Wolf of Badenoch, to the praise of God now safely deceased. He rode tight-lipped.

John the Red of Dundonald was a very different and less reputable character, huge, with a fiery head and beard, loud, boisterous, cheerful, an unlikely Stewart and taking after his Kennedy mother. He made a curious captain for the guard of his mild and inoffensive half-brother. He laughed and shouted now, at Jamie's other side — who preferred the Lindsay silence.

They had less than six miles to go, fortunately. Half-way there, they came in sight of Scone Abbey across the Tay. They all eyed it, but only John Stewart commented.

"Robert will see us fine, from yonder," he cried. "And I'll wager he mislikes what he sees!"

Three times thereafter, Jamie's keen eyes picked out silent groups of motionless horsemen, sitting their mounts beneath the cover of trees back from the roadside, wearing the Stewart colours and the Governor's badge of the earldom of Fife. None moved or made any sign as the company cantered by.

At a bend of the great river, presently, was Boat of Luncarty, a ferry and milling hamlet, with a little parish church crowning a mound on the higher ground behind. Here, on the level haughland where the progenitor of the Hays had helped Kenneth the Third to defeat the Danes four centuries before, with the outliers of the blue Highland hills not so far distant, the Highland party they sought had halted, where they could still retire into the security of their mountains if need be.

As the newcomers clattered up, bulls' horns were blown in warning and many fierce hands dropped to sword-hilts, dirks and the shafts of Lochaber axes, amongst the colourful tartan-clad warriors. These numbered about thirty, plus sentries placed on points of vantage, and all in their best array, armed to the teeth. They stared at the royal guard, tense, suspicious, ready.

It was a peculiar situation, from any standpoint — for these were amongst the best fighting-men in Christendom, and courageous to the point of folly, the pick of a mighty clan. Moreover they were here on an entirely lawful occasion, on the heir to the throne's personal invitation and under royal safe-conduct. It was unlike such to display fright, trepidation, in any circumstances; yet their alarm and tight wariness was very apparent here. It was all eloquent testimony to the state of chaos and insecurity in Scotland in the last decade of the fourteenth century, and to the reputation of the Earl Robert of Fife and Menteith, Governor of the realm for his elder brother the King.

From amongst the crowd a young man stepped forward, the only man there not wearing tartans, but dressed in approximately Lowland fashion, without armour. He was fine-featured, slenderly built, handsome in a fair way, and with a marked resemblance to the Earl David of Carrick although older by about five years, Sir Alexander Stewart, eldest of the late Wolf of Badenoch's bastard brood and, since that prince left no legitimate offspring, Lord of Badenoch in fact if not in name and character. He looked from one to the other of the leaders of the newcomers.

"No Earl of Carrick, Sir James?" he said formally — but his voice had a pleasing Highland lilt and softness. "What of our compact?"

"My lord was engaged, Sir Alexander," Jamie told him carefully. "He could by no means leave Perth. But he sent his fair salutations and asked my lord of Glenesk, here, to act his deputy. With John Stewart of Dundonald, His Grace's captain of guard. Both kin of your own, and his."

"I see. It is my pleasure to meet Sir David. I am aware of his fame and prowess, to be sure. John Stewart I know, of course — and greet kindly. But my requirement was the High Steward himself, the only man under the King who ranks higher than the Governor. And on whose invitation, I, and these, are here."

"Boy!" Glenesk barked, "who think you that you are? That you can summon the heir to the throne! And turn up your nose at Lindsay! You, Buchan's bastard!"

"Who I am, my lord, matters nothing in this issue. What matters is that the Clan Chattan accept me as my father's heir.

And that we have come South to Perth on the King's safe-conduct. Although such should scarcely be necessary for the King's lawful subjects in his own realm! Yet we are threatened by the Governor . . ."

"He has not assailed you? Nor even sought to halt you?"

"His men have dogged us since Dunkeld. Now they line the road ahead, our scouts say. The Earl Robert does not wish us to come to Perth . . ."

"But the Earl David does, by God — and we will see that you get there!" John the Red cried. "He, Robert, but thinks to scare you off, man."

"I have tasted of his scaring off methods, sir! And wish to taste no more. *Why* should he seek to do so?"

Lindsay shrugged. "He disapproves of the Earl David his nephew's appointment to be Lieutenant of the North, and Justiciar. He appointed his own son, the Lord Murdoch Stewart, to that position six years back. Murdoch durst never take it up, whilst your father lived. So the Governor has never been able to extend his rule to the northern half of the kingdom. He still would have his son Lieutenant and Justiciar. He says that the Earl David is too young, lacks experience. He would discredit his appointment. This contest David has conceived as a means of settling the feud which has been tearing apart much of the North. If it is successful, then David's reputation is much enhanced — a good start to taking up office. If it fails, or never takes place, after half Scotland has come to watch, then . . .!" He left the rest unsaid.

Jamie intervened urgently. "That is all true. But there is need for haste. Already there must be delay. The King waits. The folk will grow impatient. Let us be on our way."

Sir Alexander turned to consult with the leaders of the watching, listening Highlanders, fierce-looking men with the softest voices in the land.

"Tell them who and what I am, young man," Lindsay said loudly, as though to penetrate their Gaelic-speaking ignorance by sheer volume of sound. "Tell them that they need have no fear — the Governor will not seek to interfere with *me*."

"I have done so, my lord. And they agree. We will come . . ."

So, mounted on their stocky, sturdy Highland garrons, the Badenoch party took the road again, flanked by the superbly horsed royal guard, heading southwards at a brisk trot under the streaming banners.

18

Not a single man-at-arms wearing the Governor's colours did they observe *en route*. Evidently there was nothing wrong with the Earl Robert's eyesight, nor with his recognition of realities, when it came to the bit.

When they reached the North Inch of Perth it was to find that great park already crowded with people. A central area of about six acres had been fenced off, and at the south end of this the Clan Comyn, or Cumming, contingent was already in place, waiting, a piper strutting up and down before them. Elsewhere the spectators thronged the approximately one hundred acres of common land, riverside meadows from which the cattle had been driven for the occasion — save for the clear space left immediately in front of the Blackfriars monastery wall. The folk were entertaining themselves meantime, in good spirits, with games, dancing, fiddling and horseplay — although one or two minor fights had inevitably broken out amongst rival lords' retinues. Pedlars, hucksters, tumblers, gypsies, fortune-tellers and the like were doing a roaring trade. It all resembled a gigantic fair, in the crisp October noontide.

Leaving the Clan Chattan party, with John Stewart and part of the guard, at the north end of the railed-off enclosure, the object of much interest, staring and pointing on the part of the crowd thereabouts, Jamie Douglas, with Sir Alexander and Glenesk, rode on into the town. The streets were much less thronged now, with most of the people already assembled in the Inch. At the monastery, Jamie was in doubt as to whether to seek the High Steward in the Gilten Arbour again or in the more conventional royal quarters in the guest-house; but the sight of his henchman, Pate Boyd, talking with a group of others at the guest-house door, and a jerk of that man's head upwards, seemed to indicate that the prince's recreational activities were for the moment over. The Douglas, dismounting, led Sir Alexander upstairs two steps at a time, the Lindsay following the young men more sedately.

In a large upper room, from which emanated much chatter and laughter, they found the Earl David in the midst of a gay and richly-dressed company of both sexes, beakers and flagons of wine being much in evidence. He had his arm around the shoulders of a handsome and statuesque woman almost old enough to be his mother, his hand inside the low-necked bodice of her gown, whilst he talked animatedly with sundry others. He seemed to be in excellent spirits, certainly without any aspect of anxious waiting. The Lady Congalton was reunited with her husband, over near one of the windows.

"Come, Alex," Jamie said, as the young man from the North held back a little in the doorway. "That is he, in the scarlet-and-gold. With the Countess of Mar."

"I see him, recognise him. As he has seen and recognised me — although he gives no sign. He seems . . . fully occupied!"

"Tush — never heed that, man. It is his way with women. Even his real aunts must needs put up with it — although some appear to like it. Come!"

"I am not clad for this peacock throng . . ."

"Sakes, Alex — do not be a fool! You are worth any score of these put together — and *he* knows it! What do clothes matter? See, we shall . . ."

"Ha, Jamie my dear — I have been looking for you." A good-looking woman in her late thirties came up to them, fair, almost beautiful, though with her fine-chiselled features just slightly lined with care. "Where have you been? And who is this? Kin of my own, in some sort, I swear! But then, we Stewarts have almost a surfeit of kin, have we not?"

"Ah, to be sure — you have not met. This is Sir Alexander Stewart of Badenoch, whom I aspire to call my friend, my lady. And this is the Lady Isabel, His Grace's sister, former Countess of Douglas and now wed to Sir John Edmonstone of that Ilk."

"I might have known it. Another of my multitude of nephews — Alec's son. And the best of that brood, from all accounts. Certainly the best-looking, I'd vow! Welcome to Court, Sir Alexander — if this Court is any place to welcome one to!"

The young man bowed courteously. "My father spoke much of you, Princess. As has Sir James, here. And always much in your favour. I perceive why, to be sure."

"Gallant, Nephew! Who would have looked for the like from your wild mountains?"

"There are worse places to be reared than our Highland mountains, Lady Isabel — some nearer here, I think!"

"So-o-o! We have claws as well as smiles, Sir Alexander!"

"My lady — your pardon," Jamie intervened, with a trace of impatience. "We must speak with the Earl David. Forthwith. We have been hastening, to come to him . . ."

"Yes. It is ever the Earl David nowadays, Jamie. David this, David that! I must not delay you, and him, no!"

The Douglas bit his lip. His position at Court had grown difficult of late. He was, in fact, the Lady Isabel's man, her knight and man-of-affairs, her late husband the Earl of Douglas's former chief esquire who had remained loyal servant and friend to his widow although she had in time been forced to remarry. But ever more noticeably, in the last year or so he had tended to gravitate into the orbit of the young and masterful heir to the throne — who indeed most evidently liked and trusted him as he did few others. Whomsoever the Prince David wanted to serve him, served him — it was as simple as that. Just as he would have none near him who did not please him. Wilful in all things, spoiled in one way from earliest years, he had nevertheless come to approve of Jamie — admire would be too strong a word — ever since they had first clashed and then worked together in some measure at Turnberry seven years before, at the task of circumventing his Uncle Robert of Fife and Menteith. They were still at it, united in this at least, that the Governor had to be countered. David had plenty of aides and servants more in keeping with his own style and temperament; but he had recognised something in Jamie Douglas lacking elsewhere, and more or less purloined him from his aunt's service when he had come to set up his own establishment at Court. The Douglas was not altogether happy with this position — although serving the Lady Isabel had its own difficulties and embarrassments, especially for a happily-married man. The Stewarts were an autocratic lot; and since aunt and nephew were by no means always on the best of terms, the situation could have its problems.

Shaking his dark head unhappily, Jamie took the young Stewart's arm and led him over to the prince's group. He did not hesitate to interrupt what he conceived to be the inanities there being discussed.

"My lord — Sir Alexander Stewart of Badenoch, representing the Clan Chattan party," he said briefly.

"Ah, yes. Welcome, Cousin — I thought it must be you. Though what you may have to do with the Clan Chattan I am eager to learn! It is long since we forgathered." With no undue haste he withdrew his hand from the Countess of Mar's fine bosom, stroking her neck and dark hair as he did so.

"I greet you, my lord Earl. After six years. Clearly I find you in excellent shape and spirits! As to the Clan Chattan, they do me the honour to make me their spokesman and, to some extent,

21

guide — since they are unaccustomed to your Southron ways and tongue."

"Indeed. How fortunate they are! And where are your picturesque barbarians now? We have been awaiting them overlong, it seems."

The other young man, so strangely like the prince, drew a deep breath — and Jamie Douglas plunged in, to avert the clash.

"They are in their place at the north side of the lists, my lord. The Comyns face them. All is now in train. No need for further delay . . ."

"Our Jamie is a notable foe of delay and dalliance," the Earl mentioned conversationally. "Highly admirable, I am sure. Myself, I fear that I am less concerned over who is kept waiting — so long as it is not Davie Stewart! How is it with you, Aunt? Are you of the impatient sort?"

"For some things, yes, I think I am."

Something in the Countess's husky voice made the prince look at her quickly. But she was looking only at Alexander, with an assessing, almost lustful expression in her dark eyes. She was a strong-featured, handsome woman, well-made, with a high complexion and a smouldering aspect to her — a fairly typical Douglas. She was, in fact, sister to the murdered 2nd Earl of Douglas, only daughter of the 1st Earl of Douglas and Mar, and had inherited the Mar earldom in her own right. She was married to Sir Malcolm Drummond of Stobhall, chief of the name and brother of Queen Annabella, David's mother.

"To be sure. That I can well believe," the quick-witted prince acceded. "You hear that, Cousin? Beware — as I do! Now — we must not keep Jamie waiting — or even Clans Chattan and Comyn. Still less, my royal sire — although I cannot conceive of him being eager for the fray! Where is Lindsay? Ah, there. Uncle David — you and Moray will take charge in the lists, you with Clan Chattan, Moray with his Comyns. Lyon and his heralds and trumpeters to the Gilten Arbour. Indeed, all of you to the Arbour, to await His Grace's coming. Wines and refreshments are already there, never fear . . ."

Sir Alexander bowed briefly. "I shall return to my, h'm, barbarians and friends, my lord!"

"And I with you," Jamie said.

"You shall not," the prince declared. "I require you by my side, Jamie. Take my aunts over to the Arbour meantime."

So a move was made across the gardens, amidst much donning of cloaks and plaids against the October air. Jamie, collecting the Lady Isabel, her sisters Marjorie, widowed Countess of Moray, and Jean, widow of Sir John Lyon, now wife to Sir James Sandilands of Calder, looked around him for a fourth to escort. He found her having a brief word with Sir Alexander at the door before he hurried back to his Highlanders — Jamie's own wife Mary Stewart, illegitimate daughter of the late monarch, Robert the Second, a dancing-eyed, high-spirited creature, comely, highly attractive and of strikingly excellent figure, whom six years of marriage to the seriously-minded Douglas and two young children had totally failed to repress. She now pressed her equally illegitimate nephew's arm and came across to her husband and half-sisters cheerfully.

"Alex grows more to my taste than ever!" she announced. "Is he not good-looking? Jamie will have to keep his eyes open, I swear! He says that the Clan Chattan are sure to win, that he knows the Comyns — or should it be Cummings? — and they are not truly Highlandmen. They will break first."

"I say that the entire contest is shameful," the Lady Isabel declared. "Davie is not to be congratulated. In this, as in much else. Nor your Thomas, Marjorie — who put him up to it."

"I agree," the Lady Marjorie of Moray said. "It is to treat men like dumb animals. Like a bear-baiting or a dog-fight. I shall not watch for long, I promise you!"

"No need to come watch at all then, Marjorie," the Lady Jean pointed out.

"It will not be a pretty spectacle," Jamie admitted, "I sought to convince the Lord David against it, to be sure. But good could come of it, to be sure. Much good, for the North. An end to this terrible feuding and bloodshed."

Over at the Gilten Arbour, the high-born throng squabbled for the best seats and view-points; also started at once on the victuals. The view over the North Inch was tribute to the monkish builder of the summer-house; and of course the railed-off enclosure for the lists had been chosen to be immediately below and in front of the royal vantage point. A great stir and swell of noise arose from the crowded park, punctuated by the high and distinctly discordant strains of the bagpipes, for the Clan Chattan party had produced one of their own pipers to pace and blow before them — which caused the opposition to field two further instrumentalists to outplay their rivals. At some two hundred yards apart, the resultant din was notable, and even the royal band of fiddles, flutes and cymbals which the Earl David had thoughtfully provided failed to drown the competition.

Presently, however, a brassy fanfare of trumpets rang out, and under its imperious blare even the pipes wailed and sobbed into silence. Flanked by gorgeously tabarded heralds, the Carrick and Strathearn Pursuivants, the venerable Lyon King of Arms came pacing along the Arbour balcony, clearing a passage. When the trumpets died away, Lyon raised hand and voice.

"Silence and due obeisance from all!" he called into the hush. "Bow low before His Grace the Lord Robert, by God's will and anointing High King of Scots, our most noble and puissant prince."

Unfortunately there was something of a hiatus after this resounding introduction. The stairway up to the balcony was steep, and King Robert was lame, having been kicked on the knee by a Douglas horse when a young man, with disastrous effects on more than his walking. Bowing low, even more or less metaphorically, was not something which might be maintained indefinitely.

At last, leaning on the arm of his Queen, with his son David on the other side, the monarch appeared at the head of the stairs. Although in fact only fifty-eight he looked at least fifteen years older, a frail, stooping figure, white-haired and white-bearded, with a finely sensitive face and lofty brow but the lines of weariness and weakness etched deep. He was wrapped in a voluminous furred cloak, for he felt the cold. Limping heavily, he kept his eyes downcast, a man miscast for his role if ever there was one. At his side Annabella Drummond looked every inch a queen, tall, serene, quietly assured without any trace of prideful haughtiness. She was not beautiful like her son, but of pleasing looks and a kindly expression. She aided and supported her husband solicitously. The prince did not actually hold his father's other arm but strolled close by, smiling and nodding to all.

The King and Queen took their seats at the centre of the gallery, to the prolonged cheering of the populace in the Inch — for strangely enough Robert was popular, in a quiet way, more perhaps out of comparison with his brothers than for more positive reasons, although he had a reputation for generosity, patience, kindness, the Good King Robert who would not hurt a fly. The Queen too was gracious and accessible, much more so than was normal. And the beautiful High Steward was the people's darling, despite the nature of many of his activities. David did not sit but remained behind his father's chair, beckoning Jamie Douglas to his side.

"No sign of my Uncle Robert?" he murmured. "He can scarce expect us to wait for him!"

"As Governor of the realm he may feel so entitled, my lord."

"Then he must learn otherwise." The prince raised his voice. "Lyon, proceed, if you please."

After another long flourish of trumpets, the principal herald bowed to the King and spoke again. "By His Grace's royal command," he cried, "I declare that a judicial trial of strength and armed contest shall now take place before His Grace and all men. Between the House of Comyn, or Clan Cumming in the Erse, and Clan Chattan. This as final decision and judgement between these two tribes and contestants in the dispute which has long maintained between them, on the matter of the lands and castle of Rait and the barony of Geddes, in Strathnairn, in the province of Moray in the northern parts of this realm; whereby there has been much scaith and hurt to the lieges of His Grace in those parts, to the King's sore sorrow."

The elderly Lyon King of Arms paused for breath, and the buzz of anticipation grew, far and near.

"This contest," he went on, "will be decided by thirty champions of these tribes or clans, duly selected. They will fight here, before His Grace, as is their custom, with sword, dirk, axe and arrow, but without armour or shield other than the small leathern targe. The fight will be to the death or until one side concedes complete victory to the other, and therewith the undisputed possession of the said lands of Rait and Geddes, which Mackintosh of Clan Chattan claims the Clan Cumming have unlawfully taken from him and his. Moreover it is to be accepted by both sides that the losers will hereafter abide by this decision and disturb the King's peace no more, by placing themselves under the dominion and authority of the winners. Assurance of their full acceptance of these terms to be made here before the King's Grace by right and proper sureties — namely the noble Lord Thomas, Earl of Moray for the Comyns, of whose earldom they are vassals; and the potent Sir David Lindsay, Lord of Glenesk and Strathnairn, who has consented to act surety for the Clan Chattan of Badenoch in the absence

25

of a reigning Lord of Badenoch. My lords — in the King's name do you accept the terms aforesaid?"

The young, red-faced Moray and the older Lindsay paced out from their respective sides, bowed to the royal gallery and indicated that they did.

"So be it." Lyon turned to face the Earl David. "And do you, my lord of Carrick, High Steward and Prince of Scotland, appointed to be Justiciary and Lieutenant of the North, accede that such decision by trial of arms shall be binding and final in the jurisdiction of your northern territories hereafter?"

"I do."

"Then, my lords, it is His Grace's royal pleasure that you return to your clans and prepare them to commence the contest. You will signal when ready."

Throughout Lyon's long announcement the King had sat, head bent, eyes on his clasped hands. He did not raise either now. A less convincing picture of royal pleasure would have been hard to conceive.

Jamie touched the Earl David's arm, and pointed. Above the mass of the crowd, away to the north, could be seen waving banners and the glint and gleam of sun on steel armour.

The prince nodded. "He comes, then. Damn him — just in time!" Frowning, he jerked. "Jamie — haste you and get these Hielantmen started. Before he comes up. Quickly!"

Even as the Douglas hurried through a postern gate in the town wall, he heard the Earl of Moray shouting that the Comyns were ready. But when he reached the Clan Chattan party it was to discover consternation. One of their number was missing. They had all been present only a short time before. They had only twenty-nine men to face the Comyns' thirty. It was a catastrophe.

"Is it so bad?" Jamie demanded, of Alexander Stewart. "One man in thirty? A loss, yes — but not too great a challenge for stout fighters . . ."

"*Dia*, James — do you not see?" the other exclaimed. "It is not that. Clan Chattan would fight five short, ten short, and win! It is the disgrace. One turned craven and fled. Or been suborned."

"Suborned? You do not mean that?"

"Why not? We know the Governor would wish this contest to be stopped."

"He is coming. That is why I am here. The Lord David

wants a start made without delay. I think that he fears the Lord Robert might prevail on his father to stop the contest, even yet."

"No doubt. But we cannot start with a man short. It is not that we are weakened but that the terms of the engagement are broken. The compact was for thirty on each side, no armour, no spears or lances, no surrender, no truce or interval. If any of these terms should be broken, the trial is over and the victory adjudged to the other side. Now do you see?"

Just then, only now visible from this lower position, the Earl of Fife's column of about two hundred armed horsemen forced its way past, some way to the east, along the line of the road which threaded the North Inch, swords out to beat a way through the crowds with the flats of the blades. In the midst, surrounded by his gentlemen, the stiffly erect figure of the Governor looked neither left nor right. Curses followed him, but low-voiced, and fists were shaken, but not where they might be seen by the horsemen.

"What will you do, then?" Jamie demanded.

"We have men out, searching for the man in the crush. If they cannot find him, we must seek to enroll another. If we can."

"That will take time. The Earl David wants a start made. At once. Before the Governor . . ."

"*Could* he stop all? If the prince and the King say otherwise?"

"He is strong, harsh — and the King fears him. Moreover the King himself does not like this contest. He might well be persuaded. But, once started, it could scarce be stopped."

"Give us but a little longer." Stewart spoke briefly in Gaelic with the enormous man near him, Shaw Beg MacFarquhar, leader of the Clan Chattan group, a magnificent figure of a proud young Highlander, nearer seven than six feet tall. He turned back. "We shall seek a substitute. At once. But he must be of Clan Chattan, or linked with it. While still we search for this wretch . . ."

"Perhaps none would perceive it? Twenty-nine will look much like thirty, in a fight."

"The Cummings would see it, never fear. Every man will count, before the end. No — go back to my Cousin David, Jamie. Tell him that one man has fallen out — sick, say. We shall find another. A few minutes only . . ."

Lindsay had come up, with Sir Thomas Hay, Lord High Constable, who had an overall responsibility for supervision of trials of strength, referee. The Lord of Glenesk was frowning blackly.

"This is shameful!" he declared. "Would God I had never allowed myself to be talked into this folly. Moray will never cease to point his insolent finger at me . . .!"

"Grieve not too soon, my lord," Alexander advised. "We shall fight, and win. Even if I myself have to take part . . ."

"That would not serve, man. You are a Stewart, though base-born. All know it. No member of Clan Chattan. Such it must be, the Constable says."

"The piper . . .?" Jamie suggested.

"He is no sworder. Besides, they will need his piping to spur them on. But off with you, Jamie. We will find a man. Gain us but a few minutes . . ."

When the Douglas won back through the throng to the Gilten Arbour balcony, it was to find the Earl Robert Stewart, Governor of Scotland, standing before the King, in no very respectful attitude, and speaking coldly. He was a tall, slender man, good-looking in a stern-faced way, thin-lipped, long-featured, pale-eyed, with a watchful and severe manner. Although he had a faint impediment in his speech, his clipped voice lacked nothing in chill authority.

". . . as wrongful and ill-conceived as it is barbarous!" he was saying. "Folly and worse. I say that it must be stopped. Forthwith. You, Sire, must command a halt."

"*Must*, Uncle . . .?" That was the Earl David, interestedly.

"I am the Governor of this realm. The rule is mine . . ."

"Governor for His Grace, is it not? When the King is present in person, his word is supreme, I think? Tell me, Uncle, do you conceive the Governor superior to the King of Scots?"

The other kept his steely gaze on the unhappy monarch not on the insouciantly smiling heir. "Not superior — effectual," he said briefly, without change of tone. "The King has ordained me Governor, to rule — confirmed by parliament. Therefore *I* rule — not the King, who reigns. There is a difference, Nephew."

"To be sure. But whom the King has ordained, the King can unordain. And the Governor cannot *over*-rule the King's expressed wishes, at any time. Is that not so?"

His uncle spoke directly to the monarch. "Sire — *is* it your expressed wish that this great slaughter of your subjects should proceed?"

His brother gnawed his lip. "Not, not slaughter, Robert —

no, no. A fair fight, just — no more. To save many lives. Davie says it is the best way. To end this strife in the North . . ." The only certainty about the royal voice was its pleading note.

"Davie is young and rash, Sire. Well-meaning no doubt, but lacking in experience and judgement. You must heed sound, proven advice, not the wild notions of a lad not yet of full age."

"*Must* again, my lord! I think that you forget to whom you speak!" The prince turned. "Sire — the word is given to commence this combat. The Governor has come late. I urge you to request him to be seated and let all proceed."

"Aye, Robert — that would be best . . ."

Jamie Douglas, at the Earl David's back, touched his elbow. "Sir Alexander seeks time," he whispered, "a little time. One man of Clan Chattan gone. Bolted, they fear . . ."

"God's damnation!" the other swore, but beneath his breath, and somehow managing to retain a smiling face. "This could ruin all."

"Yes. But he says they *will* fight. Find someone. Give him time . . ."

The Governor was now appealing to Queen Annabella, as a woman, to make her husband stop the contest, adding that, moreover, the King was in duty bound to heed the advice of his appointed Governor above that of any other, even the heir to the throne, where the public weal was concerned. The Queen, who was in fact much against the entire project but desired to support her husband and son, looked less serene than usual. The prince interrupted, strongly.

"Your Grace — I am appointed Justiciar of the North. Thomas Dunbar is Earl of Moray and the Clan Cumming are his undoubted vassals. The Clan Chattan are vassals of the lordship of Badenoch, represented by Sir Alexander Stewart. All three agree on this contest. Does the Governor claim that his authority can over-rule the juridical and feudal rights of all? If he so claims, I suggest that we call for a ruling from the Lord High Justiciar of the realm, Sir James Lindsay, Lord of Crawford. Where is the Lord of Crawford?"

Although the Governor asserted that he was not interested in the opinion of Crawford or anybody else, the cry went up for the Lord High Justiciar — who was Sir David Lindsay's cousin. He was not in the best of health, and it could be anticipated that he would take some time to find.

The Earl of Fife and Menteith seldom permitted himself the luxury of anger, but he showed it now, striding up and down in front of the nervous monarch, declaring that all was folly, insolence, a deliberate affront and attack on himself. Heads would fall for this . . .

Vigorous argument and the taking of sides resulted amongst the Governor's gentlemen and the courtiers of the King — or, more truly, of the Earl David, since it was around him that all revolved. Time was well and truly wasted.

In the midst of it all, with the Lord of Crawford still not found, his cousin Glenesk appeared below the gallery, with the High Constable, to announce that all was now ready, Clan Chattan having found a replacement for one of their number who had fallen sick. A certain Perth blacksmith and armourer of Mackintosh blood, commonly called Hal Gow of the Wynd, had volunteered to aid his fellow-clansmen, a doughty swords-man as well as a sword-maker, it seemed. The Constable had approved this replacement . . .

Cheers greeted this intimation. The Earl David quickly signed to Lindsay to get on with it.

So, while argument and protest still continued, the bagpipes struck up anew and a great shout arose from the ranks of Clan Chattan, to be taken up immediately by the Clan Cumming. Not to be outdone, Lyon's trumpeters blew a high blast or two. All talk died away and all eyes lifted to the tourney-ground. Even the Earl of Fife turned to watch, frowning. Jamie Douglas heaved a sigh of relief — even though he was none too happy, himself, about the entire contest.

Hay, the Constable, flanked now by Moray and Lindsay, moved over to a platform erected in a commanding position against the town-wall and below the royal gallery, where they could oversee all. He bowed towards the King then to each of his colleagues, and raised his hand. Only the strains of the bagpipes sounded.

As his hand dropped, the two groups of contestants moved forward, at the walk, pipers pacing behind. Most of the Clan Chattan were bare to the waist, having discarded all clothing save for the philabeg or short kilt — all save one who was seen to be a short, stocky man in ordinary artisan's attire of hodden grey breeches, grey shirt and blue bonnet — the volunteer blacksmith Hal Gow, somewhat bandy-legged but immensely broad across the shoulders. Like the rest he carried on his left arm a round leather-covered targe, as shield, and a crossbow of hunter's type in the right hand. The long two-handed sword, sheathed at his back, which looked comparatively modest on Shaw Beg's tall frame, seemed huge indeed behind the smith. A cheer went up, especially for the bow-legged auxiliary champion, from the vast crowd of Lowlanders. The Cummings, being less truly Highland, retained more of their clothing, but were similarly armed and looked a fine stalwart crew, under the leadership of one Gilchrist mac Ian, or Christie Johnson.

Marching warily forward, the two leaders were watching each other like hawks as they drew closer. They had started about two hundred yards apart, which was overlong range for maximum effect for these hunters' crossbows, however short for the typical English longbows of war. Mac Ian was fractionally the first to act. When each side was some forty yards from its base, slightly in front of his extended line, he dropped on one bare knee and whipped out one of three arrows from his belt. Immediately all his men followed suit.

Shaw Beg adopted a different tactic, and swiftly. His men, who had been bunched much closer together, at his shout leapt and bounded closer still, to hurl themselves into a tight group, in approximately three layers, the lowest crouching down, the middle stooping forward, the rear standing upright. All thrust their targes out, the lowest held fairly close, the second rank out a little to protect the heads of those beneath, the standing men fully extended over the men in front. This manoeuvre, although undoubtedly often practised, took precious seconds to perform; and before the last targes were in position the first arrows were on their way. Screams rang out as three men fell transfixed, one in the rear rank through an eye, two in the middle rank through throat and breast. Their comrades closed still tighter, their targes forming a fairly continuous shield now — although, being circular, they inevitably left gaps.

Each man was provided with three arrows only. The Cummings now shot off their remaining shafts; but the toughened leather of the targes was impenetrable and they almost all fell harmlessly; but three more of the sixty found marks, one man pitching forward in the bottom rank, one hit through a gap in the middle to yell in agony, the third arrow piercing the left forearm of Shaw Beg himself, who being the tallest man there was the least well protected. He remained standing, with the shaft protruding back and front.

Five Clan Chattan fallen and their leader wounded in the first few moments.

Now the scene changed dramatically. It was the Badenoch men's turn. They had five, possibly six, fewer marksmen but their opponents were now disadvantaged in that they were not huddled together but extended in a long line, each man's targe only partially able to cover him. Gilchrist mac Ian yelled at them to close on him, and this they raced to do — but not before the Clan Chattan shafts were flying. Four men fell, in that unprotected race, two more before they could form up their targes as a consolidated shield, two more still from the final flight of arrows which found gaps and niches.

Eight Cummings down as against five — for Shaw Beg had demonstrated that he was by no means out of the fight, using his crossbow with the best of them. Now, tossing the bow away, he twisted his arm around, grasped the barbed end of the shaft, and with a vicious jerk which must have caused excruciating pain, snapped the wooden shank in two. Drawing out the remaining feathered end, he threw it from him; and almost in the same motion reached back for his great two-handed claymore. All his men had likewise thrown away their bows, and drawn swords. Yelling their slogan of "*Loch Moigh! Loch Moigh!*" they went forward at the run, in an ever-extending line, to give room for effective swordplay, the Perth blacksmith well to the fore, bow-legs or none. They left the five bodies behind, lying still or writhing in torment.

The clash, as the two sides met headlong, was shocking, to watch and hear as well as to experience, twenty-five against twenty-two. The clang and shriek of steel, the yells and screams of men, the shouts and howls of the crowd and the high discordant strains of the pipers who continued to play as they strode up and down behind their respective sides, and only some fifty yards apart now, made a frightening accompaniment to a scene of fury and heroism, savagery and anguish, bloodshed and death.

There could be no description of this extraordinary struggle, since it was really a score of different struggles, all to the death, all competing for description. In swordsmanship and axemanship and dirksmanship the two sides were fairly evenly matched; and in courage and determination there was nothing to choose from. Wounded terribly, men fought on, even when stricken to their knees. Swords and Lochaber axes falling from one nerveless hand were grabbed and wielded by the other — and when neither had the strength left to brandish such weighty weapons, dirks were snatched out to thrust and stab. Flesh and blood wilted and spouted and failed, but the spirit maintained, triumphed whilst breath and consciousness remained — worthy of a better cause.

Up on the Arbour balcony, as no doubt elsewhere around that arena, Jamie Douglas was not alone in feeling that it was shameful, almost obscene, to sit and watch this desperate encounter. He had fought long and hard on the bloody field of Otterburn, and had suffered hurt in sundry tournaments; but being an idle spectator of men in extremity and dying horribly, was not for him. Many, especially amongst the women, found the spectacle more than they could stomach, and there were hasty retirals, vomitings, even swoonings. But by no means all, or even a majority, felt this, as was proved by the shouting, egging-on, wagering, the cursing and cheering which prevailed. The King, however, crouched low, hand over his eyes, his Queen stroking the bowed head. His brother the Governor watched expressionless.

Of all the individual combats, two were apt to rivet the attention — those between Shaw Beg and Gilchrist mac Ian, and between the smith Hal Gow and a variety of opponents. The two leaders singled each other out, from the start, and went at it with tremendous vigour, despite the Shaw's wounded arm. As swordsmen there was little between them — although fighting with the five-foot-long two-handed claymores demanded sinew and endurance more than finesse; nevertheless skill of a sort was important, especially in the recovery from missed strokes. Basically a figure-of-eight motion was more effective than any indiscriminate jabbing and poking and slashing, since it enabled the wielder to remain in control of his weapon; but it had the disadvantage of predictability. Sundry variations on the theme were possible however, switchings of figure, direction, extent and level; at these Shaw Beg probably had the greater expertise as well as the longer reach — which helped to counter-act the obvious pain and increasing stiffness of his left arm. But it seemed apparent that he was going to tire soonest, if he could not finish off the combat with a vital stroke.

Hal of the Wynd, as the Perth folk called the volunteer, was in a different case. He quickly demonstrated that he was no mere rash townsman taking on his betters in weaponry, but a

33

man who knew all there was to know about swords and swordsmanship. His first opponent he disposed of in a couple of minutes. His second took longer, having a more extended reach and notably quick footwork; but a dextrous backhanded reverse stroke eventually laid him low — and everywhere men began to wager on the blacksmith personally.

Elsewhere honours appeared to be fairly equal — although Clan Chattan's extra three men did make a difference. It was an unwritten law that, although it was a battle between sides, within that context combats were single — so that two men did not assail one, and when a man felled his opponent, he waited until one from the other side was free to engage him — and usually much needed the momentary respite to regain breath.

Although there was no official interval in that dreadful battle, there came a time when, in mutual if temporary exhaustion both groups, or more accurately all sets of combatants still on their feet, gradually came to a halt. Indeed, at one stage, only the two leaders were still circling and slashing at each other. When Mac Ian tripped and fell over one of many bodies which littered the field, Shaw refrained from striking down at him but instead stepped unsteadily back a little, staggering, to lean heavily on his tall sword, panting grievously. The other rose, and he too backed away. Everywhere, men who could do so leaned on swords and axes, swaying, clutching at wounds, some doubled up in pain. Few were not covered in blood, their own or others'. The trampled grass around them was more red than green.

In this grim hiatus the pipers came strutting to the front again, to march up and down before their respective sides, blowing and playing at their strongest, passing and repassing within only a few feet of each other, weaving in and out amongst the fallen, the jangled strains of their rival instruments helping to drown other demoralising sounds — for even the most determined and stoical sufferers could not entirely still their groans and cries, and somewhere a man was screaming thinly in mortal agony. Some wounded were dragging themselves about, even in circles.

Not all the spectators were appreciative of this interval, some even claiming that they were being cheated, that this was no fight to a finish. Others, of the wagering sort, were busy assessing and seeking to count and allot the slain and survivors to their two sides; since most combatants stood, panting, approximately where they had paused and there was no clear front, this was not entirely clear. But there was no doubt that there were still thirty-three men on their feet; and of the twenty-seven fallen over half appeared to be dead. The general consensus was that there were eighteen to fifteen, in favour of Clan Chattan, still in the fight.

After only two or three minutes, the pipers' revitalising efforts seemed to be sufficiently effective for a restart to be made. By unspoken consent the two leaders moved off laterally, in the direction of the riverside, a little distance, this to make use of a clean stretch of greensward; for the blood everywhere made footwork hazardous, and the litter of bodies was a major impediment for the remaining fighters. The others were not slow at following, even though the majority now reeled, limped or hobbled.

The fight recommenced, with three Clan Chattan men waiting, disengaged.

At first, the clash seemed to be only fractionally less vigorous and furious than heretofore. But in fact, after a few minutes, it was evident that the pace had slowed. The urgency and resolve was still there, but thews and sinews and breath just could not maintain the fullest expression. Strokes were less accurate, reaction slower, footwork heavier, swords being increasingly discarded for dirks. Nevertheless, men fell faster and blood flowed still more copiously — for weary men were tardier in avoiding blows, in ducking and dodging. In the next quarter-hour sixteen men fell, ten of them Cummings. Of these, Hal the Smith slew two, though twice wounded himself now, with a gashed brow and a slit forearm. Only five Cummings remained capable of fighting, to face twelve opponents. But the terms declared that there was to be no yielding, and none there questioned it. Only up on the Gilten Arbour balcony was there some talk of calling an end to the slaughter, and that only by a minority, mainly women. The King had not once raised his head to look during the second stage.

The end came quite suddenly. The leaders were fighting only with dirks now, and therefore at closest quarters. In making an arm's length stab, Gilchrist mac Ian Cumming lost his balance and stumbled forward, actually cannoning, bent, into his foe. And this time the Shaw did not step back but drove down with his dirk between the other's bare and unprotected shoulder-blades. Pierced to the heart, the Cumming fell.

Although it is to be accepted that the others still fighting were much too busy to have eyes for anything but their opponents, somehow the fact of the fall of their leader communicated itself to the remaining four Cummings. This affected men differently. One red-bearded individual, although already bleeding from multiple wounds, it maddened to a final desperate outburst of furious energy wherein he hurled himself bodily upon his foe, ignoring the dirk-slash which laid his cheek open from ear to chin, and stabbed the other to death in a wild flurry of vicious blows — indeed went on stabbing crazily even with his man inert on the grass. But the other three reacted otherwise, recognising that fate was against them, accepting it at last, and quite literally yielding up the ghost. In a bare minute after mac Ian's fall, these three also lay twitching on the ground.

The fight was over. Eleven men of Clan Chattan's thirty, including the blacksmith, remained on their feet, although all were more or less seriously hurt; the one red-head of Clan Cumming, gibbering inanities. The pipers did not stop their playing but, unasked, changed their tunes from fierce arousal to merge their offerings to a slow and dignified coronach for the dead, no longer in competition but united in the same lament.

The High Constable, with the lords of Moray and Glenesk, turned about, bowed to the royal balcony, then stepped down from their platform and came almost hurrying to the scene of conflict.

The entire North Inch of Perth seemed to erupt in cheering.

"God's eyes!" the young Earl David cried, "that was a fight! The greatest, I say! And I am three hundred merks the richer! That blacksmith shall have it all, I swear. Come, Jamie." And forgetting all about the dignity expected of the heir to the throne, the High Steward of Scotland or the Justiciar of the North, he swung himself over the balcony-rail, hung by his hands from its flooring, dropped to the ground, landed on all fours and ran for the postern-gate.

Sir James Douglas, with a wife present, was less precipitate, bowing towards the King and more vaguely towards the princesses, before pushing his way to the stairway and down.

The monarch arose, and without a word to any, limped away. Any acknowledgement towards the bowing courtiers, the Queen made. The Earl of Fife briefly ordered a return to Scone.

Jamie caught up with the prince, who was having to fight his way through the surging, excited throng to the battle-ground. Owing to the fact that the combat had moved riverwards, they had to cross ground which had been fought over; and the Douglas, for one, all but spewed when he realised that what he, and others, had kicked and tripped over was a hacked-off arm. Despite his battle experience, he had not realised that human blood smelled so sickeningly strongly.

They reached the ultimate arena to find arguments and confusion, the triumph confined to the spectators, the victors suffering from reaction, pain, loss of blood and weariness. Monks from the Blackfriars and other monasteries were already there seeking to comfort the hurt, to staunch and bind up wounds; and a priest, kneeling in congealing blood, was administering extreme unction to the dying. The one Clan Cumming survivor was still shouting Gaelic incoherencies, to the embarrassment of all, while his wounds were being dressed. The pipers continued with their sobbing coronach; but the young Earl of Moray was involved in an argument with the Constable over what he claimed, at second-hand, was the unfair introduction into the conflict of another and especial kind of music, from a mysterious chanter, the flute-like portion of the bagpipes on which the finger-work was played. This, he asserted, according to his Cumming supporters, had been enchanted or incanted over by witchcraft or other such devilry before-hand, and played during the combat by persons unknown, enabling the Clan Chattan contestants to fight on with supernatural vigour long after their wounds should have laid them low. In token of which he held up a slender black pipe perforated with holes, which someone had picked up from the field. Lindsay was treating this extraordinary objection with hooted scorn, while the Constable looked highly sceptical; and Sir Alexander Stewart was declaring that not only had he not heard this alleged unworldly music but had never seen the chanter before, and that the Clan Chattan did not require witchcraft to win their battles for them.

On this confused scene, the prince's arrival had some calming effect. He commended the Constable's handling of the contest, congratulated Shaw Beg, through Alexander Stewart, on his well-deserved victory, dismissed the black chanter complication as nonsense — he did not like his cousin, Thomas Dunbar, Earl of Moray — and made much of the smith, Hal Gow of the

Wynd, declaring that he should have the full three hundred merks, £200, which he had won on his wagering. It seemed that the smith had agreed to act volunteer for a mere half-merk of silver, plus the assurance that if he survived the fight he would receive suitable compensation — a sporting arrangement. This royal windfall, a huge sum for any working craftsman, relieved the Clan Chattan representatives of any financial responsibility — although Sir Alexander told the tough little man that if he elected to come back to the North with or after them, to the land of his fathers, he would give him a good croft in Badenoch to be held by him and his heirs in all time coming, an offer accepted on the spot.

There was some discussion as to the circumstances which had led up to the smith's enrolment. It was now established that the Clan Chattan defaulter had been seen to hurry off eastwards, run down to the riverside and thereafter swim away across Tay; yet the man was known as a considerable swordsman, with some pretensions to gentility and certainly not lacking in courage. The assumption that he had been bought off by someone who wished to stop the contest was reinforced and logical. And the Governor seemed to be the likeliest buyer.

"It was my noble uncle, I swear!" the Earl David declared. "It has the smell of him about it! Not that we will ever prove it against him — he will, as ever, see to that. But when the reckoning comes, I shall not forget it."

"Such reckoning could cost you dear, my lord," his Uncle Lindsay warned. "I would advise that you forget it, lad."

"Not so," his nephew contended. "I have an excellent memory. And the score lengthens. One day, see you, I shall be king in this realm."

"God willing!" his uncle said.

The prince stared at him for a long moment. Then he turned to Alexander Stewart. "Come, Cousin — we shall dine together. Celebrate your victory, and mine. I swear that we have much to talk over. I am going to require a deputy in my justiciarship — for I promise you I am not going to bury myself up there in your wilderness, however magnificent!"

"I thank you, my lord — but no. We head back over the Highland line, forthwith."

"With all these dead and wounded?"

"Even so. The wounded will do better in their own country. We shall bear them in horse-litters. The good brothers at

38

Dunkeld will attend to them, tonight. They would have it so, I assure you. The dead we will carry with us, for burial in their own glens."

"But why the haste, man? Wait until the morrow, at least."

"Tomorrow might be too late, my lord."

"Too late? For what?"

"For our safety."

"Safety from whom, of a mercy?"

"From the same man as heretofore — the Governor of this realm. Think you that he will love us any the more for this day's outcome?"

"God's eyes, man — you are under *my* protection, now! The Governor will not touch you, I tell you."

"You tell me, yes, my lord — and I thank you. But is our Uncle Robert aware of it? Or heeding? You are heir to the throne, and with much influence. But he it is who still governs this kingdom and wields *power*. Men must obey his word — unless you or His Grace are there to controvert it. So, being in even less good state to withstand him than we were on our way south, we retire behind our Highland hills forthwith. Where even he dare not follow us, I think. So I promised *Mac an Toiseach Mor*, Captain of Clan Chattan."

The prince seldom displayed his anger — although Jamie Douglas at least could recognise the signs, the lifted left eyebrow, the slight flaring of fine nostrils, the increased brilliance of the smile. Now he positively beamed.

"I could almost conceive you to insult me, Cousin," he murmured. "But have it as you will, since you judge me unable to protect you and your hillmen. Perhaps one day you will learn who rules this Scotland. Jamie — have Red John Stewart and his guard escort our doubting friend back to the skirts of his precious mountains. My lords, if you are finished here . . .?"

Jamie Douglas lingered for a few moments with Alexander Stewart. "That was . . . a pity," he said.

"Perhaps. But as well to know always where we stand."

"The Earl David could be as valuable a friend as a dangerous enemy, Alex."

"No doubt. I have no wish to have him enemy, God knows. Uncle Robert is enemy enough! But first dangers first! I gave my word to the Mackintosh — as *you* once gave your word to my father, in like case. As did David also."

"I have not forgotten. So be it. But . . . you heard what he said anent a deputy in the North justiciary? Play your hand aright, Alex, and you might ride high on that tide."

"But — is it a tide I wish to rise on, Jamie . . . ?" the Wolf of Badenoch's son wondered.

II

FIVE-YEAR-OLD David Douglas frowned darkly at his father, his mother, his three-year-old sister Alison and his nurse Janet Durie, in turn; but it was at the last that he pointed his small imperious finger.

"She is bad!" he asserted. "Janet is bad. An ill woman. I will *not* go to bed with Alie. She is younger than I am and goes to bed first. Everybody knows that."

"But you are late already, Davie," his mother pointed out, reasonably. "Both of you. Janet is quite right . . ."

"She is not. I will not go." Straddling his stocky little legs widely, the heir to Aberdour, Roberton, Stoneypath and Baldwinsgill stood, rock-firm, and summoned up his blackest scowl — which could be black indeed, like the rest of him.

"On my soul, he grows more like his father every day!" Mary Stewart declared. "A true Douglas — black in manners, habits and conduct as in appearance! And so overweening as is beyond belief!"

"To be sure," Jamie agreed. "I fear it is the bad Stewart blood in him. He minds me more of his uncle the late Wolf than of any Douglas I know. And as for overweening, he is after all the grandson of one king and like to be the godson and namesake of another."

It was the little girl's turn to assert herself. "I gave Davie an apple with a worm in it," she announced informatively. "A white, curly one. He ate it in half." Her expression angelic, she sighed, with all the sympathy in the world. "Poor curly worm."

"And there, further, speaks the voice of Stewart womanhood!" her father exclaimed. "Seldom have I heard it more eloquently expressed!" Certainly the child had all the renowned

41

good looks of the female Stewarts, of exquisite features, flaxen fairness, purple-blue eyes and a grace of manner to charm the sourest.

But not, in this instance, the ill-used Davie Douglas. "I hate her," he announced simply. "And I hate Janet too."

"Sirrah!" his father declared, "for that unknightly word, *you* shall go to bed first. And if the other half of the curly worm remains uneaten, Alison shall have it!" Sternly he strode over to the children, picked one up under each arm and marched off with them up the winding turnpike stair of Aberdour Castle keep, right to the little garret bedroom within the parapet-walk, the giggling young nurse following.

When he returned to the modest first-floor hall, it was to be chided by his lively and lovely wife.

"I vow those poor bairns never know whether their father is carping at them or cozening them. Sometimes I do not know myself. I never met a man who could proclaim his mirth under so sombre a visage!"

"Would you have me smirking and leering all the while, like some of those half-men at Court, woman?" he demanded.

"I would but have you to smile, say twice a day, my love — thrice on saints' days! And fill my cup of happiness. Once at the bairns' bed-times, once at your own. The warm results might surprise you, sir!"

He achieved a grin at that, at least. "Sakes, girl — if the results were warmer than your usual at such times, I doubt if I could stand up to it!"

"Craven! Poltroon! We shall put you to the test this very night!"

"Lord — as well that I am off the morn for a spell of only hard *horse*-riding! You Stewarts are devils between the blankets, male and female!"

"At least I may send you off on your travels in suitable state to be a leal husband, until we forgather again! How many days, Jamie? And nights?"

"Nine. Ten at the most. All must be at Cortachy by Saint Gregory's Eve, 11th of March, at latest. And I with them. And you must be there by then likewise, with the Lady Isabel — since you prefer to escort her, rather than that I should! It is fell important that she should come, David says. He cannot be sure that the Lady Katherine will come, Lindsay's wife — and he would wish *some* royal support."

"I hope David knows what he is doing and where he is going, in this."

"He knows very well, that one, where and how and what," Jamie said, but sombrely again. "It is that he does not count the cost, ever. And the cost could be high, high."

"Yet you aid and abet him in it? For love of David? Or hatred of Robert?"

He did not answer that.

She gripped his arm. "Go warily, Jamie," she pleaded. "I am not the most careful of women, as well you know. But at Davie Stewart's heels you could come to sore hurt. I reckon I would almost sooner see you at Isabel's beck and call again, than his!"

"Yet you have ever supported him. And against the Earl Robert."

"Aye. But this is different, more dangerous. You know it. Being against the Governor, hostile to him in matters general, is one matter. Many are that. But plotting his downfall is another. So be careful, lad — for you are the only husband I have . . ."

Next morning early, Sir James Douglas rode away eastwards from Aberdour, with only the one man-at-arms as attendant and groom. Eastwards, through Fife, was not the way he wanted to go — just as he would have been safer with a round dozen of armed men at his back, in Robert the Third's lawless and faction-riven kingdom; but he desired to go inconspicuously, and the Governor had spies and informers everywhere, and was well known to hear tell of every traveller of any note who crossed Forth from and to Fife by either Queen Margaret's Ferry to the west or at his own Earl's Ferry to the east. Jamie therefore made his way thus early to the bustling port of Dysart, ten miles eastwards, where the Bishop of St. Andrews maintained not a ferry but a number of ferry-scows for travel and transport, across Forth, to the see's great lands and properties in Lothian, to and from which there was constant coming and going. The Archdeacon Thomas Stewart of St. Andrews, under whose immediate authority such transport came, was another of the late King's bastards, and full brother of Mary. His friendship and aid Jamie had more than once found useful.

The traveller landed, in mid-afternoon, at Haddington's little port of Aberlady, on the south shore of the firth, amidst a scowful of monks, friars and officials of Holy Church. Sir James Lindsay of Crawford's castle of Luffness was nearby, scene of dramatic events eight years before; but Jamie did not include it in his itinerary on this occasion, for Lindsay was a very sick man and unlikely to recover. Likewise, he did not make for the great Douglas castle of Tantallon, which the Governor had high-handedly taken over for his own use; Archie the Grim, 3rd Earl of Douglas, his friend, unprotesting.

His first call was at the castle of Dirleton, mid-way between these two, where he saw Sir Walter Haliburton, and presented the Earl of Angus's invitation to attend his majority celebration at Cortachy in Angus in ten days' time. If Haliburton, a fiery young man, was somewhat surprised to be so asked, his doubts were resolved when Jamie told him that David, Earl of Carrick would be present, and urged his attendance. He promised to be there.

The next destination was fourteen miles distant to the south-east, at the royal burgh of Dunbar, where Jamie arrived with the early March night-fall. Here, facing out over the open sea, not the Firth of Forth, perched in highly unusual fashion on low cliffs and jutting stacks at the harbour entrance, its masonry actually forming bridges over the surging waters, rose the Earl of Dunbar and March's principal stronghold. In rich red stone and conforming to no recognisable plan or pattern, it was a strange building which had grown over the centuries but only where the rocks and stacks permitted; so that, in fact, it seemed more like a great natural extension of the cliffs themselves, built of the same stone, than any work of man. There was no other castle quite like it in all Scotland; but then, there was no other noble quite like George Cospatrick Dunbar, either.

Jamie was received in more friendly fashion here than he would be in many non-Douglas houses; for the Earl of Dunbar it was who had in fact conferred the accolade of knighthood upon him, nine years earlier, after the famous battle of Otter-burn when, on the murder of the 2nd Earl of Douglas, George Dunbar had assumed the command of the Scots force. A man of now later middle years, moderately handsome features rather spoiled by a broken nose received at some tournament, he was an individual of moods, unpredictable, more cultured than most of the Scots nobility, but not an easy man to work with because of a highly independent mind which by no means accepted that normal restraints, loyalties and indeed laws should apply to him. He was indeed the proudest character, in respect of ancient lineage, in all the realm, tenth earl in direct male succession from the line of the early Celtic monarchs, descending on the female side from the English royal house also. Beside him, the Stewarts, Douglases, Lindsays, even the Bruces, seemed comparative newcomers on the Scottish scene, gaining their high positions by the sword, intrigue or judicious marriages with Celtic-line heiresses. George Cospatrick Dunbar let none forget it.

After being handed a sealed letter from the Earl David, Dunbar left Jamie to eat a solitary meal, in the company only of a bevy of shaggy deer-hounds, in a corner of the vast shadowy great hall lit by smoky pitch-pine torches. The Earl was a widower, his sons from home, his only daughter not on view, and the huge rambling stronghold, loud with the sound of waves, was a chilly, echoing, gloomy place where draughts constantly stirred the arras hanging against the stone walls. Dunbar owned a score of castles in a dozen counties of Scotland, the entire Isle of Man also; and it was strange that he should choose to make this one his principal domicile, dramatic history notwithstanding.

Fed and refreshed, Jamie was led by a servitor through a succession of winding vaulted corridors, their walls running with damp, which were, he could sense, bridges over the swirling tide, to a small private chamber in a detached tower, hung with tapestries and lined with books and parchments, where the Earl George stood in front of a well-doing log fire, the warm comfort contrasting notably with the spray which every few moments splattered against the shuttered windows.

"Draw in to this fire, Sir James," his host said civilly. "It is chilly again, after the softer weather we have been having. Ill conditions for riding the country."

"None so bad, my lord. I have ridden abroad in much worse. As well, since this gathering I come to tell of has been planned for the earliest date possible when the lower Mounth passes should be clear of snow. Hard weather now could ruin all."

"Aye, no doubt. Angus in fact came of age in January, did he not?" The Earl waved the opened letter in his hand. "You know what is written in this?"

"Only in general, my lord. The Earl David honours me with his confidence in sundry matters."

"You will know, then, that he seeks my aid in a league against his uncle, the Governor — whom God rot! This aid he seeks — what is it for? What does he plan?"

"That, my lord, I cannot tell. I do not know. This is what

45

the gathering at Cortachy is to debate — under the cover of the Earl of Angus's coming-of-age celebrations. A secret gathering . . ."

"Yes, man, yes — I understand that. But before I go traipsing off to Angus on this young man's caper, to my much discomfort, I must know at least in some measure what he proposes. There could be danger in this . . ."

"There is ever danger. my lord, where the Earl Robert is concerned. This is to seek to lessen it."

"A plague on it, man — that goes without saying. Do you have no notion as to what young Carrick plans? What action he envisages? He must have something in mind."

"No doubt, sir. But he has not confided it to me. I am but his messenger, in this. He does not wish it talked about at large, bruited abroad, lest it come to the Earl Robert's sharp ears. The Governor has his creatures everywhere . . ."

"Of that I am well aware also. But not in Dunbar Castle, I think!" He waved the letter. "David Stewart must require my help badly, I swear — since to obtain it he offers to marry my daughter! Did you know of that, Sir James?"

The younger man blinked. "No, my lord — no. I . . . ah . . . this is a surprise to me."

The other smiled faintly. "And to me. My daughter is but fourteen years. Young for her age. I had not considered her marriage, as yet, seriously. Certainly not that she might be the future Queen. Yet this letter offers just that. Why? What does he want of me, at that price? He knows that I have no love for Robert Stewart, anyway. Any move against him would have my sympathy. So what is this for?"

Jamie was nonplussed. On the face of it, this suggestion of marriage to Dunbar's daughter was an unlikely one. The girl was little more than a plain-faced, gawky child as yet, scarcely an attraction in herself as bride for the dashing heir to the throne. As an alliance of houses it did not seem to reveal obvious advantages. Admittedly, Dunbar was very rich, owning vast lands apart from much of this Lothian, and Man, in the Merse, Lauderdale, Annandale, Nithsdale, Clydesdale, Galloway and Ayrshire, capable of producing great numbers of men as well as riches. But these territories had never been integrated into any strategic man-raising block, united by name and clanship, as were those of Douglas for instance. Nor was George Dunbar a particularly notable warrior; indeed his record of treasonable

activities was worse than that of any other noble in Scotland —
although undoubtedly he would not call it that, since he considered himself a free agent, a semi-royal and all but independent
princeling, who contrived alliances as he would. He had gone
over actively to the English side in disputes twice already — as
indeed had his forefathers — once in 1385 and again in 1393,
when he considered his interests thus best served. In every way,
he seemed an unlikely choice as prospective father-in-law for
the future monarch. Yet David Stewart, however impulsive,
seldom made major moves without good reason. It might even
be that it was Dunbar's English links which interested the
prince, at this juncture — and the fact that Dunbar controlled
the vital East March of the border. The Governor, whatever
else he was, was consistently anti-English. Who could tell —
David might even be prepared to play with such dangerous
fire . . .

"I know not, my lord — save that an alliance with your great
and illustrious house could advantage any . . ."

"Pshaw, man — spare me that! The Stewarts have always
hated and feared my house. I think it may well be merely that,
with Douglas firm on the Governor's side, the Earl Archibald
and to a lesser extent your own father, he thinks to use me
as a counter-weight. Well, we shall discover — if I come to
Cortachy."

"I pray that you do so, sir — for the realm's sake. If it comes
to a struggle between the Earl David and the Governor, every
man's support is like to be vital. And you are one of the greatest
in the kingdom . . ."

"I do not require you, young man, to tell me of my duty
towards the realm!" the other snapped. "But we shall see . . ."

Next day Jamie proceeded due southwards through the
Lammermuir Hills, by the pass of Monynut, to the Whitadder
Water and so to Duns and the Merse. A long day's stiff riding
brought him to Roxburgh, where Tweed and Teviot joined,
forty miles without making any calls — for this was all still
within the earldom of Dunbar and March, and its lords and
lairds would do as the Earl said. Fourteen further miles up
Teviotdale, deep in the Borderland now, and wearily, with the
dusk, the traveller came to Cavers, in a hanging valley amongst
green whin-clad knolls high above the river and under the
thrusting conical hill of Ruberslaw. Here was the massive peel-
tower of a friend and distant kinsman of his own, Sir Archibald

Douglas, illegitimate son of the previous Earl of Douglas, knighted like himself on the field of Otterburn where his father had fallen. Now aged twenty-four, he was a stocky, dark young man, like his sire, of a cheerful, outgoing and uncomplicated nature. Jamie had no difficulty in convincing him to come to Cortachy. Nor did he require persuading to take the risk of offending his present chief, Archibald, Earl of Douglas, his father's successor. None of the murdered Earl James's kin and close followers were greatly enamoured of Archie the Grim, who had disappointed the entire clan by his support of the Governor. Many indeed claimed that he should never have been appointed Earl of Douglas, and that the earldom should have gone to another, notably to this Sir Archibald of Cavers' elder brother, Sir William of Drumlanrig. Admittedly Sir William was illegitimate — for the Earl James had had no lawful offspring — but then, so was Archie the Grim himself, Lord of Galloway and natural son of the great Bruce's heroic friend, the Good Sir James Douglas, greatest of the race. Jamie was not desirous of promoting any sort of revolt against his chief, nor against his own father who supported the Earl Archie and therefore the Governor; but, along with many another Douglas, he felt that their great and powerful house was not playing the part it should, and could, in faction-torn Scotland.

Sir William of Drumlanrig, whose tower rose right in the midst of the little town of Hawick, only three miles from Cavers, was presently from home, tending his lands in Dumfries-shire; but his brother assured that he would send for him and have him at Cortachy likewise, within the week. Satisfied — for these two between them largely controlled much of the Middle March, and could muster almost a thousand tough and mounted Border mosstroopers — Jamie headed on westwards the following morning, over the lofty watershed of Southern Scotland, for Moffat, Upper Nithsdale, Carrick, Kyle and Cunninghame, where he had many more calls to make. It was indeed going to take him all his time to reach Angus, nearly two hundred miles to the north-east, by the due date.

*   *   *

Cortachy was not a castle in the accepted sense, but rather a fortified private township, in the old Celtic tradition, a seat of the former Celtic Mormaors and Earls of Angus and now the temporary domicile of their successor the young George

Douglas, dispossessed of Tantallon in Lothian by the Governor. It was a sprawling, untidy establishment which had outgrown its containing stone walls and earthen embankments and ditches, set pleasingly in the green haughs where the South Esk and Prosen Water joined at the mouth of the great Glen of Clova, under all the snow-capped Highland mountains. It guarded the southern exit from the White Mounth pass from Upper Deeside, part-Highland, part-Lowland. It was crowded this St. Gregory's Eve, in mid-March 1397, but few there were Highlanders.

George Douglas was an unlikely figure to be the focus of so much stir and excitement, a pale and frail young man, almost fragile-seeming, with large anxious eyes and a diffident air — although there was more to him than might appear at first glance. His mother was the power here, Margaret Stewart, Countess of Angus, a lusty, hearty woman still, with an unusual and complicated history, countess in her own right, widow of the last Earl of Mar and mistress of the 1st Earl of Douglas. This young man was the illegitimate son of the said William of Douglas, to whom she had conveyed the earldom of Angus. He had been accepted by all to be a Douglas, not a Stewart. Undoubtedly he found his lively mother and stirring ancestry hard to live up to.

On this occasion, although friendly to all, he made little attempt to act the host. That duty was taken over with entire authority by David, Earl of Carrick — in between flirting outrageously with his hostess, who was almost old enough to be his grandmother. The Stewarts were apt to be like that. The heir to the throne was at his brilliant best, gay, witty, winning, approachable, putting all at ease — save for the women, none of whom seemed to remain unaffected by his rampant sensuality. He should have been drunk throughout, from the amount of liquor he consumed — and possibly was, although he gave little sign of it.

It was a great gathering, in those rather odd surroundings, skilfully selected and assembled, with half the nobility of Scotland represented, as well as certain members of the royal house. Not a great deal was attempted to emphasise the theme of Angus's coming-of-age; that was merely the excuse for the bringing together of so great and diverse a company so that suspicion would not be aroused in the Governor's circle. It was as well that the Earl David was so able a host, for many of the guests were antipathetic if not downright enemies, their only common ground a hatred of the Governor and all his works.

Jamie was delighted to reunite with his Mary — who actually had reached Cortachy before him, in the company of two of her half-sister princesses, the Lady Jean Stewart, formerly married to Sir John Lyon the Chamberlain and now to Sir John Sandilands, Lord of Calder; and the Lady Isabel, wife of Sir John Edmonstone. The latter's husband was not present, for he was a vassal and supporter of the Lord of Dalkeith, Jamie's father, and therefore in the opposite camp; but his wife, widow of the murdered Earl of Douglas, hated her brother the Governor sufficiently to insist on attending in person.

The banquet held in the great hall of the place, a long detached building of its own in the midst of the township, had to be a carefully managed occasion. Food and drink were available in rich profusion, and all must be satisfied; yet it was important that drunkenness on a major scale should not overtake any large percentage of the guests before decisions were reached, a difficult matter to ensure. Deliberately therefore the wines and spirits were held back in some measure, and elaborate entertainment provided throughout the meal, so that the deprivation might be the less noticeable; singers, jugglers, dancers, acrobats and the like performed without pause in the cleared space to one side of the long tables, amongst the hurrying servitors and the roaming, stealing and squabbling deer- and wolf-hounds — a lively scene under the smoky, flickering blaze of the torches. Even so, not a few of the company managed to get distinctly noisy and elevated on the light ale — or perhaps they had been indulging beforehand — to the extent of joining in with the entertainers, one pair of young lords capering up and down the table-tops themselves, weaving in and out amongst the viands and flagons, whilst Jamie's own half-sister, wife of Philip Arbuthnott of that Ilk and a bold piece, left the board to dance a wild jig with a handsome gypsy, pushing aside his partner to do so.

The Earl David, up at the transverse dais-table and flanked by young Angus and his mother, watched all heedfully whilst apparently by no means stinting himself of food and wine and jollity. Deciding that the moment had come, he rose to his feet, a resplendent, glittering figure. At a sign from him a servitor rang a bell, and gradually quiet was established. The entertainers were hustled out, the capering lordlings coaxed down from the table and the panting and dishevelled Lady Arbuthnott restored to her place on the bench between her equally disapproving husband and half-brother Jamie. Amidst sundry hushings, the High Steward and Prince of Scotland spoke, pleasantly, conversationally.

"My lords and ladies and friends all," he said, "we are here gathered for the most happy and felicitous of employment, the celebration of the coming to full years of our good friend and host, George Douglas, Earl of Angus and Lord of Abernethy. His reaching of this great age, something I myself cannot aspire to for two years yet, mark you, should be a source of joy and satisfaction to us all, and indeed to this ancient realm, in the councils of which he will now be able to play his full and important part. In urging you all to rise and drink to the health, well-being and success of George Douglas, I say that we should couple with it that of his lady-mother, whose beauty, talents and attractions grow but the more dazzling with each year that passes. I tell you . . ."

The rest was drowned in shouted acclaim, as all who were able to do so lifted to their feet to pledge the Earl and Countess in vociferous if less than decorous fashion. It was perhaps noticeable that many more eyes lingered on the mother than the son.

After a little, Angus rose from his chair, said simply, "I thank you all," and sat down again. The Countess Margaret threw kisses at large and then pulled down the Earl David at her side to salute him full and protractedly on the lips, to the cheers of the company.

Murmuring something in the lady's ear, David Stewart straightened up. "I thank the good God that this is not *my* mother!" he observed, with a joyful laugh and significant pause, and received a slap on the wrist for his pains. "However," he went on, when he could make himself heard, "something of the sort is proposed. My esteemed royal father, to express his pleasure in the occasion and his favour towards George of Angus, has graciously consented to bestow the hand of his second daughter, my sister Mary, on the said George, in betrothal. Which will make him and myself brothers, and therefore his mother perilously near to being mine!"

As the din occasioned by this pronouncement continued, Jamie looked at his wife. He had had no inkling of this. Clearly it represented a major departure in policy, David's policy, since it was unlikely that the King had done more than merely accede. It was one thing to use Angus's majority as an excuse to assemble supporters from far and near in this remote hold, altogether another to ally him intimately to the royal house in marriage. To what advantage? George Douglas was an inoffensive young man and no warrior. Nor was he particularly rich or strong in manpower. Personally therefore he was of no great value to the prince's cause. Yet this especial mark of favour must have some good reason — for the King had only three daughters and the eldest already married to the Master of Douglas, the Earl Archie's heir; and the third to Jamie's own half-brother, heir to the Lord of Dalkeith. It could only be the vital Douglas connection, then, Jamie concluded, the determination to support the Crown with Douglases, in the next generation. No doubt also as warning to Earl Archie and his son that their hold on the Douglas earldom might not be all that secure. After all, this George Douglas was a son of the first Earl, and half-brother of the second, much closer to the main stem than was Archie the Grim. Wed to a princess, he might be used conveniently to supplant the Galloway line should cause and opportunity arise. That would be it . . .

"The Earl Archie is not going to like this!" Mary whispered in his ear, indicating that she had reached the same conclusion. "Nor is Robert. But many Douglases will."

He nodded. "He is making a bid, I think, to separate Douglas from the Governor. Possibly even to challenge the leadership."

The prince was continuing. "Whilst we are on matters matrimonial, it is my further great satisfaction to declare that His Grace is likewise pleased to accede to my own betrothal to the Lady Elizabeth Dunbar, with my lord Earl of Dunbar and March's kind agreement, a match and alliance which, I am sure, will give all cause for much rejoicing." He turned towards where that Earl sat at the dais-table between the Princesses Isabel and Jean, and raised his wine-cup. "My lord, I drink to our mutual felicity."

This time there was no riotous din as reaction but something of a hush as men and women groped in their minds for the reason for this utterly unexpected and unlikely intimation. So much was involved in this. Dunbar was unpopular with most of the nobility, resented by many and distrusted by almost all. His wealth and power were not belittled; but his suitability as father-in-law of the future monarch, his unknown daughter as the next Queen, were highly questionable.

Dunbar rose, bowed gravely to the prince, sipped his wine, and sat down unspeaking.

Recognising, as no doubt he had planned, that the time had come to dispense with pleasantries and side-issues, the Earl David changed his tone and manner to a suitable seriousness.

"My friends," he went on, "these matters of kindly goodwill and celebration are to our comfort and satisfaction. But we announce them in ill times, our ancient realm in sorrowful state. My royal father's kingdom is divided, misgoverned, endangered. There is chaos and faction and discord within, and threat from without, our friends at enmity, our enemies like to seize their opportunity against us. I have secret but sure word that the English plan to beset us, taking advantage of our divided state, although there is truce, but recently renewed, between the realms."

The growl from his listeners proclaimed their predictable rising to that age-old but unfailing bait.

"At home here, as we all know, the King's law is disregarded on all hands. Men are permitted to do as they will, he who has power taking what he covets, the weak and the helpless crushed."

The prince paused at that, looking around him slowly, significantly. There were not a few of the powerful present, used to doing just as he said. Many pairs of eyes concentrated on their plates and wine-goblets. No comment was forthcoming.

"The Treasury, moreover, is empty, the King's taxes, revenues and customs uncollected or handed over as pensions and bribes and fees of support. Due and proper charges are not paid, the trade of the merchants and craftsmen is stolen, the King's roads, bridges, fords and ferries are not maintained, the ports and harbours are choked, sea-walls broken, flood-banks breached, town-walls crumbling. Even my royal mother's yearly portion, established by parliament, has been withheld these three years by the Chamberlain's deputies."

Again he paused. All knew who was now Great Chamberlain of Scotland. The growl which had remained muted over the depredations of the powerful barons rumbled satisfactorily again.

"Who is responsible for this evil state of the realm?" the speaker demanded. "My royal sire, the King, reigns, yes. So he cannot avoid some blame. He sorrows for it. But owing to age, ill-health and infirmity, His Grace is unable to *rule* his

53

kingdom as he would, and should. So he appointed a Governor to rule it in his name. That Governor and Great Chamberlain, his brother the Earl of Fife and Menteith, has ruled the land these eight years. In these years, evil has multiplied and triumphed and good has been put down, justice set at naught, the revenues squandered, place-seekers and lickspittles are raised up and honest men slighted. I say that it is enough, that it is time for change!"

A great shout greeted that declaration, and continued. Flagons, beakers and fists beat on table-tops. There was no doubt as to the support for that sentiment amongst those present, divided as they might be otherwise. But doubts were implicit.

"How?" Lindsay of Glenesk barked, when he could make himself heard. "Change, yes — but how is it to be effected? When the Governor controls all?"

Many voices echoed that vital question.

"Bear with me, Uncle and my lords, for a moment," the prince said. "There must be change. And change, to be effective, means that the Governorship must be changed. Although the Earl Robert of Fife is my own near kin, I say it. Fife must go. And although, as you, my lord, say, he presently controls all, I believe he can be *made* to go. And must . . ."

"How? How?" The demands came on every hand now.

"I have thought long on this, my friends," David assured. "I am young, yes — but I have consulted with wise heads, my royal mother in especial, who grieves sorely for the realm. I have come to the conclusion that there are four means by which we may unseat my uncle. It will take time, for we must by no means risk war, civil war amongst our people. But the four together, I am convinced, will do it. And, I say, within a year or eighteen months."

He had the keen attention of all, even the drink-taken leaning forward, ears cupped.

"Here is the gist of it. Four heads, but all linked. To be spoken to more fully hereafter. First, the English threat — for nothing will more swiftly unite our folk. The English threat — with the Governor shown to care nothing, taking no steps to counter it. Second, money, siller, the empty Treasury — and the Governor giving bribes to his friends and shown to be but lining his own pockets. Third, a parliament to deal with this, a parliament called to *our* tune, not his. Lastly, and necessarily, to detach Douglas from his support."

Into the buzz of excited comment and exclamation, Mary spoke to her husband. "I did not know that he had it in him. This, this state-craft. He is more able than I knew."

"Aye — but can he carry it further? Can he convince that all this is possible? He has made a good start, yes. But he must convince. And there are hard heads here . . ."

It was as though the prince had heard them. But then, many, no doubt, were saying or thinking the same. "My friends — you may consider that I but beat the air. Hear me, then. Take the last first — Douglas. The Earl Archibald is close to the Governor, unhappily. But he could be detached, I swear — at least in large enough measure for our purposes. His son and heir, the Master, my own good-brother, married to my eldest sister, loves Fife a deal less. He is unhappy at the role of Douglas today — as are many here. The Douglases are fighters ever, and even Archie the Grim must gravely doubt the policy of appeasing the English. Especially as much of his great lands lie along the Border, and suffer. My Uncle Robert made one great mistake. On the death of Earl James Douglas he snatched the Chief Wardenship of the Marches for himself, because of its revenues, when it should have gone with the Douglas earldom. Always the Chief Warden was Douglas. Now, with the English threat, the Border Marches come to the fore. And they are not being protected. We have, in this room, the Hereditary Sheriff of Teviotdale, Sir William Douglas of Drumlanrig, who with his brother of Cavers, all but controls the Middle March. Also here is the Earl of Dunbar and March, who controls the East March. The West March is the Earl Archibald's, deputed to his son the Master. Where, I ask you, does that leave the Chief Warden, the Governor? I say all but powerless in a most vital area. But *responsible!* If we cannot use that situation to prise the Earl Archie and the rest of Douglas further from Robert Stewart, then we are poor creatures indeed. Moreover, we now have another Douglas earl, of full age, and to be allied to the royal house, with a more ancient earldom than that of Douglas. How say you, my friends?"

There was no question about the reaction. Even the most sceptical were impressed. The Douglases were the most powerful house in the land, and essentially a Border clan. Use the Border-land and English threats thereto as lever, in skilful hands, and almost anything could be done with them. Most there indubitably had forgotten that amongst the innumerable offices and positions the Earl Robert had appropriated to his own uses was that of Chief Warden of the Marches. The Douglas brothers of Drumlanrig and Cavers were loudest in their acclaim. Dunbar looked thoughtful and young Angus uncomfortable.

"This English threat?" Lindsay demanded. "I have heard naught of any such. What substance is there to it? Other than casual raiding, which is always with us."

"I come to that, Uncle. There is substance indeed. It is like a pitch-fork, double-pronged. Carefully planned. Donald of the Isles, my esteemed cousin, has entered treasonably into what he terms a treaty with Richard of England whereby he will make an attack by sea in the West, at the same time as Richard sends a force into the East and Middle Marches. Donald, injured over Skye and the earldom of Ross which he claims as his and which the Governor conveys to his daughter's husband, will descend with his galley-fleet on the Galloway, Carrick, Kyle and Cunninghame coasts."

"When, by God?" Sir John Montgomerie of Eaglesham cried, whose lands lay in Kyle and the Ayrshire coast.

"Before summer, I am told. When the season is apt for coastal landings and campaigning . . ."

"Save us — and we do nothing!"

"I, Carrick, intend to do something, my lord of Eaglesham! As you will hear. It is the Governor who does nothing."

"Curse him . . .!"

There was uproar in the hall now, for there were many present from Galloway and Ayrshire, the fruit of Jamie's patient calls.

"Wait you, my friends — cry out not too soon," the prince advised. "My father's lands of Dundonald and Bute, and my own of Carrick and Turnberry, are thereabouts. So I am as much concerned as any here. But I believe that we can turn this to our great advantage, well before Donald is ready to strike." He paused. "We are fortunate, I think, in that Richard of Bordeaux, King of England, is a fool! Rash and arrogant, setting his own nobility, even his own kin, against him. He has had his uncle, Gloucester, arrested and slain, likewise Arundel. Which much offends his other uncle, John of Gaunt, Duke of Lancaster. Now, to distract his people's attention from his follies at home, Richard will adventure into Scotland, as he has done before. For this he requires commanders and men, for he is no warrior himself. So he must needs turn again to the stalwart Lancaster, his best soldier still. And for men, in the North, he needs the Earl of Northumberland — or Hotspur, his son. These are to invade the East and Middle Marches when Donald descends on the West. If we do not halt them first."

"Halt them with what? John of Gaunt will not halt lightly!" Lindsay asserted.

"It is my hope to halt him with words rather than men," he was told. "See you, my lord of Dunbar has the advantage over the lave of us, in that he has good friends and even kin south of the Border." The prince said that straight-faced, although most would not have done so. "John of Gaunt is one of them, Hotspur likewise. I say that we could turn this to good effect. Hotspur, the Percy, is Warden of the English East March as is my lord on our side. The Wardens meet, ever and anon, to settle Border differences. I say, with my lord's good offices, we will call a greater meeting, letting the English know that we are aware of their projected invasion, prepared for it, and requesting John of Gaunt to be present, as well as Hotspur. We could claim this meeting under the terms of the truce. On our side, as well as my lord of Dunbar and myself, we would ask Earl Archie of Douglas but also Earl George of Angus, here. Others likewise, including our friends of Drumlanrig and Cavers. This well before Donald can move. I believe we could force Lancaster to come, and thereafter prevent the venture. The Earl of Dunbar is Lord of Man. If a host was to be mustered on that isle, directly opposite John of Gaunt's Lancaster coast, with many boats assembled for transport, I think the Duke would think twice of obeying his arrogant nephew Richard. And all done with the Governor not having stirred a hand!"

There was a pause whilst men took all that in. Gradually heads began to nod in appreciation. No objections were put forward, although not a few glances were cast doubtfully at Dunbar. The prince's gesture towards him in the matter of the betrothal was now better understood, tying him to the Scots side; but not all were disposed to trust him, even so. He sat, toying with his wine-cup, a half-smile on his tough features.

"So much for Douglas and the English threat," the Earl David resumed cheerfully. "Now, as to the revenues, siller. Next to English invasion, naught effects men more than the belief that moneys are being stolen from them! The misappropriation of the King's funds is a large subject and not easily brought home to ordinary folk, I agree. But actual sums, figures, charged against a single man can be understood, and telling." He reached into a doublet pocket and brought out a paper. "Here are some, for you to remember and speak of, my lords and ladies. All relating to the Earl of Fife and Menteith, his private purse. As Governor, £1,000, or 12,000 ounces of silver yearly. As Chamberlain £200, although he is demanding £900 more for sundry expenses. As Keeper of Stirling Castle, £200. As protector of the Abthania of Dull, of the old Celtic Church, £200. From the royal customs of Cupar, £200. The same from Linlithgow. All the wool and hides from his two earldoms permitted to be exported free of the customs charged on others. There are more, many more than these. But these will serve. Remember some of them. We can use this to bring him down."

There were due cries of outrage; but likewise queries as to how this shameful catalogue could be used to effect their purpose. As Lindsay did not fail to point out, the Governor would care nothing for their mere condemnation.

"This is where my fourth charge to you arises," David Stewart told them. "The parliament. A parliament called, and these facts presented before it. An indictment of the Governor. The facts would tell, then. It could not be a true parliament, to be sure, since in effect now the Governor must call that, in the King's name — or the Chancellor calls it on the Governor's instructions — and Chancellor Peebles is in my uncle's pocket. But the Privy Council can call a Convention or General Council of the realm — also in the King's name — and I swear that I can muster sufficient votes thereon to carry the day, to outvote my uncle if he objects. There are seven members of the Privy Council here present. This will be the last of our steps against the Governor, and we must all ensure its success. Persuade all our friends and kin. Convince the people that we can, and must, unseat him. Especially the churchmen. The Church votes in the Estates are vital. We shall not put down Robert Stewart without them. He has much offended many of the clerics. Peebles the Chancellor, Bishop of Dunblane, is his man; but Bishop Trail of St. Andrews, the Primate, does not love him, and is close to my mother the Queen. Glendinning of Glasgow, and other bishops, are likewise against him. We must all work hard on this. By then I believe the English business will be settled, and my uncle discountenanced therein. The Douglases, also, should be deserting him, if I judge aright. We can do it, I say. A year, eighteen months . . ."

The gathering was getting noisy now, with enthusiasm mounting. But there were still some hard heads.

"An indictment of the Earl of Fife on this of moneys might be passed by such Convention, my lord — yet not achieve our aim." A new voice spoke, that of Sir James Sandilands, Lord of Calder, fairly recently become the husband of the widowed Lady Jean Stewart, and so one more uncle of the prince, a solid and influential man of middle years. "He might well bow to it, but no more. Not stand down. And we should be little the better."

"True. But after such vote, we can further force him, I believe. It will require a device, but will serve almost certainly. The Council must first declare misgovernment of the realm. This against my royal father — who already admits as much, to his sorrow. He will then acknowledge it to the Council, but declare that his officers have failed him, in especial the Governor, and charge the parliament or Convention, to judge the matter and put it right. This a royal command. The Convention would then *have* to arraign my uncle. And since the King had thus expressed no confidence in him beforehand, the vote could scarcely be other than against him — after this of the moneys."

That produced the loudest cheering of all. Lindsay had difficulty in making his strong voice heard.

"When you have unseated the Governor, Nephew, who will then govern in his place?" he demanded.

Smiling genially, the younger man spoke briefly, simply. "*I* will."

As all digested that, some with glee, some with sober approval, some with doubts, the prince turned to look along the dais-table to where his aunts sat on either side of Dunbar. He caught the Lady Isabel's eye and raised his brows.

That princess, now in her early forties, her lovely face showing the lines of strain and sorrow, nodded and moistened her lips. With some reluctance she spoke.

"My lords. My lords, I say . . ."

Her comparatively soft tones quite failed to penetrate the clamour of talk until the Earl of Dunbar banged his flagon on the table for quiet. She went on.

"Hear me, my lords. I speak as one close to His Grace the King, and much concerned for the welfare of this his realm. Hear a woman's voice, if you will. I say that what we have heard tonight should rejoice us all. I say indeed, thank God for

59

my nephew the Earl of Carrick and High Steward. That he is such as he is. Thank God that the heir to the throne is grown to man's stature in fashion as he has, strong, able, vigorous. For too long this kingdom has been weakly governed, and all have suffered for it. I say it, who have reason to know — although it has been my own royal father and brother from whom that weakness has stemmed. Kindly and gentle, they have not been of the stuff of kings. But at last we have one who is. My other brother, the Governor, has brought the realm to its knees. If it is to be saved, it must be saved soon, swiftly. I have come far to say this, and at some cost to myself. I urge that you support the Earl of Carrick with all your strength and will. The Earl of Fife can be put down from the high place he has held for too long — and must be. He has done . . . enough harm." Her voice choked a little at that, and for a moment it seemed that she would not go on. Then she rallied. "Unseat him, my lords, for the realm's sake and your own sake — and mine! And raise up in his place him who will one day be your rightful king."

There was a sympathetic murmur as she ended, into which the Lady Jean, her sister, exclaimed, "I say the same."

Mary whispered to her husband. "She did it well, in the end. I know how she dreaded it. To speak thus. And she has ever had her doubts about David. But she did well."

He nodded. "Yes. Her hatred of the one much outdoes her doubts of the other. I feared that she might fail him. But, no . . ."

The prince, assessing the approval which greeted his aunts' support, as indication that the royal family was largely behind him, judged the moment apt to bring the talking to a close. "I thank you both," he said. "Indeed I thank all here for heeding me so patiently, for showing that you are with me." He raised his wine-cup. "Drink with me," he urged. "Drink to His Grace, to the downfall of Robert Stewart and the reform of the realm's government."

All, enthusiastic, more soberly in general favour, or positively doubtful, must needs drink to that cunningly worded toast — since to fail to honour the King's Grace was as good as high treason. So all present were, in a measure, committed.

Summoning back the entertainers, and further supplies of wine, the Prince of Scotland sat down, prepared to enjoy the rest of the evening.

III

THE BORDERLAND WAS a joy to behold, with the spring green stippling the trees, the golden gorse ablaze on every knowe, the corn-spears beginning to thrust up, the lambs and calves frisking on the hillsides, the cuckoos calling in the valleys and all the Cheviots, snow-free to the summits at last, looming a purple-blue barrier to the south. Few failed to respond, in some measure, however subconsciously.

Jamie Douglas whistled tunelessly as he rode, with moderate content and no immediate responsibilities. He had done all that he could, and success or failure lay on more important shoulders than his own. He was not a wagering man, and would not have liked to stake a lot on the outcome of this day, one way or the other. But at least it was action of a sort, a start in putting to the test David Stewart's theories and plans, after much labour, persuasion, bargaining and drumming up of support. By this night, they should know if it had been worth while or mere wasted — and dangerous — effort; whether Scotland was likely to take the first faltering steps on a new course, or not.

The Earl David, at least, could not complain of lack of interest in his project — too much interest, rather. His own retinue was a distinguished one, for as well as the Earl of Angus, and the lords of Errol the Constable, Keith the Marischal, Eaglesham, Calder and Glenesk — although Sir David should now more properly be called of Crawford, since his cousin Sir James thereof had died of his sickness leaving no nearer heir and he had become chief of all the name of Lindsay — it included Bishop Walter Trail of St. Andrews, the Primate, Bishop Matthew Glendinning of Glasgow, the Archdeacon Thomas Stewart of St. Andrews, and the Abbot of Melrose, all entitled to sit on the Privy Council. Not far behind, but keeping a careful distance, was the Earl of Douglas's cavalcade, also illustrious, with the Master, the Lord of Dalkeith, Jamie's father, the lords of Mordington, Strabrock and other Douglas barons plus the Bishop of Galloway and the Abbots of Dundrennan and Newabbey.

This was fair enough, indication that Archibald the Grim took the business sufficiently seriously to come in some strength. But what was less encouraging was the fact that, not far behind the Douglases, rode still another glittering contingent — and this, like David Stewart's, under the royal banner of the Lion Rampant of Scotland. The Governor himself, Earl Robert Stewart of Fife and Menteith, had elected to come, uninvited, to this meeting at Haddonstank. As nominal Chief Warden of the Marches, of course, none could question his right to attend, furiously angry as he was known to be over this arrangement entered into with the English outwith his authority.

The meeting, whatever it effected, could hardly fail to be lively.

Haddonstank, on the Redden Burn, four miles east of Kelso but on the south side of Tweed, was the recognised meeting-place for the East March Wardens. Situated on steadily but gently rising ground, where the Borderline swung away southwards from the great river, it was just a few hundred yards inside Scotland. Because of the welter of Cheviot foothills behind, it seemed to turn its back on England and the South, to look out northwards over the farflung, extensive and undulating plain of the Scots Merse, a rich and fertile land of corn and pasture in marked contrast to the high heathy moors of North Northumberland, to make Englishmen's mouths water in contemplation — the goodly heritage of George Dunbar.

Today the broad shelf of grassland, normally cattle-strewn, was as busy and as colourful as any fair — as indeed to some extent it was, for these periodical Days of Truce were accepted as something of a holiday by the Border folk on both sides, and people who had no connection with Wardens' meetings and cases to be tried, flocked from far and near to attend, to meet friends, to make bargains, do business and possibly witness a hanging or a scourging. Packmen, pedlars, dealers, begging friars and the like seized the opportunity to ply their trades, and vendors of ale, wine of a sort and even hot cakes and shellfish did a good traffic. Always tents and pavilions and shelters were erected for the Wardens and their followers; but on this occasion the number of these was vastly increased, and to add to the colour, vivid and variegated heraldic banners flapped in the breeze above many, as above the men-at-arms' camps and horse-lines.

When the Earl of Carrick's company arrived half-an-hour before noon, George of Dunbar and March was already there, he being responsible for arranging the meeting. His opposite number, Sir Henry Percy, the famous Hotspur, English East March Warden and heir of the old Earl of Northumberland, was also present; and the two, who were old friends, indeed kin, had all ready and were drinking wine together. Hotspur, a gallant figure now in his late thirties, was well known to most of the Scots notables, for he had been taken prisoner after Otterburn in 1388 and had thereafter spent over a year in Scotland whilst the new castle of Polnoon was being built for his captor, Sir John Montgomerie of Eaglesham, its cost being the price of his release. He was a cheerful character, however arrogant, and good company when he considered that company up to his exacting standards — for to be sure he was one of the foremost champions of England, indeed Christendom, in the lists if not necessarily on the battlefield. He now greeted David Stewart with an easy, half-mocking deference, and Montgomerie his former captor with real warmth. He had a distinct burr, almost stammer in his speech — but none would dare call it a hesitancy or impediment.

These greetings were still in progress when the Earl of Douglas arrived, and he and his entourage were included in the welcome. Archie the Grim, although still a formidable, not to say daunting, character, at seventy-three had mellowed somewhat. Tall though bent, like a great stooping eagle, beak-nosed, iron-grey, harsh-voiced, irascible, he nevertheless was less feared than formerly, although few could ever be close to him — including his silent, watchful, scarcely likeable son, the Master of Douglas. The Earl's hot temper was proverbial, but he was reckoned an honest man, insofar as his position as head of the most powerful house in Scotland permitted, his long-term support and even friendship for the Governor wondered at but accepted as an idiosyncrasy — and possibly, conceivably, implying some virtue in Robert Stewart not generally discoverable. He greeted the heir to the throne warily, was barely civil to Hotspur, looked pityingly at Angus, ignored Dunbar entirely, and clanked and stamped about in half-armour and great spurs, hawking and spitting, glaring at all and sundry but not actually attacking anyone. More diplomatic Douglas relations were left to James, Lord of Dalkeith and Morton, a grave, courteous man in his mid-sixties, statesman rather than warrior, comfortably built, reputed to be the wealthiest noble in the kingdom. Jamie was, as almost always, quietly proud of his sire, who tended to show up well in most company, although he had chosen to adhere to the opposite side in the Scottish dichotomy from his illegitimate son. That Dalkeith supported the Earl Robert, as at least capable of holding a strong hand on the chronically unstable helm of Scotland, instead of the King's nerveless grasp, was apt to be a source of unease, not only to Jamie but to others who liked and admired him, not least the Lady Isabel Stewart, to whom he had acted protector on her husband's murder. He was, moreover, known to think but poorly of the Earl of Carrick.

The Governor's arrival could have provided a dramatic moment — save that there was little of the overtly dramatic about Robert Stewart, however much so his actions might be, on occasion. Cold, reserved, disapproving, he gave no impression of being emotionally involved in any way as he rode up to the meeting-place, save in a general distaste for all he saw. Soberly but richly clad, spare of figure, upright of carriage, he remained in his saddle, waiting until others came forward to receive him suitably.

David did that, cheerfully unabashed. "So, Uncle — you honour us with your presence!" he called, but without haste or coming close. "Excellent. I am glad that you have come to recognise the importance of what we seek to do."

"I recognise folly, insolence and youthful rashness, Nephew," the other answered thinly. "As I have had occasion to do ere this! And so am come, to seek undo such ill as folly may breed, in affairs best left to men of full age and experience."

"Ah — that is kind! To come aid us, in our immaturity. All here will be grateful, Uncle, I have no doubt — including the Earl of Douglas, whose immaturity and inexperience I had scarce recognised! Sir Harry Percy, here, you will remember . . . ?"

"Where is Lancaster? John of Gaunt?"

"He is not yet here. But he is not far off, I am told. Come — a cup of wine while we wait . . ."

The Earl Robert ignored that, and urged his horse aside,

over to where the undifferenced banner of Douglas waved above a pavilion — the only one, presumably, in which he was prepared to bestow his person.

"It looks ill," Angus said unhappily. "He is set against us. He will ruin all."

"Never think it," the prince assured. "He can do little here against us, without offending his friend Douglas — I shall see to that! Jamie — you are able to enter the Douglas tent unannounced, to speak with your father, if naught else. Go you, and try to hear what goes on between them. I need to know how the Earl Archie will behave, if I can. How he is disposed towards the Governor's strictures. John of Gaunt is an old friend of Douglas's, I am told, but mislikes my Uncle Robert. Watch and listen, for so long as you may . . ."

Jamie Douglas had indeed no difficulty in slipping into the Earl of Douglas's large pavilion, for the Master was standing in the doorway, with his overweight brother known as Sir James the Gross, and with them he was on good enough terms. Within, it was uncomfortably crowded, many of the Governor's supporters having followed their master in. Jamie's presence went scarcely noticed. The Lord of Dalkeith was talking with the two earls, and his son moved as close as he might, waiting ostensibly for speech with his father. It was not easy to hear all that was being said, however, for the noise of the general chatter.

It was sufficiently clear that the Earl Robert's displeasure was not being confined to his nephew, and the Douglas was finding it necessary to defend his own presence there in no uncertain fashion, Dalkeith as ever seeking to pour oil on troubled waters. Archie the Grim was barking out that he must needs protect his own interests, not only as West March Warden but because lands of his own were being preyed upon by English raiding parties, and especially by the impudent English garrison of Roxburgh Castle. The captain there was indeed demanding no less than £2,000 of compensation from him for his son James's breaking down of Roxburgh bridge — and this five miles within Scotland! Moreover, the Percy was claiming actual rights of use and want within Ettrick Forest, *his* Forest, seeking damages from him, Douglas, for having fired his camp there. To such a state had matters come in this Borderland . . .

Testily the Governor replied than none knew better than he that the English were insolent ever. But far more was at stake this day than any mere Border bickering. The due and proper rule of the realm was being challenged.

With the Douglas earl spluttering that the continued occupation of Scots' castles by Englishmen, and demands for thousands of pounds compensation, was scarcely mere bickering, Dalkeith soothingly suggested that it was all a question of which to deal with first, the cause or the effect. If they could strike at the roots of the English trouble, rather than the branches, they would achieve the more.

This seemed to mollify both men somewhat, since each evidently considered it to substantiate his own contention. The Governor's further assertion that his nephew's head was swelled altogether too large for a youth not yet of full age, and required to be reduced not a little, was accepted. But when he added that the young man was a fool and a dangerous fool, Dalkeith demurred, declaring that he believed him far from a fool; and that the danger could well lie in treating him as such. Rash and impetuous, yes — but these were common failings in young men of spirit. Safer to deal with him in such fashion, than to deem him fool and so underestimate him. Was that not why they were here? This point of view seemed to irritate the Earl Robert, who snapped that he required no advice as to how to deal with his brother's son, and was not going to have an arrogant stripling summoning English leaders to meet him, without the authority of the kingdom's Governor. He alone was competent to deal with Lancaster — as he would demonstrate. Why the proud Plantagenet had consented to come in the first place, he did not know. But if come he did, it was not for young Carrick to deal with him.

Archie the Grim was declaring that he did not care who dealt with his old gossip John of Gaunt so long as he obtained his rights, when a cry from outside intimated that the Duke of Lancaster approached. As they all trooped out to watch, Dalkeith perceived his son's presence.

"Ha, Jamie — I heard that you were here. You would be, to be sure. You have a habit of being where trouble is, these days — if not stirring it up! What are you at, here? What does the prince think he can achieve?"

"Much, my lord. For the good of the realm. Much that the Governor has not done, and appears to care naught for."

"Concerned with Lancaster?"

"Yes. In part." Jamie was wary. For though he loved and

66

admired his father they were seemingly on opposite sides in this, as in much. "But since you support the Governor, sir, we shall not agree on it."

"I do not support him blindly, lad," the older man said, low-voiced. "Nor wholly. Where what he does seems to be in the realm's interest, I support him, yes, in the cause of good government, of *any* firm government. He *is* the Governor, and until another is appointed it is all true men's duty to support him insofar as their consciences allow."

"How can you say that, in honesty, sir? When so much that he does is evil, oppressive, dishonest, contrary to all good conscience. You, a man of religious faith . . ."

"Perhaps, Jamie, I see things less clearly-cut, at sixty-seven years, than you do at twenty-seven! Kings and rulers cannot be judged by the same standards as ordinary men, they frequently must do deeds, in the interests of government, which would be wrongful in lesser men. You will learn as much, if so be you grow in wisdom with the years! All is not conveniently black and white, lad. I love not Robert Stewart — but the nation had *no* government until he took it in hand. Remember that. He has many faults — but so have I, to be sure. Even you may have one or two! We must make do with what we have, in matters of state."

"Thank God, then, that we have a prince and heir to the throne who is otherwise. Who will rule honestly, fairly."

"You think so? How good to have your young certainty. Does David seek the rule, then? Think to replace his uncle?"

Jamie bit his lip. "In due course," he said, more carefully. "His time will come."

"No doubt. But he would hasten it a little, perhaps? And hopes this meeting with Lancaster might aid in that?"

Unwilling to be questioned further, the young man made for the tent-door. "As to that, I cannot say, my lord. Ask him yourself. I must go to him, now . . ."

"Hear this, son," his father said, at his back. "I am not so thirled to Robert Stewart that I would seek spoil young David's chances, this day or other, should they seem to me to be for the realm's good. And you can say the same for Archie Douglas. We are no creatures of the Governor's. I made a compact with Archie, you will recollect, lang syne, to support him so long as he sought to counter his friend Fife's excesses. That stands — but our interest is the realm's, and Douglas's, weal, not Stewart's. Mind it."

Jamie turned to look at his sire for a moment, searchingly; then nodding, moved outside the pavilion.

A splendid cavalcade, ablaze with heraldry and banners, under the great standards of the Plantagenet leopards and of Lancaster, was quite close at hand, perhaps two hundred strong, approaching from the south-west, from the woodlands of Haddonrig, emitting the music of instrumentalists as it came. Sir Henry Percy and the Earl of Dunbar were already moving out to meet it.

Jamie hurried through the crowd to where the Earl David waited, some way apart from the Governor and Douglas.

"See there," the prince said. "We have achieved our first aim. We have brought John of Gaunt to parley with us. He would not have come, I vow, had he not been prepared to treat. Now I needs must play my fish to best advantage. But the invasion will not take place, I think, and Donald of the Isles be disappointed. Islanded, indeed!" He turned. "Well, Jamie — did you discover aught?"

"Only that the Governor deems himself alone able to deal with the Duke of Lancaster. Intends to do so. But that the Earl of Douglas and my father are by no means wholly thirled to him. They will choose their own course, as they see best. Best for the kingdom. And for Douglas."

"Ah! Then we must see that my uncle learns a lesson — and that Douglas is well served. Eh, Jamie Douglas?"

The leaders of the newly-arrived English party had dismounted, their musicians still playing a rousing air, and were now approaching on foot, with the Wardens Percy and Dunbar. These two had their instructions to bring the visitors directly to the Earl David; but, from his flanking position, the Earl Robert stepped forward to intercept.

"My lord Duke — welcome to Scottish soil," he called, having to raise his voice — something that man very seldom permitted himself — although his words remained clipped, flat as ever.

John of Gaunt paused, half-turned and inclined his head. He was a heavily-built, florid man in his late fifties, with prominent features which might have been graven in stone, and an imperious mien and bearing. Splendidly dressed and bejewelled, with gold-braided tunic and fur-lined travelling cloak, he was the fourth son of Edward the Third, born in Ghent, and had for a time assumed the crown of Castile, in right of his wife, moreover succeeding his brother, the Black Prince, as Duke of Aquitaine.

"My lord," he acknowledged, briefly.

"It is our pleasure to see you once more — and in more comfortable state," the Governor went on, with rather obvious lack of warmth. The last time that Lancaster had been in Scotland he had been taking judicious refuge after the revolt of the peasants led by Wat Tyler, in 1381, in which he was suspected of having a hand — although a few months later he had led an armed host over the Border on a limited raid which almost got to Edinburgh.

Lindsay of Crawford gripped the Earl David's arm. "He is seeking to oust you, here," he declared. "To take command of the meeting."

"Let him be," the prince said. "He will find that difficult. He has little that Lancaster wants — whereas I think that I *have*."

"Greetings, my lord Duke!" the Earl Archie cried — who had been both host and opposing commander to the Plantagenet on various occasions.

The other inclined his head but did not answer. He looked towards the Earl of Carrick. That young man took a couple of steps forward, as acknowledgement and encouragement; and gravely Lancaster resumed his onward pacing, a man of inbuilt dignity and formal behaviour. David of Carrick, although less powerful than the Governor, nevertheless held precedence there, as heir to the throne, High Steward and second man in the kingdom. Only to him could the Duke speak, in the first instance.

"Cousin — well met!" the younger man said genially. They were not any sort of cousins, in no kinship at all; but the term emphasised their special status, both sons of kings. Fife could have said the same, but had not. "You have ridden far today? You are not wearied, I hope? Your presence here gives pleasure and satisfaction to us all. Your fame precedes you."

John of Gaunt eyed the speaker keenly and took his time to answer. "I thank you," he said. "I am not wearied. Your letters I read — and understood. I deemed it best to talk with you." Clearly the Duke was a man of few words.

"Best, yes. We have much to discuss. First, however, wine to refresh you. My tent is yonder. But — here is my lord Bishop of St. Andrews. And my lord Bishop of Glasgow. Likewise, my lord of Crawford. Of Erroll, the Constable. Of Calder. Of Eaglesham . . ."

After the introductions, as Lancaster was led into the prince's pavilion, the Earl of Douglas stamped over to join them, muttering into his beard. The Earl of Fife however, did not. Expressionless he watched, and then turned and pushed past the Lord of Dalkeith, back into the Douglas tent, alone.

* * *

It suited both parties that the proceedings should seem to take the form of an ordinary Wardens' meeting, within a recognised framework. Face had to be preserved, dignity maintained intact, if anything real was to be achieved. This way was best, enabling the true principals to seem merely to sit in on the transactions, making their interpolations as and when it suited them, masking the significance of their contributions under the guise of advice and guidance. Moreover, for David Stewart, it had the very important advantage that it forestalled any move by the Governor to chair or manage the meeting. The two Wardens were automatically in charge, and since it was being held on Scottish soil, the Earl of Dunbar and March opened the proceedings.

George Dunbar was no more a wordy man than was Lancaster. The proceedings were held, as usual, in the open air, so that as many as possible might see and hear justice being done according to the special Border law. He commenced by declaring that this was a duly constituted court of justice for the East March of the Border, binding on both sides thereof, called as was their right and duty by himself and Sir Henry Percy of Northumberland. They were privileged to have with them on this occasion the lord Duke of Lancaster, uncle to King Richard, on the English side; and David, Earl of Carrick, High Steward and Prince of Scotland on the Scots side. Also the Governor, the Earl of Fife and Menteith, honoured their deliberations with his presence. Let the first issue be raised.

A typical Borderline case was put before them, in which one Wattie Home, in Thortersyke in the parish of Birgham, in the Scots Merse, claimed that Samuel Payne, known as Fenwick's Sam, in Chatton-on-Till, had crossed the March on the night of November 15th last, St. Margaret's Eve, and driven off from his outfield five of his best kye, two in calf. Because his, Home's, wife was labouring with their first child at the time, he was unable to follow up the raiders until the child was born, which was a day and a night later. When he rode over the March into the Vale of Till with his friends, to regain his beasts, as was his right, they were assailed by Fenwick's Sam and his neighbours, to the effusion of blood, and were driven off and sorely pursued back to Scotland, contrary to all the law of the Marches. He now claimed the return of his beasts, with the two calves, plus due compensation.

Sir Henry Percy then called Samuel Payne, in Powsall Rig, Chatton-on-Till, who admitted that he was known as Fenwick's Sam and that he had, on the night stated, taken the said kye from Thortersyke over in the Scots Merse, this because of injury done to him by the said Walter Home, at Bellingham Fair three months earlier, over the sale of a broken-winded nag. He asserted that the said Wattie Home was no better than a Scots rogue and thief and well-known as such. Moreover he could not claim hot-trod rights to recover the kye, since as all knew it was necessary for the trod to be hot that it should be ridden within twenty-four hours of the alleged offence. This had not been done; indeed it was nearer forty-eight hours than twenty-four before the Homes crossed the March. Therefore their lordships should dismiss the claim as incompetent.

All this in the broadest of Border accents, unintelligible to certain of the illustrious hearers, who indeed looked thoroughly bewildered.

The two Wardens eyed each other, Hotspur raised one shoulder fractionally. Dunbar nodded, and demanded whether Fenwick's Sam had never heard of the *cold*-trod, whereby action could be taken for recovery within six days?

The Northumbrian was vehement that there was no such thing.

A debate developed over the legal effectiveness of the so-called cold-trod, Borderers on both sides joining in loudly, until Hotspur held up his hand.

"Enough!" he cried, in his slightly stammering though commanding voice, "or we shall be here all day, on this one issue. My decision is this. The cold-trod, right or wrong, can be debated on another occasion. In this case I say that the man Home was entitled to remain with his wife over the birth of their firstborn, and in a difficult labour. He should not be penalised thereby. He followed the trod as quickly as he was able, and should not have been assailed. But Sam Payne was not necessarily to know this. Therefore my judgement is that the kye be returned, lacking the two calves, which Payne has nurtured since November. And no compensation to be paid." He raised eyebrows at Dunbar.

That man nodded. "Accepted," he said. "But since Home is tenant of a vassal of my own, I shall pay him compensation for the calves. This for judgement. Next?"

There was no argument by the litigants, nor delay in bringing forward the next case. It was fairly straightforward. Returning from the last Day of Truce six months earlier, when the Wardens had met at Cornhill-on-Tweed, one Pate Swinton, dealer in Kelso, had in the ale-house of Mother Shipley at Learmouth, struck the complainer John Robson also a dealer, of Branxton, known as Robbie Doddie, whereby he was unable to ride abroad on his lawful occasions for the space of many months — indeed could not be present today on account of the said injury, wherefore his claim was being presented by his brother. The man Swinton had ridden fast over the March, after the offence, and no punishment nor recompense had been obtained. Such was demanded now, the offence being committed on an undoubted Day of Truce.

Pate Swinton, who admitted the assault, pointed out that he had been grievously insulted by the said Robbie Doddie, himself a notour horse-coper; moreover, he had been drink-taken at the time.

Dunbar imposed a fine of one silver merk to the Warden's Fund and two silver merks compensation to the injured man, Hotspur agreeing.

It was during the succeeding hearing concerning a trespass committed on ground which was debatable, that is, where the Borderline was less than distinctly defined on a hillside on Steer Rig near Old Halterburnhead, that signs of restiveness amongst the more important onlookers became too apparent to ignore. The Earl David nudged Dunbar's elbow, and that man, catching Hotspur Percy's eye, intervened to declare that he would appoint two commissioners to proceed to the spot in question, there to decide whether the offence was in fact committed on Scots or English ground, and whether the offenders paid fealty to Scots or English feudal barons, or both, as some were contending. He hoped that Sir Henry Percy would do likewise. If agreeable, case continued until commissioners reported.

Hotspur acceding, looked round. "My brother, Sir Ralph Percy, to speak. In another matter," he announced, almost without pause.

The quality, if not the local Border folk present, drew deep breaths. Now they would get down to matters of some moment.

Sir Ralph Percy was a very different man from his gallant and extrovert brother, quiet, thoughtful, restrained. He had been badly wounded at Otterburn nine years previously and still walked with a pronounced limp.

"I speak to this, my lords," he began, almost apologetically, "since my brother is Warden here and so may feel prevented from speaking to it with freedom. But the matter concerns his interests, and those of our father, the Earl of Northumberland. I hereby make complaint against Archibald Earl of Douglas, his son Sir James, called the Gross, and others, servants of theirs, that they did violently attack and burn the camp of my brother, Sir Henry Percy, within the Forest of Jedburgh, on the 20th day of October last, to the death of four of King Richard's lieges, the destruction of much valuable property and the theft of nine good horses. For which shameful and warlike act, due reparation is demanded, punishment required upon the offenders, however illustrious, and assurances given that such assault will not be repeated."

There was silence round that great circle as men considered the significance of that statement.

The harsh, gravelly voice of Archie the Grim broke the hush, and strongly. "It will not have escaped the notice of you all, my lords, that the alleged offence was committed in the Forest of Jedburgh, in Scotland, and against Englishmen. Moreover, on *my* property! On whose authority were Sir Henry Percy's men in Jedburgh Forest, far beyond their own borders. And what doing?"

Sir Ralph looked at his brother, who nodded and took over. "Easily answered, my lord," Hotspur said. "They were hunting buck in that part of the Forest near to Roxburgh Castle, known as Sunlawshill. As was their right. As all know the Forest extends far beyond Jedburgh, and the offence was committed in that part which comes within the demesne of Roxburgh Castle. Which castle is held by Sir Philip Stanley, under my overall authority, for the King of England . . ."

"God damn you, Percy!" the Earl Archie snarled. "Roxburgh is in Scotland."

"But held by King Richard, as is Berwick Castle, and so agreed and accepted under the terms of the current truce, renewed three years ago, my lord."

"No. No, I say! No truce gives Englishmen the right to ride abroad at will in Scotland, and on *Douglas* property. To hunt *my* deer. To fray with my servants."

The Percy shrugged. "Are Douglas deer excepted from the truce? That truce, my lord, confirmed the *status quo* at date of renewal. Roxburgh and Berwick Castles, with their demesnes, were and are occupied by English garrisons, and as such are covered by the terms of truce." He turned to look directly at the Earl of Fife. "You, my lord Governor, signed that renewal, in the name of your royal father. Can you deny that this is so?"

Robert Stewart moistened thin lips. "I signed, yes," he said coldly. "The truce confirmed the *status quo*. But it gives no especial rights or privileges to Englishmen in Scotland."

"Is it an especial privilege not to be attacked by Douglas bravoes when on peaceable and lawful employ?"

"Mind you words, sirrah!" Archie the Grim exclaimed.

The Governor stared blankly but said nothing more.

"If my words offend, Douglas, show me how they err," Hotspur went on. "You cannot deny the attack and damage. You cannot deny that the east portion of Jedburgh Forest has long been the demesne of Roxburgh Castle. You cannot deny that the English occupation of that castle is confirmed by the truce which your Governor signed. If you have any quarrel, it appears that it should be with him, not with us!"

"Insolent!" Douglas swung on Lancaster. "Do you permit your spokesman so to insult us, on Scots soil?" And when John of Gaunt made no answer, he turned to Robert Stewart. "You, my lord Governor — teach this arrogant Percy to curb his ill tongue. And not again to challenge Douglas on Douglas territory — or suffer another Otterburn, by God!"

"I did not call this meeting," Fife said. "I did not invite Sir Henry Percy on to Scots soil. Address your complaints, my lord, to him who did!"

Every eye turned to the Earl David. That young man smiled pleasantly. "Let us discuss this matter reasonably, my good lords," he suggested. "It seems to me that the Earl of Douglas has much right on his side. He is undoubtedly feudal superior of the Forest of Jedburgh, and the deer in that forest his. If the Percys were indeed hunting buck therein, then he or his had the right to interfere. If that was, in fact, the true reason for the English presence there? After all, I would have thought that

Sir Harry had a sufficiency of deer to hunt in his own wide territories?"

There was silence at that, from Hotspur as from all others.

"I put it to you, Sir Harry," the prince went on, conversationally, "that when the Douglases came upon your men, they were not indeed hunting but clad and equipped for war. Wearing steel jacks and helms, not hunting green, bearing lances and swords, not greenwood bows."

Hotspur shrugged. "In the lawless and ungoverned state of Scotland, all who venture abroad are well advised to go so provided!" he gave back. "Whether so be they hunt, journey or attend Wardens' meetings!"

"Ha! So you claim that Scotland is misgoverned? Or was it ungoverned?"

"Why, I do, my lord — since that is my experience. And that of others."

All glances swivelled back to the Governor, as breaths were held. That self-contained individual did not rant or bluster. He merely turned to where John of Gaunt sat stroking his jowelled chin.

"My lord of Lancaster — restrain this man," he snapped.

The Duke gave a single shake of his grizzled head. "Sir Harry Percy is Warden of this March, and may speak his mind here," he said heavily.

"I insist, sir," the Governor declared, steely-voiced.

"No-one insists to *me*, my lord."

"In Lancaster perhaps not, sir. In England, even. But you are here on Scottish soil. And I govern in Scotland. I insist that you restrain your Englishry. I will not be insulted by any soever, on my own territory."

"Any more than will I!" Archibald Douglas cried.

Lancaster rose from his wooden bench. "Then I shall leave your territory, and gladly, my lord," he said evenly. "But . . . I do not promise that I will not be back! In different garb!"

David Stewart spoke up. "My lords, my lords — here is no cause for offence, I swear. Probably the fault is mine. I may have seemed to accuse Sir Harry of sending his men into Scotland on warlike intent. Spying out the land, or something such. That was not my mind. Merely that they seemed not to be hunting, from what I have heard. But with all this talk of English invasion imminent, we Scots are perhaps over delicate."

Men eyed each other wonderingly. To most present indubit-

75

ably this was the first they had heard of any projected invasion. Lancaster, who had been turning to move away, paused. Moments passed, without a word spoken.

With an easy laugh the young prince waved his hand. "Forgive us then, Sir Harry. And do not accuse my good uncle of misgovernment! And you, my lord Duke, be pleased to sit again, I pray. For we have much to discuss yet, have we not? Of more profit."

Most of the English who had seats had risen automatically when their leader did. Now they sat down, one after another, and the Duke, dignity suddenly at stake, appeared to decide that it was probably less feeble to sit again than to remain standing uncertainly, alone.

"This of profit, then," he jerked, resuming his seat. "Let us have it."

"To be sure. If the Lords Warden will permit? And leave Sir Harry's claim meantime, for another. This concerns a claim also against the Earl of Douglas and his son, this time made by Sir Philip Stanley, English captain in Roxburgh Castle, for £2,000 compensation for the destruction of Roxburgh bridge. My lord Governor, do you wish you speak to this?"

His uncle stared out of these colourless eyes, mouth like a trap. But as all watched, he had to speak. "I know nothing of any such," he said flatly. "Nor can conceive it possible."

"Ah. Yet the claim is made, Uncle, and falls to be considered." David did not add that the claim had been made only two days earlier, direct to the Scots Warden, and Dunbar had been instructed to keep quiet about it.

Percy spoke. "Sir Philip Stanley cannot be present but has given me the terms of his claim. The moneys are for the cost of rebuilding the bridge, and for inconvenience and delay caused by lack of the bridge."

"Insufferable!" the Governor said.

"My son destroyed that bridge, as he did others, for good and sufficient reason," Douglas asserted. "For the better security of this realm. It is a Scots bridge, built by Scots hands, within Scotland and on my land. How can any Englishman claim anything concerning it."

"The bridge served Roxburgh Castle across Teviot, my lord. All who travel to Roxburgh, from the South, from Berwick, even from Kelso, must use it."

"Preciseiy. That is why it was destroyed."

"And why we who hold Roxburgh and Berwick, by treaty, demand compensation."

"You do not hold these Scots castles by treaty, but by armed invasion and conquest."

"The signed truce is a treaty, as is its renewal. Confirming, whilst it lasts, the *status quo*."

"Damn the truce and the *status quo*!"

"You damn the man who signed it, Douglas!"

David appeared to come to the rescue of his uncle again. "We must not wholly blame what seems to be an ill-made treaty or truce on he who signed it," he objected, moderately. "The greater good of the whole realm, of the two realms, was no doubt paramount over Douglas and Border interests. Was it not, my lord Governor?"

Only the quiver of Robert Stewart's slender nostrils betrayed his fury. "Enough of this folly," he jerked. "No such claim is to be considered."

"The claim is against Douglas," Percy insisted. "On behalf of King Richard, not myself. I but speak for his captain of Roxburgh." And he looked at Lancaster for support.

"The claim is fair," that man nodded.

It was Robert Stewart's turn to rise to his feet. "This is not to be borne," he said. "Such English arrogance is beyond belief."

"Are you speaking to me, sir?" Lancaster demanded. "Watch your words. I would have you know that . . ."

"Dunbar," the Governor ordered, breaking in. "Close this travesty of a meeting. I will have no more."

"How dare you interrupt my speaking, sir!" John of Gaunt exclaimed. "No man in Christendom may do that. I am not finished . . ."

"But I am! And this is Scotland, where *I* rule. The meeting is closed — as it should never have been opened."

"And I say no!" Lancaster thundered. "I have not come so far to be spurned aside thus."

"Will you outface me, sir? Me, the Governor?"

"Aye, will I! Governor of what? A sub-kingdom of which my nephew is Lord Paramount. As was my father. And his. Mind it. And mind who I am, man. I am Duke of Lancaster, Duke of Aquitaine, former King of Castile and Leon, nearest heir to the throne of England. You will give me the respect that is my due."

"I will give you nothing, sir — save permission to leave my borders, and forthwith!"

77

David Stewart stepped in once more. "My lord — *I* asked the Duke to come to this meeting. So that, in some measure, he is my guest, under my safe-conduct. In due course I shall escort him honourably over the March. When we have finished our deliberations."

"Then do so speedily."

"In my lord Duke's good time, Uncle. After all, he outranks us both in dignity, does he not? Not, I say, in this fable of English paramountcy, but as duke — where we, to be sure, are but earls!" The prince's smile indicated what he thought of such titular niceties.

"Young man," John of Gaunt said ponderously. "Hitherto I have discovered nothing to have made my journey from Lancaster worth the making. I have been miscalled, and I find all profitless. It is not my custom to suffer such treatment. I warn you all, I have the means to demonstrate my displeasure."

"No doubt, my lord Duke. You have already intimated as much, I think. Did you not say that you did not promise not to return, and in different garb? I took that to mean, at the head of an army? As you have done ere this."

Plain speaking at last, however pleasantly enunciated.

"You may take it as you will, sir."

"A threat, a palpable threat!" the Earl of Douglas asserted, grinning fiercely. "Will you cross swords with me again, my friend? In your other garb?"

"Hear who speaks of threats!" Hotspur cried. "Was it not Douglas who threatened another Otterburn, a little back? Invasion of England. War, in fact."

"To be sure. Two can play that game, Percy. You think to march into Scotland at will. What of your truce, now? What of this *status quo*?"

"You dream, Douglas — dream! You are getting old — an old man's delusion . . ."

"Old enough to recognise an insolent pup in need of schooling!" The Douglas–Percy feud seemed in no danger of dying. "Why think you my son broke down Roxburgh bridge? And others along Teviot and Tweed, Jed, Rule and Slitrig Waters? To hold up and hamper projected invasion, that is why! Invasion planned by you and Lancaster, to link with Donald of the Isles' descent upon my lordship of Galloway, in the west. That is why. We know it all."

In the succeeding hush the wheepling of curlew on the moorland rising behind was the only sound. It was out, now — the reason behind this entire assembly. And the Earl Archibald had been forced into the making of the disclosure, not David Stewart. Jamie Douglas looked at the prince with enhanced respect. It had all been masterfully done, the others, however illustrious, little more than puppets to dance to his skilful manipulation.

The Earl David's gaze was directed, not at Douglas, Percy or Lancaster, but at his Uncle Robert — on whose account everything had been plotted and guided, of course. As far as was possible with that sternly disciplined and unbending character, the Governor was looking almost bewildered, at a loss. Clearly no hint of the English invasion threat had reached him, despite his multitude of spies — as had been David's major preoccupation. That the Douglas had kept it to himself, as requested, was in fact the most hopeful indication of all, proof that Archie the Grim could be detached from the Governor's party, that he resented still the Chief Wardenship having been filched from him and then left contemptuously neglected; proof that he recognised misgovernment, especially in the policy towards England and in the terms of the truce which had been used to hurt him so. He might only be teaching his former ally a lesson, of course. But it all represented a notable advance for the Earl David's cause.

That young man saw the moment as ripe for the further and final pressure. "My lord Duke has come here to speak to this matter of invasion talk, I think," he observed. "No doubt he will dispel all such fears as groundless?"

Lancaster took his time to answer that. "If we are threatened, we protect ourselves," he said, at length, carefully.

"To be sure. So must all. But Scotland poses no threat to England, at this time. Has not my uncle here signed this notable truce? It may not comfort Douglas and the Borders, but at least it must comfort England!"

"What but a threat to England, my lord of Carrick, are the many Scots troops massed on the Isle of Man, opposite my Lancaster shores? Troops and ships."

"Ah, that. You have had your answer from the Earl of Douglas. My seditious cousin, Donald of the Isles, in what he deplorably calls treaty with King Richard, assembles galleys and birlinns for a descent on Galloway and the West March. The word is that King Richard will despatch forces to join him, over our Marches. But on this we are confident that you can reassure us. So my lord of Dunbar, who is also Lord of Man, takes due precautions. Against the Islesmen. For Man is but twenty miles from Galloway. In sight, indeed. No threat need be looked for, towards *Lancaster*. Which is somewhat further off, is it not? Thirty miles?"

They eyed each other levelly for a few moments. This was what John of Gaunt had come for, this and nothing else. All the rest was, in a sense, unimportant, but play-acting, setting the scene.

"I am well pleased to hear it, sir," Lancaster said, at length — although he scarcely sounded it. "No such venture was envisaged. No such invasion. Whatever your barbarian Donald might devise."

"I was sure of it, my lord Duke. We may take it, then, that the only threat to our peace comes from the Islesmen? No English will support them?"

"Have I not said so, sir?"

David laughed, in friendliest fashion. "We are great sticklers for words, in Scotland. One of our many weaknesses. There is a word for it, which escapes me! You said, my lord, that no such invasion was *envisaged*. Not that no invasion would take place! A mere equivocation, admittedly. As though, when I said that no threat need be *looked* for from the Scots forces on Man, I meant that there still might be *un*looked-for developments! It would be a pity to misunderstand, or suffer ambiguity — eh, my lord Duke?"

The other frowned. "There need be no misunderstanding. I am a man of plain words. And not used to having my word doubted, sir."

"Of course not. And I the last to doubt it. Then, all is as it should be. We have the word of John of Gaunt, Duke of Lancaster, that there will be no English invasion over the Scots March; and you have mine that the Scots forces on Man will move only against Donald's Islesmen. What more might any desire? Your journey has not been wasted — nor that of any here. Eh, Uncle?"

The Governor, who had listened to this exchange in tight-lipped hostility towards all concerned, inclined his head slightly but did not commit himself to speech.

"The claims against Douglas?" Hotspur put in. "King Richard's and my own?"

"I suggest that you reconsider them, sir," David answered,

with just a touch of asperity. "Sir Philip Stanley likewise."

"Saints of God, yes!" the Earl Archibald agreed.

"*I* might reduce my claim somewhat," the Percy admitted judicially. "But I cannot commit my liege lord Richard to do so."

"No? I swear King Richard knows naught of this. But, since the claim is only made in his name, no doubt the Duke here, his uncle, can modify it. Especially as the bridge was broken in error, as it were. To counter this supposed invasion. After all, my lord of Douglas will have to build it up again!"

John of Gaunt shrugged. "We shall not bicker over a bridge," he said. "Forget the matter."

"Well spoken, sir. That, then, can conclude our business, my lords . . ."

"Save for *my* claim against Douglas," the persistent Hotspur reminded. "In this pass, I will accept £1,000 for damage to my camp, horseflesh and men, in Jedburgh Forest . . ."

"By God you will not!" That came out like an explosion from the hitherto genial, patient and smiling prince. In the twinkling of an eye, he was transformed to the personification of blazing royal rage and startling authority, quite frightening to see. "Jedburgh Forest may be Douglas's, but in the final instance it is the territory of *his* liege lord, my father, the King of Scots. Not one merk of £1,000 will I allow that Douglas or any other pay to any Englishman for rights claimed therein. Is it understood, sirrah?"

Surprise, shock even, registered on every face, shading to consternation and alarm where English, to delight, glee, where Scots. The Percy, dumbfounded at last, found not a word.

"My lord of Dunbar," the prince went on, crisply. "Close this meeting, if you please. I thank all who have attended. My lord Duke, I shall now escort you over the March — and consider it an honour." Most evidently in complete control of the situation, the Prince of Scotland called for horses.

After briefest leave-taking, variously stiff, and with the Earl David riding off with Lancaster in a southerly direction whilst Percy headed eastwards without delay and the Governor north-westwards still more expeditiously, Jamie Douglas found his father at his side.

"Well, son," the Lord of Dalkeith said, "that was a remarkable accomplishment. I have seldom seen the like, in a long life. Your prince has more to him than I had reckoned."

"*Your* prince also, sir."

"To be sure. We seem like to have a new kind of King in Scotland! It was masterly, from start to finish — especially the finish! As good as a play-acting."

"It was no playing," Jamie assured. "That was a bid for the governance of this realm. Before ever he ascends his father's throne."

"No doubt. And Robert Stewart perceived it as such. He will not take that kindly, mark you."

"No. But David, having planned thus far, will not be out-smarted easily."

"I hope not . . ."

"*You* hope not, Father — you who have supported the Governor hitherto? Do you change sides, then?"

"I told you before, lad, it is no question of taking sides. I seek first the weal of the realm, then the weal of Douglas. After this day, few will doubt where both lie! As, to be sure, was the prince's whole purpose."

"Will the Earl Archie then think as you do?"

"Need you ask? You heard him. His interests are made to seem to suffer most from the Governor's actions, or lack of action. The mockery of this truce. The danger to the Borders and Galloway — all now lifted by the heir to the throne! Who himself still accuses none of anything. What sort of a son has our sorry monarch produced?"

"One who intends to see justice and good government in the land."

"I hope so — I hope so, indeed. I hope that he is not . . . *too* clever, for his own and the kingdom's good."

"Why should he be?"

"He moved men around like pawns on a chess-board this day, Jamie. And few men, proud men, like that. The Governor he made look a fool and less than competent — and he is no fool. Lancaster he manipulated into committing himself not to invade. Hotspur he led on to his own destruction. Dunbar he used. All before other men. Today David Stewart demon-strated his ability, yes — but he made enemies in doing so, powerful enemies. He is going to need friends, lad, *friends* — not enemies."

"He made friends of Douglas, at least . . ."

IV

THEY DREW REIN on the long, rounded hill-crest and gazed down thankfully, all but wonderingly, on the vast green amphitheatre with the wide loch at its centre, so little to be anticipated in that seemingly illimitable wilderness of rock and peat and heather. Farflung, the bare hills reared on every hand, with here and there to be glimpsed the misty blue outlines of higher, farther mountains. To come across an enclave of greenness in the barren midst, not the emerald warning of bog and moss but the kindly green of hayfields and pasture, of water-meadows and even strips of tilth, of spreading birch-woods and the darker richness of Caledonian pines, was a joy and relief to the eyes of weary travellers. The entire Highland scene was beautiful, of course, although somewhat inimical to Lowland eyes; but the lofty moorlands of Braemoray, north of Strathspey, were particularly daunting, extensive, unrelenting, and all that August day Jamie Douglas's party had been traversing their heather wastes without sign of settlement, or even a house or the works of men — although not without sign of man himself, for well behind them, not always visible but ever present, the shadowy figures of men, many men, dogged them, dismounted wild Highlandmen, but apparently well able to keep up with the mounted Lowlanders on this rough terrain, even though the travellers had wisely exchanged their fine horses for shaggy, sturdy sure-footed garrons, six days ago back at Dunkeld in Atholl, on entering the true Highlands. Jamie at least knew who those shadows would be, and what they portended — for he had been here before.

"What place for a castle, by the Powers!" Pate Boyd exclaimed, pointing. "Whoever built yon hold must have misliked his fellow-men! Forby, it is a large place. What good can it serve, hidden away here?"

"More than you might think," Jamie told the prince's tough henchman. "This Lochindorb may seem lost, far from all. But, in fact, just to the north, beyond that ridge and col, is a notable hub of routes, coming out of sundry glens and passes, from the Laigh of Moray, from lower Strathspey, from Strathdearn and Strathnairn and Inverness and the Great Glen, as well as this we are on from upper Badenoch and the South. Whosoever holds Lochindorb Castle can control most of the North-East. That is why Edward of England, the first of the name, curse him, built it! The place was a small Comyn hold before that, a mere hunting-house. But Edward was a notable soldier and campaigner, whatever else, and saw its value. Like the late Wolf, who perceived that he might rule the North from here. And did."

In the midst of the roughly circular loch which lay in the centre of the great green hollow of the hills, a small island projected, wholly occupied by the towers and walls and battlements of a sizeable courtyard-type castle, with gatehouse-keep, flanking towers, curtains and outer and inner baileys. A flag flew from the gatehouse parapet, blue-and-gold, for Stewart. They rode down towards the loch, thirty well-armed horsemen of the royal guard, under Douglas and Boyd. It represented long journey's end.

"They will have been warned of our coming — unless Sir Alexander differs greatly from his late father," Jamie informed. "They maintain look-outs on every hill-top. And no doubt these behind us have sent a messenger hastening ahead."

That this was an accurate forecast was soon proved by the fact that boats were to be seen, presently, pulling out from the castle-island, a large flat ferry scow for horses and a smaller craft. These, and only these, were waiting for them at the jetty beside the scattering of rude cot-houses and cabins which comprised the castleton, at the mainland shore opposite the island; clearly no access to the castle was possible unless boats were despatched therefrom.

The young man who awaited them, with a group of gillies, at the jetty, was clad in simple short kilt, shirt and calfskin sleeveless jerkin, like the rest, but by his bearing and features was obviously of a different background — Sir James Stewart, youngest brother of Sir Alexander, now in his twentieth year, and good-looking in a raffish way. The late and alarming Earl of Buchan, the King's brother and so-called Wolf of Badenoch, who had for so long ruled these parts as Lieutenant and Justiciar of the North, had produced no legitimate offspring, for sufficient reasons though a surplus otherwise; but this family at Lochindorb, five sons, the children of the Lady Mariota de Athyn, his concubine, he had singled out from all the rest by knighting them all at an early age, in a gesture part-defiant, part-mocking, part-significant, so that they had constituted a kind of ruling family of the North. This one, probably the most presentable, next to his eldest brother Alexander, of a wild bunch, had become comparatively friendly with Jamie Douglas when he had been a hostage, if not prisoner, here seven years before.

"Jamie Douglas — it is yourself!" he cried, in a sibilant Highland lilt. "And nothing changed, by God — save that you are better escorted than once you were! We wondered who came, so well provided with steel, whatever."

"To be sure, friend — one learns caution if not wisdom, with the years. And you — you are a man now, and a brave one, I swear. Around the age I was then. When last I was here. I trust I find you all well at Lochindorb? It is three years now since your father died. But I saw Alexander near a year back, at the North Inch fight at Perth."

"Aye, that was a notable ploy — would I had been there. But someone must needs keep this place, when Alex is from home. As he is now . . ."

"He is not here? A plague — we have travelled a long way to see him. He is not far off . . .?"

"Far enough. He is in Lochaber, with Andrew and Duncan. With swords unsheathed! Would God I was with them, instead of biding here looking after my mother and sister . . ."

"Lochaber! Dear God — so far! Is it this of Alastair Carrach MacDonald?"

"The same — the murdering brigand! He lays Lochaber waste."

"It is partly on his account that we are come. This is ill news. We shall have to follow him — Alexander. Follow your brothers . . ."

"Not this night, whatever," the young Stewart declared. "Come you over to the castle. My mother will joy to see you. She ever thinks well of you, often speaks of you. As does Margaret . . ."

85

So Jamie and Boyd were rowed over to the island, leaving their troop of thirty men-at-arms at the castleton.

The Lady Mariota de Athyn welcomed Jamie most warmly, almost embarrassingly so. Now in her late forties, she was a large, generous, cheerful and handsome Highland woman of character, one of the chiefly Mackays of Strathnaver, improbable to a degree as a notorious courtesan who had set the tongues of Scotland wagging. The fact was that she had been a good wife to the Earl of Buchan, although he could not marry her, having been wed to the heiress Countess Euphemia of Ross and Buchan at an early age, although he had never lived with her. The Lady Mariota had loved that extraordinary man, accepted all the difficulties and contumely that went with concubinage, made an excellent mother to his children, maintained this remote northern home of his, and exercised a beneficial influence upon one of the wildest characters ever Scotland had produced. She and Jamie had got on well, from the first. He had always treated her with respect, as wife and chatelaine.

Now she embraced him affectionately, comprehensively, and not really in motherly fashion, kissing him, holding him at arm's length for inspection and then pressing him back to her ample bosom for further kisses. He did not exactly struggle to be free — but would have preferred that the cynic Boyd should not have been an interested witness. Moreover, she was a strong woman.

When they could exchange more than breathless incoherencies, and he had muttered conventional sympathies over the death of the Earl — since when he had not seen her — he launched into an explanation of his presence there, and with an escort of the royal guard. He came on behalf of the Earl David — of whom the Lady Mariota in general approved — on an important, composite and quite difficult mission. The prince was seeking to unseat his uncle, the Governor, in a lengthy and elaborate campaign carefully thought out. In this cause it was necessary that the heir to the throne's own credit should be maintained and enhanced. One of the weaknesses of his position was that he had made scarcely an adequate Lieutenant and Justiciar of the North, indeed had not as yet so much as shown his face in these parts — this because of his great and many commitments in the South and the demands of this campaign. Jamie did not emphasise the large demands on the prince's time of whoring, drinking and general merry-making, although no doubt the lady, who was not unfamiliar with the Stewart character, could assess that for herself. The Earl David had had to leave all in the North to deputies, up till now, notably Sir Alexander, her son. But it was important that, at a parliament or general council of the realm to be held in a few months' time, no stones should be hurled at him on account of any seeming neglect of his duties as representative of the Crown up here. So he planned a major visit or progress through the Lieutenancy before the winter set in; and he, Jamie Douglas, was here in the nature of a forerunner and smoother of the paths.

The Lady Mariota expressed herself as delighted at the prospect of seeing the prince again, and hoped that she would have the pleasure of entertaining him at Lochindorb.

Jamie's acknowledgement of that was somewhat preoccupied. The difficulty was, he pointed out, that there must be no *trouble* during the Earl David's tour. The situation demanded that it should be more in the nature of a triumphal progress, the holding of a few selected justice ayres, the appointment of sheriffs and officers, and so on. But no fighting or disputes. As for this wretched Alastair Carrach, Donald of the Isles' brother, his raiding and ravaging from the West, this must be stopped at all costs. Undoubtedly it was being done as a form of reprisal for Donald's intended descent on Galloway, and linking with the English, being countered by David.

Their hostess pointed out that this was what Alex and her other sons were now doing down in Lochaber, seeking to deal with Alastair Carrach. He had attacked and captured the royal castle of Urquhart, near Inverness, and left Maclaine of Lochbuy installed as keeper. Then he had retired again down the Great Glen, and was now dispossessing the Camerons and running riot around Arkaig and Lochy. Her boys were doing all they could, and manfully.

Jamie shifted his stance uncomfortably. "I am sure of it," he agreed. "And their prowess is not in doubt. But it is a matter of time, see you. The prince must make his progress here in the North before the onset of winter when the passes are closed and the rivers in spate. Not later than October. Less than two months now. And there must be no warfare, or the echoes of warfare, to mar it. His enemies would seize on that. So there is no time for any campaign against this Alastair. We must gain our ends . . . otherwise."

"Otherwise?" the lady repeated. "How think you to do that, Jamie my friend?"

He looked away. "Terms," he said. "We must come to terms, I fear."

"Terms! With Alastair! Save us — you do not know what you say! This is not like you, Jamie."

"No," he agreed unhappily. "But these are the prince's commands. I am sent to treat with the man and get him out of Scotland and back to his isles. At almost any price. And swiftly."

"Here is foolishness. Alastair will not be bought off cheaply, if at all. And no trust be put in any treating with him. He is a hard man. My lord knew how to deal with him. He would never have dared this raiding whilst the Earl lived. Cold steel he understands, only that. If not that what have you to offer him?"

"Sufficient, perhaps. This is no ordinary raiding, see you. It is not, in truth, Alastair whom we have to buy off, but his brother Donald. The Lord of the Isles is angry that his plan against Galloway and Man was brought to naught. We know now, what we had not understood earlier, that he intended to seize Man. And to keep it, to incorporate it in his island kingdom. And to use his alliance with King Richard to win complete independence from the Scottish Crown. So now he sends his brother raiding, not so much for gain, or in Highland feuding, but against the Crown. Why think you Alastair assailed and took a *royal* castle — Urquhart? That is not raiding, but a gesture. If Donald is making gestures, it is for a purpose — for he is no fool. So perhaps he will talk, bargain."

Doubtfully the woman shook her head. "And *you* think to bargain, to outwit Donald of the Isles, Jamie?" Undoubtedly that was not meant to be insulting, but there was no mistaking the implication.

He shrugged, and sought to change the subject.

Next morning early they left Lochindorb, returning as they had come, over the empty heather hills to mid-Strathspey, at Duthil on the Dulnain, young James Stewart glad to escort and guide them to his brothers, as excuse to get away from Lochindorb. Nothing was said about the shadowing hillmen who had dogged their heels the day before, minions undoubtedly of one of the Stewart half-brothers — for the Wolf had left a varied and sufficient progeny to ensure a kind of dynastic leadership

88

over all these vast territories. These men had followed them from the vicinity of Ruthven Castle, near to Kingussie, another of the Wolf's strongholds, and thus far the party reached that evening, with Stewart insisting that they spend the night there. It was a grimly amusing situation for Jamie, not only in that these same shadowers, who had found them too strong a company to interfere with on the way north, now must needs act hosts, after a fashion; the fact was that last time Jamie Douglas had been within these walls, it was as an ill-used prisoner in a cell. The Sir Andrew Stewart who then captained this fortress was now away in Lochaber with Sir Alexander, and only a surly half-brother by some undistinguished paramour, Rob Stewart, was in charge. Although considerably older than Sir James, and clearly disliking having to offer hospitality, however elementary, to the Lowlanders, he did not argue — an interesting commentary on the power and supremacy of the Lady Mariota's offspring over the rest of the Wolf's numerous brood. Considering this oafish Rob, it did not fail to cross Jamie's mind that he also was, nevertheless, a grandson of King Robert the Second and no more illegitimate than were Sir Alexander and his brothers.

Ruthven was a very different place from Lochindorb, set on a lofty mound amidst the flooded water-meadows of Spey, strong and quite large, but internally more like an encampment of gypsies, a sordid caravanserai, than a powerful baron's castle. No chatelaine kept this hold, however many slatternly women roosted therein. The visitors were glad to escape, with the sunrise.

They rode south by west through a lovely land, one of the fairest, so far as scenery went, in all Scotland, following the waterlogged meadows of Spey by Nuide and Ralia, through hanging woodlands of birch and forests of ancient and gnarled Caledonian pine, fording foaming, sparkling rivers, and with the great mountains ever shouldering close, a place of deer and wolf and wildfowl, of eagle and buzzard and blundering capercailzie. Where Glen Truim came in from the south, down from the lofty bare pass of Drumochter, the Spey took a pronounced bend almost due westwards into what seemed almost a new valley. This they followed, through Cattanach and Macpherson country. All the way they would have been challenged, obviously enough, for it was a fairly populous land, with cattle in all the open woodlands and the cabins of the clansfolk sending up their columns of blue woodsmoke into the August air; but young Sir James bore aloft his father's dread banner of Buchan and Stewart colours, which clearly still represented authority hereabouts. Following a well-defined drove-road, one of the main Highland routes into the West, they made fair progress, and camped for the second night a few miles beyond the foot of long Loch Laggan, Spey far behind now. They were here on the watershed of Highland Scotland, on the edge of the great lordship of Lochaber.

By noon of next day they were beginning to see traces of Alastair Carrach MacDonald's work, in the Braes of Lochaber, burned homesteads and cabins, slaughtered cattle, here and there the unburied bodies of men, women and children, not a few hanging from roadside trees. The local folk now remained in hiding, but the condition of the corpses indicated that the killing had been done possibly a week previously. Eventually they came across a couple of cowherds, Camerons, who either recognised the Stewart banner or else were of bolder stuff than their fellows, who told the travellers that the word was that the accursed Islesmen were now ravaging and butchering in the Arkaig and Glen Loy areas, to the west, and that *Alastair mac Alastair Mor* — the Gaelic name for Sir Alexander Stewart — had followed them this way five days earlier.

They pressed on with enhanced urgency, their way fairly consistently downhill now through long Glen Spean, with the tang of the western ocean not infrequently in their nostrils, on the breeze, to add its piquancy to the prevailing scents of heather, pine, bog-myrtle — and burning.

By evening, they came down the frothing, spouting, cataract-strewn Spean to the more open levels of the lower end of Glen More, the Great Glen of Scotland, between Loch Lochy and Loch Linnhe, the latter but an arm of the Firth of Lorne and the Sea of the Hebrides. Emerging from Glen Spean, now indeed they were challenged, and fiercely — but by Badenoch men, Macphersons attached to Alexander's force. On ascertaining young Stewart's identity, although they eyed the Lowlanders with undisguised suspicion, they provided an escort to convoy them the few miles further to the main Badenoch camp. There had been no major clash with the Islesmen as yet, they reported.

The travellers came up with Alexander Stewart, at length, at Gairlochy where Spean joined Lochy under the abruptly-rising hills of Locheil and Wester Lochaber, here forming the west wall of the Great Glen. This was the traditional gathering-place of the Clan Cameron. Alexander and his brothers were waiting here for the fullest assembly of the Cameron manpower, for they were under no illusions as to the size of the task ahead in seeking a confrontation with the Islesmen. They had brought about eight hundred men from Badenoch, mainly Mackintoshes, MacGillivrays and Macphersons, of the Clan Chattan federation; but it had become very evident as they progressed that Alastair Carrach had far larger numbers with him than had been reported previously, possibly as many as 3,000 — and none underestimated the fighting qualities of the Clan Donald Islesmen, sea-rovers of the toughest breed. So every Cameron that Lochaber could produce was going to be required. Some nine hundred of them were already assembled, under the chieftains of two of the three branches, the MacGillonie of Strone and the MacMartin of Letter Finlay. But more, many more, were needed; the question was whether Alastair Carrach would give them time to muster. He was up the long side-glen of Arkaig, to the west, but known to be retracing his steps.

Alexander was as delighted as he was surprised to see the Douglas again — even though his brothers Andrew and Duncan were less so. He eyed the royal escort thoughtfully however.

Jamie was interested to see how very much in command the other was, without in any way making a display of it. Slighter, finer-made and superficially at least, gentler than any of his brothers, he nevertheless exercised his authority seemingly effortlessly — over the wild-looking Cameron chieftains also. His father, to be sure, had been Lord of Lochaber as well as Badenoch, through his lawful wife, who had inherited ancient Comyn lordships; and now Alexander was accepted as lord in his place, here in the North at any rate, whatever the Governor and parliament might say. Being a deputy of the Justiciar, too, enhanced his authority, giving him legal power; but it was the power of personality, of blood and birth, and of the sword, which really counted. However, his quiet air of mastery and leadership was obviously innate, a personal attribute rather than stemming from his position. Jamie had never had occasion to see him as a commander, hitherto, and was impressed.

But it was not long before they came to disagreement, nevertheless. When Alexander heard about the proposed coming to terms with the island invaders, he was as critical as his mother had been, declaring the whole notion as impossible as it was unprofitable. Alastair would never treat, especially when he was in a position of strength, as now; besides, he required to be taught a lesson, not encouraged in aggression. His own cousin he might be, in blood, but he would hang him for a pirate and murderer, if he could lay hands on him.

"That would not please the prince, Alex — whose cousin he is also," Jamie pointed out, as they paced back and forth along Lochyside in the August gloaming light. "And you are here as the prince's deputy, in part. Alastair may deserve hanging — and David used to be a great one for hanging folk in the name of the realm's weal, in his father's Carrick! But, for policy's sake Alastair, and through him his brother Donald, must be kept quiet meantime, until David gains the governorship. Then it may be different."

"And what, my friend, will keep Alastair Carrach quiet, whatever, in this situation? He lives by the sword, the dirk and rapine, a captain of pirate galleys and gallowglasses; cold steel and the torch's flame the language he talks and understands. He may be a king's grandson — as are some of the rest of us! — but his standards are those of a jackal. You saw what he has done in Glen Spean and Glen Roy?"

Jamie nodded. It was on the tip of his tongue to say that his friend *ought* to know how to deal with such, since his own father had been the prince of jackals of all the land, a greater pirate and blood-letter than ever Alastair MacDonald could hope to be; but that would be to defeat his own case, for the Wolf at least had known how to keep the Islesmen in their place, and would have hooted at the Earl David's project in derision.

"See you, we — or at least the prince — has something to offer," he explained. "It is a most privy matter, but I can tell *you*, so long as no others learn of it. The offer, though made to Alastair, is for Donald's consideration. It is the earldom of Ross, no less. Donald has ever claimed it, in his wife's right. The Governor saw that her sister gained it, and through her, her weak son, the present Earl, who is wed to the Governor's daughter. Murky work. Once the Governor is unseated, David is prepared to support Donald's claim, and to move the King to support it. All the earldom save Easter Ross and the lordship of Ardmeanach and Cromartie, which the present Earl should be left. So Donald would get all Skye and Wester Ross. Is that not sufficient price for Alastair's return to his islands? That is what I am empowered to offer."

The other stared at the speaker for a long moment before commenting. "Changed days for Jamie Douglas!" he said, at length. "Is your Earl David corrupting you? You named it murky work, what Robert Stewart did with the Ross earldom. Is this less murky?"

"It is . . . statecraft."

"Perhaps. But less than honest, I think."

"Why should it be? If David is to oust his Uncle Robert from power, and keep him so, he is going to require friends, many and powerful friends. Or allies. If he could make his peace with Donald, he could be a most powerful friend. They are full cousins, after all . . ."

"The prince has over many full cousins! And Donald the least likely as friend. And the most dangerous. Better to have him as declared enemy, I say. See you, Donald is different from all others in this realm, Jamie — he considers himself *outside* it. He seeks independence from Scotland. Once, his forebears were Kings of the Isles — he seeks return to that state. And to advance his territories, to recover all that once was the great Somerled's — the earldom of Ross, yes, and much more. This Lochaber. Much of Argyll. Indeed, most of the North-West. And if he does gain all that, as price for his support of David, think you he will be content? Donald is clever, and of boundless ambition. I do not think you know what you attempt, you and your prince."

"*Your* prince likewise, Alex! And Donald's. One day to be King — and before long, perhaps, for King Robert is in poor health. And David is clever too. He has outwitted Donald once, at Haddonstank. He can do so again . . ."

"And does he intend to, in this of the earldom? Is it only a cheat?"

Jamie frowned. "No. Or not that I know of. He offers to bargain . . ."

"At *my* cost!"

"Yours? Why that?"

"I should have thought that easy to understand, friend. Lochaber was my father's, and is now mine, by right. Donald makes no secret of claiming it — why Alastair is here now. Not only that. The earldom of Ross flanks all the lordship of Badenoch to north and west. Alexander Leslie, the present Earl, is a quiet man, little menace. But let Donald of the Isles establish himself here on the mainland, and it will be constant war. As

Earl of Ross little of Badenoch will be secure from his ambitions. War not only with me and mine, but with the mainland clans — Clan Chattan, these Camerons, the Mackenzies, the Grants, the new Frasers, the MacMaths. Can you not see it? This may look like statecraft from Stirling or Perth. But from here it is the promise of war and bloodshed."

The Douglas looked at his friend concernedly, perplexedly. "Surely you mistake?" he objected. "Fear unnecessarily?" But he said it without conviction, for he did not underestimate Alexander's wits nor shrewdness.

The other shook his almost delicately handsome head. "No. Here we have cause to know Donald MacDonald better than you in the South do. And it is we who will suffer, in the first instance. I warn you, Jamie — say nothing of this your mission to my brothers here, as *I* will not. Or I fear not only for the mission but for your safety!"

"They would threaten the heir to the throne's envoy?"

"They are my father's sons — and see your Lowland affairs as little concern of theirs. Whereas Donald and Alastair are! And these Cameron chiefs I scarce think have ever heard of the Earl of Carrick!"

"Must I hide, then, within my escort of the royal guard? In *your* camp, Alex?"

"Not so. But — keep your lips closed on what you have told me."

"But I must get to Alastair. For that I have come all this long road."

"How do you propose to do that, my friend?"

"Go seek him out — what else? Up this Arkaig, where you say he is."

"He may welcome you less warmly than you think."

"Never fear — *he* has heard of the Earl of Carrick, if the Camerons have not! And I have my guard."

"Thirty against 3,000! Do not rely on Alastair's courtesy. He is a man who strikes first and talks afterwards! I fear for your mission as much as I fear its consequences." He looked away, at the now darkling hills, and slowly he spoke. "I do not know that I can allow it, Jamie."

From anyone else that would have brought forth a fairly harsh and unequivocal response. But these two knew and respected each other. Nevertheless, Jamie frowned blacker than he knew. "You would not seek to *halt* me!"

Alexander Stewart sighed and changed his tune a little. "See here — I think you still do not understand the position, Jamie. This is war we are at, here in Lochaber. Alastair has laid waste much of our land, and must be stopped, punished. He knows that we are here, waiting for him, and marches back down Arkaig — though he takes his time, sure of himself. He is much stronger in men than am I. We await reinforcement, more Camerons and the like. He will know that also. Think you he will delay and parley whilst we grow stronger? Accept your word and withdraw, whilst we sit here? His galley-fleet awaits him in Loch Linnhe; he must pass us here to reach it. Will he be prepared to believe that you can hold back us, and the Camerons, after what he has done to their glens? Not fall on him as he emerges from the *Mile Dorchaidh*, the Dark Mile, at the mouth of Arkaig? *I* would not so believe."

"You are set on fighting, then?"

The Stewart inclined his head. "I fear so. That is why we are here. You cannot assemble hundreds, thousands of Highland fighting-men who have seen their glens smoking, and then turn and say that talking will serve, that they should go home peaceably. Could you do that with Douglas mosstroopers? I do not know. But clansmen — no. You know the Cameron motto? *Chlanna nan con thigibh a so's gheibh sibh feoil.* Sons of the hounds, come here and get flesh!" He paused. "Jamie — give me two days. Till tomorrow night, at least. I shall then know better Alastair's position, his strength and my own. If I can check him, even in a limited fashion, he will be the more ready to talk, perhaps. That I *must* attempt — or my name and repute as Lord of Badenoch and Lochaber is discredited. Give me until tomorrow's night."

Douglas shrugged. "It seems that I have little option, does it not? Very well. Till tomorrow night . . ."

*   *   *

Jamie did not have to wait so long. By mid-forenoon next day reports were coming in of Alastair Carrach moving down Loch Arkaig-side with all speed now — and significantly, on both sides of the loch. Latest word put his forward parties at near Ardachvie on the north side and at the River Mallie crossing on the south — but three miles from the foot of the loch. Not only that, he had scouts out ahead in both the entrances to the glen, which could only indicate a tactical move. He was looking for a fight.

Arkaig was one of the many long valleys which branched westwards from the Great Glen, probing for nearly a score of miles into the mountains towards the western sea, but coming to something of a dead end well before reaching salt-water. It was a reasonably fertile and populous glen by West Highland standards, the main holding of the MacGillonie Camerons. But it differed from most similar east–west valleys in that it was something of a hanging valley, averaging some 150 feet above the Great Glen level, and all but blocked at its entrance by a great intrusive wedge of hill called *Torr a Mhuilt*, a glacial deposit. Two narrow exits skirted this land-mass to north and south, the former the main entrance to Arkaig through the constricted mile-long ravine known as the Dark Mile, a rocky and gloomy trough, wood-hung, threaded by the twisting, awkward drove-road. The southern pass was much more open, and through it the River Arkaig itself found its way, but the road did not follow it nevertheless, because that river, in its mile-long descent presented a mixture of cataracts and flooded flats, still more difficult to negotiate than the Dark Mile's constrictions. Both represented awkward exits militarily, and it looked as though Alastair was going to use them both. Alexander meantime, of course, had pickets lightly holding both.

He summoned his leaders, Jamie attending — but it was clear that this was not to be any council-of-war; only the details of his tactics remained to be worked out. He spoke to them in the musical sibilant Gaelic, so Jamie understood none of it, though gaining just a hint here and there from the finger pointing to various features of the landscape as he went on. He was interrupted frequently, especially by his brother Sir Andrew, with evident doubts, questions and suggestions; but clearly he held firmly to his own theme and decisions. These seemed to be accepted in the end, and presently his bearers hurried off, shouting for their own lieutenants.

Alexander turned to Jamie. "We must do the best we can," he explained. "Alastair divides his force — which might aid us. Or again might not. We do not know which route his main body will take — by the Dark Mile or the river. I think the river. We do not even know his full strength. I am sending companies to seek block both passes. But he will expect this — it is what any man would do. So there can be little surprise. All I may do is not to commit *my* main strength at first. Only comparatively weak parties into the passes, under my brothers. To delay

Alastair, and at the same time perhaps make him over-confident. He is a confident man, and has had these weeks all his own way. Pray that he remains that way, today!"

"And where *will* you place your main strength?"

He pointed. "Hidden, up there on the ridge of yonder hill, *Torr a Mhuilt*. In the birch-scrub and hollows. From up there I will be able to see down into both passes, in some measure. Can send my strength where most needed. Alastair will not know my numbers, either. It will provide little enough of surprise, but it may just serve."

"You are still determined to fight? Why not let me talk, instead?"

"No, Jamie. You may talk if we are defeated! I have drawn the sword, and must use it — or cease to lead Highlandmen."

The other shrugged. "As you will. What would you have me do then?"

Alexander eyed his friend keenly. "I would have you aid me this day, Jamie. In some small degree. Will you?" That was a question and no plea; but the Douglas could not fail to sense something of appeal.

"How aid you?" he asked, warily. "*I* am not here to fight."

"No. I do not ask you to fight. Only to, to make a gesture. See you, oddly, *you* in fact represent the only true surprise with which I can confront Alastair Carrach — cavalry. The Islesmen do not fight horsed — Highlanders seldom do. They cannot carry horses in their galleys. He may have captured a few garrons, for use as pack-animals for booty — that is all. His is a foot host — as is mine. But you have come with thirty horsed men-at-arms, of the royal guard. Armoured, and with banners and pennons . . ."

"Thirty only! A mere escort, not a fighting force . . ."

"True. But in this camp there are over a score of garrons — my own and my brothers' and some of the chieftains' riding-horses. Around here I could raise more, many more. There are plenty of garrons — only they are not used for fighting. We could mount men on them, contrive what would look like lances and banners, at a distance. Add these to your thirty. Then you could take up your stance on the high ground, where you would seem to threaten Alastair's flank. Let yourself be seen, a quite large cavalry force, ready to ride down upon the Islesmen. I believe that would cause him some alarm, give him pause."

Jamie stared. "You mean that I should just stand? On a hill? Do nothing? Play-acting . . . ?"

"To be sure, my friend. That is all I ask."

"But . . . I should feel the greatest fool."

"The hero of Otterburn, eh? But if the Douglas is prepared to come all this way to talk with Alastair, surely he is prepared to show himself? As being at least fit for more than talking."

The other chewed his lip. "Is there such a place? Where such stand could be made? Where cavalry could hope to operate?"

"There is, yes. Part way up the River Arkaig, on the south, the Achnacarry side. At the widest part of the pass, high above, is a lesser ridge, a half-mile back from the river. If you lined the crest of that. See you, I believe Alastair will come that way, with his main force, not through the Dark Mile. At this season the flooded meadows will be dry, passable. He will be laden with booty, his people sure of their strength. The Dark Mile is difficult and narrow. They would be much more strung out and apt for ambush. I will seek to trap him, nevertheless, by the riverside. And if cavalry, which he cannot have looked for, hold the high ground, he will be much distracted. Will you do it, Jamie?"

The Douglas spread his hands. He could not say no.

"My thanks. It may mean much. And Jamie — do not show yourselves until the enemy is well forward, so that he cannot change his advance. Now, sufficient of talk. Let us be doing . . ."

*   *   *

On the high bare heather slopes of the *Meall an t-Seamraig* ridge, with much of Lochaber spread below and the lochs of Lochy, Linnhe, Eil and the farther Firth of Lorn shining in the afternoon sun, Jamie Douglas looked back at his motley following, which straggled over a large area of the hill. From thus close-at-hand it certainly did not look like any sort of cavalry force — a gypsy encampment on the move, rather. The thirty troopers looked the more formidable and effective in contrast; but for the rest, it was an almost laughable sight. Alexander had scraped together almost a hundred beasts, of a kind, shaggy garrons and work-horses for carrying peats in panniers, in the main, some rather better riding animals, many mere ponies whose low-slung bellies brushed the high heather and whose riders' feet were apt to all but trail the ground. The said riders were as heterogeneous as their mounts, largely old men and boys unfit for the Cameron fighting strength, rounded up at short notice from herding, peat-cutting, from the cowshed and the cabin door, armed with every variety of weapon, however rusty and antique. They seemed cheerful enough, most appearing to look on it all as in the nature of a holiday — although none could speak other than the native Gaelic and so were unable to communicate with the Lowlanders. Not that there was any fraternising between the two parties anyway; the royal guard men-at-arms, in their gleaming breastplates and helmets, could scarcely have shown their scorn and disapproval more eloquently even if they had spoken the Gaelic.

Pate Boyd, riding beside Jamie, gestured. "This rabble wouldna frighten a coven of auld wives!" he asserted, not for the first time. "Guidsakes — we'll never hear the end o' this when we get back hame!"

"From a sufficient distance they may look better, Pate. But as well that we are only to stand and watch! That low ridge ahead — this guide keeps pointing to it. I take it that is where Sir Alexander would have us stand."

From up here, facing north, they could not see down into the short, deep valley of the Arkaig River, the swelling of hill ahead, a mere long fold in the heather rather than any ridge, preventing. There was a distinct dip, wet with black peat-hags, before it; and here Jamie ordered his curious company to wait, whilst he rode on with Boyd and the Cameron guide. Nearing the crest, if so it could be called, they dismounted and went carefully forward on foot.

They were unprepared for what they saw. Although it was comparatively level up here, really only a sort of heathery plateau, the terrain changed entirely before them, the ground falling away in a long and continuous grassy slope, quite steep, scored by small watercourses and dotted with carpets of bracken. At the foot, possibly six hundred feet below, there was a belt of green levels, no doubt flooded in winter but now meadowland of a sort, then the river, quite wide, and the opposite hillside rising much more abruptly, clothed with hanging woods of oak and birch. But it was not the sudden prospect of the Arkaig valley which surprised them so much as what went on within it, the violent activity of men. The valley-floor was full of men. Battle was already joined.

"Dear God — it is started! We are too late. Or Alastair early. Look — they are fording the river. There — and there.

These must be the Islesmen. Alexander was to be up the hill there, opposite, he said." Jamie shook his dark head as though to clear it of indecision. "Pate — back with you. Bring up our people. Mounted. On to the crest. Quickly. Spread them out in line abreast. Mix our men-at-arms amongst them. A long line, so that they seem more than they are. Haste you . . ."

While he waited impatiently for his horsemen to come up, Jamie sought to comprehend the most evidently confused situation below, half-a-mile away. There appeared to be roads, or tracks, on both sides of the river, and both were crowded with men over a long stretch. At first he assumed that these represented the two embattled forces, Alexander on the north side, the Islesmen on the south. But many were to be seen splashing across the shallows from south to north, and not being opposed; so clearly Alastair's men must be on both sides, having advanced along each bank. It was not easy to see just what was happening on the north side, for the woodlands came down almost to the river there; but it seemed that fighting was proceeding on the lower slopes, amongst the trees. Continual splashes in the river — and they must be large splashes to be visible at this distance — puzzled him at first. Then he realised that these were being caused by rocks, and possibly logs, being rolled down upon the Islesmen by Alexander's men on the higher ground.

Evidently then his friend was using the hill opposite, this *Torr a Mhuilt*, as a sort of fortress, and had coaxed Alastair Carrach into the costly task of assailing its steep side. Sound tactics for the weaker side, forcing the other into the difficult role almost of a besieger against a strongly-entrenched garrison. But though this might inflict heavy losses on the enemy, it could hardly result in Alexander's victory — for if the cost proved too great, the Islesmen could always withdraw their attack and, with their greater numbers, merely sit around the foot of the hill waiting, like any other besieger. Eventually Alexander would either have to come down and fight it out on the less advantageous low ground, or else try to steal away quietly, by night. Both of which would mean defeat. It was, in fact, a defensive strategy.

Jamie had reached this conclusion when his horsemen came pounding up around him, scarcely in the long and careful line abreast formation he had commanded. His men-at-arms sought to carry out the order, in some fashion, but the Gaelic-speaking contingent had either not understood or were otherwise minded. These came in bunches and groups, to yell and point at the scene below and brandish weapons and shake fists, a sufficiently aggressive demonstration but lacking any appearance of a disciplined cavalry force. Some indeed promptly urged their beasts, and their friends, on down the hill towards the battle.

Jamie shouted and gesticulated for these to come back and for all to line up as arranged — but he might as well have saved his breath. He called for his single trumpeter to sound a summoning blast or two — and though this, echoing and re-echoing amongst the hills, did have the effect of turning most heads in his direction, it produced no other positive result save to increase if possible the warlike ardour of his ragbag throng, who presumably took it as some kind of challenge or encouragement. It occurred to him indeed that the fighters down in the valley-floor might consider it in the same light, since undoubtedly they would hear it also.

"We will never hold the critturs!" Boyd asserted, coming up with Jamie's own horse. "They will be off, down there, like a pack o' gangrel curs."

The Douglas mounted, fists clenched, staring downhill. Clearly Boyd was right. Everywhere the Cameron riders were edging forward raggedly, in ones and twos and little parties; only the royal guard sat their mounts on the ridge, as ordered.

"It will be a massacre!" he exclaimed. "These fools, with their hatchets and dirks — the Islesmen will cut them to pieces!"

"Nae mair'n they deserve, the witless, godless heathens!"

"No! They are fighting for their homes, their folk. Look up there, at Arkaig-side burning . . ."

But Boyd did not glance up the long smoking glen to the west. "There they go!" he shouted. "They're off, the crazy-mad spawn of . . ." The rest was lost in the fierce and prolonged yelling of the rest of the Highland horsemen as with one accord now they surged forward, after the group of about a score who had started the downward rush.

"God Almighty!" Jamie cried. "We cannot sit here and watch. Watch our friends fight and die, and do nothing. Damnation — I am going down! Trumpeter — sound the Advance." He drew his sword and raised it high. "Forward!" he shouted.

Pate Boyd cursed obscenities behind him but did not hold back. And whatever their feelings in the matter, the out-

101

stretched line of the thirty royal guardsmen dug in their spurs, lances brought forward to the ready.

This was the craziest cavalry charge since Bruce's campfollowers made their wild rush at Bannockburn. In no sort of order, scattered over a wide front and brandishing their diverse weaponry, they thundered downhill bellowing their wrathful challenge. The Lowland men-at-arms fairly quickly managed to coalesce into something of a recognisable formation, but this was well towards the rear. Jamie discovered himself to be shouting "A Douglas! A Douglas!" in true Border style, and though it was not taken up by his following, he kept it up.

It was as well that the Highland garrons were sure-footed creatures and used to coping with treacherous conditions. There were a few spills amongst the unaccustomed horsemen but somehow the vast majority reached the bottom of the hill and plunged on across the soft level meadowland, a disorderly, yelling rabble.

At least their spectacular eruption on the scene had had a major effect on the enemy. The tide of men splashing across the river's shallows had all but died away, as all were called on to turn and face the new threat. And if the charge was a wild and headlong one, the defence was as little co-ordinated, likewise strung out along the riverside over a considerable distance in no formation or commandable state. The Islesmen were in greatly larger numbers than the horsemen, but they were at some disadvantage through being stationary in the face of violent impetus, lacking any strategy for dealing with such unprecedented attack, and being insufficiently concentrated to take concerted action.

The clash, inevitably, was less impressive than the approach, the impact individual rather than general. Momentum carried the shouting horsemen through, in the main; but once that momentum was spent, at the river's edge, the attackers tended to be at a loss. Many, indeed, flung themselves down from their mounts, unused to fighting on horseback, and hurled themselves into battle on foot.

Confusion reigned.

On a scene of utter chaos, Jamie Douglas suddenly perceived that he and his men momentarily could represent the only ordered and disciplined entity present, and as such might exercise a major influence on events. He could see a point in the long enemy line, a knot as it were, where it was thickest, densest, and where there seemed to be less disorder — the leadership almost certainly, possibly Alastair Carrach himself with his chiefs. With instant decision he turned in his saddle, reining up a little, to wave up the cohort of the royal guard behind, using the clenched-fist close up signal, swinging his arm up and down on either side.

"Back me! Back me!" he cried. "Tight. Arrow-formation — arrow, I say!"

Probably few if any heard him; but these were trained cavalrymen and knew very well what was intended. Swiftly they closed in behind into a solid phalanx, with little lessening of speed, and Pate Boyd and the under-officer spurred up alongside Jamie. He brought down his sword in a slashing gesture forward, pointing towards that knot of the enemy leadership some three hundred yards away, half-left a little further up the valley, kicking his beast into a full gallop.

The Islesmen were no cravens and amongst the fiercest fighters in the land. But they were wholly unused to the terrifying task of standing up to a charge of semi-armoured cavalry and had no tactics to deal with it. There might have been two hundred or so men clustered round what were now clearly the chieftains of the invading host, and only thirty men bore down upon them. But those thirty were on pounding, turf-scattering, snorting horses, long lances levelled now, and wearing steel breastplates and helmets. The waiting half-naked men wilted and broke before ever impact could be made.

Jamie, keeping his eye firmly on the chiefly figures, evident from their arms and attire and barbaric jewellery, drove unswervingly at these. They did not linger for him much longer than the rest, but scattered likewise. His beating, seeking sword never so much as made contact with any as they darted away in all directions, desperate to get from under lashing, flailing hooves. In a matter of only moments the leadership group of the invaders was no more, dispersed.

As the river-bank loomed up, Jamie sought to pull up and rein round, urgently, in danger of being ridden down by his own followers; but training told, and the men-at-arms managed to swing away right and left, and wheel about, retaining something of formation.

"After the leaders!" the Douglas yelled. "Hunt them down. Only them. The leaders . . ."

Now indeed all *was* confusion on that south side of the

Arkaig, as the Lowlanders rode off after the individual fleeing chiefs and all semblance of a front on either side was broken. Jamie was gambling on preventing any overall enemy command from being able to operate and control the situation; but he recognised the risks and dangers inherent. He and his were still vastly outnumbered, this side of the river; and though the Islesmen had been scattered, few casualties had actually been inflicted. Moreover, he himself had now little in the way of control over his people — although the trumpeter still clung close and his blared summons could fairly quickly recall the men-at-arms to his side. Their surprise had been highly effective, but if the enemy rallied now all could be as swiftly lost.

It was at this critical stage that, of all things, music took a hand in the struggle. Suddenly, above the shouting and clash, the sound of bagpipes came sobbing and shrilling up the valley, turning Jamie's head as it turned many another. There, down-river but on this south side, a host was coming into view, marching westwards, led by half-a-dozen pipers. Banners of a sort waved above this also, and steel gleamed in the sunlight. From the direction, it could only be Alexander's men, more Camerons presumably.

The effect on the Islesmen was dramatic. Any possible rally was halted there and then. Reinforcement for their foes was just too much, at that moment. Men began to disengage, to turn and flee, in ones and twos and small groups, some westwards towards Loch Arkaig again, some across the meadowland to the hills from which the horsemen had descended.

Promptly the noise of battle began to increase on the north side, amongst the woodlands, as the attack there was stepped up, to coincide. The trickle of flight became a flood. Soon all the invaders who could move were streaming away from that highly unconventional battlefield, casting weapons from them, abandoning booty, every man for himself. Moreover, the panic quickly spread across the river. There, too, flight became general.

It was not Alexander himself but young Sir James Stewart who came hastening up behind the pipers — and his company proved to be only superficially like a fighting-force, in fact a similar collection of old men and boys to Jamie's own, another example of Alexander's talent for improvisation.

The elder brother was not long in coming leaping down through the birch-woods of *Torr a Mhuilt* to splash across the

Arkaig shallows to them. He ran up, to grasp Jamie by both arms.

"My friend, my good friend!" he cried. "A joy, a very triumph! I thank you, I thank you with all my heart! A victory, a notable victory — and all yours, Jamie. You took Alastair wholly by surprise — aye, and myself also! Your charge of cavalry won the day. How can I sufficiently thank you, friend?"

Embarrassed, Jamie shook his head. "It was no charge. Only the merest chance," he asserted. "We could do nothing else. They plunged on, out of hand. I could not control them . . ."

"You controlled them sufficiently to make Alastair Carrach turn and run, man! I asked you only to stand and show yourselves — and instead you charged, and won the battle for me! The Islesmen will not rally now, this side of the Hebridean Sea — I shall see to that. Thanks to Sir James Douglas . . .!"

Protest as he would, that was the way of it. Jamie was a hero again, and nothing that he could say would alter it. Even the other Stewart brothers relaxed much of their hostility.

Alexander was right, at least, about Alastair Carrach being unable to rally his forces. No doubt he tried to, but, harried by Alexander's men, now being continuously reinforced by new Cameron contingents coming from all over Lochaber, he was unable to make a stand. Moreover, his galley-fleet lying there in Loch Linnhe, beckoned men enticingly. Within forty-eight hours he was sailing back to his isles, a discredited man.

Jamie, of course, had no opportunity to deliver his message from the Earl David — nor indeed did it seem any longer necessary. Circumstances had changed radically — and he had had his part in changing them. What the prince would say to it all was debatable — but the sooner he was informed the better.

The Lowland party rode with the returning Badenoch contingent as far as the northern mouth of the beetling Pass of Drumochter, and left them there to head southwards, with the plaudits and thanks of Alexander Stewart loud in their ears. However much of a hypocrite Jamie felt, he was glad of that young man's esteem nevertheless. He recognised him as a figure it would be unwise to underestimate on the Scottish scene. Unfortunately the chances that he and his cousin David might come to a clash was distinctly possible — two Stewarts of similar spirit if very dissimilar natures. Though if he, Jamie Douglas, could do anything to prevent it, he vowed to himself that he would do so.

V

IT WAS STRANGE to be back amongst the Highland hills again, and in Alexander Stewart's company likewise, so soon, however different the circumstances. Strange too how different the land itself looked, after a bare two months interval, if possible even more colourful, more beautiful. Already the mountain tops wore caps of snow, their lower slopes with the heather turning from purple to a rich sepia, and further down still the tracery of the birches changed from delicate green to pale gold. The October air was like wine. It was good to be off, footloose as it were, on this special mission for the prince, instead of proceeding on to Elgin and Inverness with the large, slow-moving and far from harmonious official cavalcade.

Jamie Douglas had been thankful when, at Lochindorb, the Earl David, concerned with the continuing delays in their progress through his Northern lieutenancy, had decided that the itinerary must be curtailed drastically. The Governor himself, no less, with a large entourage, had insisted on accompanying his nephew on this Highland tour, and could nowise be dissuaded or prevented. With as result an inevitable sourness and ill-feeling throughout, as well as a general slowing up. Just what the Earl Robert's purpose had been in coming on this prolonged and uncomfortable peregrination was not entirely clear; presumably he suspected David of designs which could damage his own interests—and with reason, of course; possibly he felt that he could act as a brake and counter-influence on the young man's all-too-evident ambitions. But the effect had been depressing, and restricting in results as in pace. And to none more galling than to Jamie Douglas, towards whom Robert Stewart never attempted to conceal his chill hostility.

A large part of David's design in making this progress was, of course, to try to ensure the support of the northern magnates in the forthcoming struggle for power. Naturally it much hampered him to have his rival with him, and in consequence, many of the intended interviews with the lords and chiefs had either to be abandoned or conducted at second-hand, by envoys sent out on detachment as it were. Jamie had been so used on not a few occasions, primed with appeals, promises and disguised threats. It was not work greatly to his taste, although he proved fairly successful at it. The word of his dramatic intervention into the battle on the Arkaig had spread far and wide throughout the Highlands, exaggerated out of all recognition, and he now found himself accepted as something of a major military leader, a reputation which no denials from him could eradicate, and which the Earl David found a distinct asset. He had been as delighted as he was amused at the result of Jamie's August excursion in the North, which had enabled him to preserve intact the bargaining powers of the earldom of Ross and at the same time bring pressure to bear on Donald of the Isles — who indeed had further drawn in his horns and agreed to the gesture of theoretically punishing his brother for unauthorised raiding on the mainland by allegedly committing Alastair Carrach to token imprisonment on the isle of Islay for a year. Also the royal castle of Urquhart had been yielded up again to the King's officer — in this case Sir Alexander Stewart.

The slow progress of this less-than-happy joint Lieutenant's and Governor's tour had meant that, if indeed the travellers were to get back safely to the South before the snows came down from the mountain-tops to choke the passes, a large part of the programme would have to be abandoned. It had been intended to return from the Inverness area by the vast and populous territories to the east, by the sheriffdoms of Banff and Aberdeen and the great earldom of Mar. That was now ruled out, and Jamie in consequence sent on this independent journey, to the Countess of Mar and her husband Sir Malcolm Drummond, at Kildrummy in Strathdon, thereafter to find his way home on his own. He had been glad to go — and Alexander, as Deputy Lieutenant, glad to accompany and escort him through the seventy-odd miles of wilderness — for he, of course, was even less popular with the Governor than was the Douglas.

So the two friends, this time with a bodyguard of a score of running gillies, Clan Chattan men, trotted south-eastwards through the glowing October uplands with a great relief from cramping restrictions and strained relations, and a consequent almost carefree cheer. Affairs of state and the power struggle could be forgotten for the moment, and the natural friendship and mutual esteem of spirited young men allowed its head.

They had crossed Spey and threaded the Abernethy Forest to climb the eastern skirts of the great Monadh Ruadh range beyond, up and up on to even higher lands than Lochindorb. Spending the first night in the narrow gut of steep Glen Braan, they had crossed over the desolate heights to the south, the very roof of Scotland, by Tomintoul and the Lecht passes through the Mounth, by a route which would be impassable in little more than a week or two. By testing even their sturdy garrons, not to mention the tireless gillies, they reached the lower lands around Corgarff at the head of Strathdon for the second night. And now they were riding down that lovely strath, eastwards still, amongst the gentler hills of the wary Forbes clansmen, immediate destination not far ahead.

Kildrummy Castle, principal seat of the mighty earldom of Mar, was strategically sited to dominate more than one route through the Mounth passes from the lowlands of Aberdeenshire, Angus and the Mearns. Strongly sited on the hillside above the Don, and protected on all sides save the approach by steep ravines, it was a great and powerful hold, larger than Lochindorb or any other further north, from which its owners ruled a territory large as many a Continental princedom — all the Mars, Braemar, Cromar, Midmar, Formartine and the Garioch, with much of the Firmounth and parts of Strathbogie besides. Although theoretically under the authority of the Lieutenant, because oft he mighty masses of the Monadh Ruadh mountains which soared between, the earldom of Mar was in practice almost independent. Hence this visit.

The travellers came to Kildrummy in mid-afternoon, and were received in very cautious fashion by the steward, being scrutinised and interrogated at some length from the gatehouse drum-towers before being admitted. Clearly Highland caterans were less than welcome here.

It seemed that the Countess of Mar was out hunting stags, and Sir Malcolm her husband had left to visit his Strathearn domains far to the south-west.

The young men were disappointed, for Malcolm Drummond,

Queen Annabella's brother, was an important man to win to the support of the prince in the forthcoming struggle. It might seem strange that he should require to be coaxed to his nephew's side, but there was sufficient reason. First of all, he did not love any of the Stewarts — had been brought up so. His aunt, Margaret Drummond of Logie, had been Queen and second wife to David the Second. Although admittedly a lady of doubtful virtue, the King had known that when he married her — she had, after all, been his chief mistress for years before his first wife died. But when King David himself died, his nephew and successor, Robert Stewart, treated her and her family vilely; and the Drummonds did not forget. Moreover Sir Malcolm hated the Douglases — or at least the present Earl Archie, considering that he had wrongfully supplanted his wife in titles and estates. He had married Isobel Douglas, sister of the late Earl James, and Countess of Mar in her mother's right; but she had been excluded as heiress of Douglas in favour of Archie, Lord of Galloway. So, a man with a grievance, he found little on the Scots governmental scene to attract him, and seldom appeared at Court or council. Nevertheless he was powerful, when he wanted to be, not only because of his wife's great earldom of Mar but on account of his own large Drummond lands in Perthshire. He was a strangely proud man, yet had never sought to be created Earl of Mar, in his wife's right, as was his entitlement.

However, when that lady returned from her hunting, she at least greeted the visitors warmly — and Alexander notably more warmly than Jamie. They had met before briefly, of course, prior to the North Inch contest at Perth, when the Earl David had been fondling her, in his usual fashion with attractive women whatever their age. She was a handsome creature, now in her thirty-ninth year, dark and tall, of statuesque build, big-bosomed and with a hot eye. The so-pronounced swarthy Douglas colouring gave her almost a Latin look, and she was as forthright in manner as most of the clan.

"So, my young friends," she declared, when she came down to join them for the evening meal. "You bring me Stewart requests, do you? Seeking favours? Brave knights!" She had changed from her hunting attire into something more suitable for evening wear — or at least for some sort of evening, though whether it was apt for this occasion was a matter of taste, for the rich gown was so low-cut and off-the-shoulder as to provide a challenge to masculine susceptibilities and the laws of gravity both. How it kept approximately up was a mystery which continued to preoccupy the two guests. Momentarily they expected to see one or both of the great white breasts burst out of the purely token grip of the bodice whenever the Countess drew deep breath or laughed, both of which she did frequently and heartily. Now and again she hitched the material up somewhat, but with a casual lack of concern. She ate and drank heartily too, and gave the impression that the evening might not be altogether uneventful.

Jamie allowed Alexander to answer this first verbal challenge. His position *vis-à-vis* his friend was a little uncertain here. He was the prince's man and direct envoy; but he was only an unimportant knight and small Douglas laird in fact, the lady's brother's former esquire. Whereas Sir Alexander, although a bastard also, was son of a royal earl, grandson and nephew of kings, Lord of Badenoch and moreover acting Deputy Justiciar of the North.

The other demonstrated a sort of wary courtesy and charm. "We did not fear too greatly, Countess, since we have heard only good of your ladyship, to rival your beauty. Moreover, does not the Earl David look on you as his friend?"

"Does he? You tell me, sir."

"Er . . . that is my understanding. He spoke most kindly of you, Lady Isobel."

"My husband's nephew will speak most kindly of any who can serve him — *while* they can serve him! Being a Stewart — like yourself, Sir Alexander." She chuckled throatily. She had a deeply husky voice.

Dragging his eyes from the endangered bosom, the other glanced at Jamie.

"Yes," the lady went on. "Let us hear a Douglas on this."

Jamie coughed, applying his gaze to his rib of cold venison. "The prince ever speaks well of you, madam," he said, with as much certitude as he could summon up.

"That comforts my heart, Sir James. Yet he sends you two to ensure my support? He conceives it necessary — but does not come himself."

Neither guest was in haste to answer that. Jamie spoke, at length. "His lordship conceives you his sure friend, Countess. It is more to your husband, I believe, that he sends us. It is unfortunate that Sir Malcolm is not here."

"Ah. So he is sure of me, but not sure of his Uncle Drummond — is that the way of it? He knows my husband's opinion of the Stewarts, so keeps his distance and sends you?"

Her guests applied themselves to their viands, aware that they were not doing very well, and that this woman was shrewd as well as bold, formidable in fact.

"Come," she went on cheerfully. "No need to look so glum. It is always as well to know just where one stands, is it not — where the Stewarts are concerned, in especial! Have you come seeking anything of *me*, a mere woman? Or is it Malcolm only your prince needs?"

"No, Countess — by no means," Alexander assured in his softly pleasing Highland voice. "It is you who are Mar, not Sir Malcolm. You who control this great earldom and all its powers and men and resources. Sir Malcolm and the house of Drummond are important also, and the prince seeks their aid. But Mar is of much larger influence, and could mean much to his cause."

"David Stewart wants those powers and men and resources for his own purposes? Why should I lend him them — even though it does suit him to call himself my friend?"

"It is not the men and resources he wants, lady, but your support. The votes of your vassals at a parliament. In the spring, in April most like, he intends to challenge his uncle the Earl Robert for the power and governorship of his realm. He is going to need every vote that he can raise, and all possible support in the land likewise. Mar comprises many lordships, not a few votes. And a large number of knights' fees . . ."

"I see. So that is it. David Stewart would displace Robert Stewart, the young lion for the old fox — and his love for me comes down to votes in a parliament!" She actually snorted. "Is there any reason why I should so aid him?"

"The young lion will be your king one day, lady."

"Perhaps, perhaps not. Only if he wins his fight. If Robert wins, then *he* will no doubt be king one day, instead. What of those who supported David, then? Safer to support neither, is it not? I fear that you have shown me no reason why I should risk all for David Stewart."

Alexander looked towards Jamie.

That young man frowned. "Lady Isobel," he said, almost challenged, in his jerky forthright way. "You have no cause to love the Earl Robert, I think?"

"That is true, at least," she agreed.

"He it was who made sure that you did not get the Douglas earldom, at your brother's death. He it was who, I believe, had your brother, my master, foully slain at Otterburn."

"I have heard that tale, yes. But there is no certainty, no proof."

"No proof — but he gained most from the Earl James's murder. And the murderer was slain in turn, secretly, before he could talk. And the slayer was in the Earl Robert's pay. Your brother's widow, the Governor's own sister, believes that he did it. Is your ladyship less . . . concerned?"

She eyed him levelly. "You speak very directly, sirrah. But the Douglases are apt to, are we not?"

"I judge that you would wish me to do so, Countess."

"Perhaps. Then tell me, as directly, what I gain by supporting David Stewart, Sir James."

"Vengeance on the Earl Robert. And a better, more honest, rule in this kingdom."

"What makes you believe that exchanging David for this uncle will better the rule? I conceive the one no more honest than the other."

"I believe it — although I cannot prove it, any more than I can prove that the Governor slew Earl James. But I have known the prince since he was but a boy. He has his failings, but I believe him honest in his wish to govern well the realm which will one day be his own."

She looked at him for long moments, silent. Then she laughed, and bit into her venison with strong teeth. "We shall see," she said, mouth full.

Alexander felt the need to change the subject. "It much interests me to be in this house, Countess," he said. "For another reason, as well as the delight of your company. It was here that a forebear of mine suffered grievous betrayal. My great-grandmother, Marjory Bruce, with her stepmother the Queen Elizabeth de Burgh, and her uncle, Nigel Bruce, were betrayed here to the English invaders, Nigel to his execution, only a few months after the good King Robert's coronation. It was an evil chance."

"No chance, my friend. The smith here, one Osborne, bore a grudge against his master, Gartnait of Mar, for some slight. This was his revenge. Although Gartnait himself escaped. That slight cost the King his favourite brother, his wife and daughter eight years in English prisons — aye, and his sister Christian, Gartnait's wife also."

"A dastardly deed. I hope the smith suffered for it, in due course?"

"Oh, he did. And quickly. Oddly, at the hands of the English themselves — who seem to have misliked traitors also. Osborne had covenanted with them for a large sum in gold, for the deed. They paid him by melting the gold and pouring it molten down his throat." She laughed. "No doubt they slit him open after, and retrieved their outlay!"

"Lord . . .!" Jamie muttered.

Later, they sat before the great log fire and listened to a silver-voiced singer render the haunting ballads of the North-East, accompanying himself on a harp. The Countess sat on a deerskin-piled settle between the two young men, wine goblet in one hand but the other free to touch and stroke and caress Alexander on her left. Jamie, at the other side, was sufficiently aware of this, but managed not to feel deprived or resentful that he was not equally favoured. If Alexander found the process distasteful, in a woman old enough to be his mother, he did not show it. But when the minstrel exchanged his harp for a fiddle and the Lady Isobel, evidently still more affected by that sobbing, romantic music, leant still further over to her left so that one magnificent breast at last escaped from its tenuous confinement to rest heavily white on the Stewart shoulder, Jamie felt that in merest friendship he ought to seek the other's rescue. When the musician paused, he cleared his throat and announced that Alexander himself was a notable performer on the fiddle, and singer likewise, and should demonstrate his skill.

Their hostess took this, as it were, in her stride however. Expressing unqualified delight, she imperiously summoned the minstrel over to the settle, to give his fiddle to their visitor, who would play it there at her side, without disturbing himself or her. This Alexander proceeded to do, however cramped the accommodation and possibly distracting the attentions on his right, and demonstrably to the satisfaction of their chatelaine, seemingly unperturbed.

After some time of this, and finding his role unrewarding, and moreover tending to nod off, what with the heat of the fire, the large meal and a long day in the saddle, at the end of a Gaelic love-song of infinite yearning, Jamie got to his feet and sought the Countess's permission to retire. This she graciously granted

— whilst keeping her strong hand pressing Alexander firmly down in his seat.

Jamie had one more try. "We shall be riding early on the morrow, Lady Isobel," he informed. "For I have other calls to make and little time to make them. I hope that I may give the prince a favourable answer as to the valuable support of the earldom of Mar?"

"A mercy — what an hour to consider such matters, man! The Douglas single-mindedness carried almost too far, I vow! A weak woman, I have not yet reached a conclusion on this important issue. But . . . seek you your couch, Sir James. Sir Alexander will sing me another lay or two, and then we shall have some small exchange and see if we cannot come to agree on the matter. I am hopeful of a mutual accommodation — eh, Alex? So, off with you, and a good night to you."

Jamie looked down at his friend, who smiled up at him guilelessly but made no suggestion of a move.

Thoughtfully he left the private hall and found a sleepy servitor to light him to his tower chamber. Here, then, was a side of Alexander Stewart new to him. Hitherto he had no knowledge and insight on his friend in relation to women, other than unfailing courtesy towards his mother and sister. It seemed that he was either susceptible or opportunist — or both. He could well understand that the other's almost delicate good looks and engaging manner could have great attraction for the opposite sex, especially for older women; even the hint of steely and wholly masculine determination beneath the mild and slightly diffident exterior could probably have its fascination. But on this evening's showing, the inclination was two-sided. He was a Stewart, of course. Did such seemingly mutual partiality add up to weakness or strength? It might be important to know.

Jamie was pondering thus as he undressed for bed when there was a knock at his door. Assuming that he was perhaps misjudging his friend after all, he went to draw the door-bar — a precaution he had early learned not to neglect in an imperfect world. But he found not Alexander Stewart but a smiling young maid-servant there waiting on the draughty stair-landing. She slipped inside and bobbed a sort of curtsy — in the process the voluminous plaid in which she was wrapped opening to reveal that she was wholly naked beneath, a rounded, buxom creature of very definite femininity, strongly but comfortably made.

"Her ladyship sent me to warm your bed for you, sir," she

114

explained cheerfully. "She wouldna have any guest o' hers deprived!"

"Indeed. That was kind in her — and in yourself, lass. And I am grateful," he declared. "But when weary, as I am this night, I sleep better alone, see you. My good wife assures me that, after a long day ahorse, I twitch grievously — to my bedfellow's discomfort!" Turning the young woman around, he guided her back to the door — although for both their sakes he did not fail to run his hands appreciatively over her generous curves and undulations, and patted her substantial bottom as he propelled her out. "I thank you. Both. An undisturbed good night to you!"

The Countess of Mar, then, had not been quite so lost in lust for Alexander as she had seemed — or at least did not forget her chatelainely duties towards her other guest.

In the morning, despite what might have been anticipated, both Alexander and the Lady Isobel were early on the scene — earlier than Jamie indeed. More hunting, it seemed, was on the programme, this being the best time of the year for upland stags, just before the rutting season started. Fond as he was of the chase, Jamie had more to do than hunt deer this October; but it transpired that Alexander was otherwise minded — at least the Countess evidently assumed that he was accompanying her on the day's expedition.

When the Douglas could get his friend alone, it was to learn that this was indeed the parting of the ways. Alexander felt that, here on the verge of the Lowlands, his presence was no longer necessary, or in fact advantageous, for Jamie's further calls, in Angus and the Mearns. He had played his part for his Cousin David, would stay a little longer at Kildrummy and then return over the mountains to his duties in Badenoch.

The other eyed him with his direct Douglas gaze. "You find it to your liking here?" he asked — and sought with only partial success not to make it sound like an accusation.

"Why, yes," Alexander acceded, with no hint of embarrassment. "The Lady Isobel is good company, and kind, when you come to know her. I find her something of a challenge."

"Is that what she is? I would have called her a masterful woman — of the sort I would admire from a distance!"

"Masterful, yes. And all woman. As I said, a challenge."

"Almost as old as the Lady Mariota, your mother, I swear."

"Four years younger. She told me she is thirty-nine. And so

115

has almost twenty-five years of experience of being an attractive woman! Is there not something in that, some dare, some gauntlet to be picked up? Much more so than with some milk-and-water wench or untried virgin. No?"

Jamie shrugged. "A matter of taste, let us say. I prefer something ten years and more younger."

"You prefer Mary Stewart! But I have not that good fortune and felicity. Every man to his inclination. But, you should be grateful, Jamie, for mine — for your prince's sake. I think that I convinced the Countess last night to throw the whole weight of Mar behind David. And to urge her husband thereto, likewise. Whilst you but slept!"

"M'mm. Aye, well . . ."

Presently Jamie Douglas rode away alone southwards for the Dee and the Cairn o' Mount pass to the Howe of the Mearns and the land of the Lindsays and the Ogilvys, leaving his mild-mannered and delicate-seeming friend and his forceful, mettlesome hostess to their sport. Not for the first time, he wondered about Alexander Stewart — almost as much as he wondered about David Stewart.

VI

"THIS ACCURSED WEATHER!" David Stewart exclaimed, beating fist on the window-ledge of an upper room of the Blackfriars monastery at Perth. "Snow — in April! It is damnable. This could ruin all — all we have worked so hard to achieve. Infernal, devil-damned snow!"

"I think not, my lord," his cousin Alexander said soothingly. "It commenced only at noon yesterday. Insufficient time to harm us greatly."

"But it is heavy, man — heavy. Look at the size of those flakes, of a mercy! If it has blocked the passes again, or some of them, we are lost. It could have been a close enough thing as it was. This could hold up and delay many. Even turn some back. Defeat us."

"Will it not be apt to hold up the Governor's supporters equally as much as your own, my lord?" Jamie Douglas asked.

"Not so. My uncle, having held the rule all this time, has his support all around him, near at hand. Those who love him least have stayed at a distance, furthest away; those who fear him most — for who could love the man? — remain close. Moreover his earldoms of Fife and Menteith, with Strathearn also, which he dominates, are nearby. Snow will not keep these away. Whereas *my* friends, from the North, from Galloway, from the far ends of the realm . . .!"

"I say that you fear unnecessarily, Cousin," Sir Alexander contended. "I know the snow, and the Highland and Mounth passes, better than you do, since I live amongst them. There is no wind today, and it is the wind which blocks the passes — drifting snow. Days and nights of wind. This snow will not last nor lie long — not in April, almost May. Prolonged rain would have

117

been worse, for that could flood the glens and make the rivers impassable. I say that few, if any, from the North will be turned back. Delayed a little only . . ."

"Few is all that is required to defeat us," the Earl David asserted. "Delay also."

"Could it not be postponed?" Jamie asked. "Even a day or two might serve."

"A parliament, duly called under the Great Seal with the required forty days of notice, cannot be postponed. Not when all the principals are already assembled. It would require the King in special Council — and Robert still dominates the Council."

The three young men stared out at what they could see of the white expanse of the North Inch of Perth. It was exactly thirty months since the extraordinary clan battle had been fought there; and on the morrow, 28th April 1399, the town was the chosen venue for another sort of battle, less bloody perhaps but of much greater significance for the entire kingdom. It was not like David Stewart to be gloomy or depressed, but so much was at stake, the culmination of months, years of work and planning.

The prince shrugged and mustered a rueful smile. "Well, what will be, will. And meantime, I keep a lady waiting — and an impatient lady at that! Eupham Lindsay is a hot piece in more ways than one. As well, perhaps, since it may well be chilly in yonder Gilten Arbour!"

The other two exchanged glances. Jamie coughed. "My lord — the Earl of Dunbar and March is arrived. Here, in this very building. Is it wise . . .?"

"George Dunbar, I think, will scarce be haunting the Gilten Arbour summer-house in a snowstorm!" He paused. "Besides, he may be the less concerned, presently! And he is a dull fish. So — I leave you, my friends. Pray you to your various saints that the snow stops. And at tonight's banquet keep sober, since I may need you . . ."

The prince gone, Alexander looked thoughtful. "What think you he meant when he said that Dunbar might be the less concerned presently? I thought I heard a strange note there?"

"I do not know." Jamie frowned. "But I mislike this of Mistress Eupham Lindsay. At this moment. She is, after all, niece to Sir David Lindsay of Crawford and Glenesk, the King's good-brother. And the Lindsays are proud. To be playing with her now, betrothed as he is to the Earl of Dunbar's daughter.

118

Dunbar may be dull, but he is prouder even than the Lindsays — and more powerful. This could be folly, I say."

"He plays with many women, Jamie."

"Aye. But he might choose them with more care . . .!"

Even although many parliamentary attenders had not yet arrived, the refectory of the Blackfriars monastery, the largest apartment in Perth, was thronged for the King's banquet that night, so that it was difficult to see where the others would have been fitted in had they been in time. But more than mere numbers are requisite for a successful evening's entertainment, and this occasion was ill-starred from the start.

Although Lyon King of Arms, as master of ceremonies, had been carefully busy, at Earl David's instigation, in seeking to seat judiciously the membership of the two great factions, as far as these were known, there were other sub-factions, private feuds and various divisive causes, in an appallingly discordant realm. Due consideration for precedence and complicated pride of birth and rank had to be balanced likewise, and there were inevitable complaints, resentments and clashes amongst the guests long before the people at the dais-table came in to take their places. Although this had been foreseen, and music and entertainers brought on from the very start, to help damp down and disguise hostilities, the atmosphere nevertheless was more reminiscent of two armed camps than of a celebratory feast. Although none knew exactly what was likely to transpire, there was little doubt that goodwill and harmony would require much cherishing.

Jamie Douglas and Mary Stewart sat well down the third of the three lengthwise tables — for however close to the prince, the young man held no official position and was, of course, not a commissioner to the parliament; indeed he could not have found any justification for being present had not his wife been an illegitimate sister of the King. Sir Alexander Stewart chose to sit between them — although he indeed could have occupied a somewhat higher place as *de facto* though not *de jure* Lord of Badenoch and acting Deputy Lieutenant of the North.

Jamie was anything but at ease as they waited, much aware of the brittle atmosphere, concerned that there might be serious trouble; but his companions appeared to be happily carefree. Mary was of a cheerful and non-worrying disposition; and Alex, despite his sensitive appearance, seemed to be able to shrug off apprehension, secure in some inner confidence.

"There are a deal too many of David's unfriends here," Jamie declared, not for the first time. "Or, leastways, too few of his friends come. There is Sir John Stewart of Darnley, now, with Sir David Dennistoun. Sir John Ramorgnie, too . . ."

"Is Ramorgnie not friendly with David? I have seen them together."

"Aye — but I do not trust him. He is a deal too clever, that one. And his lands are in Fife. Like yonder Sir Walter Bickerton of Kincraig. I trust none of the name of Bickerton."

"Jamie is scarcely the most trusting of mortals," his wife confided. "Sometimes I wonder if he wholly trusts *me*! Even with quite elderly admirers! As well that he considers you harmless, Alex! Perhaps it is a Douglas failing?"

But Jamie was in no mood for banter. "There are too many *Douglases* here for my comfort!" he added. "At least, those following Earl Archie."

"But the Earl Archibald is less firm in his support of the Governor, is he not?" Alexander said. "Since that business on the Border and the trouble with Percy and Lancaster."

"Yes. But when it comes to the vote tomorrow, I fear that he will side with the Earl Robert. Out of old custom and friendship. So my father believes. And his son, the Master of Douglas, has taken a mislike to David, more's the pity, although he is his good-brother. Over some slight . . ."

"Ha — here is Eupham Lindsay, looking sleek as a cat at the cream!" Mary observed. "The whisper is that David is so besotted with her that she is growing ambitious."

"Ambitious? You mean . . . ?"

"Marriage," his wife nodded. "*I* do not think so, knowing my nephew. But that is the talk. Elizabeth Dunbar is a dull child and will never satisfy David. But Eupham Lindsay is scarce of the rank to threaten her."

"He'd never marry her. His wife will one day be Queen. But he could offend the whole Lindsay clan with this folly . . ." Jamie paused. "The saints be praised — here's two Douglases we can rely on, come in time. Will of Drumlanrig and his brother Archie of Cavers. They are sure, at least . . ."

The dais-table occupants began to file in, from the Prior's door at the back of the refectory. Jamie's own half-brother, suddenly greatly enhanced in status, came first, with his wife, the Lady Elizabeth, second of the King's daughters. Then the Master of Douglas, with the elder sister, the Lady Margaret;

and George, Earl of Angus with the Lady Mary, the youngest. There followed three of the princesses of the previous generation, two with their husbands, Sir David Lindsay and Hay of Erroll, the Constable, although the Lady Isabel, former Countess of Douglas, was alone. Then, after a pause, came the Earls of Moray, Ross, Dunbar and Douglas, with the senior Bishops of St. Andrews, Glasgow, Aberdeen and Dunkeld.

Jamie, counting pros and cons, glowered blackly. His calculations were scarcely encouraging.

Finally the awaited fanfare of trumpets heralded the monarch, the music and entertainment ceased, and all rose. The King of Arms led in five persons, the Earls of Carrick and Fife, nephew brilliant in white satin and gold, uncle soberly fine in black and silver; then King Robert, noble in appearance but undistinguished and untidy as to dress, leaning heavily on his Queen's arm, Annabella on the other hand leading a small, wide-eyed boy in scarlet velvet, the Prince James, born unexpectedly five years before and now the monarch's joy and consolation — although joy is too happy and positive a word ever to use with reference to King Robert the Third.

"Why have they brought the child?" Mary whispered to her husband. "Late as this. Is he not a poppet!"

"There will be a reason, you may be sure."

The King, bowing but eyeing the throng nervously, seated himself in the high chair at the centre of the dais-table, with David on his right and the Queen on his left, then the little prince between her and the Earl Robert — who sat as far away from the child as he might without having to be too close to the Primate, Bishop Trail, of whom he much disapproved. This last raised a beringed hand and declared a Latin grace-before-meat, before all resumed their seats.

"David looks in good spirits," Alexander commented. "A deal more cheerful than the Governor."

"He is ever that. And the more spirited the less the cause!"

"Jamie is ever a fount of cheer, himself!" his wife confided.

The banquet thereafter proceeded normally and without incident, other than the odd squabble between antipathetic neighbours which the music and singing was sufficient to cover up. As course succeeded course however — although April was a difficult month for game and fish — and the wine began to flow ever more freely, disagreements became more vehement and black looks were more common than amiable converse, even up on the dais. Presently Jamie found the Earl David's eye upon him, with the summons of an almost imperceptible jerk of the head.

He made his way unobtrusively round the side of the refectory, amongst the busy servitors, to the back of the dais where he could approach the prince from behind, to bend discreetly.

"Get Dennistoun out of here, Jamie," David murmured. "He is drunk and ripe for mischief. He is picking on Montgomerie of Eaglesham — who is sufficiently hot-tempered as it is. Anything of trouble could spark off a blaze here now. Get him out."

"But . . . how can I, my lord?" the other demanded in an anxious whisper. "He is much senior to myself. Chief of his name. And of the Earl Robert's party."

"Tell him . . . see you, tell Montgomerie also. Tell him I command it. Both to leave, in the King's name, to settle their differences outside. The guard then to take Dennistoun in charge. Montgomerie can come back. Speak with Montgomerie first. Quickly now, man."

Doubtfully Jamie moved down to midway along the second table, where he whispered to the angry Sir John Montgomerie, Lord of Eaglesham, whom he knew well since Otterburn days. That man seemed disposed to question the command, but a glance at the dais-table, and the prince's nod, convinced him. He rose — and at his rising, Dennistoun, across the table, also got to his feet, presumably taking it as challenge. Jamie indeed had to do little persuading with the younger man, for with Montgomerie gesturing far from kindly towards the nearest door, he was nothing loth. Fists clenched threateningly, he turned to stumble in that direction, pushing servitors aside roughly.

Jamie pressed back into his seat Sir Thomas de Eglinton, who would have gone with his friend Montgomerie, and then hurried to the door himself, to alert the guard there, and his colleagues outside. In the end, the entire contrivance went naturally enough, for Dennistoun had barely got through the doorway before he began to lay violent hands on Montgomerie, so that the guards' duty to prevent fighting in the monarch's vicinity was plain and straightforward, scarcely requiring Jamie's relayed instructions from the prince to take Sir David Dennistoun of that Ilk into custody meantime for his own good. There was something of a scuffle before the protesting laird was led away. Jamie advised Montgomerie to wait a little while before returning to the banquet, for appearance's sake.

When he himself re-entered the chamber, it was to find the music and singing stopped and the King of Arms on his feet and declaring,

". . . all love and royal goodwill and for the better repute and report of this his realm. His Grace therefore decrees and ordains that the style, title and degree of duke in this kingdom of Scotland be herewith established, to rank above that of earl, as in other kingdoms of Christendom, that henceforth none such Englishman as the Duke of Lancaster or other shall seek to claim superiority or precedence over princes of this our more ancient realm, to their just offence. In pursuance of which royal ordinance, His Grace the King hereby is pleased to nominate his entirely well-beloved son and heir, David, Earl of Carrick and High Steward of Scotland, to be known and styled hereafter as Duke of Rothesay, with all such honours, privileges and dues as may be deemed suitable to support that rank . . ."

Lyon's fruity intonations were lost in the surge of comment and speculation, as the company demanded of each other the meaning of this wholly unexpected and unprecedented development, and what advantage there was in it for the prince.

"Further . . . further, I say," Lyon went on loudly, "His Grace appoints and ordains his well-beloved elder surviving brother, Robert, Earl of Fife and Menteith, likewise to be a duke of Scotland, with the style and title of Duke of Albany . . ."

Again the swell of remark and exclamation, louder now.

"Silence, I say — silence in the King's royal presence! In consequence of these elevations, the King's Highness is graciously pleased to appoint his second and entirely well-beloved son, the Prince James here present, to be Earl of Carrick and Lord of Renfrew, in the room of his brother, with all due appurtenances. And likewise the Lord Murdoch Stewart, His Grace's nephew, absent through indisposition, son of the said Duke of Albany, to be Earl of Fife — although not of Menteith. All as from this day henceforth, by royal command."

David Stewart rose to his feet, smiling, and bowed low to his father, then to his mother, and waved an all-embracing genial hand to the company — which mustered a somewhat ragged and less than enthusiastic cheer. It was then seen that the little boy, James, was also standing and bobbing his head. Their Uncle

Robert evidently felt himself compelled to do likewise, although he dispensed with the smiling.

"Now, what is the meaning of this?" Mary demanded of her husband new back at her side. "Did you know of it, Jamie?"

"No. Nothing. It is a strange device. But since I swear the King did not think of it himself, it must have been David's, or Robert's doing. Yet David is not one for styles and titles. He must have seen this as a means to sweeten his uncle, to cozen him perhaps? For even if it was the Governor's notion, it could not have been contrived without David's agreement. Robert *was* angry, at Haddonstank, when Lancaster sought to take precedence of him, as duke. But . . ."

Lyon was not finished yet. "These appointments, the first dukedoms in this realm of Scotland, will be confirmed and celebrated, as is fitting, before God's altar in the abbey-church of St. Michael at Scone tomorrow, at noon. Which means that the parliament to be held thereafter will be of necessity postponed until the hour of three in the afternoon . . ."

"Ha! There is David's hand, at least! Delay for four hours," Jamie muttered.

"Moreover, His Highness, in his gracious favour and love, desire to honour two of his most important and puissant subjects, to make acknowledgement of their long and excellent services to his realm and person. Therefore he calls Archibald, Earl of Douglas, father of his daughter Margaret's husband, likewise to the rank and style of duke of Scotland. And Sir David Lindsay, Lord of Crawford and High Justiciar of this realm, to be belted Earl of Crawford."

This new announcement achieved a deal more interest and excitement than had the previous ones — especially the last. For although dukedoms as such meant little or nothing to the Scots, being a wholly alien conception, earldoms were very much otherwise, being part of the nation's very fabric and polity, positions of vast hereditary power and influence. The earls of Scotland, fourteen in number hitherto, were a tight and exclusive group of the supreme nobility, based on the ancient Celtic mormaorships, and semi-royal in a way that their English counterparts were not. They were, in fact *Righ* in the Gaelic, sub-kings, giving point and meaning to the monarch's proud title of *Ard Righ*, or High King of Scots, king of these kings. No new earldoms had been created since that of Douglas in

1357, and that had been a special case and had aroused a furore as an unsuitable precedent, not one of the antique Celtic patrimonies. Now Crawford was being elevated to this jealous estate, the Lindsays raised to dizzy heights.

Sir David Lindsay rose and bowed, clearly surprised, bewildered, indeed.

"Nephew Davie again?" Mary wondered. "Buying Lindsay to his side?"

Jamie was fingering his chin thoughtfully. "I would scarce have thought it necessary. Lindsay is on his side, anyway. He hates the Governor. Look at him now — the Governor. His face . . .!"

Certainly the new Duke of Albany was showing grievous displeasure frozen on his handsome features.

"I wonder if it is not Douglas's elevation, rather than Lindsay's, which hurts him most?" Alexander suggested. "A dukedom, level with his own. Moreover, must it not mean that the King, and therefore David, is seeking to bind Douglas to his side, thus? Our David has not been idle!"

"Is the Earl Archie drunk, think you?" Mary asked. "He has not risen. See, he sits there grinning and shaking his head."

Others too were noting the Douglas's behaviour, notably Lyon, who was looking significantly at the Earl.

"My lord of Douglas," he called. "You heard the King's most gracious appointment? Do you make due acknowledgement?"

Into the sudden hush, Archie the Grim hooted a harsh laugh. "I heard!" he cried. "But . . . na, na! I'm beholden to His Grace. Och, aye — beholden. But by his royal leave, I'll just bide the way I am, man!"

Lyon gasped — and not only Lyon. "But, sir — a duke! A duke, do you hear?"

"Sir Duke! Sir Duke!" the Earl quacked. "Why no' Sir Drake, Sir Drake?" His hoarse laughter, on top of his efforts to sound like a duck all but choked him — and laughter in turn swept the assembly. In braid Scots the word duck is pronounced juke.

Lyon, looking appalled, banged his baton of office on the table. "My lord," he exclaimed, "do I understand that you *reject* His Grace's honour?"

The other leaned forward, smile gone. Indeed he had seldom looked more grim. "Not reject, sirrah — but decline. Aye, humbly decline. With my thanks. For if I became this new-fashioned duke, who then would be Earl of Douglas? Tell me that!"

There was silence then, as his fellow-guests stared, at each other, at the King and his son, at the Governor and back to the old Earl, weighing the implications, the significance and the consequences of this unprecedented disclaimer. Even Jamie, although he sensed the danger, knew a surge of sheer elation. Never, surely had the power and pride of the house of Douglas been more vividly if crudely demonstrated, the Stewarts more clearly put in their place.

"Oh, dear," Mary murmured. "Now what will happen?" But her eyes danced.

David Stewart required none to point out the danger — nor how to deal with it. He slapped down his open hand on the table-top, to make the goblets and flagons jump, and throwing back his beautiful head, laughed silvery mirth.

"God save us — and bless the Douglas!" he cried. "Juke! Juke! Here's a joy! My potent goodsire-to-be, in no doubts as to who is to be Earl of Douglas! Not the Master yet awhile — no, no, not the Master yet!"

"Clever!" Alexander commented, beneath his breath. All knew that the Earl did not get on well with his son and heir, the moody Master of Douglas — who, as the two Stewart dukedoms foreshowed, as heir would become Earl if his father was Duke.

But Mary, brows raised, was following a different line. "Goodsire-to-be?" she repeated. "You heard what he said? What does that mean?"

"A slip of the tongue? The Earl is his *sister's* goodsire."

"David does not make slips of the tongue," Jamie jerked, tensely.

The prince proceeded to prove him right — and effectively to banish from men's minds the possible injury to the royal authority and patronage implied in that rejection of the duke-dom. Still standing, he went on.

"This, my lords, ladies and friends, would seem a suitable moment to acquaint you with my, h'm, felicity. As all know, I had the honour to be betrothed to the Lady Elizabeth Dunbar, daughter of my good friend the Earl of Dunbar and March. This, because of purely personal reasons, and owing to delay because of youth, has been broken off, with no least reflection on the young lady concerned. And it is now my pleasure to

126

inform you that I am to be wed, and shortly, to the Earl Archibald's daughter, the Lady Mary Douglas. You will rejoice with me, I am sure!"

The breathless pause which greeted this announcement was rudely broken by the noise of a chair being forcefully pushed back, as George, Earl of Dunbar and March, rose abruptly to his feet, white-faced. He stared around him, threw a curt nod in the direction of the monarch, and stamped out of the apartment without a word to any. The Earl of Douglas grinned.

In the clamour of talk which followed, Jamie looked at his wife, sombre features working. He could find no words.

"Our Davie outdevils the Devil!" she said. "But he will overstep himself one day, I fear."

"If he has not already done so," Alexander added. "Dunbar is too powerful a man to offend so. Tomorrow, how will he vote, he and his?"

"David assesses Douglas as a deal more powerful — tomorrow and every day. And would bind him close," the young woman said. "But . . . it is not well done."

"It is damnable!" Jamie declared. "I it was who took his offer of betrothal to Dunbar. This is beyond all. And to say nothing of it . . ."

Mary touched his arm and nodded. Near the foot of the first table there was a commotion. Sir William Lindsay of Rossie, illegitimate half-brother to the new Earl of Crawford, and his daughter Eupham, were also in process of leaving the room, and angrily. It was forbidden, of course, to leave any function at which the King was present without specific royal permission; but the calls of nature had to be met, especially with so much wine being consumed, and it was usually politely assumed that such departures were thus motivated and only temporary.

"So — the whisper was true!" she said. "The Lindsays *were* ambitious. And now see their hopes dashed. But to prevent more lapsed votes, their chief is made earl!"

"Even David would not be so cynical as that!" Alexander protested. "Although it is no doubt no accident that the earldom was announced tonight, before the parliament . . ."

Their exchange was halted as the new Duke of Albany got to his feet to speak. He seldom so indulged, being no orator and preferring to wield power from the background.

"Your Grace," he said, although he did not look along at his brother, and spoke without the least hint of warmth, "believing this advancement in style and rank to be advisable and to the advantage of the realm in its rule and governance — which rule and governance are my responsibility — I accept it with due approval. I say, however, that my friend the Earl of Douglas was right and wise in declining such elevation. I advise that the dignity of duke should be restricted wholly and only to members of the royal house, lest unnatural envies and intrigues as to station be aroused. I am rejoiced also that my lord of Douglas's daughter is to wed my nephew, and so in God's providence may one day be Queen-Consort — which day, it is to be hoped, will however be long delayed. The lady is well known to me, and I am satisfied that she will be an excellent and steadying influence on the prince, of whose youthful spirits we are all aware . . ."

"To be sure, Uncle Albany — to be sure!" David called out cheerfully. "But you need not make the Lady Mary sound quite so . . . venerable! She is but six years older than myself, I believe!"

If there was considerable amusement at this significant sally, the Governor demonstrated none — nor did the Earl Archibald. "Such steadying being also in the realm's interests," Albany went on levelly. He paused. "But these matters, although of some import, are minor compared with the business of the morrow. I have agreed to the calling of this parliament because there is a dangerous spirit of lawlessness, and denial of due authority, in the land, fostered I fear by persons who should know better and who manifestly therefore lack due responsibility of judgement. This parliament must take fullest steps to crush such hurtful spirit and dangerment to the good government of the kingdom. To which end I will address myself tomorrow — and expect all others to do likewise, and enact accordingly. On pain of my direst displeasure, as Governor of this realm." He stared round the suddenly sobered gathering with a kind of chilly menace which left no doubts in the minds of practical men that stern reality as distinct from clever manipulation had belatedly come to this banquet. "Mind it tomorrow, I say, lest much that you all deem secure held in your hands is wrested out of them, to your sorrow." Again the telling pause. "That is all I have to say — save that the hour grows late and tomorrow will demand clear heads and firm wills. Roystering can await another occasion. With Your Grace's permission I will now retire — and advise those who have any part to play in the parliament to do likewise."

As the Governor turned to move from the table, King Robert raised his gentler voice, for the first time that evening. "Aye, Robbie," he said. "I'm for my bed, my own self — and you will be pleased to await my departure, see you." And as the company all but gasped audibly at this extraordinary assertion of the royal identity, the monarch added, "I agree that the morn's parliament is important, fell important — otherwise I'd not have called it. But I'd remind you, remind all, that dire displeasure is *mine* to display, on this realm's behalf. Not yours, Robbie, nor yet Davie's, here, but mine — so long as I wear the Crown. Your advice I shall ay cherish, and whiles act on. But the Lord's anointing is on my head, God help me, and mine only. Mind *that* tomorrow. I bid you all a good night."

As the King heaved himself up, with his wife's aid, and Lyon gestured urgently for the trumpeters to sound, Robert, Duke of Albany stood stiff, silent, expressionless, whilst everybody else rose hurriedly. Men, it might have been noted, bowed lower than they had done for many a day as their sovereign lord limped off, even David, Duke of Rothesay.

"Who won this night's jousting, then?" Mary Stewart wondered — and received no answer from either of her escorts.

*   *   *

The service of installation of the new dukes, conducted by Bishop Trail the Primate and the Abbot of Scone, was solemn and impressive, but there was an unreality about it, a sense of play-acting whilst more major matters loomed large. Few conceived these titles and dignities as of any vital importance, whereas the clash which must follow between the two beneficiaries could shake the kingdom. No great numbers attended.

Jamie Douglas reined over to the prince's side as the company formed up outside the abbey for the ride back to Perth. "Pate Boyd has just brought word, my lord, that the Countess of Mar and Sir Malcolm Drummond have arrived at St. Johnstoun, with their train. Also the Bishops of Aberdeen and Moray, and the Lords of Arbuthnott and Philorth and the Thane of Cawdor."

"Praise God for that — for some of them, at least! They are all going to be needed. You heard of George Dunbar, damn him?"

"That he has ridden off for his Borders, aye. With his lairds. And so you lose his votes. That . . . could have been avoided, my lord," Jamie declared with dour emphasis.

The Duke smiled. "Perhaps. But I think I made a fair exchange — in the parliament and Council, as well as in my purse, if not in my bed! As to that last, we shall have to see, Jamie. You Douglases are dark ones, in more than your faces! Ah — there goes my puissant sire. Heaven grant that he did not use up all his hard-won resolution last night! Keep me informed, Jamie, as to all arrivals, right up till the end, the vote. I will give orders that you may come and go, by the Prior's door." And he spurred off.

The parliament was held in the same Blackfriars refectory as the previous night's banquet, and for the same reason. There was little room for spectators here, but David had arranged for space to be reserved, and seats, for certain special onlookers, notably such royal ladies as wished to attend, and countesses in their own right who would have been entitled to be present as commissioners had they not been women. Despite the weather— although the snow had now disappeared — there was a fair attendance, seventy-odd votes being represented.

The King presided in person, as was the correct if not invariable procedure; but the Chancellor acted as chairman, a sort of programme-director. Old Bishop Peebles of Dunkeld had died, and the Governor had swiftly ensured that another nominee of his own, Bishop Gilbert Greenlaw of Aberdeen, succeeded him in this post of chief minister, an able and ambitious cleric who could be relied upon to be on the winning side. The line-up of forces appeared to be very evenly divided, although there were a number fairly doubtful of allegiance and the prince's faction still hoped for sundry belated arrivals.

After prayers for God's guidance on their deliberations, and loyal expressions towards the monarch, the Chancellor outlined the agenda. Because of the unavoidable delay in starting, the proceedings would have to be extended over two days, with His Grace's permission. The detailed business of sheriffships, revenues, customs and taxes, trade, foreign envoys and the like would be held over till the morrow, and this day's consideration devoted entirely to high policy in the rule and governance of the realm.

No comment, indeed profound silence, greeted this pronouncement; and the Bishop, coughing slightly, went on after a pause, with more than a hint of nervousness evident in even his assured and sonorous tones.

"Your Grace," he said, "there has been much talk, some of it malicious and ill-informed, of misgovernment, misfeasance and impolicy, in the realm. To put an end to such talk and accusation, my lord Duke, Your Grace's Governor, agreed to this parliament making specific enquiry into the matter that the truth of the situation may be established beyond a peradventure. He who has ruled the land these ten years has nothing to hide nor any regrets to make. Contrariwise he is entirely confident of his rectitude and the fairness and honesty of his rule. Although, to his grief, he has certain charges to make against, against persons here present."

"My lord King," the Lord of Eaglesham, bold man, called, "is this clerk from Aberdeen making a homily on behalf of the Governor? Or conducting the business of this parliament?"

The groundswell of both agreement and dissent rose, making ominously evident the deep divisions and passions represented in that room. Jamie Douglas, standing near the door behind the dais, silently cursed Montgomerie's impatience. This was no time for hot words and losing tempers, with so much so delicately balanced.

The monarch raised a hand in an uncertain gesture, but made no comment.

"Sire — my lords — bear with me," the Chancellor pleaded. "All must be done in due and decent order. It is proper that, since the rule is being challenged, he who has borne the rule must make his attitude and position clear. My lord Duke, whilst permitting this discussion and voicing of opinions, in no fashion accepts that he is open to censure or obliged to heed it. As duly appointed Governor, his is the rule, his the authority, and decision therefore his alone."

"His alone, then, the blame!" That was Sir Malcolm Drummond of Stobhall — and Jamie gave thanks at least that he was thus early coming out on the right side, and strongly, hopeful for the Countess of Mar's attitude.

"Perhaps, my lord. If blame there be. But who can apportion blame, save he who knows all the facts behind the decisions? And only the Governor is in that position."

The groan that went up at that was promptly drowned in cheers from the opposition. The two dukes sat silent throughout, watchful, waiting. It was some time before it was perceived that the monarch's hand was raised again.

Silence gained, King Robert spoke, in his mild and slightly hesitant voice. "My lord Chancellor — there is truth in what you say. But you mistake, mind, when you say that the Governor permits this discussion. He can neither permit nor refuse, see you. The King in parliament is sovereign. The *King* therefore permits this discussion. Aye, and there's another bit. You said that the decision in rule is the Governor's alone. That isna so. The rule and governance of this realm is vested in the Crown. The Crown may decide to rule by the hands of others. But the decision is the Crown's — aye, and the responsibility likewise."

Of all there, probably only his wife and son had ever heard John Stewart speak thus firmly, and with authority undeniable however unhappy the voice.

Glancing across to his Queen, amongst the watching ladies, the King drew a long, tremulous breath. "See you, my lords of parliament," he went on. "If my brother Robert, now of Albany, has no regrets to voice, *I* have. If this realm has been misgoverned — and I accept that it has — then I must bear the responsibility since I am its ruler, not Robert. He has but governed in my name. If there has been ill done, then this parliament must say so and condemn it. That is your duty, aye your duty. You must censure such failure in the rule. And censure who is responsible — myself."

There was confusion, almost consternation, amidst cries of No! No! But Jamie noted that David Stewart was smiling quietly. This, then, was no surprise to him at least.

There was a pause. The monarch seemed to have completed his extraordinary intervention. Nobody appeared to know just what to do now, least of all the Chancellor, who kept looking towards the Governor for guidance — and receiving none.

Jamie saw David turn and sign towards his other uncle, by marriage, the new Earl of Crawford. Somewhat doubtfully the Lindsay stood up.

"Sire," he said, "this taking on your own royal shoulders of the blame for the misgovernment, and what is amiss in the land, is noble, most noble. Though few would say the fault was Your Grace's. Yet it is true that if there is misrule in a kingdom, the King must, in the first instance, bear the responsibility. If matters are to be righted, then the righting must start at the head. This parliament is called so to do, that your realm may regain its health, and the rule of law, justice and peace be restored. Therefore parliament's blame must be declared and recorded, and censure passed on . . . on the guilty. Before there can be betterment, reform."

From his throne the monarch held out empty hands. "So I recognise, my lord. So indeed I do command. Censure there must be, unmistakable. And it is necessary that the censure of parliament must be passed upon myself, as head of the realm's government at fault. For all to perceive. I, I command that you proceed to do this, my lord of Crawford." If those strange words were sufficiently strong, certain, the voice enunciating them was not.

"Yes, Sire. H'mm." The Lindsay looked around him. "I move, then, that this parliament of our Scottish realm here assembled declares solemnly that there has been grievous mis-rule and wrongous handling of the nation's affairs these sundry years past. And hereby makes due censure of the King's Grace, and his government, as responsible therefor." And he sat down abruptly.

"And that motion I second," Sir Malcolm Drummond called strongly.

"As do I," Montgomerie added.

The stir and excitement was intense. Never before, so far as anyone there had heard tell of, had the King of Scots been publicly and formally censured in his own presence. Even though it was by royal command, and presumably within the power of parliament, it seemed little short of high treason, almost of sacrilege.

The Chancellor-Bishop, chairing his first parliament, looked about him in unhappy agitation. "Is there any contrary motion?" he quavered. "Is any otherwise minded?"

As men shuffled and eyed their neighbours, suddenly aware of the danger, that any denial of this censure itself would in fact be a disobedience of the King's expressed command, and therefore likewise to be rated as treasonable, a dry cough from the Duke of Albany drew all eyes. That self-contained man did not rise, but spoke flatly.

"Before any such motion can be accepted or rejected, it is necessary to establish that there has indeed been the mis-government alleged. Unless this is proven, there can be no cause for censure." He made that sound like a douche of cold

133

water, so that the heady temperature in the refectory dropped immediately by degrees.

Thankfully the Chancellor seized on this lifeline. "True, my lord Duke, assuredly. Before my lord of Crawford's motion be put, if its relevance is contested, such must be spoken to. My lord Earl, do you so speak?"

Crawford snorted. "What need of that, man? Everyone knows the realm has been mismanaged for years. Lawlessness is on every hand. The Treasury is empty. The sentences of sheriffs and justice-ayres are not carried out — I, as High Justiciar can vouch for that! Men mete out their own justice. Lands are raided. What more establishing do you need?"

"My lord Chancellor, these are general assertions," Albany observed. "Not specific charges. Not evidence, as the Justiciar knows well — or should. Indeed, even as such, they would seem rather to indict the High Justiciar himself, for failing to enforce due justice in the land."

"How can I, Stewart, when the very Governor himself flouts all law and justice!" Crawford cried hotly. "The power and force of the realm is in *your* hands, not mine."

"Specific charges — and named witnesses to speak thereto, my lord Chancellor," the Duke went on frigidly. "We have heard sufficient of wild accusation. Else I leave this travesty of a parliament for more profitable activity. And not only I!"

In the ominous growling from both sides which greeted that threat, David, Duke of Rothesay rose from his seat, smiling as ever.

"Your Grace, my lord Chancellor, my lords all," he said easily, "I agree entirely with the Duke of Albany. Enough of generalities. Likewise of hot words. This is the King in parliament assembled, the weal of the realm our only concern. But our solemn duty also. None of us enjoy the laying of blame and the passing of censures — in especial upon our own close kin and friends, to say nothing of our liege lord. It is distasteful to all men of goodwill. Let us, then, dispense with blame and accusation, and confine ourselves to a calm and reasoned consideration of facts and problems, that we may ensure due amendment, if this is necessary, in all amity."

Warily men weighed that, his own supporters equally with Albany's and the uncommitted, doubtful of such sudden sweet reasonableness.

"Let us be done with this issue as swiftly as possible," he

went on. "And I crave your sympathy in having thus to make dispraise and denunciation of my own royal father's government. To prove its failure, as at present administered, it is only necessary to present to you certain proven cases of ill-management to the realm's hurt. Not by any means all. As herewith. The Treasury is empty and owing moneys to many. In especial the sum of 10,000 merks, being four years payment due to Her Grace the Queen, secured nevertheless on the customs of certain ports and burghs, including those of this same St. Johnstoun of Perth, of Dysart, Montrose and Aberdeen. Yet these customs have been uplifted each year and duly paid to the Lord High Chamberlain of the realm. This in time of peace when no major charges have been required of the Treasury. Many other such defaults I could list — but one is sufficient for our purposes. My lord Chamberlain may, to be sure, assure us that such customs, dues and taxes have not reached his coffers. But if so, since they have been uplifted from the shippers and traders, who hold papers to prove it, then failure in government is evident."

There was silence in the chamber. Silence likewise from the Chamberlain — who, of course, was none other than the Governor himself and who certainly did not fail to perceive the trap set for him. If he denied that he had received the moneys, then his system of tax-collecting was grievously at fault; if he had received them, but had not paid them out in accordance with parliament's express provision for the Queen's expenses, then he was still more at fault. And where were the moneys gone, with the Treasury empty?

When none other spoke for him, Albany shrugged. "There are many calls on the Treasury," he said, without rising. "Were my nephew more conversant with the difficulties of government, he would know of these. Such as the payment of life pensions, heritable pensions and pensions of retinue — these last to ensure supplies of armed men for the defence of the kingdom in case of need — payments made to many of those lords here assembled! There are payments of clerks, officers of state, keepers of castles, notaries and the like. There is the upkeep of embassages and the sending of envoys to other Courts. The repairs of fortresses, ports, bridges. Many more. I do not come to parliament armed with clerks' books and papers; but such can be seen hereafter by those so minded."

"To be sure, my lord — to be sure. None would expect the King's Chamberlain to act as clerk. And with so great and many moneys amissing, it would be beyond all reason to bring to mind even a few of these piddling matters. But, as it happens, I am in a position to aid you in this, in some small way, to recollect some of these grievous items at the realm's charges. Such as 12,000 ounces of silver paid yearly, for the Governor's support; £200 yearly for the Chamberlain's support — with £900 more required as sundry expenses; £200 yearly from the royal customs of Linlithgow, for the Governor's support; £200 from the customs of Cupar, likewise for the Governor's support; £200 yearly for the support of the Keeper of Stirling Castle, my lord Duke of Albany; £200 yearly to the Lord Protector of the Abthania of Dull — which some here may never have heard tell of, but which is an office connected with the ancient Celtic Church of this realm which has been non-existent now for two centuries. That former Church is fortunate in having as the Protector of its Abthania none other than my lord of Albany — than whom none could be more sure a shield, you will agree! I could considerably further aid the Governor's memory — but here is sufficient, I think?"

As the catalogue was spelled out, faces had grown grimmer, and a muttering noise, almost a snarl, accompanied the final stages of the recital, all but drowning the prince's mellifluent tones. Some of it undoubtedly emanated from the Governor's own supporters, resenting this damning attack. But the shock sustained by many of the uncommitted was probably the more telling, whilst David's own adherents sought to cover their glee by cries of shame and the like.

But glee was suddenly quenched, on the prince's side at least, as the door opened to admit a new group of commissioners to the parliament, still travel-stained from long and muddy riding — the Bishops of Moray and Ross and the Abbots of Deer, Kinloss and Fearn. The churchmen's votes could be vital to the outcome today, and all these five could be guaranteed to support the Governor. Jamie all but groaned.

The interlude, with the newcomers from the North bowing to the King and then taking their seats, gave Albany opportunity to collect his thoughts, if that was necessary; and when he spoke he did so carefully, precisely.

"Again the Duke of Rothesay fails to recognise the realities of government, Sire," he said. "These sums accrue to me, or more properly to my offices, in respect of the various and many offices I administer in Your Grace's service, all of which are

136

costly to operate and which could demand much greater payment were they in the hands of others than myself. Even that of the Abthania, which requires the administration of wide lands of the old Church. I would remind all present that as well as Governor I fulfil the duties of High Chamberlain, Captain General of the forces of the Crown, Keeper of the Great Seal, Keeper of Stirling Castle, Custodian of the Royal Mint, Justiciar of Fife and Strathearn and Chief Warden of the Marches. Others likewise. All these demand much expenditure of moneys. Mind it."

"Dear God, Sire — I had no notion that your noble brother and my good uncle was so imposed upon, so overburdened by the duties of your government!" David cried, as though astonished. "All this, on the shoulders of one ageing man! Small wonder if that government has broken down. Surely Your Grace and this parliament must needs relieve the excellent Duke of much of this crushing weight of responsibility! Lest he collapse entirely beneath the load!"

"Your Grace's government has *not* broken down, Sire. And I require none of this young man's false sympathies!" Albany snapped.

"My lord Duke is too conscientious," his nephew insisted, kindly. "Nobly prepared to bear more than his share, not only in matters fiscal. In the still more vital affairs of the realm's security from assault and invasion he is sorely overwhelmed. He has just reminded us that he is Chief Warden of the Marches and commander of Your Grace's forces. Yet, less than a year past, he did naught to counter the threatened invasion of the English under the Duke of Lancaster and Sir Harry Percy — if he knew aught of it — and the matter had to be dealt with by, h'm, other hands. At considerable cost and danger to certain of your lords. Moreover the Governor, all unwittingly I make no doubt, had renewed the truce between the two realms, in a fashion most disadvantageous to Scotland, maintaining the *status quo* whereby the castles of Berwick and Roxburgh remained in English hands, thus permitting Englishmen to ride abroad on Scottish soil and even to demand compensation for damage done by Scots hands to Scots works, to wit the bridge of Roxburgh, from Scots subjects. In especial, to the Earl of Douglas his cost. Is that not so, my lord Earl?"

The sudden indrawings of breath from all around indicated that the moment of truth had come, at last. All eyes turned on

137

Archie the Grim's long crouching figure. So much depended on which way the great house of Douglas jumped now. Albany's old friend, almost his only true friend in the years past, could muster or sway up to a score of votes in that parliament.

"Aye," the Earl grunted, grinning, without rising from his seat.

Men waited, and then gazed at each other as they realised that that was all that the Earl of Douglas seemed to be going to say. Stir, disquiet, question surged over the assembly.

Even David Stewart looked less assured than he had been — although his uncle Albany was frowning uncertainly also.

Jamie Douglas cursed his chief below his breath. The old man had always been an awkward character, unpredictable save in that he could be relied upon to be difficult. But with so much at stake for all, this was too much.

The prince recovered himself. "My good-father-to-be agrees," he observed, and mustered a laugh. "As Warden of the West March, who should himself have been Chief Warden — he could hardly do otherwise. And with a claim for £2,000 sterling against him by the Percy! Moreover, when the realm is in danger from over the Border, Douglas does not shrink his duty."

"The realm was in no danger of invasion," the Governor intervened shortly. "John of Gaunt was concerned and mustering troops because my nephew's late friend, Dunbar, was landing large numbers of men on his Isle of Man, opposite Lancaster. And the Percy is ever raiding across the March, no more than a brigand. As for the truce, I could not alter the *status quo* without mounting an armed expedition against Roxburgh and Berwick — war, in fact. I either signed, or provoked a new war. Which would Your Grace have preferred?"

As the monarch, thus shrewdly appealed to, shook his head and tugged at his grey beard, a clatter from the ladies' enclosure distracted attention momentarily. Looking thereto, Jamie saw that it was the Countess of Mar who had dropped her crucifix and chain. He was surprised to perceive also that, stooping to pick it up, her glance was directly aimed at himself, and the slight jerk of her head was as unmistakable a beckon as it was imperative.

The prince smoothly used the slight interruption to make up for his father's lack of answer by declaring that the invasion had been planned by the English *before* Dunbar's force moved to Man, to coincide with a descent on the Douglas province of

138

Galloway by Donald of the Isles and his barbarous hordes.

Jamie slipped round behind the benches to the ladies' seats, where he managed to insinuate himself to the Countess's side. He had not seen her since that day at Kildrummy in October.

"See you," she said to him quietly but urgently, "*I* cannot speak in this man's assembly. But I have something that could be said. Against Robert Stewart. Tell Alex Stewart to come to me, quickly. He can speak to it. Then tell your prince to call him."

"Your husband, Sir Malcolm . . .?"

"He hates Douglas — and this could benefit Douglas. Get Alex — he has his back to me, here, or I could sign to him."

Jamie moved down and whispered to Alexander, sitting amongst the lords as Lord of Badenoch. He recognised that he must be very conspicuous doing so; but David was still speaking and he was known as the prince's man. Moreover, he was by no means the only messenger who had moved between principals during that session.

David finished speaking about Donald of the Isles, and the further invasion of Lochaber and the North-West by his brother Alastair Carrach, which the Governor had done nothing to halt. Donald himself was not present, although entitled to be. Nobody took up his cause, and Albany declared that if the King's government involved itself in Highland feuding it would have time and strength for little else. Jamie moved close to the prince.

"My lord," he murmured, "the Countess of Mar says to tell you to call on Alex Stewart to speak."

"She does? Why?"

"For your benefit, she says."

"Why should she be concerned? It could be a trap. She may be my mother's brother's wife — but I do not know that she loves me."

"I think she would not trap Alex, my lord."

"Ha — you say so? Is it so? Very well . . ."

The Governor was ever brief, and Bishop Trail, the Primate, had risen to speak, pointing out that Alastair's incursion was no mere clan feuding but a major assault on part of the kingdom, in which an establishment of Holy Church, the Valiscaulian Priory of Ardchattan, was assailed, to its loss and great injury. If Holy Church could not rely upon the King's government to give it protection, then it must reconsider its attitudes and support.

Although many of the assembled company appeared less than concerned with the Church's problems, David rose to declare his sympathy, and pointed out that the Islesmen's threat had been lifted thanks to the valiant efforts of Sir Alexander Stewart of Badenoch, ably assisted by Sir James Douglas of Aberdour, whose efforts on behalf of the realm, including the relief of the royal castle of Urquhart, deserved the thanks of all present. To scattered acclaim, he suggested to the Chancellor that Sir Alexander should speak.

Alex had just got back to his seat. Men considered his slenderly graceful person keenly. The fame and dread of the Wolf of Badenoch was still sufficiently fresh in all minds to endow his son with more than usual interest, and his delicate good looks were the more intriguing.

"Your Grace and my lords," he said, with his soft Highland intonations, "I fear that the defeat of Alastair Carrach was a very minor matter — save in the splendid charge of Sir James Douglas with a troop of the royal guard and some Lochaber clansmen, which saved the day. Scant credit accrues to myself." He paused. "But with Your Grace's permission, instead of dwelling on this, I would now ask a question of whosoever is best informed to answer it — a question I believe relevant to this discussion on government. I would ask whether or no, after the death of the late second Earl of Douglas at Otterburn, the Countess of Mar, that Earl's sister, was offered a large part of the Douglas lands, including the Forests of Ettrick and Jedburgh, by the then Earl Robert of Fife and Menteith, in return for her acquiescence in the said Earl Robert's taking to himself of the castle of Tantallon and the Chief Wardenship of the Marches, with their revenues — both hitherto included within the earldom of Douglas? Which great lands were assumed by the Countess — but later taken from her, the said Earl Robert and the Crown assenting. I ask if this is the fact, since it bears heavily on the administration of justice and officers of government in this realm?"

The choking cry from Archibald, Earl of Douglas, all but drowned the last of that lilting query.

"I do not believe it!" he bellowed, rising to his feet. "This, this young whelp of an excommunicate freebooting father —

140

how dares he! None would so use *me*, Douglas!" But it was at his old friend the Governor that he glared.

"My lord Chancellor — I suggest that the Earl of Douglas directs his spleen elsewhere than at my humble self," Alex said. "The Countess of Mar is here present. Although she may not intervene in this parliament's debate, at least, with His Grace's permission, she can answer or no what I have said is true?"

"Well, woman — is it true?" Archie thundered, not waiting for any royal permission.

"It is true." Isobel of Mar's voice might be husky but her words were clear enough. "Robert Stewart offered me such compact. And then broke it when it suited him. Can he deny it?"

"I confirm or deny nothing," Albany said levelly. "Earl James of Douglas died ten years ago. Before I was Governor. In the previous reign. What arrangements may have been made in the matter of his estates and offices are long done with and no concern of this parliament."

"They concern *me*!" Douglas grated. "Have I nursed a viper to my bosom all these years? Why have I never heard tell of this?"

"Because it did not concern you," Albany said. "You were not Earl of Douglas then, I'd remind you. Likewise I'd remind you *how* you became Earl of Douglas!"

"Christ God . . .!"

"Your Grace, Your Grace," David intervened, loudly for him, and necessarily. "I agree with my lord Duke of Albany. This matter, although interesting no doubt, is of no immediate concern to our discussion. I suggest indeed that we have discussed sufficiently. If you, my lord Chancellor, and all present, are satisfied that there has been enough evidence of the King's government's mismanagement — as I am satisfied — then let it be put to the vote of parliament without further debate. I am sure that the Governor would not delay further."

There was a long moment of silence, with the Earl Archibald still on his feet, scowling blackly, and Albany pointedly looking elsewhere. The latter shrugged.

"Then I call upon the Earl of Crawford, if still so minded, to put his motion," the Chancellor said, though doubtfully.

"Gladly," Lindsay exclaimed. "There has been overmuch of talk, I say. I move, as before, that this parliament declares that there has been grievous misrule, and hereby makes due censure on the King's Grace and his government as responsible."

"And which seconder?"

Before Sir Malcolm Drummond of Montgomerie could rise, Archie the Grim, already on his feet, spoke. "I second that, by the Mass! Aye — Douglas seconds!" That was almost a shout.

The entire assembly seethed. The Governor had lost Douglas. For a full minute there was pandemonium in that refectory.

At last the Chancellor, banging with his gavel, made himself heard. "Quiet! Quiet, I say, my lords — in the King's royal presence! Is there any contrary motion?"

"Aye! Aye!" came from various parts of the chamber.

"My lord Earl of Ross. Your motion?"

"The direct negative, sir," Albany's son-in-law declared, in duty-bound. "That this parliament has fullest confidence in the King's Grace and his government, in especial in the Governor, the Duke of Albany."

"I second," Sir William Lindsay of Rossie cried — and none failed to note that here was a house divided also, with Crawford's brother voting against his motion. That was the price paid for Eupham Lindsay, no doubt.

"And I," the Bishop of Moray added, with a quick glance at the Primate. "Holy Church must ever support the King's Grace."

When the uproar died down, the Chancellor said that he would take the vote on the negative first. All who supported the Earl of Ross's motion to show hands.

Decision at last. It is safe to say that, as well as the Chancellor's tellers, practically everyone in that apartment was counting hands — and turning to scan their neighbours keenly, speculatively. Indeed not all hands went up at once; clearly what others did was important to many. When not only the Earl of Douglas but also the Lord of Dalkeith, kept their hands by their sides — the Earl of Angus and the Douglasses of Drumlanrig and Cavers were, of course, sure for the prince — not a single Douglas vote could be counted for the negative, something none would have prophesied only a short time before. On the other hand, despite the new earldom conferred on their chief, fully one-third of the Lindsays raised their hands. The Stewarts themselves were divided right down the centre, and it would be hard to compute which side had the advantage. The church-men's vote, so important, looked to Jamie to be on the whole favourable, with well under half of the bishops and mitred abbots raising beringed hands. Of the few royal burghs represented, only those in Fife, Menteith and Strathearn showed for the negative. Nevertheless, there was a solid mass of Central Scotland lords and knights-of-the-shire, many in receipt of the Governor's pensions, or vassals of the earldoms of Fife, Menteith, Strathearn, Lennox, Atholl and Ross, about whose allegiance there was no doubt.

"I make it thirty-five — no, thirty-six — against us!" Jamie exclaimed excitedly, at the prince's back. "Dear God — it is enough, is it not? There are more than eighty present . . ."

"Wait you," David said steadily. "Some cautious folk may abstain. Seek safety in that."

"Your Grace, my tellers count thirty-six votes for the direct negative of my lord of Crawford's motion," the Chancellor announced. "I now call upon all in favour of the said motion to show."

Again not all who had not yet voted put up their hands, at first. Led by the Earl Archie, Douglas did, a fine phalanx that swelled Jamie's heart. Five Mar vassals likewise. The Primate and fully half the churchmen. All the remaining burghs — for the prince was popular with the people and the Governor was anything but. The South-West was fairly solidly in favour. But it was soon apparent that there were indeed to be abstentions. No fewer than six Lothian and Merse representatives sat still heads down — these were the Earl of Dunbar and March's vassals. Some few churchmen did likewise. Surprisingly, the Lord of Calder, new husband of the King's sister Jean, had not voted although his sympathies had been taken for granted. Similarly Thomas Earl of Moray and Sir Patrick Gray.

Jamie all but shook his fist at these last, as he counted. "Thirty-four, thirty-five, thirty-six, thirty-seven, thirty-eight. God is good — thirty-eight, my lord! You have won! A curse on those faint-hearts — but you have won!"

"A-a-aye!" David let out a long sigh. "Won — but only just. By only two votes — and thanks to Isobel of Mar! One vote, truly, for the Chancellor himself has not voted, and he is for my uncle. Or *was*! One vote — by what a margin to rule a realm!"

"My lord King," the Chancellor reported, "my tellers agree on thirty-eight votes in favour of my lord of Crawford's motion, as against thirty-six negative. I do therefore declare the motion to be carried. That this parliament declares misrule and mis-

143

government, and censures Your Grace and your government."

Amidst the mixture of cheers and cries of anger and dissent, a new voice, clear and strong pierced the din. "My lord Chancellor — since the difference is so small, I take leave to challenge the vote of one man — Sir Alexander Stewart, who has voted for the motion." Sir John de Ramorgnie, the expert on laws, from Fife, sitting near Albany and one of his vassals, spoke authoritatively. "Sir Alexander is not entitled to vote. He only *claims* to be Lord of Badenoch. He is illegitimate. His father was Earl of Buchan and Lord of Badenoch; but being base-born he succeeds in law to neither the one nor the other. None accept him as Earl of Buchan. Why should we do so as Lord of Badenoch?"

"A plague!" Jamie muttered. "Mary said that Ramorgnie was not to be trusted."

David answered the protester, almost conversationally. "Sir John — I think you err in this. Sir Alexander was born out of wedlock, yes. But so were many here. Some even claim that my royal sire, and the Duke of Albany were so born!" He smiled. "Sir Alexander voted as representing the great lordship of Badenoch, one of the largest in the realm. None other seeks, or dares to seek, to represent that ancient lordship. Is it to be forever without suffrage? My uncle, the Earl of Buchan, left no legitimate issue, and Sir Alexander is his eldest son. Moreover he has but recently served the realm well indeed, against the Islesmen. Without the help of any from Fife! I say that he has the right to vote."

"Nevertheless, my lord Duke, he is not *de jure* Lord Badenoch."

"Then His Grace the King, sirrah, can make him so by a lift of the royal hand! He is his nephew, after all." David looked at his father.

The monarch raised his head, sighed, and waved a vague hand. "You are answered, sir. Sir Alexander of Badenoch's vote stands."

There was another intervention. Sir James Sandilands, Lord of Calder, rose. "My lord Chancellor," he called, "I wish your clerk of parliament to note in his writings that I, for one, abstained from voting. Not because I was not in favour of the motion in general, but in that it included in its wording a censure of the King's Grace, in person. This I can by no means countenance. I will never have it said that Calder made public censure of his liege lord!"

144

Others of the abstainers hastened to add their voices to that.

The King raised his hand again, but only continued banging of the Chancellor's gavel gained him silence. "Nevertheless, my lord of Calder, and all my good lords and subjects," the monarch said in a strained and unsteady voice, "I accept that censure as just. Upon myself, as having failed to ensure good government. And on those who have governed in my name. The will of parliament has been expressed. It now behoves me to offer new arrangements of government for parliament's approval." He looked about him distinctly nervously. "It is my wish that the office of Governor of the realm be abolished — in that there can indeed be only one governor, he who wears the Crown. This office has proved to be an unfair burden on my good brother, who has borne it these many years. In its place, since I myself am, by God's will, infirm and of poor health, there will be a Lieutenant of the Crown, who shall rule in my name but subject to my authority at all times. To this high and onerous position I appoint — if I have the approval of parliament — my well-beloved elder son David, Duke of Rothesay, heir to my throne and High Steward of Scotland. I am confident that . . ."

Despite the impropriety of interrupting the King's speech, a tumultuous cheering drowned the royal words, and continued. Robert Stewart sat still, utterly expressionless throughout, as he had done indeed throughout the voting also.

When quiet was restored, the King went on. "I am confident in my son's ability, goodwill and love of justice. But because, as my lord of Albany has said, he is inexperienced in the art of government, I would appoint a special council of his own, a Council of the Lieutenancy, to aid and advise him. On which council, distinct from my own Privy Council, I would wish to see his uncle the Duke prominent. Also my lord of Crawford, High Justiciar; my lord Bishop of St. Andrews, Primate; my lord of Douglas, Chief Warden of my Marches; and others, experienced in administering the realm's affairs. All for the better rule of my kingdom." The monarch sat back, as though exhausted. "Is this, then, approved by this parliament?"

There was a muttering and nodding of approximate agreement. But the Chancellor, wishing to see things done in order, was declaring that a motion should be moved and passed, when he was interrupted by the thin, severe voice of Robert of Albany.

"I so approve," he jerked. "I wish my nephew well. And now,

if Your Grace will permit, I shall retire. There has been a sufficiency of talk." And with a brief bow to the throne he turned and walked with stiff dignity to the dais-door, and out.

In the commotion, with several of his closer supporters apparently desirous of following him, David Stewart took charge.

"Sire," he said, "my lord Duke is right. It is sufficient for this day, is it not? Your Grace is wearied, I can see. This session has been adequately decisive. We assemble again tomorrow. I propose that Your Grace adjourns the sitting until then."

Thankfully his father nodded, and heaved himself out of his throne. Hurriedly Lyon came forward, and the trumpeters reached for their instruments. All rose.

As the fanfare blared out, men bowed and women curtsied, it was not so much on the limping monarch that eyes were turned but on the new ruler of Scotland. Very much aware of it, David Stewart smiled brilliantly and waved a genial hand. But Jamie Douglas, standing behind, noted that the other hand was clenched tight behind his back, knuckles showing white.

VII

S IR JAMES DOUGLAS rode fast across the fair land of East
Lothian, between Lammermuir and the sea. He was in a
hurry, and yet loth to arrive at his destination. The wide,
undulating landscape of the coastal plain had never looked
finer, with the corn turning to gold on all the rigs in the mellow
August sunlight, the cattle sleek in the vales of Peffer and Tyne,
and the lambs on the green foothills strong and well-grown. It
was country to be savoured and enjoyed, not pounded through
with drumming hooves; the most rich and fertile in the land — a
land which had had four months of fair and reasonably honest
government, four months of the longed-for relief from oppres-
sion and lawlessness, at least in theory. Yet Jamie rode as
urgently as he had ever ridden during the long, unhappy regime
of the Lieutenant's uncle.

It was late in the warm afternoon, and he had been in the
saddle for thirty-five miles, from Linlithgow, where the Duke
of Rothesay was presently amusing himself with the Lady
Matilda Douglas — not the Lady *Mary* Douglas, the Earl
Archie's daughter, whom he had married at Bothwell Castle in
May, but the younger and more ardent wife of Sir James
Douglas of Strabrock, keeper of the royal palace of Linlithgow,
the Lady Mary being bestowed well out of the way at Turnberry
in Ayrshire. That Jamie was on the way to remonstrate with the
neglected bride's father was purely coincidental, and no more
satisfactory in that young man's estimation.

The traveller, with his two troopers of the royal guard, had
no time to call in at his own little castle of Stoneypath Tower,
tucked within a Lammermuir glen; nor yet at the mighty castle
of Tantallon on the sea cliffs, now safely back in Douglas hands,

147

having been taken from Albany and restored to the Earl of Angus and his mother. He drove on, east by south, along the south shore of the wide sandy estuary of Tyne, by the fishers' boat-strand of Belhaven, until the red-stone towers and battlements of the strange sea-girt fortress of Dunbar rose ahead of him. It was over two years since he had acted messenger here before.

The situation could hardly have been more different from that stormy March day when he had found George of Dunbar and March roosting almost alone in his draughty, wave-splashed hold. Now, in the genial evening sun and dark-blue calm of the whispering sea, the place was transformed. And not only thus, but in that it was seething with men, an armed camp in fact. Far too many men were there to be able to get into the castle itself, and the little town and all the slopes around were full of Douglas men-at-arms and mosstroopers. Jamie had come fearing to find the place under attack.

Asking for the Earl of Douglas, he was directed to the castle itself — and his heart sank. Clattering across the lowered drawbridge above the tide, it fell still further as he perceived signs of warfare, splintering, broken arrow-shafts, the blackening, fly-buzzing stains of spilled blood. Frowning, he rode in under the gatehouse arch, his dark features sufficiently Douglas-like to demand no challenge, whatever his escort's royal liveries might do.

But when, dismounted, he requested to be taken to the Earl Archibald, he was eyed strangely and told that he should see the Master. He was taken along the same vaulted corridors to the very room where previously he had been interviewed by the Earl George, to find it full of booted and spurred Douglas lairds sitting at meat, with the Master and his fat brother Sir James the Gross, at the head of the table, and no sign of their father.

Jamie and the Master were scarcely friendly; indeed it might have been difficult to find anyone who claimed real friendship with Archibald, Master of Douglas and Galloway, a self-contained, silent, brooding young man of now twenty-seven years, bullet-headed, heavy-featured, unsmiling. But they got on well enough, indeed had some dark Douglas affinity. James the Gross, however, he cordially disliked.

"What brings Davie Stewart's errand-runner here?" the latter exclaimed, in his squeaky, curiously high-pitched voice.

"No good, I swear! You'll find no loose women for him here, if that's your mission!" And he chuckled an unpleasant laugh.

"Quiet!" his brother commanded. "So, Jamie — welcome to Dunbar. Too late for the tulzie, I fear. How may I serve you?"

"It was your father I came seeking. My sorrow that it is too late. Is he not here?"

"He is above. Taken to bed. Sick."

"Sakes — the Earl Archie sick? Who would have thought that! I am sorry . . ."

"He is an old man — seventy-four years now. This ploy has been overmuch for him. At the height of the storming, himself in the van, he took a seizure, fell choking. We got a monk of the Red Friars here to bleed him. Yesterday. Maitland, George Dunbar's nephew, surrendered the place this morning."

"And is he . . . recovering?"

"We do not know. He has his wits again, in some measure — but does not speak. The monk says that he must not be moved or troubled."

"An ill chance. So hale and stout a man."

"What was your business with him?" the younger son demanded.

Jamie hesitated, then shrugged. "I was sent to tell him not to assault this castle. Not to do damage to any of the Earl of Dunbar and March's properties. At the Duke's . . . request."

James the Gross hooted.

His brother toyed with his meat. "Do you think that he would have heeded you?"

"I believe he would. Since it is the Lieutenant of the Crown's wish. And for good reason."

"We had good reasons for coming here. The best."

"Perhaps. But the situation has changed . . ."

"Dunbar is still turned traitor. Gone to England. Is working with Hotspur Percy, to raise a force to come back and spread devastation. Against his own countrymen. Why should David Stewart seek to protect him? From Douglas? He threw Dunbar over and chose Douglas, but a few months ago."

"It is scarce that. But he, the Duke, has now the safety of the kingdom to consider. And there is grave danger. King Richard of England is deposed, some say dead. The Duke has just had word that Bolingbroke, John of Gaunt's son, has now had himself proclaimed King, as Henry the Fourth . . ."

"Richard? The Plantagenet dead? Is he not in Ireland?"

"He was. When John of Gaunt, Duke of Lancaster, died, Richard confiscated his estates and declared his son, Henry Bolingbroke, forfeit and outlaw. His own cousin. Henry was in France. He came home, and set up the banner of revolt. Richard had gone to Ireland, yes, to put down some rising there. He returned — and Bolingbroke was waiting for him. Defeated him at Flint, and took him captive. Now he is deposed, or abdicate, or may be dead. And his Lancastrian cousin is king."

"Stirring tidings," James the Gross commented. "But what is it to do with us? Or Dunbar?"

"Bolingbroke — or Henry — is a very different man from Richard. He is strong where Richard was weak. A fighter not a talker. And popular with the people where Richard was not. He represents real danger to Scotland. One of his first pronouncements as king was to declare himself Lord Paramount of Scotland!"

"That old insolence and folly of Edward Longshanks!" the Master said.

"Folly and insolence, yes. But threat also. Why should he make that old claim about paramountcy now? So soon? The Duke believes that he contemplates an invasion of Scotland. What better way for a warrior-king to commence his doubtfully-lawful reign than by a military campaign? To win his people's support and rally his nobles behind him."

"If that is so, then the sooner he perceives that the Scots are warned, ready, and indeed striking first, the better." The Master said that flatly but heavily. "Teach him to think again. As we are teaching Dunbar that treason is costly!"

"The prince thinks otherwise. He was much concerned when he heard that Douglas was moving to assail Dunbar Castle. He sent me at once, when he was told. We did not believe that you could have gained entry thus soon — so strong a place."

"The hold strong, yes — but not the man who held it. Sir Robert Maitland. Dunbar left it in his keeping, his nephew, and took the rest of his family with him into England. Maitland is a weakling. And his manors in Lauderdale and Lothian are surrounded by Douglas lands. So he yielded — for a consideration! After but one sally."

"But — what authority did you have to attack Dunbar Castle? What business of Douglas?"

"You, a Douglas, ask that?" the fat young man demanded. "Dunbar is a forsworn traitor, a friend of the Percy. Con-

150

trolling all the Merse and much of Lothian, from here. A menace to the realm — but to Douglas first."

"You did not seek the Lieutenant of the realm's consent before you attacked."

"Seek Davie Stewart's consent! In the Borders! Have you lost your wits, man?"

His brother intervened. "Have done, James. You ask our authority? Have you forgot that Dunbar is Warden of the East March? Gone over to the English. And as Chief Warden, is it not Douglas's duty to ensure that his desertion is made good, and punished? You — nor even my peculiar good-brother — will not deny that?"

Jamie shook his head. He, and no doubt the prince also, had overlooked the fact that, since the parliament at Perth, the Chief Wardenship had reverted to the Earl Archie, and that therefore he was supreme authority on the Border — under the Crown.

"The Crown conceives that the situation requires more delicate handling than this," he said carefully.

"Are *you* the voice of the Crown now — to Douglas? I shall require more than Jamie of Aberdour's words to convince me of that!"

Jamie was in a difficult position and knew it. This stolid young man did not get on well with his ebullient brother-in-law — brother-in-law twice over, since he was married to David's sister, as well as David being now wed to his. And with the old man ill, he now wielded the full power of Douglas, a difficult, moody, serious-minded but obstinate individual — and Jamie's own acting chief.

"I but bring you the prince's message," he said. He had been going to say command, but thought better of it. "He wished you to leave Dunbar Castle alone, and allow *him* to deal with the Earl of Dunbar's treachery."

"Then he is too late. And he should have come himself, if he seeks to over-rule Douglas and the Chief Warden, not sent you. But no doubt he is too busy with his pleasures and his whores, shaming my sister within months of her wedding." He paused, glowering. "But sit down, man. Eat. You may bring unwelcome tidings but you are still a Douglas . . ."

Jamie was indeed hungry and weary, after nearly forty-five miles of hard riding. He sat and ate gladly enough. He could not really dislike Archibald Douglas as he did his brother.

"How does the Earl do?" he asked, as he ate. "You say he does not speak. How long . . . ?"

"Who knows at his years? I have never known him sick before. He ever laughed at sickness. Always the man of iron!" If there was a hint of bitterness there, it was scarcely to be wondered at, in a young man who had himself suffered much sickness. The Master had had a hard time with his fierce father who, besides being scarcely an affectionate parent, had never made any secret of the fact that his favourite was his first-born but illegitimate son, the late and famous Sir Will of Nithsdale.

"May I speak with him? Give him the Duke's message?"

"No. He is not to be troubled with affairs, with anything. And if he could understand you, he could not answer you. You must needs deal with *me*, Jamie, now. As must your Duke."

"M'mm. What then shall I tell him? The Duke?"

"Tell him what you will — since it is too late to alter anything. But . . . aye, tell him that I am leaving Dunbar Castle, as he requests! To go about my further business as Chief Warden of the Marches. Tell him that."

"Your father's business, surely?" Jamie amended. "Since he is the Warden . . ."

"Not so. *My* business. I am the Warden. He passed it on to me. I have been Chief Warden for two months."

"You . . . ?"

"Why not? I had been Deputy Warden of the West March for three years. And this is no task for an old man."

"But . . . he did not inform the prince?"

"I do not know. Why should he? It is a Douglas matter. David Stewart could do nothing about it, even if he cared."

As Jamie digested that, it occurred to him that the other had put some significance into his phrase earlier as to going about his further business as Chief Warden. "And this further business you speak of? Can you tell me that?"

"Why not? It is but further to my duty here. We cross the Border. The morn's morn."

"You what? Cross the Border! You mean, in strength? Invade England!"

"Invade is a large word. But in some strength, yes. Make a demonstration of strength, indeed. It was needed before — and from what you tell us about the new king, it is now needed even more."

"But . . . man, this is crazy-mad! For Douglas, the Chief Warden! A reiving, a cattle-raid, is one thing. But this — this would be an act of war! But without the Crown's authority. Against the Crown's wishes, most certainly."

"And is Dunbar not engaged in an act of war? He and Percy are mustering men to invade *Scotland*. This we know for sure. In the vales of Aln and Till and Breamish and Coquet. And now you say that this new King Henry is calling himself Lord Paramount of Scotland and may lead an invasion likewise, to rally his people. Is not this the time to show these folk that the Scots are not waiting tamely to be trampled on? Make them think anew?"

"Arouse them to greater fury, you mean — Henry, at least. What more likely to fix him in his determination, to play into his very hands? Do this, and he has the most excellent excuse for retaliation. In greatest strength. It is folly, I say."

"I say otherwise. And, to be sure, it is what *I* say that signifies!"

"You cannot do it. Not now. Not when the Duke has but newly replaced his uncle. Before he has had time to set the realm to rights. When nothing is ready for war . . ."

"Now, indeed. Now is the time. Can you not see? The truce has just expired. The new English king cannot be ready either. Moreover, there is plague in England, bad plague. It has spread into the North, to the Yorkshire dales and Durham and Northumberland. They, the English, are in much fear of it. They will never look for a raid, in such case."

Jamie stared at the other, helpless.

"Go tell Davie Stewart that," James the Gross advised. "Aye, tell him to join us. A change of sport from wantoning and drinking!"

"Better — come with us," his brother amended. "We ride in the morning. So stout a fighter as Sir Jamie Douglas would be better employed than riding messenger."

"Ride where?"

"Across Lammermuir and the Merse, to Birgham on Tweed. There, tomorrow night, I meet with Will of Drumlanrig and Archie of Cavers, Rutherford of that Ilk, and others likewise. To double my strength."

"And then?"

"Cross Tweed and go seek out George Dunbar."

"Your father — had he intended this?"

153

"To be sure. It is at his summons that the others come to Birgham, not mine."

Jamie pondered. Will and Archie Douglas were his good friends, knighted with him at Otterburn, Will Warden of the Middle March and Archie Sheriff of Teviotdale. They were men he could talk to, important in their own right. They might heed him. Aid him to dissuade the Master from this folly. It was worth the attempt.

"I will ride with you as far as Birgham," he agreed.

*　　*　　*

On the morrow, leaving a small party in charge at Dunbar and another to convey the stricken Earl back to Threave in Galloway when he was fit to travel, they set out southwards, about five hundred strong, all mounted, a tough and fast-moving column of Border mosstroopers. Through the quiet Lammermuir hills they rode, to the headwaters of the Whitadder, to follow that lively river down to the low ground at Preston, and then to strike directly across the green and rich Merse, by Duns and Leitholm and Eccles, to the wide Tweed valley, and so to the riverside township of Birgham.

When Jamie saw the series of encampments, their banners, the long lines of tethered horses and the camp-fires, his spirits sank despite the spirited scene. He did not fail to recognise that the chances of success for his self-appointed task were small. Here was a much larger force than he had looked for, all set for war — and composed of warlike Borderers whose whole background and tradition was embued with raiding and reiving across the March; and who, moreover, had been held in, to some degree, for years by the series of official truces. To hope to turn back this exultant martial array by sweet reason and pleas, without a blow struck, seemed suddenly improbable to say the least.

And so it proved. His friends of Drumlanrig and Cavers were glad to see him, assuming at once that he was taking part in the adventure and hailing his adherence as like old times. When he disillusioned them, and endeavoured to convince them that this was an ill-considered and highly dangerous project, they were astonished and clearly considered that his judgement was at fault. It was not merely that Douglas had ordered it, they asserted; but this move of Dunbar and Percy had to be countered, before it got out of hand and set the entire Borderland on fire. There was no question but that the English were mustering. If the Mersemen refused to resist them, as was possible with their own Earl and Warden leading the invasion, then the rest of the Scots Borders would be in the gravest danger, their flank turned, their ancient enemies pouring in on them from behind. They it was who would have to bear the brunt of the bloodshed, pillage and rapine, not the Lieutenant of the Crown and the rest in faraway Linlithgow, Stirling or Perth. It was David Stewart's fault that it was happening, in the first place, by his having offended Dunbar and retained the dowry-moneys for his daughter. He could scarcely object to the Borderers defending themselves. This threat had to be halted before it properly began.

Jamie, of course, could not altogether refute their arguments, for there was much truth in what they said. And to assert that, for the greater good of the kingdom, the longer view should be taken, was neither popular nor entirely convincing. Moreover his position was complicated by the fact that he was only *assuming* that the prince would be opposed to this cross-Border raid; for of course nothing had been known of the project when he left Linlithgow. His own remit had been to dissuade the Earl of Douglas from attacking Dunbar Castle. He presumed that the same reasoning would be against this unofficial invasion — but he had no specific instructions to that effect.

When it was obvious that nothing he could say was going to alter the situation, Jamie came to a decision. He could conceivably do more good by staying with the raiders, seeking to influence them against possible follies and excesses, than by hurrying back northwards to Linlithgow — where David would be in no position to do anything swiftly effective anyway. He sent back his two royal-guard escorts with a message to the prince, and signified to the Douglas leadership that he would remain with them, although critical of their course.

The Master eyed him, at that, with a hint of grim humour — almost the first resemblance to his father that Jamie had seen in the man — but shrugged acquiescence. His Teviotdale friends clapped him on the back.

The waiting Teviotdale and Jedburgh party — which included Sir William Stewart of Jedworth, the Laird of Rutherford, Turnbull of Bedrule and a famous freebooter known as Outwith-the-Sword Turnbull — had had the good sense not to camp at the riverside and so be visible from across Tweed, but inland a short distance where they were screened by woodland. In typical Border fashion, a wait was made until the small hours of the next morning when, with a pale waning half-moon adding its wan light to a not very dark night, a flying column was sent quietly across the ford of Tweed nearby, to surround and isolate the village of Carham on the far side, to ensure that no alarm emanated from there. Then the main force, some 1,300 strong, splashed across the shallows into England.

Their first concern had to be the Castle of Wark some two miles further downstream, a powerful hold belonging to the English Crown, which dominated this stretch of the river in general and in particular served for the exaction of tolls for the fords and ferry between there and Coldstream, a source of much revenue, though little more popular with the local English than with the Scots. It was not a fortress of the calibre of Berwick or Roxburgh, but it was a strong place with a sizeable garrison under a renowned and veteran keeper, Sir Thomas Grey. It was not a comfortable place to leave free to menace their rear and possibly to interfere with their use of the forts on return. The present hope was to surprise it at what was ever the most vulnerable hour for any fortified strength, when the new day began, with its cattle being driven out from their night's security in the outer bailey, night-soil being ejected and forage and fuel being brought in from outside — moreover with the night watch weary and off their guard, duty over, and the day staff still sleepy-eyed and less than alert. Many a stronghold had been surprised and cheaply won in these circumstances.

In the event, the surprise was otherwise. The Scots, halting to wait for sun-up in nearby woodland, did observe the drawbridge lowered and a quite numerous herd of cattle being driven out to pasture. A swift-moving troop under the Master himself galloped forward to capture the bridge before it could be raised again and the portcullis lowered against them. This they achieved — but the surprise was to find that there was little or no subsequent resistance. It transpired, in fact, that the castle was practically empty of its garrison, Grey and most of his men having been summoned to a great muster-at-arms being organised by Sir Ralph Percy, brother of Hotspur, at Wooler, the chief town of Glendale, where the Glen joined the Till, about a dozen miles to the south-east, leaving only a few men at Wark. These put up only the merest token fight.

The Douglases, naturally, were much heartened by this speedy and painless success, an excellent omen and proof, the Master claimed, that their raid was timely and necessary. They would now drive on for Wooler and break up Percy's muster before it could become a menace.

But before they rose, it appeared there was a task to be performed here. Wark, ever something of a threat to the Scots, must be burned, razed to the ground. It was too good an opportunity to miss, and worth spending a little time on. Moreover, it would serve as an excellent warning to Percy and Dunbar.

Jamie protested strongly. To destroy the castle would serve the Scots cause nothing. But it must seriously anger the English, the new King especially — for it was a royal castle. A raid was one thing; but deliberately to raze a major stronghold which had yielded without bloodshed was altogether another. Henry Plantagenet could not fail to seek to avenge that — his credit quite forfeited otherwise.

These contentions were rejected. The forenoon was devoted to the methodical and thorough demolition and burning of Wark, its castle and supporting castleton, of manor-place, cot-houses and mill. A small detachment was despatched back over Tweed with the cattle, ever dear to Border hearts. At noon the advance was continued, due southwards over Wark Common, for the Bowmont Water, leaving a great column of black smoke soaring into the August sky.

That ominous beacon had its effect. All the way down the twisting valley of the Bowmont Water and through the wide vale of Till and beyond, the Scots found the folk fled before them, cottages, farmsteads, whole villages and manors hastily abandoned — and the Master of Douglas found it difficult indeed to control his mosstroopers and prevent them from indiscriminate pillage and helping themselves — after all, that was what Border raiding was all about, on whatever the scale. And he was not the old Earl, lacking his authority. The pace of the advance slackened inevitably.

At least they took suitable military precautions, riding in four distinct groups, with constant liaison — an advance-guard under the redoubtable Out-with-the-Sword Turnbull, old in experience of such reiving and knowing this territory like the palm of his hand; a strong flanking force to east and west on the heights above the vale; and the main body in the centre, following the rivers, where lay the villages and townships —

although sending back many a little party with cattle, horses and plunder.

Long before the dozen or so miles to Wooler was accomplished, it became obvious to Jamie — and to others likewise no doubt — that they were going to be in no position to fight any major action, with numbers being steadily depleted and with the minds of most preoccupied with plunder rather than battle. Fortunately for them, it appeared that Sir Ralph Percy did not realise this, or else was very doubtful about his musterers' ability to put up any sort of effective opposition, for Turnbull's scouts presently sent back information that the quite large numbers of men assembled on the Glendale flats were in fact streaming away southwards towards Alnwick. When, in the late evening, the Scots eventually arrived at Wooler, it was to find not only the encampment but most of the little town deserted.

Douglas took over the abandoned camp, and his men made merry in the town and surroundings.

The Glendale area, with Doddington, Chatton and Chillingham, was richer than the land they had traversed hitherto, and as good as a magnet for the mosstroopers. Sleep, save for the hopelessly drunken, was scarcely considered that night, with such plentiful pickings to be had for the minimum of effort. Women too were soon discovered. The Master and his colleagues did not appear to be greatly concerned, their attitude being that since this raid was in the nature of a demonstration of strength and readiness, it did not matter if there was little or no real fighting, so long as the English in general were suitably intimidated and alarmed. Their cause could be as well served by pillage and destruction as by actual bloodshed and battle. Jamie, with no hankering after either, nevertheless felt, and said, that this was mistaken policy. But then, the entire expedition was a mistake, in his opinion.

In the morning the leaders of the Scots force had the greatest difficulty in rounding up their followers into any coherent array. Pillage and rapine are highly infectious states of mind, and men with almost unlimited booty available were naturally intent on getting it safely back home. Since none were actually paid to be there, giving only armed service to their lords and lairds, they tended to see their duties in a different light from hired or professional soldiers; also Borderers were renownedly of a fiercely independent mind. Moreover, many of their lairds were similarly inclined. Had there been any sign of serious opposition,

158

any hostile threat evident, it would have been different. Not many more than half of the original numbers were accounted for by mid-forenoon. When Out-with-the-Sword Turnbull himself sent word back that his advance-party was so sorely depleted as to be unable properly to carry out its scouting and protective functions, the Master bowed to the inevitable. He ordered a retiral to the Tweed.

If the outwards journey had been a slow progress for an armed advance, the return was more so, with vast numbers of cattle to be herded along — and more being added all the time, for it would have been a poor Borderer who would see any available left behind. It took them all day indeed to reach Tweed, at less than two miles in the hour, spread wide over the country-side, no longer any sort of coherent force but an agglomeration of drovers. Such farms and homesteads and hamlets as had escaped in the advance now went up in flames. A whole land blazed and smoked behind them.

More than once Jamie Douglas almost left the others in disgust and frustration, to ride northwards on his own, back to Linlithgow. But he told himself that he would see them safely out of England, at least. He had good friends here, and he *was* a Douglas.

The business of getting the herds across the fords of Tweed was a seemingly endless nightmare, and took most of the night in fact. There were thousands of reluctant and weary beasts to force and steer and harry over, with many breaking back in mid-stream in bellowing panic. Fortunately the water was low, so that a number of fords could be used, some not normally available, between Wark and Birgham.

On Scottish soil thereafter they rested until well into the following forenoon, all along the riverside — for such huge numbers of cattle took up a great deal of space. They had left a rearguard behind them, of course, as necessary precaution.

When eventually they moved off again, westwards now, it had to be by innumerable stages along the Tweedside drove-road, for they could not trample widespread and roughshod across the land here as they had done in the Auld Enemy's territory. Jamie thankfully decided that his presence was no longer required, in any way, and took his leave.

"Go back to your prince, Jamie," the Master said, in farewell, "and tell him that Douglas has taught both traitors and pro-claimed Lords Paramount a lesson! At no cost to his realm. Tell

159

him that the English have been given warning that the Scots are ready and in good fettle. Aye — and tell him to appoint a new Warden of the East March forthwith — and that a Douglas one would be advisable! Say that I suggest your Uncle Will of Mordington."

"All that I shall tell him," the other agreed. "But I do not promise that my news will rejoice him!"

"Then he knows not when he is fortunate. We do his work for him, while he whores and idles. Tell him so."

Jamie rode with his Teviotdale friends of Drumlanrig and Cavers as far as Edenmouth, and there left them to follow up the Eden Water while they continued up Tweed. He was making for Ednam, a barony belonging to the Lady Isabel Stewart, former Countess of Douglas, gifted to her by her father at her wedding and one of her main sources of revenue. He was still her knight and kept an eye on her affairs, for he admired her greatly and owed her much — and her present husband, Edmonstone, although amiable was elderly, drunken and lazy. He would take the opportunity to look in on Ednam on his way home, since it was near at hand.

In the event, he found quite a lot demanding attention there, with the old steward dead and the new one less effective as yet; and he delayed overnight and most of next day, for it was an extensive property with much requiring decision. He had just finished, and left for the north, when, a mile or two on his way, the new steward came pounding after him at the gallop. He had just had word, the man gasped, that a large English force had crossed Tweed and was hot on the heels of the Master of Douglas, pausing for nothing.

Jamie cursed. He had feared something of the sort, and Archie Douglas's over-confidence. They would be in no state to fight effectively now, their force disintegrating and dispersed. The Teviotdale contingent would have left Tweedside to follow up their own river, at Kelso — for Jamie knew that the Master intended to head westwards for Douglasdale in Lanark's Upper Ward by following Tweed right up almost to its source and then crossing over the watershed to Clydesdale.

What to do? He could not just ride off homewards and leave his friends and fellow-clansmen to their fate. On the other hand, one extra sword would be of scant benefit. One thing he might try — he could hurry after the Teviotdale party, warn them, and possibly bring them to the aid of the Master. The probability was, if the English followed the others up Tweed, those in the long side vale of Teviot would know nothing about it — not for some time, at any rate.

Decision made, Jamie turned back for Ednam, hurriedly rounded up a dozen sturdy Mersemen there, and with these set off at top speed south-westwards for the Teviot.

On the outskirts of Kelso, with the sun setting before them, they halted discreetly when they could see from the higher ground that the town seethed. Enquiries from cottagers elicited the information that the English were in fact in the town, at the junction of Tweed and Teviot, and appeared to be going to spend the night there whilst their leaders went on to consult with their countrymen garrisoning Roxburgh Castle. A kind of hell was loose in Kelso, according to their informants, with folk fleeing; but so far the town had not been set afire. Possibly the invaders were reserving that for their return journey. The English force was said to be under the joint command of Sir Robert de Umfraville, Deputy Warden of the English East March and Sir Thomas Grey, Keeper of Wark.

At least this pause ought to give the Master of Douglas a breathing-space, a little more time to organise some defensive action. But it by no means lessened the need for swift reinforcement. Jamie turned his horses' heads westwards again, to keep well to the north of Kelso. Roxburgh Castle, sitting at the joining of the waters, had to be avoided also. In the shadow of the August dusk they rode on, round the great crescent-shaped haugh of Floors and so back to Tweed about three miles above Kelso, where they crossed the ford at Trows and so reached Roxburgh Moor well west of the fortress. In a couple more miles they came to Rutherford, and here Jamie roused up Sir Robert of that Ilk and his five sons whom he had parted from the previous noonday, quite unaware of the English presence so near. The old man, although preparing for bed, promptly sent his sons out to reassemble his men. They would ride as soon as they might, up Tweed after the Master.

Jamie hurried on southwards now through the night, to ford Teviot at Nisbetmill and so to ride up Jed to Jedburgh. Here they had some difficulty with the town-watch before they could get at Sir William Stewart in his house in the centre of the burgh. But when reached, he agreed immediately to muster as many citizens as he could mount, and to ride north likewise. Over the Dunion Hill by a drove-road to Bedrule in Rulewater they proceeded, after midnight now, there to rouse the Turnbull laird and have him summon the many other Turnbull lairdlings of that remote valley. Then on, up Teviot again, to Denholm-on-the-Green and Cavers. Despite the small hours of the morning, Jamie's friend Sir Archibald, illegitimate younger son of the late James, Earl of Douglas, left his new wife's bed to take over the task of warning the rest of the Teviotdale Douglasses, including his brother Drumlanrig at Hawick, whilst the weary group from Ednam rested.

By sun-up four hundred men were assembled in Hawick's Sandbed, most of them the same who had just returned from the raid into England. Jamie gladly resigned the initiative to his friends. The brothers decided that, in the circumstances, the Master, once warned, would almost certainly try to keep ahead of the pursuit until he could win into the wilds of Ettrick Forest proper, where he might make the land fight for him in some measure — with six hundred or so against 2,000 he would need to do so. Presumably, to free his hands and gain speed, he would send off the great cattle droves into side-valleys and hidden hollows all the way up Tweed — although this must further deplete his numbers. If this estimate was correct, he would leave Tweed where the Ettrick Water joined it, near Selkirk, and follow up the lesser river to its confluence with Yarrow — for Yarrow provided an alternative route over the empty hills to the west and eventually Douglasdale — with the forest thickening and the hills heightening and steepening. If he could get that far. There, if he chose his ground well, he might make a successful stand; there was nowhere similarly suitable before that. The Rutherfords, Jedburgh men and Turnbulls should have been able to join him before that. So much depended on how long the English might linger at Kelso and Roxburgh — although they must be equally well aware of the need for haste.

So the Teviotdale force rode for Ettrick by the most direct route, up over the rough hills by Stirches to Ale Water at Ashkirk, and again climbing, by the Haremoss heights and Hartwood to Selkirk Common. It was a dozen hard miles before the wooded vale of Ettrick opened before them, with, deep below, the little town of Selkirk nestling snugly in its enclave of the great forest. By then it was nearly noon.

This was Pringle country, vassals of Douglas, and at the Haining of Selkirk the aged Pringle laird gave them urgent tidings. The Master of Douglas was at Foulhopehaugh, at bay, with an English force caught up with him. He, Pringle, had already sent his sons, with as many Selkirk men as could be raised at short notice, to his Earl's son's aid. But by all accounts they were vastly outnumbered.

Foulhopehaugh was some two miles to the south-west, where Yarrow joined Ettrick, but on the other side of both rivers. Because of the woodlands, it was not visible from Selkirk. Thitherwards the Teviot force rode at speed.

Will and Archie Douglas said that the Master, when he could flee no further, would have taken up a defensive position where the Foulhope Burn came down to the haugh just below the junction with Yarrow, to use the burn and the damp and soft ground of the haugh as protection. Unfortunately it had been a dry season and the flats would be less soft than usual. They splashed across the Town Ford and swung left-handed along the farther bank.

They heard the noise of battle some way off — so, at least, the Master was not yet defeated. His friends would have ridden hot-foot straight on, to assail the English rear — for here they must be behind them; but as ever, Jamie urged caution, consideration. They might achieve more by less headlong measures. His reputation from Lochaber, however unwarranted, gained him their heed.

The entire terrain, save for the level haugh itself, was densely wooded with tangled scrub and old pines, poor ground for gaining any prospect. But there was a knoll to the west, a low outlier of Harehead Hill, which would overlook the haugh near the rivers-meeting. It was tree-clad also, to the summit, but it should provide some sort of viewpoint. A little reluctantly the others agreed to rein right-handed to make for this.

The trees on the knoll at least gave them some cover from view, likewise. Leaving their men at the east side of it, the leaders rode up to the crest.

The scene that met their gaze, in the early afternoon sunshine, was not at first glance that of a normal battle between two sides. It was, in fact, a furious and widespread confusion down there on the river's flood-plain. There was no line, no front, no recognisable sides as such, merely a vast number of isolated tussles, individual fights often between quite small groups, covering much of the south end of the haugh. Which was friend and which foe it was almost impossible to say, from any distance, with the innumerable struggling clusters and knots surging this way and that and facing in all directions. Banners and pennons seemed to have been discarded. Bodies lay or crawled everywhere. The battle was being fought on foot, even by the leaders — which presumably meant that, dry season or not, the haugh must be too soft still for cavalry tactics. Certainly it could be seen that the levels were split and scored by many ditches and water-channels. The Ettrick, coming down from the high hills so close at hand, was very liable to spates.

One thing was clear about that fight however. The struggle was taking place on both sides of the Foulhope Burn — which must mean that the burn had in fact failed as a defensive line and therefore that the Scots were in general, losing ground, getting the worst of it. Clearly there was no time to be lost.

"Down at them!" Will Douglas exclaimed. "No more delay, in God's name!"

"Aye — they're in sore trouble," his brother agreed. "Come — quickly!"

"Wait," Jamie advised again. "For just a little." He pointed. "See — their horses. Left yonder, to the north, 2,000 of them! And under scant guard. There's our opportunity!"

"Eh? You mean . . .?"

"Send down some of our people, horsed, first. While the rest wait here, hidden. Say a hundred — we can spare that. To gallop down, shouting, to a little way north of the horse-lines. Then, at the foot, swing southwards, right-handed. Drive directly on to the pack of their beasts. Panic them. Send them bolting down on the battle, 2,000 galloping horses! Break up the fighting."

"Lord . . .!"

"Then charge down our people from here. On foot, shouting, into the midst of it. No battle left, after that, perhaps!"

"Save us, Jamie — what a ploy! But . . .?" Sir Will looked doubtful. "What if they do not bolt? The horses? Or bolt in the wrong direction?"

"They will bolt. *I'll* lead. If we keep well to the north, at first, then turn on them. They will not stand. They will shy, turn tail, flee. Bolt southwards. They will not plunge into the river. Nor be apt to climb this hill. They will take the open haugh."

"Yes, yes," Cavers cried, "come, then . . ."

The three young knights ran back to their men. Will shouted for roughly five score to follow Sir James of Aberdour, the rest to dismount and come with him up to the crest again.

"Do not charge too soon, or you might turn the horses back on us," Jamie panted, as he vaulted into his saddle.

He led his party to thread the trees northwards till they came to the tail of the little ridge. Drawing rein for a moment there, where they could see the low ground clearly, he jerked his instructions. Then, drawing his sword, he raised it high and dug in his spurs. It crossed his mind that he was becoming expert at leading false charges.

Downhill, in a fairly compact mass, they thundered, yelling A Douglas! A Douglas!, not directly towards the long lines of the English horses but angling north-eastwards. So far as Jamie could see, no more than a score or so of men had been left in charge of the animals. These began to scurry about, in agitation, at the sight of them coming. He had no time to observe whether their eruption on the scene had had any effect on the battlers to the south.

Reaching the levels, he sought to wheel his party round into a sort of sickle-shaped front, facing south, with the higher, westernmost end furthest forward, to counter any possible tendency of the English horses to bolt that way, uphill — all this without pausing. His men were not trained cavalrymen, but being mosstroopers all they were born horsemen, and quickly perceived what was required. Still shouting, and waving their swords, hooves drumming on the softish ground, they swept down on the great mass of riderless mounts.

There was no question as to the panic — and panic is just as infectious amongst horses as amongst men. The few guards left with them had no hope of exerting any sort of influence, much less control. Well before the Douglases were upon them, the first ranks of the horses were turning and rearing, whinnying and lashing out in terror at their fellows blocking their escape from the pounding, yelling, steel-waving menace. In only moments all was indescribable chaos, with animals kicking, screaming, falling. Jamie was suddenly afraid that he and his men were in fact going to crash into a solid if heaving wall of struggling horseflesh. He began to pull in on his reins in incipient panic of his own.

But, just in time, the danger eased as the alarm spread to the farther side of the pack, and the beasts there, with nothing in front to stop them, swung away and went plunging off southwards, reins trailing, stirrups and saddle-cloths flapping. The jam of unhappy creatures thereby easing, slackening in that direction, every tossing head turned that way. In mere seconds that inchoate lashing mass evolved into a coherent movement, a flood that streamed away southwards shaking the entire haugh with the beat of 8,000 hooves. What happened to the guards in it all was not to be known.

Thankful that there had been no dire pile-up, Jamie and his men cantered on behind the stampede, throats hoarse with shouting, flats of swords beating at the rumps of any laggards — not that there were many of these. It was far from smooth going, of course. The ground was soft and pitted and scored by ditches and dried-up runnels. Some of the English beasts had fallen or been trampled down. There were isolated thorn-trees, and driftwood from spates, to be negotiated. It was a hectic, crazy, headlong scramble.

The first realisation for Jamie that they had reached the battlefield itself was when he began to see blood and men's bodies and weapons beneath his own mount's hooves. He risked a glance upwards, westwards. A horde of yelling Douglases were already plunging downhill, on foot, over quite a wide front. It would be only a matter of moments until the impact. He had neither time nor opportunity for further attention.

If the battle had seemed unclear, confused, before, now it ceased altogether to be a battle. No fighting could continue under the headlong onslaught of 2,000 maddened horses. Men on both sides were indiscriminately swept away, knocked over, trampled on and dispersed, under the flailing hooves. Those who had time to flee before the clash did so, desperately, uphill into the trees or actually into the river — these latter in the majority. The Ettrick was not very deep here, save in patches, and probably few drowned. Most splashed or swam to the far side, tending to lose swords and battleaxes in the process. Others clung under the near bank or stood about in the shallows, at a loss — this applying to the Scots and English alike, leader and led, for the moment at one in seeking escape from the terror. By the time that the seething flood of horseflesh had swept over the battleground and onwards unflagging, there was no semblance of a fight remaining — nor any real probability of it being reconstituted and resumed in the immediate future, whoever had been winning; especially as now the Teviotdale hundreds descended on the littered field in a fairly coherent and solid force, to find themselves in complete mastery of the situation without a blow struck. As surprised as anyone by the abruptly total cessation of hostilities, they halted, to stand about in a kind of stupor. It was a little while before men went to peer at, aid and attend to the trampled wounded — all the wounded, since it was almost impossible to distinguish friend from foe still.

Jamie was able to disentangle himself and his followers, and pull up, after another couple of hundred yards, to turn and trot back, himself not a little appalled by the results of his action.

Drumlanrig and Cavers and the other Douglas newcomers, however, although slightly dazed by it all, were far from appalled. They came running to hail him, shouting their praise and plaudits. But sitting his panting, trembling mount, he shook his head.

"It . . . it is shameful! Terrible! No victory this. I . . . I have ridden down friend and foe alike!"

"You stopped the battle, man. Left us holders of the field. Saved the day . . ."

"Ignobly. Where are our friends? Where is the Master? Have I trampled him to death, with the others?"

None could answer that — though more and more of the Teviotdale men were examining the fallen.

Those who had fled successfully into the river and woodland began to reappear, clambering out of the water and emerging from the trees — or some of them, for these were nearly all Scots, the English naturally not anxious to place themselves in enemy custody. It fairly quickly became evident that larger numbers on both sides had managed to win clear than at first might have been thought. Hundreds of very wet Englishmen were now streaming away southwards on the other side of the river, and no doubt many more were doing the same through the forest glades.

Amongst those struggling out of the Ettrick, on this bank, were some whose fine half-armour or gleaming shirts of mail revealed them to be leaders or of knightly rank. One stocky figure, black hair plastered over his features, became recognisable as the Master of Douglas and Galloway. Thankfully Jamie flung himself down from his saddle and went hurrying to meet him.

"God's eyes!" the normally stolid heir to Douglas declared, gasping, and dripping water. "What a — a broil! Saints a mercy — it's a miracle!"

"You are unhurt? And your brother? God be praised! I feared, I feared that . . ."

"*You* feared, man? What think you *I* feared! Seeing that crazed host of horses bearing down on us. I near . . . shamed myself! I vow it! How did you contrive it? Was it of a purpose . . . ?"

"It was all Jamie's doing, Archie," Sir Will exclaimed. "He devised it. Led it. We saw you were much outnumbered, losing ground. He rode down hill, with five score men, and herded their horse-lines down upon you. To end the battle."

"Lord save us — here's a ploy! Jamie Douglas! But . . . how came you here, man? You left us at Birgham . . . ?"

"I heard, at Ednam, that you were being pursued by Umfraville and 2,000 horsed English. So I came after."

"He came after *us*, Archie. Roused all Teviotdale, to come to your aid," Sir Archibald of Cavers amplified. "You have him, and him alone, to thank for your deliverance."

"Not so," Jamie contested. "I merely brought the news. And this, this of the bolting horses, I perhaps misjudged. I insufficiently considered. How I put at risk my own friends equally with the enemy. And even these English deserved better than to be beaten down by brute beasts . . . !"

"Nonsense, Jamie. This is war, not a tourney," the Master averred. "We were all but lost, could not have withstood for much longer. You saved Douglas this day, my friend."

"Aye, he did. He did."

Embarrassed, Jamie shook his head. "This is folly! Besides waste of time. We should be ensuring that the English do not rally again — not talking here. All could yet be lost. They will still outnumber us."

"They will not rally now, I think," the Master said. "Not sufficiently to challenge us. They are dispersed, wide-scattered. And if I know them, they will before all seek to recover their horses — and that will take much time. They are Borderers too, and lost without their mounts. Besides, they will need them to get back to their own country. I do not see another attack on us. For all that, we must *see* that they do not. Will — your men are fresh. Divide them into two companies, to keep the English running, on both sides of the river. Keep them from joining up, for as long as you can. I will gather my people together again. See to the wounded and prisoners. There is much to be done, yes . . ."

It was only later that Jamie discovered that the victory — if so it could be termed — was far from one-sided. Indeed, on balance, it might be more truly said that the advantage was with the English. Their casualties were undoubtedly lighter. And it seemed that, before ever the Teviotdale contingent had reached the scene, the Scots had suffered a severe reverse. The earlier reinforcements from lower Teviot, those Jamie had warned first, under Rutherford, Turnbull and Stewart of Jedburgh, had coalesced into a single force of about two hundred and fifty, and following directly on the Master's route, had fallen into an English trap. Umfraville, a veteran campaigner, had ambushed them at Faldonside, where wooded hills came down close to Tweed between the confluences of Gala and Ettrick Waters, and, hopelessly outnumbered, they had been overwhelmed, only a few escaping to bring the news to the Master. Old Rutherford and all five of his sons had been captured. Likewise Out-with-the-Sword John Turnbull and other Turnbull lairds. Sir William Stewart also. Where they were now was not known — presumably held somewhere in the rear, or already sent back under guard to England. The Master would send out scouting parties to try to find them, or recover them — but feared for the result.

The toll of those fallen in the battle was grievous; but Jamie, perhaps foolishly, was relieved to discover that most, on the Scots side at any rate, had already fallen before ever the horses made their impact. The fate of the already-wounded, under those stampeding hooves, did not bear thinking of, however.

It was a distinctly grim-featured young man who eventually took his leave of his Earl's son and other friends, laudatory as were their farewells, sent off his Mersemen home to Ednam, and rode alone northwards, by Tweed and Gala Water, for Lothian and Linlithgow.

VIII

"AYE, JAMIE — a bad business," Rothesay nodded. "Fool-ishness, I agree. A beating of the air. My good-brother Archie lacks his father's wits and his strength, no doubt. But — look not so glum, man! There is no great harm done." David Stewart certainly did not look nor sound glum — but then he seldom did. He appeared to have listened to Jamie's tale of the abortive Border raid and its consequences with only a part of his attention.

"Might it not do *much* harm, my lord?" Jamie insisted. "The harrying in England. The destruction of Wark. With this new King Henry already threatening us. This cannot but grievously offend him. Give him excuse, if he needs it, for retaliation. Invasion . . ."

"It will not help, to be sure. But Henry Plantagenet may have more to think about than Douglas raiding or Dunbar's treason, as it transpires. But, come, down here. Leonora is installed in the tower there meantime. Until we contrive more suitable accommodation."

They were walking down from the upper or palace courtyard of Stirling Castle, on its lofty rock, to one of the lower groups of buildings — for the rock-summit's uneven surface meant that the fortress was built on various levels. Jamie had arrived at Linlithgow the previous evening, to discover that the Duke had moved unexpectedly to Stirling, where his father had come evidently from Turnberry. He had come on, and the prince had welcomed him gladly enough, in good spirits, but seeming to be only marginally interested in what he had to report on the Dunbar and Border incidents. He was clearly much more eager to show him his latest divert, as he described her.

Jamie, still in his travelling clothes, dust and all, tried again.

170

"Perhaps, my lord Duke. But, although the Master of Douglas is my own kin, and I like him well enough, there is danger surely in letting him have his head thus. He is claiming to be Chief Warden of the Marches now, in his father's room; and as such could rule all the Borderland, where *your* father's realm joins England. A most delicate province. With a spirited English king, that could spell trouble indeed. For although he does not look it, nor sound it, he is rash, headstrong . . ."

"Young Archie rash? That dull fellow! He is as rash as you are, Jamie Douglas!"

"It was a rash act, was it not, to storm Dunbar Castle? Rasher to invade England without warrant. There was no need to burn down Wark Castle, the King of England's own property. And then to allow his men to stray far and wide, stealing cattle and pillaging, in enemy country when the English were already mustering . . ."

"Aye, indiscreet, no doubt. But he lacks experience. He will learn. I will have a word with his father."

"How is the Earl Archie?"

"Recovering, I am told. He is at his house of Threave, in Galloway. But see now — here is my Leonora's lodging."

The prince produced a key, and opened the heavy door of a flanking-tower of the most northerly range of buildings, perched on the very edge of the precipice above the flood-plain of Forth. Immediately a puff of hot air came out, with a thick, throat-catching smell, strange, feral. Jamie, like all others, was used to strong smells, mankind being prone to emit them in fair variety; but this was different.

"Is she not handsome?" David demanded, gesturing.

The vaulted basement of the tower was lit only by two arrow-slit windows narrow and unglazed; but though dark, there was no difficulty in seeing the great tawny shape crouching on the straw-covered stone floor behind the interlaced iron grating, any more than in hearing the deep-throated snarling growl. Involuntarily Jamie started back before the glare of yellow, unblinking eyes and the savage grin of white teeth, of a full-grown lioness in tail-lashing menace.

"Fear not!" the prince said. "She will not eat you — not yet! Eh, my beauty?" And he held his hand out to the brute, through the bars.

The lioness did not move. But the rumbling growl lessened nothing.

"Do not do that!" Jamie exclaimed, pulling at the Duke's arm. "She could have your hand off in a single bite! For God's sake . . .!"

"Not so. I feed her. She learns to know me. I should have brought some meat." But he withdrew his hand. "I sent to Barbary for her. Some time ago. She reached Dumbarton the day after you left."

"But . . . but why? What want you with this creature?"

"*You* would scarce understand that, my sober Jamie! I shall be the Lion of Scotland, one day. Fit that I should have my lioness! Besides, I like taming wild females — and I find most of our Scots ones over-eager to please! Leonora will teach me much of use, I feel sure."

Jamie shook his head, wordless.

"I shall build her a travelling cage. On wheels. So that she may go where I go. Perhaps even a litter-cage, to be carried between horses so that she may travel the faster — if I can train horses to accept her. We shall have some amusement with this lady from Barbary, Jamie, I swear! How think you my Uncle Robert will enjoy Leonora's company? He was never one for females, to be sure — save as conveyors of lands and earldoms! I shall watch his sour face, with interest! Tomorrow. I have had shackles made for her, for all four paws, so that she cannot leap. A collar and chain likewise. That she may walk abroad with me. Until I have tamed her. We shall try them out, tonight."

"But — how will you put the shackles on? How?"

"The way the Moors do in Barbary. And as they did in Rome, lang syne. A great net is thrown over the creature. It struggles — and the more it does so the more entangled it becomes. Until it is wholly bound. Then the shackles are put on the net and cut away. Wasteful in nets — but they are only rope and easily remade."

"Lord! All this for what, my lord?"

"For my pleasure and satisfaction, man. There is more in life than stern duty and endeavour, than statecraft and power over men, than pious devotion or even the gaining of riches. Does your Mary, my aunt, never tell you so? I vow *she* is well aware of it! Although her brother Robert has never discovered it. Nor yet my unhappy sire. My Uncle Alex, now — he was different."

"Aye, the Wolf would have approved of your lioness!"

"No doubt. But Leonora may have her uses also. We shall see." David paused. "You are not overtired, Jamie?"

"Tired? No. Why?"

"How far to Aberdour? Twenty-five miles? Thirty? With a fresh horse you could be there before sundown. Easily. And back here, with your Mary, soon after tomorrow's noon. No?"

"Mary? Why Mary, my lord?"

"Because I have a task for my favourite aunt. See you, to my sorrow my mother is fallen sick. Has not been able to accompany my father from Turnberry. Nothing grievous, so far as I can learn. My royal sire is sore lost, here, without her. He requires a woman's sustaining hand ever at his elbow, I fear. Especially for such occasions as this. He is in a sorry state, to tell truth. I had the devil's own task to get him here, at all. I cannot seem to act nurse to him, before all, to keep him right in tomorrow's ceremonial. Moreover, a hostess is required. My own wife would not serve for this. She scarce knows my father, nor he her. Besides, she something lacks the, the graces, that one! She is going to demand a deal of training to make a queen, one day! To act suitably at the King's side, it must be a princess. So I have sent for my Aunt Isabel, from Edmonstone. My father approves of her, better than his other sisters. But she must have a lady-in-waiting. Not only for the appearance of it, but to pass on *my* instructions anent my father. Someone with quick wits, and no shrinking flower! For this is going to require careful handling. Mary has acted lady-in-waiting in the past. And her wits are quick enough for any, I swear!"

"But — why? What is this great occasion?"

The Duke shut and locked the lioness's door. "It is a strange business, Jamie — but one which I cannot afford to neglect. We are to have a visitor to my father's Court. No less than King Richard the Second of England, indeed!"

"King Richard! But . . . but is he not dead? I thought that he was slain. At Pontefract."

"So it was given out. So indeed it may be. But now there is another story. True or false remains to be seen. It was your friend Alex Stewart of Badenoch who sent me word. He had heard the tale that the deposed but rightful King of England had arrived, of all places, on the isle of Islay, at Donald of the Isles' castle of Finlaggan. It seems that he said that he had effected his escape from Pontefract where Bolingbroke held him, crossed England to the west coast, and there took ship for the Hebrides. He and my cousin Donald, to be sure, had long been in league, traitorously so — Donald made treaties with Richard like an independent monarch. So he fled to him, as secure haven."

"Is there any truth in this? Surely word would have leaked out of England if Richard had still lived, had escaped? It may be but an impostor . . ."

"This I must seek to find out. If I can. But meantime, my hand is forced. For I have since learned that my Uncle Robert has also heard the story — sooner than I did, it seems. And acted upon it, swiftly. Presumably for reasons good for himself. He invited this alleged Richard Plantagenet to his own castle of Doune, in Menteith. And the man has come there. He arrived five days past, Donald with him. Now, why has Robert done this? And why has Donald agreed? My uncle never acts without sufficient reason. Nor, indeed, my Cousin Donald. They make an unlikely pair, in collusion. Hitherto they have been at each others' throats! Now Donald is in Menteith, with this mammet calling himself King Richard. As Lieutenant of the realm I had to act. I do not trust either of them so far as I can spit!"

"You fear some plot?"

"I most certainly do. Robert has not forgiven me, nor my father, you may be sure. And Donald was humiliated over the affair at Haddonstank, having to call off his invasion of Galloway, and then his brother's defeat at Arkaig. They would both unseat me if they could. Anything that brings those two together is dangerous."

"I see that, yes."

"So I am taking a risk. In my father's name I have commanded the man to be brought here. To be presented to the King of Scots as King of England. He will be received and treated as King. And once here, he will bide here! I shall see to that. He will not be allowed to become any sort of puppet in Robert's hands, nor in Donald's either. Robert cannot refuse this command. If he is indeed King Richard, then he cannot sojourn in Scotland without the King of Scots express permission. So tomorrow my father receives him, in state, as rightful King of England."

Jamie shook his dark head helplessly. "But is that not direly dangerous, my lord? Risking the repute of the Scots Crown? If he is proved an impostor, then how foolish you will seem. And your royal father."

"That is a hazard, yes. But none so grievous. And there are advantages, other than taking the initiative from Uncle Robert. See you, so long as Richard, the lawful monarch of England, is held to be alive, and *recognised* as such by his fellow-monarch of Scotland, then Henry of Bolingbroke remains a usurper. And this is to Scotland's much benefit. It must lessen Henry's authority with his nobility and people, tend to divide the English, offer a rallying point for Henry's enemies. Also possibly prevent Papal recognition — for Richard was the Lord's Anointed. If Henry indeed plans to invade Scotland, then this may give him pause."

"Ye-e-es." Jamie emitted breath in a long sigh. "But might it not have the opposite result? Might he, Henry, not invade Scotland just to show what he thought of this claim? Even to demand that the other be handed over? As price of his withdrawal from our land. Henry, from all accounts, is not the man to lie down under threats."

"If his nobles remain doubtful of his Crown's legality he would scarcely dare, I think. Leaving such unrest behind him. The house of Lancaster has no especial right to the throne. Richard had other uncles than John of Gaunt. No — with Richard still alive, Henry is in a difficult position. And we shall *keep* him alive! Meantime, at any rate. It should prove an interesting situation."

As they climbed back to the palace-yard, Jamie Douglas remained sceptical. Doubts, of course, were his weakness.

*　　*　　*

The Great Hall of Stirling Castle was loud with talk, rumours, surmise, as the high-born throng stirred and eddied. Jamie moved amongst them, listening, though not too obviously. Snatches of conversation and argument he overheard indicated that confusion was general, clear-cut opinion all but non-existent. Most seemed to assume that the Mammet, as he was already being called, was an impostor, and the reasons for him being received otherwise a mystery. But whether it was in Albany's interests, in Rothesay's, or in Donald MacDonald's for that matter, was roundly debated. That there was a deep plot of some sort was apparently accepted. Some complained even at being thus summoned to attend on such an evident sham.

The royal trumpeters were filing in at the back of the dais, with a gorgeously-clad pursuivant in brilliant blazonry, the recently appointed Rothesay Herald, Ninian Stewart of Kildonan. These blew a fanfare, and the herald in ringing tones announced the entry of the high and mighty Lord David, Duke of Rothesay, High Steward, Prince of Scotland and Lieutenant of the Crown.

There was a little delay and then a curious scuffling and clanking sound. In at the dais doorway backed two distinctly alarmed-looking servitors in the royal livery, pulling on chains. Suddenly one stumbled forward and all but fell as the chains went slack, whilst his colleague leapt as though bitten. Into the Hall after them, at a hampered, crouching, belly-down rush came the lioness, shackles dragging on the stone floor, tufted tail whipping from side to side, fangs bared, rumbling deeply in its throat. Behind, holding a gold-tasselled lead attached to the animal's jewel-studded collar, strolled David Stewart, magnificent in cloth-of-gold and scarlet, smiling genially.

Men gasped and exclaimed, some women screamed. The stumbling servant only just managed to get out of the creature's path in time. The strange group came forward to mid-dais, as the herald and trumpeters drew hastily aside. Then, at a flick of the prince's free hand, the attendants circled back, with their leashes taut, to pull strongly to halt the brute's onward movement. Still smiling, the Duke stooped to pat the slow-swinging, ears-flattened yellow head — while everywhere breaths were held. The lioness showed more of her great white teeth in a lip-curling snarl, but the man did not cease to stroke, and the snarl sank to a low muttering sound. Straightening up, David turned to take a raw leg of mutton from a third servitor at his back, and stooping again, held it out to the beast. At first it turned its fierce head away, and the rumbling deepened in its chest. Then abruptly it flashed back and snapped the offering from the prince's hand. Head hanging low, it sought to move off sidelong, with the meat, towards a corner. Restrained by the leashes and shackles, it sank down to the floor, mutton between its mighty forepaws, and started to tear at the red flesh. Instead of the growl, a throaty purring sounded.

David Stewart stood up, and waved casually towards the trumpeters.

A spontaneous if ragged cheer rose from the watching company — from the men, at any rate.

The trumpeters produced another fanfare — but loud and

strident as it was it by no means could drown the hoarse coughing roar as the lioness started up again, angered, meat dropped, yellow eyes gleaming. The Duke stooped, to speak soothingly. The trumpeting died away but the building-shaking roars continued for a little, accompanied by the prince's silvery laughter. Lyon King of Arms, who had come in behind during the fanfare, perforce waited until the alarming challenge at length faded, before he announced, in noticeably less ringing fashion than was his usual, the arrival of the puissant and right royal prince, Robert, *Ard Righ*, by God's grace High King of Scots.

Again there was delay. But at length the monarch came limping in, on the arm of his sister Isabel, former Countess of Douglas. He wore, although untidily, a splendid purple cloak embroidered with gold and trimmed with fur, and on his brow the royal golden circlet as crown. He peered short-sightedly at the waiting company, looked askance at the lioness, and veering well away from the brute's vicinity, made for one of the two chairs-of-state set in mid-dais, bowed sadly to the perfunctory cheers, and sat down. The Lady Isabel seated herself on a stool at his elbow, and her illegitimate half-sister Mary came and stood behind.

Jamie made his unobtrusive way to the rear of the dais.

Lyon stepped forward, made obeisance to the monarch, and turned, hand on high.

"I am commanded by the King's Highness that His Grace is now pleased to receive the august person of the high and mighty prince Richard, by God's grace King of England," he cried.

Into the stir the trumpets blared out again — and once more the roar shook the hammer-beam timbers of the roof. Clearly Leonora did not like trumpets. Fortunately this was a fairly brief fanfare. King Robert half-rose in agitation, with Isabel and Mary Stewart seeking to calm him. David stood, at ease, waving the gold-tasselled leash gently to and fro.

At the far foot of the Hall the main door was thrown open and another herald strode in, equally imposingly garbed and likewise supported by trumpeters — Sir John Stewart of Ardgowan, newly-created Albany Herald. This time, the instrumentalists' flourish being so much further away, only produced a tail-swinging snort. The newcomer announced the most noble and excellent Lord Robert, Duke of Albany, Earl of Fife and Menteith, Justiciar of Fife, Menteith and Strathearn and High

177

Chamberlain of Scotland, escorting his guest Richard, by the Grace of God, King of England.

Three men entered, two and one. Albany was in his usual dignified and sober black-and-silver, stiffly upright. At his side walked a heavier though slightly stooping figure, with notably pale features, peculiar heavy-lidded eyes, long fair hair to his shoulders, a down-turning moustache and a small pointed beard. His dress was nondescript and far from kingly, but he too wore a simple gold circlet round his brows. Behind, considerably more eye-catching than either, came Donald, Lord of the Isles, in the full panoply of Highland dress, vivid tartans and flashing jewellery.

All eyes were on the stranger nevertheless. Most there were undoubtedly surprised to see so comparatively young a man; for though Richard Plantagenet had been on the throne for twenty-two years, he was now but thirty-three. This man, although he held himself with a careful dignity, had little aspect of a king — but then, neither had their own monarch. All searched his features for an answer to the question, true or false? He had a pursed-up, slightly petulant mouth and a nervous frown. The trouble was that none there had ever seen King Richard. He had only once crossed into Scotland, and that was in 1385 when he had come with fire and sword, burning Melrose, Dryburgh and Newbattle Abbeys and many towns— for which invasion Otterburn had been delayed retaliation. He could only have been nineteen then. Anyway none of the few who might have seen him were here present.

People drew aside to allow the trio clear passage up the Hall; but the stir and eager whispering was very evident. Attention was concentrated on them and their progress, until a sudden, angry snoring snarl jerked every glance elsewhere. The clank of iron shackles, and the scuffle and thud as one of the Duke of Rothesay's servitors was pulled off his feet, ensured a change in concern. The rumbling growl continued.

Jamie Douglas, standing behind, was one of the very few who could have observed David Stewart's quick foot movement. He had shrewdly kicked the partially devoured leg of mutton from between his lioness's paws at a moment when the brute had her head raised, and thereby successfully resumed possession of the centre of the stage, as it were. Leonora was up on her feet again, tail lashing, meat back between her jaws.

The three newcomers had faltered in their dignified pacing,

178

staring, obviously only just become aware of the great animal's presence. As the menacing noise continued they came to a halt, astonished.

The prince waved an encouraging hand, smiling. "Come, Uncle," he called. "Fear nothing. You and your guests are entirely safe, I do assure you!"

It was cunningly, wickedly done — and the narrowing of Albany's eyes and tightening of his mouth revealed his full recognition of the fact. He grasped his companion's elbow and all but propelled him onwards to the dais at an increased pace.

Jamie exchanged glances with his wife behind the throne. The lioness sank down, to resume her interrupted meal. The King emitted something like a groan.

It was noticeable how well to the far side from the prince the new arrivals made their ascent to the dais. Distinctly to the King's left front, they stood, and bowed — if Albany's could be called a bow — and so waited.

King Robert cleared his throat and hoisted himself unsteadily to his feet. "Brother — I thank you," he said thickly. "Cousin Richard — I greet you well. Welcome you warmly to my Court. I, I rejoice that Your Grace has survived the assaults of evil men — aye, evil men. And found secure refuge in this my realm."

The other bowed again. "I thank Your Grace, from my heart," he said, in a very slightly lisping voice. "I throw myself upon your royal compassion and mercy. Until such time as I shall win back my rightful throne." That came out in something of a rush, as well it might.

There was a silence as all considered the implications of that last sentence made thus so soon.

"Oh, aye." King Robert looked about him doubtfully.

Albany spoke. "Sire — it has been my pleasure and privilege to succour and aid King Richard, and to bring him into your royal presence. With the help of our nephew Donald, here, Lord of the Isles."

"I saw Donald," the monarch said. Although the Islesman was not actually an outlaw at present, he was not far off it, and dubiously welcome at Court.

There was another pause. Oddly enough, the Duke of Rothesay had now turned partly away from the central group, and was stooping, to murmur at his lioness. He was clearly not enthusing over the new arrivals.

The Lady Isabel, who had risen with her brother, now touched his arm and glanced towards the second chair-of-state.

The King nodded. "Cousin Richard," he said, "here is my sister Isa, umquhile Countess of Douglas. Woe is me, my lady-wife is sick. See you — sit here, by my side."

Bowing to the princess, the visitor seated himself on the second chair without a word. Albany moved over to stand at his side. The King glanced over towards his son, got no response there, and sighing, resumed his seat.

The silence returned, save for the crunching of a sheep's leg-bone. Men fidgeted.

Donald of the Isles spoke up. "Uncle — I hope that I see you well? And grieve to hear of my royal aunt's sickness." His gentle Highland voice belied his reputation. "It is long since we forgathered. I welcome this opportunity to visit your Court from my island territories." It was the civil speech of a fellow-ruler rather than any subject.

The King pulled at an already slack lower lip. "To be sure," he muttered. "But your brother — yon Alastair. He did much mischief. He took possession of our castle of Urquhart. To our displeasure."

"Alastair is young, sire. Headstrong. I have him confined on Islay . . ."

David Stewart snapped his fingers, ostensibly at the lioness but looked quickly towards Jamie, and jerked his head barely perceptibly. That man moved the two or three steps over to his wife's side, and whispered briefly. As he stepped back, Mary spoke quietly to her half-sister. Isabel murmured in the King's ear.

"Aye, then," the monarch said, when Donald had finished. "That is as may be." He turned. "Now, Richard — I'd have you to meet my son and heir, David, Duke of Rothesay and Lieutenant of my realm."

The prince strolled forward and bowed elaborately. But it was to his father that he looked. "Your Grace." Then he turned his head slightly — but sufficiently to make the distinction clear. "My lord Richard — here is a notable occasion. So miraculous an escape from peril. So unexpected a sanctuary for you to seek, in our dangerous northern kingdom! We are honoured indeed!"

"I thank you, my lord David. I rejoice to see you. I have heard much of you."

"Little to my good, I fear!" He raised an eyebrow towards his

Uncle Robert, and grinned. "But perhaps it was from *your* uncle that you heard it?"

The other hesitated for just a moment. "I, I hear it on all hands," he said. "Your lordship's fame is widespread."

"You are too kind, sir. It was your Uncle Edmund I meant, of course. Edmund, Duke of York."

"Indeed, my lord? I did not know that you were acquainted with York. I assumed that you meant John of Lancaster."

"Ah, yes — John of Gaunt, God rest his soul. We met, to be sure. But I should think that it was my Uncle Albany here who made the greater impression on *him*! They found much to . . . debate. As no doubt Duke John reported to you?"

The other moistened his lips. "The Duke of Lancaster reported nothing to me, my lord."

"Ah . . ."

Albany intervened. "Sire, our nephew Donald was most fortunate in having on his island a lady who had met King Richard when in Ireland recently. Before he returned to deal with his cousin Henry Bolingbroke's shameful treason. This woman, Irish, wife to one of the MacDonald chieftains, rejoiced to see His Grace of England again, and to discuss with him the situation prevailing in Ireland. A happy chance."

"Indeed, yes," Donald agreed. "Sadly as the King's position had changed in the few months, whatever."

"Most . . . fortuitous," David commented. "It interests me greatly to learn why our distinguished guest chose to come to Scotland, a realm which he has called barbarous and with which he has been at war? Rather than to France, shall we say, where his good-brother is King?" Richard had married fairly recently, as his second wife, the child-sister of the mad King Charles the Sixth. "Or to Ireland, from which he had just returned, and where he had an army."

King Robert looked unhappy at this only slightly veiled public testing of the visitor. "Cousin Richard will tell us all these matters anon, Davie," he said. It was not often that he thus asserted himself. "We mustna weary him, new-come."

"I came here, sire, because I had little choice," the other said, carefully. "I escaped from Pontefract Castle and fled, with the help of two loyal servants, to the west. Across the moors and fells to Furness in Lancaster, in secret. At Cartmel, the good Brothers found for me a small craft sailing for Man. I dared not go to a larger haven, where I might be sought for. At Man was

181

a MacDonald galley sailing back to the Sudreys — to Islay, my lord Donald's isle. None to France or Ireland. My lord and I had had dealings. I journeyed there, and he entreated me kindly."

"A notable progress, sir," David conceded. "We all congratulate you, I am sure." He glanced at Mary Stewart, one eyebrow raised.

She spoke quietly to her half-sister, and Isabel spoke to the King.

"Aye — that is so," the monarch nodded. "Before we retire to eat, Cousin, I'd have you to meet certain of my great lords and kin, here present. My good-brother the Earl of Crawford. My nephew the Earl of Moray. My brother's good-son the Earl of Ross. My lord Bishop of St. Andrews. Aye, and others . . ."

The coming to the dais of these notables set the lioness off on a further angry growling — to considerable alarm. But since it was clearly the High Steward's and Lieutenant's animal, none might protest — save one, Robert Stewart.

"Sire," Albany declared. "This ill-disposed and ill-trained brute-beast, seemingly my nephew's, may be well enough at a fair or in a bear-pit — but is insufferable and unsuitable at your royal audience. It stinks! I pray you, have it removed."

The King looked almost relieved. "Aye, Davie — it's an unco' fierce creature that. I'd liefer it was . . . elsewhere, lad."

"Why, surely, Sire — if that is your wish. But my uncle need not be so fearful. And as for being unsuitable, what could be more suitable at a royal audience than a lion, the proud symbol of your Crown and of the royal house of this realm? It could even be more rampant! Perhaps we could find a leopard for your Plantagenet guest? And it might be, some less forthright animal for the Duke of Albany. A jackal, perhaps . . .?" And with a happy laugh, the prince bowed and sauntered back, to superintend the far from straightforward exit of Leonora.

During the upheaval and subsequent presentation of notables, Jamie moved close to his wife again, behind the thrones.

"I do not understand what David is at," he muttered. "Is he drunk, think you?"

"He is always drunk — and never drunk!" Mary said. "You know that. He is using the lioness to distract attention from the Mammet and his uncle, to upset them — for his own purposes . . ."

"I know that, yes. It is not the lion I mean. It is this of the

182

Englishman, king or none. David told me that he was to be accepted as Richard Plantagenet — a matter of policy, he said. Against Henry. Now he seems to be throwing doubt on him before all. Seeking to catch him out. Spoiling his own policy . . ."

"If I know Davie, it is all planned. I think he covers himself, in case the Mammet *is* proved an impostor. The King to accept him, yes — but if aught goes wrong, as well it may, David Stewart knew better! And all here to witness. And to make Robert look a fool . . ."

"His father likewise."

"I fear most consider the King a fool already. Though he is scarce that . . ."

The repast that followed, held in an ante-room, was not a banquet but a more modest and intimate meal for only about a dozen or so of the royal family and guests. The Lady Isabel, deputising for the Queen, and Mary seated on her left, were the only women present. The alleged Richard Plantagenet sat between Isabel and the King, with Albany at his brother's other side. David sat across the table, flanked by Donald of the Isles and Crawford. Jamie Douglas did not sit at all, standing throughout behind the prince as acting cupbearer — just as Sir Andrew Moray of Pettie, the hereditary cupbearer, did behind the King.

It was not a riotously successful meal. Indeed, had not David kept things going with wit, sallies and toasts, all barbed but genially so, it would have proceeded largely in silence. Donald was a good talker, and intelligent, and did his best; but he was largely shunned by all save the prince, looked on askance. Isabel also, with her instructions from her nephew, sought to engage the Mammet in conversation to discover what she could as to his *bona fides* — with scant success. Civil enough, he was not forthcoming. Throughout, primed by Mary with points relayed by Jamie from the prince, she asked leading questions in as innocent a way as she could, questions which one who was not King Richard could have difficulty in answering. At the end she was little the wiser, the guest parrying not so much skilfully as blankly — although on occasion he did vouchsafe a reply which sounded genuine, and indicated intimate knowledge of Richard. The trouble was that none might cross-question, or persist in probing in converse with a monarch, even a displaced one. If he was genuine, he was one of the Lord's Anointed. So long as he claimed to be so and they were not in a position to prove otherwise, the position remained in a kind of deadlock.

Oddly enough, he who perhaps ought to have been in the best position to judge, the other and true Lord's Anointed, seemed to be well enough content and well-disposed towards the newcomer. It might be that his own personal inadequacies and sense of being found wanting made him sympathetic towards the other, in fellow-feeling for a man overtaken by events too large for him. Whatever the cause, he appeared to get on well with his guest, and in fact throughout treated him as a fellow-monarch — which made it all the more difficult for others to do less.

None, however, felt like prolonging the meal unduly. Albany was the first to show evident signs that enough was enough — but even he, with two monarchs present, could not rise from the table until they did. He did work on his brother, nevertheless, declaring sufficiently loudly for the visitor to hear, that if they were to get back to Doune Castle before dark it was full time to be on their way.

The King was nodding acceptance when his son across the table cleared his throat.

"We must not detain Uncle Robert nor yet Cousin Donald, Sire," he said. "Perhaps they will wish to see the Lord Richard to his quarters in the North Tower before they take leave of him? It will be my pleasure to conduct them thither."

His father looked nervous. "Oh, aye," he said.

Albany sat up straight. "What mean you by that?" he demanded. "His Grace of England returns with me to Castle Doune."

"Ah, but no, Uncle. All is prepared for him, here at Stirling. As is suitable."

"He is my guest . . ."

"He is His *Grace's* guest, surely. Whilst sojourning in His Grace's realm. Would you have Richard of Bordeaux in any lesser place than the King's house, now he is in the King's care? We shall care for him very well, I assure you."

Albany rose to his feet and turned to his brother. "Sire — this is *not* suitable! King Richard is well settled in my house. He must remain with me."

The King looked unhappily between brother and son. In head-shaking disquiet he turned to the man at his other side. "Cousin Richard — how say you? Will you bide with me? Or with my brother?"

184

The other swallowed and looked no more happy than the questioner. "I . . . I am in Your Grace's hands," he said. "I am much honoured by Your Grace's goodwill and hospitality. I . . ."

"Good," David declared. "Well said, sir. All then, is settled. If His Grace permits, we shall proceed then to the North Tower and the Lord Richard's privy comfort. And no longer delay my lords of Albany and the Isles!"

As King Robert rose to his feet, he turned to his brother. "Davie is the Lieutenant now, mind . . ." he said, wearily.

The North Tower was that in the basement of which the lioness was immured.

IX

D AVID STEWART NOW *wanted* it to snow. At least it was not raining. It was cold enough for snow, but there had been frost again that morning, as for the last few days. Jamie Douglas argued that white frost would be better than snow, anyway.

Apart from the weather, all appeared to be as it should be, everything practically in readiness; the vast canopy as secure as it could be; the fires laid and the charcoal-braziers set up, with ample fuel stacked; the long lantern-lines hung from post to post and torch-poles planted; the evergreen shrubs and little fir-trees set out in their tubs in clumps and groves and mazes, with love-seats in the midst; the statuary disposed judiciously; the many trestles placed ready to be laden. Men worked busily everywhere, carrying, hammering, strengthening, their breath steaming in the slightly misty air, as the prince and Douglas, Pate Boyd at their heels, strolled around inspecting.

It was an hour past noontide, on Hogmanay, 1399.

"I would not concern myself too greatly over snow, my lord," Jamie said. "It will do very well lacking that, I think. It is wind that I fear. We should be praying all the saints that the wind does not rise! To blow all this into the Forth!"

"You are a Job's comforter, on my soul!" the prince declared. "Why should a wind arise? Today! We have had scarce a bellyful all winter. Besides, the tentage is strong enough, stronger than it may look. I have had them roping and staying it all week. It will withstand a fair blow."

"An ordinary blow, perhaps. But if a north-west wind off yon Hielant hills sweeps down over the Flanders Moss and hits this castle-rock, there could be down-draughts that could flatten this frail canopy, see you. Worse, if a side-blow, *round* the rock, came underneath, it could lift all up and over the castle itself, your ropes and all!"

"God's wounds, man — have done! You grow worse, I swear!" The Duke turned. "Is not Sir James the most devilish gloomy woemaster in all Scotland, Pate?"

His henchman grinned, and wisely held his peace.

They were standing on the greensward directly below Stirling Castle rock on the south-west side, beside the curious geo-metrically-stepped King's Knot, centre of the King's Garden. It was a large parterre, over four hundred feet square, raised above the level of the rest in extraordinary fashion, octagons within squares of turf rising to a sort of central plateau, round which the rose-gardens were laid out. It was of ancient, some said prehistoric, origin, sometimes called the Round Table from its alleged connection with King Arthur, its summit often used for declamations, play-actings and the like. All around it, for the past week, workmen had been busy transforming this park and garden. Tentage and the tough canvas and sail-cloth used for pavilions had been erected on poles to cover a large area with a multi-coloured canopy — although not entirely covered, for there were gaps and strips left open to the air so that smoke might escape. A long covered-way of more sail-cloth led zig-zagging down from the castle; and another such corridor from the main area went northwards, around the rock-base, for a couple of hundred yards, to a shallow hollow, always water-filled in winter. Towards this the trio walked.

The hollow had been artificially enlarged, as far as its rocky surroundings permitted, and posts bearing pitch-pine torches placed all round it, whilst in the centre a model of a Highland gallery or birlinn had been set up on the ice, almost full-size and looking very fine. But it was the ice itself that held David Stewart's attention.

"See — it is melting. A curse on it — water on top!"

"It usually does, at noontide. It will freeze up again at night-fall — unless the weather changes. Better without your snow, my lord, I say."

"Snow would make it look finer."

"Melting snow on yonder canopies, dripping down, would please none . . ."

Out of character, David was fretful, unrealistic, like a spoiled child, angry that he could not control the weather as he did so much else. He turned, to hurry back and on up to the castle again, his two companions exchanging glances. Money had been outpoured like water for this occasion. None could remember having heard of such lavish spending. The prince was determined to celebrate the start of the new fifteenth century in spectacular fashion, to emphasise the new era represented by his assumption of power, and to show Christendom, England in especial, that Scotland was no impoverished, backward kingdom which Henry Plantagenet or others might assail with impunity. Nowhere else would the year of our Lord, 1400, with all its hopes and possibilities, be welcomed in such style.

The entire town of Stirling was packed with people, to say nothing of the castle and the nearby Abbey of Cambuskenneth and sundry monasteries. Everyone who counted for anything in Scotland had been invited to attend; and since the invitations were in the joint names of the King and his Lieutenant, few had seen fit to refuse, however inconvenient and difficult might be much of the journeying at this season of the year.

Many of the principal guests, of course, had been at Court over the entire Yuletide season, and a lively, not to say hectic interlude it had been, with nothing stinted in victuals, entertainment or display. Indeed not a few declared that this Hogmanay cantrip could scarcely be other than an anti-climax in the circumstances, with little left to contrive. And where all the siller was coming from, nobody knew — for the Treasury had been empty when David had inherited it, and he had scarcely stopped spending since.

It was this aspect of the situation which intrigued Sir Alexander Stewart of Badenoch, newly arrived from the North with a group of Highland chieftains, whom David, for some reason, had been urgent that he should bring. He had not taken long to forgather with Jamie and Mary in the prince's own tower's topmost storey.

"I do not know," Jamie admitted. "About moneys he reveals little, although in most matters he is frank enough. Certainly he is constraining the customs-farmers hard. For years many have been filching moneys right and left, imposing heavier dues than they should and handing on less to the Treasury than was due. The merchants and guilds of the burghs have long complained, but the Governor, Albany, did nothing. He was too deeply in the like business himself. Now David is making the collectors squeal. But I cannot think that all his money can come from them."

"There is a tale that the Church is aiding him," Mary put in. "Bishop Trail is his friend and may help."

"Holy Church give him moneys for spending so?" Alex wondered. "I think he must have others to turn to."

"Not his father, at the least," Mary said. "The King is ever short of siller. The Stewarts never had much of their own, and needs must marry it! As did I! And *your* father, Alex. But not John. Annabella Drummond brought him little."

"David wed a Douglas," her nephew-of-a-sort pointed out. "Can it be her money he spends so lavishly?"

"I think not," Jamie said. "The Earl Archie was too canny to let his new good-son get his hands on more than the dowry-money. He is not pleased with the way his daughter is being treated, I think."

"How is the old man? I heard that he was sorely sick."

"Better. He is here. But not the man he was. I fear it may not be long before we have a new Earl of Douglas."

"David kept the money he got as dowry for his proposed wedding to the Earl of Dunbar's daughter," Mary added. "How much, I never heard tell. But they say it was a deal. And now that Dunbar has fled to England, and breathing threats, he can be called a traitor — and no moneys need be paid back to traitors! I do not think that Davie has much to learn from Robert!"

"That was ill done . . ." Jamie agreed heavily.

The timing of the evening's festivities presented something of a problem. It was dark soon after four in the afternoon, and the programme could begin any time thereafter. But the New Year did not come in until eight hours later. Since quite an ambitious procedure was planned, it was important that at least a major proportion of the company should still be sober enough to appreciate and take part. Which meant no early start. On the other hand, if justice was to be done to the refreshments provided, as well as the laws of hospitality not outraged, feeding could not be delayed until late at night; yet to provide an extra banquet in the castle, before moving down to the King's Knot garden, would spoil the effect for later. No large proportion of those attending could be provided for in the castle anyway, numbers being what they were, and the majority therefore had to make their own arrangements in the town. So only a modest meal was set before the principal guests in the late afternoon, with the liquor supply strictly limited — to considerable complaint — and all were instructed to assemble in the great hall at ten o'clock.

It was still not snowing at that hour — but neither was there wind nor rain, and the frost was beginning to sparkle in a rising half-moon. Folk had come variously garbed, some as for winter outdoor activities, others in Court or evening dress — although few of these had omitted to come provided with warm cloaks. Despite all precautions, some were already noticeably drink-taken, if not drunk. Jamie Douglas and his wife were, as usual as it were on duty, he to act general factotum to the prince, she to attend on no fewer than three of her half-sister princesses, present without husbands. But meantime their services were not required, and they waited, along with Alex Stewart and the generality of the palace guests, in the smoky but warm great hall. The less privileged perforce had to wait outside on the level tourney-ground fronting the castle gatehouse — although here large bonfires had been lit to give at least the illusion of warmth.

Promptly, as ten struck on the town bells below, a resplendent figure appeared from the dais doorway, clad in the gorgeous tabard of Lyon King of Arms, but below it baggy striped pantaloons, on his head a fool's cap-of-bells and in his hand instead of Lyon's baton a notably large and springy bull's tool with which he made great play. In ringing if falsetto tones he commanded,

"Silence, lords and gentles — silence, obeisance and humble duty for their sublime Majesties the King and Queen!" There-after he belched loudly and cut a caper.

The somewhat doubtful laughter, and remarks on the phras-ing of "Majesty" instead of the accustomed "Grace", a Con-tinental style, was lost in music, not the usual brassy fanfare of trumpets but the cheerful cascading melody of violins playing the lightsome measure of a favourite jig. In came a company of a dozen fiddlers dressed in the copes and chaubles of high clerics, with mitres on their heads somewhat askew, and dancing as they played. And after a suitable gap, the royal couple appeared, wearing gleaming crowns and the magnificent purple and furred robes of monarchy, the King's beard long, brushed and snowy, the Queen's hair glittering with jewels and piled high up through her crown. They also came skipping and swaying to the music, though in a more stately fashion, skilfully adjusting to only every second beat of the rhythm. But stately

190

movements or none, the motion inevitably swung open the splendid cloaks of both quite frequently — to reveal that the King possessed a woman's shapely bare legs beneath and a definitely black triangle at the groin despite the white beard, while the Queen boasted particularly sinewy and hairy legs and well-developed masculinity above. The faces of both were not exactly masked, but coated with a sort of paste, ruddy for the monarch and white for his consort, very effective.

"I see that we are to have a lively evening!" Mary commented, into the cheering and laughter. "If this is paid for by Holy Church, then I fear that stream is like to dry up!"

"Cousin David has a nice wit," Alex observed. "I daresay his father will forbear comment. But what of his mother? She is here?"

"Yes — although less than well. She will chide him, but gently. Jamie — do not look so shocked! It is but Up Halie Day and Twelfth Night guizardry a night or two early! The Lord of Misrule . . ."

"It is unseemly. An ill mockery of the Crown, when the Crown needs propping up and supporting, not pulling down. Yon is young Michael Stewart, son to your own half-brother, Sir John of Bute, the Sheriff. Who ought to know better."

"Is he so? From what is to be seen, _I_ would not have known! But no doubt you have the better of me, there. Are you equally knowledgeable as to the lady, Jamie?"

"Not so. But she could do with a skelping, I say."

"And I say, not from you, my dear!"

Out after the pseudo-regal pair came a column of gaily-clad revellers, led by the Duke and Duchess of Rothesay. David was resplendent, dressed all in white satin, seeded with Tay pearls and gold — which might on some have looked effeminate but on David Stewart certainly did not. He appeared to have made no provision for cold or inclement weather. At his side, the Lady Mary Douglas, looking positively dowdy by comparison, her sallow features good enough but heavy, unsmiling, her clothing rich but worn without grace. Behind came the dark-eyed, good-looking young Prince James, now aged six, walking alone, with a sort of wary excitement, followed by his three sisters and their Douglas husbands, the Earl of Angus, the Master of Douglas and Sir James, Younger of Dalkeith, Jamie's legitimate half-brother. Then the three princesses of the previous generation, the Ladies Isabel, Marjorie, Dowager of

Moray, and Gelis, widow of Sir Will Douglas of Nithsdale. The last seldom indeed attended Court, having become something of a recluse although she was the youngest and most beautiful of the King's sisters. Behind trooped the other important house-guests. Not all smiled so happily as did Scotland's High Steward.

The capering master-of-ceremonies turned, and raised his peculiar baton to quieten the fiddlers. David bowed low in an elaborate genuflection towards the mock King and Queen.

"May it please Your Serene Majesties," he said. "We shall all follow you down to the Round Table of your renowned ancestor King Arthur, where due entertainment and refreshment will be provided. My royal sire and mother will come to pay their respects later. Proceed, Highnesses."

The music struck up again, and preceded by the Lyon-fool, they all streamed out into the chill night air, to pass down through the upper and lower courtyards, the inner, counter and outer guards and through the gatehouse arch to cross the drawbridge to the forecourt tourney-ground, where the great throng waited by the light of bonfires, the steam of their breath rising into the air like a cloud. Much cheering greeted their arrival, but the light was insufficient to reveal much of the style and costume of the leaders. No pause was made here, and the tabarded guide swung away right-handed with his busy skipping musicians, towards the edge of the dark void which was the southern rim of the castle-rock. Reaching this lip, he paused for a few moments as a shadowy figure materialised out of the gloom, uncovered a hidden charcoal brazier, lit a pitch-pine torch therefrom and tossed it high into the air, blazing.

As folk exclaimed and the fiddlers jigged, there was an astonishing reaction to that signal. All down the steep path that zigzagged back and forth across the rocky face of the hill, torches flared up in the darkness, hundreds of them on their poles — which implied hundreds of men waiting there to light them from little hooded braziers. Admittedly they did not all burst into flame at the identical moment; but the pitch-impregnated turpentine-pine bunches of slivers took fire in almost every case immediately, and the effect was extraordinary. The town did not extend round to this side of the rock, only the royal park, so that all had been a pit of gloom, with the half-moon to the east. Now this brilliant alleyway of light led down into the gulf, beckoning, conjuring a myriad coruscations from the hoar-frost — yet making the surrounding night seem but the blacker.

Loud acclaim greeted this transformation, and the descent commenced, between the twisting and turning double line of torches. Mary had gone to join the princesses, but their nephew seemed to have no need for Jamie's services meantime, and he remained with Alex Stewart, now joined by his Highland chieftains, all in manifest wonder and delight at what they saw.

The progress down the cliff was a lengthy process for so large a company, for the path was inevitably narrow and a little slippery, with innumerable sharp dog's-leg bends, and fairly steep even so. Fortunately there were guard-rails at the danger-points. There was fully 350 feet of descent, practically sheer, and the track had to pick its route this way and that, sometimes making quite lengthy traverses along shelves and ledges to find a passage. Some few of the guests had come this way, of course, on previous occasions, to the King's Knot gardens; but it is safe to say none had done so of a winter's night.

When the front of the long, chattering procession was two-thirds of the way down, and the path slanting ever more towards the west now, a shout went up ahead. There was a great pressing forward and questioning, to learn what this heralded — clearly those in front could see round the contours of the great rock something as yet invisible to the majority. But that there was a widespread glow of light, and growing brighter, was evident.

When Jamie and Alex rounded the bend in the cliff, with less than another hundred feet to descend, even the former was surprised by the effect, although he had helped in its con-trivance. The little plain below and in front, really a wide terrace of the castle-hill before the undulating grasslands of the New Park and the Raploch Moss, looked tonight like a veritable fairyland, the province of the little folk, brownies, trolls and the like of which the minstrels were so fond of singing. This was caused by the light of many hundreds more torches shining and filtering through the great acreage of tenting and coloured awnings, diffusing, blending, irradiating. Even the smoke — for pitch-pine torches are by no means smokeless — seemed to be disciplined by the gaps and lanes in the covering, and thereafter, shot through with reflected tints and rosy hues, coiled and eddied upwards in unnatural or supernatural fashion into the frosty air as though with its own curious and infernal life. Bonfires by the score were beginning to blaze all around the

193

perimeter, their leaping flames contrasting with the mellower glow from under the canopy. The glitter of the frost added the final touch of unreality to a scene such as never before had been beheld.

The entry to the covered area itself, thereafter, was productive of even louder cries and gasps. For here, suddenly, they were in another land, a land of light and warmth and growing things, of plants and shrubs, bushes and trees, gleaming statuary, sparkling fountains and grassy paths, all beneath a multi-hued heaven on which painted gods and goddesses disported themselves with marked abandon and from which tinsel stars and planets dangled and spun in the heat eddies. The warmth came from the many glowing charcoal braziers, almost smokeless, and although smoke did come from the torches, the draught system coped remarkably well. The curious physical feature of the raised turf platform, the King's Knot itself, or part of it, was hidden by screens.

The weary fiddlers were now superseded by the music of hidden instrumentalists in the groves and shrubberies, playing gentler, softer music. It did not take long for many of the guests, after the initial impact, to discover the presence of numerous tables, amongst the tubs and bushes, laden with food and drink in great variety and lavish quantities, and to descend on these in force. Although not a few were distracted by the large central fountain spouting red-coloured jets and sprays, which proved to be wine.

The master-of-ceremonies, after allowing a little time for these delights to be perceived and sampled, leapt up on to the edge of the oddly-shaped grassy mound, its geometrical intricacies not so obvious from here as from high above, and there performed a few cart-wheels and similar gyrations to attract attention, singularly ridiculous-seeming in his dignified herald's tabard which tended of course to fall over his head and envelop him. Then, having gained the notice and heed of at least a fair proportion of the company, he beckoned the mock King and Queen up, with much bowing and scraping, on to the Knot, where he led them to twin thrones at one side, where he prayed them to be seated. As they sat down, the rear legs collapsed under both chairs and the pair toppled over backwards with a spectacular waving of their own white legs in the air, to the edification of the beholders. It took an unconscionable time to right them, during which it was amply proved, to the satisfaction of even the most distant or short-

194

sighted, that not only the lower quarters of the couple were bare. Considerable fuss was made too about fixing the legs back on the chairs so that the royal pair might gingerly reseat themselves, their herald reassuringly patting them the while and carefully arranging the purple robes so that they remained parted from the waist downwards. Then, clapping his hands, he gestured towards the screened half of the mound.

The curtaining was thereafter drawn aside by invisible hands, and there, lit by more torches on particularly high poles, was a scene which immediately held every eye and had the effect of stilling all the chatter and laughter remarkably. A great circle of standing-stones was set on the inner and higher tier of the Knot, which was some 200 feet square, tall, stark, timeless, fifteen of them, with two lofty portal-stones or pointers facing east, and near these a large horizontal recumbent, flat like table or altar. Stern, immutable, the monoliths stood, as though they had been there for generations untold — although in fact they had been brought from far and near and erected there, with infinite labour, only two days before — and some aura of awe and power and even menace about them, speaking to the race-memory in them all, kept the gathering silent.

The hush was broken, for the music had died away, by the sound of a strange chanting which rose and fell, singing sweet yet somehow relentless, quietly emphatic. From beyond the Knot, from a thicket of bushes contrived there, emerged a slow-moving shadowy procession; first white-robed figures with mistletoe wreaths around their white headcloths and snakeskin girdles; then the chanting choir, men and boys clad in the skins of wolf and deer; then four young men wearing only loincloths, their glistening bodies painted with broad vertical stripes of black and white, pacing spaced out to form a square and each holding the realistically-devised head of a snake. Each snake was stretched out so far, until its tail was clamped in the mouth of a second serpent, the young men rippling their serpentine chains in lifelike fashion as they walked. The second four snakes' tails joined at a single central girdle composed of more of the coiled reptiles, and this around the white waist of a fair and completely naked young woman of most lovely form and carriage, walking in mid-square and sobbing as she walked. Behind came more choristers and two further white-garbed Druid priests carrying long and curling bulls' horns.

The procession moved deliberately on round the perimeter of

the stone-circle, to halt outside the tall portal-stones, the chanting continuing. Its members, and the company, waited tensely, the girl's sobs punctuating the singing. Then, infinitely slowly a great shining disc began to appear beyond the circle, at the far side of the Knot. Of beaten metal, painted red, unseen torches before and behind made it seem to glow. Actually this rising sun had to be to the west of the circle, since all the crowd was gathered to the east; but this detail in no way detracted from the illusion. As gradually the disc rose, so rose the volume and tempo of the chanting.

When at last all the round sun was visible, seeming to hang between the twin horns of the portal-stones, the now fierce chanting was cut off abruptly and into the quivering silence which succeeded sounded the hollow booming ululations of the bulls' horns, an unchancy, sepulchral resonance. The chief of the Druids paced slowly forward through the portals to the recumbent table-stone and there turned to face the company. He raised his left hand high.

While the horns continued to wail and moan, the four young men drew the weeping girl out after the priest, into the circle. With stylised motions they took her in hand, lifted her between them and laid her, writhing, on the altar, where each held her flat by wrist or ankle.

The Druid raised his right hand, and in it was seen to gleam the blade of a long knife. When it was at the full height of his arms, and now gripped by both hands, he paused. The horns ceased to sound.

The choristers burst out into a single brief yelping shout, and down flashed the knife. There was a high thin scream. Then the silence returned.

Blood, red and wet-looking, had somehow appeared on the gleaming white breasts. Leaning forward the priest dabbled a hand in it, and turned to sprinkle each of the young men at the far side of the altar in turn. Then, moving round, his back to them and the altar and sacrifice, he held both reddened hands up and out towards the sun, and so remained.

A triumphant savage hymn rose now from the choristers, who also paced on into the circle. Unseen hands closed the curtain-screen once again.

Men and women turned to eye each other strangely, as a vast corporate sigh rose on the night air. There was none of the normal applause or clamour.

"That was . . . telling," Alex Stewart said, a little thickly. "Oddly conceived. Forgive one reared in the ignorant and barbaric Highlands — but what did it signify?"

Jamie moistened his lips. "There is an ancient tale that this Stirling was once an important centre of Druidic sun-worship, under the name of Mons Dolorum, the Mound of Pain, later Snawdoun. This mound, now the King's Knot, was the sacrificial shrine. David but puts the clock back some score of centuries."

"He himself devised this?"

"To be sure. Prompted by the man who has become his dark shadow."

"Ramorgnie, you mean?"

"Aye, Sir John de Ramorgnie, the Prolocutor-General. That man is evil. But clever — too clever. And bold. Ambitious. He has come to be ever in the prince's company of late, pandering, urging, whispering. Yet he was and is Albany's vassal, from the Howe of Fife. I believe that he is still Albany's man."

They looked to where Rothesay stood, amidst a high-born throng, his wife no longer with him, replaced by a bevy of more demonstrative and alluring ladies, at his elbow a darkly handsome man of early middle years, slender, elegant in crimson and silver that contrasted with the fair prince's white satin.

"You credit Ramorgnie with a hand in this?"

"Oh, yes. He is a great scholar and student of history and legend — the darker the better. I say that it was a bad day when he was put on the prince's Council, as its secretary — at Albany's instigation I have no doubt."

Jamie would hardly have admitted it, of course, but part of his dislike of the lawyer and Prolocutor might well have stemmed from the fact that in some degree he had begun to supersede the Douglas in David Stewart's close service. As tonight.

Alex shrugged. "Ramorgnie would need a long spoon to outsup Cousin Davie," he said. "Albany himself is not here tonight?"

"No. Invited, with all others, of course. But he keeps his distance from Court now — save at Council meetings. Although he has no lack of spies and informants, I swear!"

A wheepling on a flute drew all eyes to the agile master-of-ceremonies, who waved and announced that their sublime and serene Majesties were pleased to welcome to their Hogmanay Court and presence two more terrestrial sovereigns, the earthbound King and Queen of Scots and King Richard of England, whom all the powers of the upper and nether world preserve and protect.

All turned, to see King Robert and his wife, with the Mammet, come limping down, with a group of attendants — and now it was not the King who leant on Annabella's arm, but the reverse. The Queen was indeed grievously changed, and though she still held herself with calm dignity, her pale frailty was evident. And emphasising this sad physical deterioration, as the newcomers emerged into the brighter illumination, it could be seen that immediately behind the royal couple, with the alleged Richard Plantagenet, came hirpling the Earl of Douglas, walking with the aid of a stick. He had always had a stooping, almost crouching stance, a stooping eagle had been one punning description; now he was merely a bent old man, thin, his great shoulders shrunk. Archie the Grim was grim no longer. His Duchess-daughter now was with him, holding his arm. In that group the Mammet looked almost robust, if depressed somewhat.

The King's party mounted the Knot, to group themselves around the three chairs placed opposite those of the mock-royalties. Somebody fetched a stool for the old Earl.

Jamie heard his companion draw a quick breath, as a variation in the light-and-shadow revealed that one of the ladies behind Annabella was Isobel, Countess of Mar. He glanced at his friend.

"Her ladyship has her husband with her, this time," he observed. "That is Sir Malcolm Drummond at Crawford's side."

"Indeed," Alex said evenly. "I have yet to meet Sir Malcolm. The Queen looks ill. I am sorry, for she is much needed. By both husband and son, I think." He paused. "And that, then, is your Mammet? I do not see him very well, from here — but he looks younger than I had thought."

"Richard would be but thirty-three years."

"Would be? You still believe this to be an impostor?"

"Who knows? Say that I cannot quite believe him to be the King. Nor does the prince. But his father does, I think, and accepts him as something of a friend."

"The King is scarcely a fool, however weakly he acts. He must have his reasons."

"Fellow-feeling, perhaps, for another man in distress."

"But surely he would have discovered the man's falsity by now, if he sees so much of him? It must be evident whether or no he *knows* the close things of Richard's life?"

"He does know much. See you, the prince, to try to discover the truth, has had his spies and informants in England to make enquiry — especially when he heard that King Henry himself seems to be in some doubt on the matter. And the spies have uncovered a strange story. It seems that Richard of Bordeaux had a favourite chaplain, of whom he was very fond. Called Master Richard Maudlyn, or Richard the Magdalene. He was notably like the King in looks, almost a double. Indeed they were whispered to be half-brothers, both sons of the Black Prince, this Maudlyn illegitimate. It seems that on occasion they would exchange clothing, and this Maudlyn play the monarch and the King the priest — a useful means of discovering much of interest for a ruler. So, it seems, none can be fully certain which it was that was slain at Pontefract, Richard or this chaplain. Or whether the Mammet here is indeed king or priest."

"Save us — what a coil!"

"The prince considers the Mammet to be Maudlyn, not King Richard. He never calls him Sire or Grace, but only the Lord Richard, whatever others do. Yet it serves his purposes to hold him here, little better than a hostage or prisoner, as possible threat against Henry. For there is a party unfavourable to Henry in England, who are prepared to support the notion that this *is* Richard for their own ends. And this could help keep Henry Plantagenet from Scotland's throat."

"I suppose that there is nothing so strange in all this. *We* are both bastards . . ."

A blowing of horns halted their talk, and drew all eyes to the King's Knot again. The curtains were drawn aside. The stone-circle was still there — since its great monoliths could by no means be moved without enormous labour — but within it a very different scene was portrayed. A throne was set up in the midst, with a noble-looking man sitting, having shoulder-length hair and a small square beard, wearing a curious long coat, girdled with a gold belt and ornamented with intricate Celtic patterning, on the breast a most peculiar beast embroidered, never known to man, having a long snout, curled feet and tail and a lappet on the crown of the head. Around the throne were grouped many men, all clad in these long coats almost to the ankles, some being warriors bearing swords and spears, with small square shields, others holding aloft banners and poles topped with curious devices, the mysterious Pictish symbols of double-disc and Z-rod, crescent and V-rod, serpent and Z-rod, mirror and comb, tongs and the like. These designs, which everyone knew from the many symbol-stones scattered about the land but none could interpret, established the group as their ancestors the Picts, presumably with one of their kings. The men spoke by turn, and the king answered — but in a language none there could understand, even the Gaelic-speakers. In the background harps thrummed softly, vibrant. Then the sound of chanting voices began to filter through and supersede both talk and harping. This chanting was very different from that of the previous interlude, sweet, harmonious but assured as it was dignified. Once again light grew in the west; but not a sunrise this time, merely increasing illumination, widespread, refulgent. And to be discerned outlined against it a cross, black against the light, held high. This cross grew in size and clarity, and up on to the Knot from the far side came more pacing figures. First a youth, holding aloft this tall cross; then a man dressed in a simple white girdled robe, tonsured at the front of the head in the fashion of the Irish Celtic Church, and bearing a crozier; then four choristers wearing swords and bearing torches.

This party paced steadily towards the throne, and before it all the Pictish warriors drew their swords, lowered their spears and waved their strange symbols. But the cross-bearing singers neither paused nor wavered. Before the King of the Picts himself a threatening frieze of pointing spears barred the way, and the walkers perforce halted. But the white-robed cleric took the tall cross from the acolyte and gave him his crozier, and holding the crucifix directly before him strode on into the spear-points. One by one these wilted and sank as the cross turned them aside, and its bearer came right up to the throne, there to hold his cross right over the head of the sitting man.

"Hail, O King Brude, son of Mailcon, in the name of the One, the True and Almighty God and of His son Jesus Christ!" he cried, in a strong, clear voice. "I am Challum, son of Felim, son of Fergus the King, son of Connail King of Tirconnail, son of Niall of the Nine Hostages, High King of Ireland. Sometimes called Columb, the Dove. I bring you and yours light, O King, light in your darkness, peace in your war, love in your land, joy in your hearts and life everlasting. I have come from across the Western Sea to bring you this mighty gift — the Cross of Christ."

The seated man leaned forward to stare at the newcomer, pulling at his square beard. But the bearers of the strange symbols set up an angry shout of protest, and bore down on this Challum the Dove, or Columba, using their poles like lances. To each in turn the cross was presented, and one after another the double-disc and Z-rod, the crescent and V-rod, the serpent and Z-rod, the mirror and comb and the rest, fell back and down, and their priestly bearers shrank away abashed.

King Brude of the Northern Picts rose from his seat, held a hand up for silence, and then sank on his knees before Columba and the cross. The missionary-saint laid his hand on the other's brow, making the sign of the cross, and the *Te Deum* rose in triumph from the acolyte and torch-bearers.

The curtains were drawn once more.

"That, now, I can conceive of Holy Church paying for, and gladly!" Alex commented.

"It was well done," Jamie admitted. "But . . . look at His Grace."

King Robert was sitting forward in his chair, enthralled, tears streaming from his eyes. He turned to his wife, hands extended. Jamie had never seen the monarch so moved.

"David has pleased his father in this, at least," Alexander nodded. "How much does the King approve of his son's activities, now he is Lieutenant?"

"Little, I think. But, through the Queen and Bishop Trail, he can moderate David at times, as he never could his brother Albany. So there is that improvement."

"You do not sound so enamoured of your prince as once you were, Jamie. You are disappointed?"

"Aye, I am disappointed. It is not what I had hoped for. David is better than his uncle — but with all his gifts it should be more than that. He has it in him to rule well — but scarce takes the trouble to do so. He is too greatly taken up with his own pleasures and devices, his women in especial, ever the women! Clever as he is, he is young, to be sure — perhaps too young to be wielding the supreme power in the realm. When he is older, belike, he will make a good king. God willing . . ."

An angry coughing roaring heralded the arrival of the lioness. It had been deemed unwise to attempt to bring her on foot down the narrow winding cliff-path, where she could so easily have jettisoned her keepers. So she came in the wheeled iron cage David had had constructed for her — and which she did not like, and demonstrated the fact loudly. The cage had to be drawn by men, since they could get neither horses nor oxen to abide in the creature's near vicinity. This carriage likewise could not be brought down the steep path, so it had to make the long round-about journey down through the town and then back round the base of the castle-rock, Leonora the while making entirely clear her disapproval of all. She particularly did not like flaring torches.

The animal's arrival in the midst of the throng created the usual stir and more, her roaring, loud, fierce and continuing. Efforts to quieten her were quite ineffectual; indeed they made her worse. The prince himself could probably have soothed her — for there was an extraordinary empathy between the young man and the beast, probably because he was the only one who showed no fear of her; but he had disappeared from the scene meantime. Raw meat had been brought for the creature, but she would have none of it. Jamie tried to calm the brute, since she knew him better than most, but without success. The King was making distressed gestures, the inspiring effect of the St. Columba episode being negated by this roaring din. In the absence of better remedy, Jamie ordered the keepers to drag the cage and its occupant to some distance off north-westwards, round the rock, at least out of the crowded area and the torches' glare — where, however, although muted, the noise continued.

When he got back to his former stance, Jamie found Sir Alexander Stewart gone although his Highland chieftains were still there. Then he perceived him up on the Knot, moving quietly in behind the royal party. Mary was up there, with her princesses. But it was not to Mary's side that Alex found his way but to that of the Lady Isobel of Mar. So that pot still simmered.

The master of ceremonies captured attention in his own capering fashion and the curtains were pulled aside again — after a much briefer interval this time. Jamie had been wondering about the timing, for it could not be far off midnight by now, the vital hour.

On this occasion the scene was much more brightly lit, and more formal. In the centre of the stone-circle was set a notably large circular table, garlanded, with lesser tables grouped around. Behind it were erected twelve poles topped by banners, and beneath each hung a full shining suit-of-armour, of plate and chain mail, with plumed helmets and shields painted with colourful heraldic devices. The tables were set with flagons, chalices and beakers.

Trumpets sounded, the first heard that night, and up on to the Knot filed eleven finely-dressed men, each supported by a small page carrying his knight's sword. All were clad identically in cloth-of-gold tunics, long parti-coloured hose, with curling-toed slippers, and wore gold chains round their necks with crucifixes. These took their seats on either side of a central chair at the round table, their pages standing behind.

Another fanfare announced the arrival of a file of eleven good-looking young women, dressed all in white, red rosettes in their hair. Laughing and calling to each other musically, these went to sit at the side tables.

A longer, louder flourish of trumpets heralded a splendid figure, alone save for two pages behind, in complete shirt of chain-mail painted glistening gold, a red rampant lion stitched on the breast and a gold circlet around the fair brows. He had a cloth-of-gold cloak slung behind. It was David Stewart, looking every inch a king. As the knights and ladies stood, he waved to them left and right, and with dignity took the central chair.

There was only the briefest pause, and David raised his hand. There followed the clash of cymbals and discordant shouting, and from the side came a new procession. First there were warriors with spears and drawn swords, armoured. Then a statuesque woman of magnificent build which even the shapeless brown sackcloth in which she was garbed could not hide, long dark hair unbound, who walked head down and hands clasped low before her — but held in those hands nevertheless a rope which led back to a tethered man who stumbled along behind, with two soldiers cracking whips over his bent head. He was in one of the long coats of the Picts, and on his breast was painted a great bull, head down to charge, flanked by the crescent and V-rod devices.

This curious group moved on up to the round table, where the seated twelve watched, silent. There the guards fell back, and the woman turning, jerked the rope and gestured fiercely at the captive, pointing to the ground. The man wailed, and cast himself down, prone, clenched hands out in supplication. The woman moved, to place a foot on his neck, and thus faced the table again.

"My mighty lord Arthur," she called, in ringing tones, "I, Vanora, your unworthy wife, greet, acclaim and worship you. I have sinned against you, and against my marriage vows, and am no more worthy to be your queen. I deserve death and shall embrace it. But I have brought you, on my way to the grave, Unuist, High King of the Cruithne, or Picts, with whom I betrayed you. Into your hands I deliver him. And his people. To do with as you will. And not only him, but these also." She swung about, and pointed to where two more long-coated men had materialised, not bound these but standing free. "Nechtan the Second, King of the Northern Picts; and Loth, King of the Southern Picts. These come of their own free will, to yield themselves to you, Arthur, that you may rule over a united land, of Alba, Strathclyde, Lothian as well as Dalriada — the kingdom of the Scots. This, my dying gift, in restitution for a great sin. Now, my lord King, I present myself for your stern justice. I crave but one boon, husband — that you and you only strike the just blow with your own blade. Here!" And dramatically the woman wrenched open the sackcloth gown to bare her fine bosom.

David rose — and all others with him. He paced slowly round the table to his erring queen's side. Standing before her, he looked at her unspeaking. Then, leaning forward, he reached out to take the drawn-aside gown in both hands and jerked it apart and down, so that the stuff dropped to her feet, leaving her there completely naked, but upstanding, proud. And after another brief pause, he twitched off the cloth-of-gold cloak from his own shoulders and with a flourish draped it round her ample gleaming form.

As cheers arose from his knights and cries from the young women, with applause from the audience, he placed an arm around Vanora's or Guinevere's shoulders. Then he turned to the prostrate Pict. Stooping, he raised him to his feet, and spoke.

"Unuist, High King of Pictland, I greet you in peace," he cried — and had to raise his voice considerably, for, whether by coincidence or because she recognised his tones from afar, the lioness roared the louder. "I, Arthur Pendrachan, accept your homage and forgive you your sin, as I have forgiven the sin of this woman, my wife. I hereby take you into my peace." He turned. "And you also, Nechtan and Loth — your submission and fealty I accept, your love I seek. Your lives I return to you, all three. You shall remain kings, lesser kings, or great earls;

and with my Kings of Strathclyde, the Nordreys, the Sudreys and the Cattenes, shall rule this united realm of the Scots under me, as the Council of the Seven Kings or Earls. For all time. This I declare in love and peace."

The woman and the three Pictish monarchs all sank to their knees before him, and stirring music struck up from all around, ragged at first but soon harmonising. Raising the kneelers one by one, but without delay, David, arm-in-arm with Vanora, led them to the round table — rather more quickly than he had moved heretofore. He picked up chalices and handed them to the four — and was only just in time to grasp his own. A bell began to toll solemnly up on the castle, the music died away, and percolating through the lioness's grumbling growls sounded the pealing of all Stirling-town's church and monastery bells.

When the castle bell finished its twelve strokes — although the other pealing, like the roaring, continued — David Stewart raised his voice and cup again.

"My friends all," he cried, "great and small, rich and poor. It is the Year of Our Lord Fourteen Hundred! I give you all a good and better New Year, a good and better century, and a good and better Scotland, God willing!"

To deafening cheers that toast was drunk, by all who could find the wherewithal, and acclaimed by the rest.

Jamie Douglas thereafter pushed his way through the noisy throng and up on to the King's Knot, to reach and embrace his wife, amongst all the rest of the embracing, exclamation and cheer.

David came over from the stone-circle to embrace his father, kiss his mother, less warmly his wife, and then any and every woman available. Congratulations were showered upon him, the old Earl Archie croaking that he had just managed it in time, nevertheless.

The King rose, raised up the Queen, and bowed left and right. Then, at the prince's signal, a corps of torch-bearers and musicians hurried forward to form up and conduct the monarch and his party, with all such as preferred to accompany them, back up to the castle. They moved off slowly, at the King's limping pace.

This royal departure was the signal for the entire character and tone of the proceedings to change completely, from order to disorder, from a disciplined programme to licensed chaos, from normal behaviour to general abandon. As though to set the ball rolling, the tabarded master-of-ceremonies ran over to the pseudo royal couple and began tearing off the King's beard, crown and wig, and then the purple robe, to reveal a strapping wench all white beneath — who promptly raced off, squealing, pursued by a shouting throng of men. Others dealt similarly with the queen, who, naked, revealed much muscular and masculine endowment, and bounded off before a mainly female pack led by some of the erstwhile damsels of Arthur's Court. Soon caught, this young man, fortunate or otherwise, was dragged off and held under the wine-fountain — which had been turned off during the tableaux but now was spouting redly again. Some of the ladies fell in with him, shrieking laughter. His former female partner and following disappeared into the bushes and did not reappear.

Jamie was watching this changed scene with mixed feelings when a panting at his elbow revealed a distinctly breathless Mary.

"Save us!" he exclaimed. "You back? I saw you go off with the princesses. Here is no place for you, lass."

"They did not need me any more. And I was not going to miss the rest of it," she declared. "I noticed that *you* did not follow the King and Queen!"

"My place is with the prince — or so I thought!" he told her, but a little doubtfully.

"And I say mine is with my husband on a night like this, no?"

"Then keep close, girl — or you may get more than you look for!"

"That I shall, never fear. Already, coming back to you, I have had hands grabbing at me. Torchmen, servitors, even."

"Aye. This Hour of Misrule decent wives and mothers should be safely in their own houses."

"But not their lords and masters?" She looked around on the wild and colourful scene. "Where is Alex?"

"I do not know. I have not seen him since the King Arthur affair."

"M'mm. I noticed that one of the royal party did not go back with the King and Queen — the Countess of Mar! Although her husband accompanied his sister Annabella."

"Aye, well. Alex will gang his ain gait. As will his Cousin David."

They looked towards where the prince was eating and drinking, at one of the many tables, with a noisy party, and paying marked attention to one especially, the former Vanora or Guinevere — who appeared not to have found opportunity to add to her clothing in the interim.

"Who is the woman?" Jamie wondered. "She has a strange voice."

"She has more than that! But, did you not know? That is the wife of the new English envoy. I fear that her spouse may be less than enchanted."

"Aye — that could be unwise . . ."

Some dancing followed, led by the prince and his lady-for-the-night. Most who could joined in with enthusiasm, Mary and Jamie glad to take part. But before long it became too rowdy for any comfort, with too much drink taken amongst the dancers, and the licence for disorder and misrule adopted too literally. David himself withdrew, although without any evident displeasure, and his party with him. Calling out, he announced that those who still had control of their feet would now go skating — if they could find their way.

And so a laughing throng headed north-westwards into the bushes — and in almost less time than it takes to tell, were lost and dispersed. That maze had been cunningly devised, most of its grassy paths, amongst the tubbed shrubs and evergreens and fir-trees, false leads, circuits and blind alleys, the widest leading nowhere, the true tracks narrow and well disguised. Also there were distractions, hidden musicians, arbours, grottoes, sequestered seats, groups of statuary, some well lit with lanterns, some deep in shadow. Even Jamie, who had been at the making of it, could not recollect his way around in lamplight and gloom.

With a spirited and mainly youthful company of both sexes, less than fully sober and in a state of arousal and excitement, that maze accounted for many casualties — as it was intended to do. Couples, and trios for that matter, went exploring and did not return, protesting ladies went skirling off down dark lanes and their cries soon were heard no more, grinning men coaxed and beckoned from corners and entries.

The lioness's roars at least had some virtue here, since they helped to establish general direction. By their aid, a proportion of the prince's party managed to win through, in laughing pairs and groups. Many were the strange and stirring sights stumbled upon in the process — including a brief vision of Alex Stewart grappling with active white limbs which Mary at least had no doubts in identifying as those of Isobel of Mar.

The survivors now issued out from the great canopied area. The difference in temperature was dramatic, the effect of the wide spread of awnings and tentage, with the braziers and fires, quite extraordinary — although some draughts had been inevitable. Most there had tended to forget that they were outdoors on a cold winter's night. Now the tingling frosty air struck them like a blow, and the hoar decked all nearly as white as the snow David had foolishly hoped for.

There was no difficulty in finding the way now, for an avenue of lanterns led the couple of hundred yards further to the pond. But David, when he had assembled a number from the maze, insisted on first going to collect the still grumbling Leonora, over at the shadowy base of the rock.

This took time; no dealings with that animal could be rushed. With David present the creature stopped its growling, and even purred tentatively for a little. But it was suspicious of most of the company — a mutual sentiment — and at first would not come out of its cage. The rapport between prince and lioness had now advanced to the stage whereby he — but he alone — could lead it about on a leash, in suitable conditions with folk keeping their distance. She still had to wear shackles, to be sure, but David had had a lighter set made, less clankingly irritating to the brute.

At length the progress to the pond was resumed, with the Duke of Rothesay and his charge given a wide berth in the lead by the rest. Jamie ventured much nearer than the others when the prince signed to him — and noted with some satisfaction that Sir John de Ramorgnie kept well away.

"Back to the Knot, Jamie," David said. "There are not nearly sufficient folk here for this of the galley. Bring along all you can — not through the maze, but round above. It has been too successful, I fear! Bring all sober enough to come."

Simple instructions as these were, Jamie found it no easy task to carry out. There were still many revellers back in the centre of the canopied area, but these tended to be intent on their own chosen entertainment, or else too drunk to heed. Coupling, dancing, fighting, eating and drinking, even sleeping, Hogmanay merrymakers were not all inclined to abandon it at short notice, even on the Lieutenant of the Crown's relayed command. However in time he did manage to gather together a somewhat unruly company which he led round-about back to the pond.

When they arrived it was to find skating in full swing, to the music of instrumentalists hidden in the galley in the middle. A large number of wooden skates had been provided, and though not all were expert, or even in a state to perform adequately, at least this left more room for those who could. David was doing a sort of graceful *pas de deux* with Mary — his voluptuous Vanora apparently being no skater, and now evidently feeling the cold not a little, as well she might with only a cloth-of-gold cloak to protect her. The Prolocutor-General was however doing his best to keep her warm meantime. The lioness was out on the ice also, tethered to the galley and seeming at something of a loss.

With the arrival of the newcomers the fun developed fast and noisy. More refreshments were produced from the ship, and the wine flowed. Bonfires blazed all around, and wild dances about them became the order of the night for non-skaters.

Jamie really began to enjoy himself, for he and Mary were excellent on skates. Especially when Alex Stewart and the Countess of Mar joined them, anything but shamefaced, and they made a quartet for figure-skating and races and dancing. The prince favoured them with his company off and on — but he had other things on his mind, and disappeared now and again into outer darkness.

Wines and spirits however, although an undoubted aid to gaiety, in time become the enemies of skating, and even dancing. As more and more of the company began to have difficulty in keeping upright, David, drunk himself of course but as usual revealing little of it, decided that if climax was not to become anti-climax, it was probably time to come to a conclusion. He clambered up on to the prow of the galley and shouted for quiet.

"My friends," he called, "we have an ancient custom in this land, handed down to us by our distant ancestors, lost in time, known as Up Halie Days, or the end of the holy days marking the Twelfth Night of Yuletide. This is a time of girth, or sanctuary, wherein none may be apprehended or punished for breaking the law. I have given command, with the King's agreement, on this especial Yuletide, not only that none should be taken into custody, but that all in custody already should be released. This in all jurisdictions in the land, justiciars', sheriffs' and barons'. An amnesty, token of our new age and rule in Scotland."

There was a dutiful rather than an enthusiastic cheer, plus some muttered comments.

209

"In the past, as sign and promise that the new start was made and the old done with, it was the custom to burn a longship or galley, with all that spoke of strife, hatred and ill, in it — as is still done in some parts, they say, in the Orcades and elsewhere. We shall do so here. Follow me to the fires, for torches, my friends. It is not yet the true Up Halie Day — but we can celebrate it in advance!"

Now there was real cheering, as everyone thronged to the bonfires. Climbing down from the ship, David released the lioness tied there, and led her a discreet distance away, to secure her to a tree. Then he went to the nearest fire, to pick up and light one of the many torches lying ready. The musicians had emerged from the galley, and with these to play them on in a stirring, dancing tune, the prince raised his flaming brand high and led the torchlight procession back round the pond to the eastern side and then down on to the ice towards the vessel.

Now could be seen a new feature. Up on the high curving forepeak of the ship where David had recently stood, two figures had replaced him. Seen clearly in the light of the now innumerable torches, these drew all eyes, opened all eyes wider. Both were notably clad, one slender in black-and-silver, the other large, almost burly, in full Highland panoply. As the procession drew close the identity of these was evident to all. Dummies they might be, but they had been most skilfully made — Robert, Duke of Albany and Donald, Lord of the Isles, uncannily lifelike, unmistakable.

Something of a hush fell on the laughing, singing, skipping throng although the music continued. The prince smiled benignly.

"Did you know of this?" Mary demanded of her husband. "It is dangerous."

"I knew of Donald. The galley is meant to be his. The device of the Isles on the sail. And he as good as an outlaw. But not this of the Duke Robert. That is bad, too much. A great folly. It is bound to come to the Duke's ears . . ."

"Come, Jamie. We must speak to him. Get him to remove Robert's effigy, at least . . ."

They were not alone in their concern. Sir John de Ramorgnie was already at the prince's side, hand on his sleeve, making urgent representations. It was not often that Jamie Douglas joined forces with Ramorgnie, but he and Mary did so now. But to no effect. Laughing, David waved them away.

Reaching the galley, the prince turned. "So let us end the

troubles of this kingdom!" he cried, and hurled his torch. It rose in a flaming arc, showering sparks, to fall within the galley's hull. After it sailed a few others — but not all.

David looked round, narrow-eyed, most pointedly at those who still held torches in their hands. He did not speak, but his glance was eloquent.

With a sudden whoosh the combustibles in the open vessel caught fire, and roaring flames leapt up. In moments the galley was an inferno from end to end.

Shrugging, Jamie tossed his torch in with the rest, Mary and the others following suit. All drew back, for the heat was intense.

The prospect of the burning vessel there on the ice was impressive, exciting, somehow basically frightening. The great square sail caught alight quickly, and the dread device of the black Galley of the Isles painted thereon was consumed in a broad sheet of flame, the single mast and rigging taking longer to go. Almost the last to be enveloped was the lofty prow with the two so real-seeming figures standing there. For a little they seemed as though imperishable; then abruptly they were alight together, their turpentine-soaked clothing erupting. A long sigh arose from the watchers, but no words. The musicians had stopped their playing. Even the prince was silent. Only the lioness growled her anger and fear at the blaze.

David was the first to recover himself. He laughed loudly, just a little forcedly for him. "Thus ends misrule!" he cried. "Let each and all witness! Now — back to the Knot. The night is young yet. This year of Fourteen Hundred must be well launched. Jamie — take Leonora back to her cage. You she will not eat — I think! Come, all."

"I think that I have had sufficient," Mary said, when the others were moving off. "Our own bed calls, husband!"

"Aye. Enough is enough — and more! I must get the lion first. But — keep your distance from the brute, lass."

"You are sure you are safe with it, Jamie? I would leave the creature where it is, tethered."

"No, no. It knows me, knows that I am not afraid of it. Besides, it is shackled. And it is not far to the cage. Where is Alex?"

"Alex is gone again. And the Countess with him. He is a Stewart, after all! As am I, Jamie Douglas! Haste you with that roaring creature — but have a care. I wish it did not make such ill noise . . ."

X

THE TWO BROTHERS, both Sir James Douglas, rode hard through the Lothian countryside in the early darkening of the February afternoon, Candlemas 1400, behind them a hastily-gathered force of some two hundred Dalkeith men-at-arms and retainers. It was by pure chance that Jamie was with his legitimate brother. He had been summoned to Dalkeith from Aberdour, their father being seriously ill again, and declaring death imminent. And then had come the urgent message from Archibald, Master of Douglas, from Edinburgh Castle where the Lieutenant of the Crown had recently appointed him Keeper. The English were invading Scotland, under Hotspur, the traitor Dunbar with them. Not in major force yet, so far as was known, and not King Henry. Reported numbers varied, but about 10,000 seemed to be the figure. They were already through Dunbar's Merse and into Lothian, nearing Haddington indeed. It might well be but the spearhead of a larger invasion under the King. He, the Master, was hastening to meet them, with all the force he could muster at short notice. He called on all possible support, to join him at Haddington, the East Lothian county town, at the earliest moment. The old Lord of Dalkeith had recovered his spirits wonderfully at these reviving tidings, and insisted that his sons should leave his bed-side forthwith, gather as many of his adherents as they could, and be off, while his younger son, Will, mustered more from further afield, to follow on later.

Sir James, Younger of Dalkeith, although nominally in command, deferred to his elder bastard brother in most things. Jamie's experience in matters military especially, was much the greater; and his reputation as some sort of hero, however unwarranted, was a major factor with men to lead. They rode side-by-side, therefore, but Jamie would take the decisions.

They came to Haddington, over the bleak wastes of the Gled's Muir, with the dusk, to find the town gates shut and the burghers putting the place into a hasty state of siege-defence. The Master of Douglas had moved on, watchers shouted to them, on to Traprain. The English were assailing Hailes Castle of the Hepburns and had burned Spott and Stenton and the Lammermuir townships. It could be Haddington next, unless Douglas stopped them.

In the gathering gloom the Dalkeith contingent pounded on eastwards, the abrupt bulk of Traprain Law, old Pictish King Loth's one-time hill-top capital, looming vaguely ahead four miles, its lofty flat summit outlined against a flickering ruddy glow which could only be the burning Lammermuir villages. At the sight, men's hands tended to loosen swords in sheaths.

Halfway to the hill, they swung leftwards down to cross the Tyne by the Bere Ford. The Haddington folk had said that the Master of Douglas would do this likewise, to approach Hailes, not by the normal road but by the higher ground of Pencraik Hill on the north side of the river, as precaution in case of English scouts and patrols. Jamie commended this caution in his less-than-cautious young chief.

Hailes Castle was in a curious situation for a quite major stronghold, set deep in a narrow valley below the north face of Traprain Law, on the south steep bank of the Lothian Tyne, which here ran through what was almost a gorge. The road threaded this ravine, and the castle was therefore in a position to close that road at will, one of the main highways from Dunbar, Berwick and the Border to Haddington and Edinburgh — and likewise to levy toll on travellers, cattle-droves and the like. It had its own strength, despite being thus overlooked by high ground, for owing to the constricted nature of the gorge and valley no enemy force could deploy effectively around its rock above the river. Evidently the English had discovered this.

The Dalkeith party came up with the larger force on a wooded spur of Pencraik Hill, a lesser height directly opposite Traprain, from which they could look down on the castle in the valley some two hundred feet below. The Master welcomed them with relief, even though he was frankly disappointed in their numbers; but Jamie's unexpected presence partly made up for this, for he had not forgotten his rescue at Foulhope haugh in Ettrick and

213

had acquired a high opinion of Jamie's abilities in the field. He made no pretence of treating the other Sir James as commander, although the pair of them were the two senior representatives of the house of Douglas in the younger generation, and were moreover linked by marriage, both to daughters of the King. The Master had some 1,200 men on Pencraik Hill, so, welcome as was a reinforcement of two hundred, it was not much with which to tackle 10,000.

Nevertheless, Archibald was sufficiently aggressively-minded, as befitted a Douglas leader. "At least you have come at the right time," he told them. "Fortunately, the enemy is divided, for the night, and show no signs of knowing that we are here. I chose to come by this Pencraik, to keep our presence secret — even though it is on the wrong side of the river. Fighting in the dark will be difficult, but it may yield us some advantage — which we shall need, by God!"

"To be sure," Jamie agreed. "What do you purpose? It will not be so dark, besides, with those fires."

The Master pointed directly downhill first, to where the castleton of Hailes, the cabins and cot-houses of the Hepburn retainers, had been set alight and blazed redly.

"Part of their force is there, sitting round the castle. They have made three attempts against it already, a shepherd here tells me, but without success. I think that they will try again, under cover of darkness, when archers cannot repel them." He raised his head and hand to look and point eastwards by north. "Yonder is the town of Preston, and the mill-town of Linton. The English main body is camped there — you can see their fires. There is no room for them all in this narrow valley. They are over a mile away. We could move down quietly, and attack these around the castle — Hepburn perhaps sallying out to aid us. And, pray God, surprise and defeat them before help could arrive for them from the town. How say you?"

"A bold and notable tactic, Archie," young Dalkeith declared enthusiastically. "The fires will show them up, but not our approach. Dismounted, and quiet, we should win close before ever they learn of our presence. Eh, Jamie?"

His brother fingered his long chin. "It might avail, yes. But . . . see you, why not rather assail the main body in their open camp, rather than this tight detachment in the difficult valley?"

"Eh? But, man," the Master protested, "there are thousands

there! My scouts say so. Three or four times as many as here around the castle. Why pit our smaller strength against the greater?"

"Sufficient reasons, I think. These are men encamped for the night, no longer girt and standing to arms. Moreover, encamped at a town, they will be dispersed for a surety, scattered, seeking drink and women, pillaging probably. Whereas those below are tightly grouped and still in fighting trim. Also, you must cross the river to get at them — and you will not do that, with many hundreds, in the darkness, silently or easily. Again, surprise and break up the main body, and this detachment will be loth to continue the invasion alone; but defeat it only, and the main body is still there, still many times your number, and alerted against you."

"Aye, you are right. That makes good sense. How then may this best be attempted?"

"I know this country. I have lands nearby, at Stoneypath, in Lammermuir. The river leaves this valley a mile on, and curves round to the north before turning east again for the sea. In that curve, this side of it, lies the mill-town of Linton, then the kirk-town of Preston. We cannot attack from the east therefore, the Tyne barring the way. Nor down this valley itself, in case there is coming and going between the camps. But if we go north-about from here, on this high ground, by Markle, then divide into two and come down upon both ends of the mill-town and the kirk-town from the Markle slopes, we should do best. It is the town's pasture there, open grass slopes, so that we can make a mounted assault, at least to start with. Always best against a dispersed and surprised enemy."

"Very well. I do not know how this land lies. But — let us pray that Hailes Castle does not fall, meantime."

"That is a hazard we must risk. But this business may not take so very long, see you. Given luck . . ."

The order was passed through the quiet waiting ranks to mount and move. It was quite dark now, but the various glows in the sky, from the distant foothills villages, from the burning castleton and the many camp-fires at the mill-town and kirk-town of Preston, provided some illumination in an arc to east and south. With its fluctuating and modest help the long column of 1,400 horsemen picked their way slowly north by east over the rounded summit of Pencraik Hill, on tussocky grassland with cattle and sheep continually moving off in alarm before

215

them. They contoured round a north-going spur of the hillside beyond, and then were faced with a complication. In the wide further valley was the small monastery of Markle, and a community clustered around it, below quite a steep escarpment. This now proved to be on fire likewise, the flames dying down to a red glow. Presumably therefore the English were there also. It meant that they must veer off eastwards, or risk giving the alarm, even a clash. There was the advantage, however, that it indicated that the enemy were more split up than ever.

Eastwards, they could not go much further before the slope dropped away, before them and the camp-fires gleamed around the south end of the double township, known as Linton, where there was a group of mills along the waterside, with an inn and the mill-hands' cot-houses. The larger part of the place, where was the parish church, another mill and more houses, was half-a-mile to the north, and not quite so easy to ride down upon, because the river began to curve away again and an incoming shallow valley from the Markle direction intervened. There appeared to be as many camp-fires in this more distant Preston vicinity. It takes a lot of riverbank ground to camp 7,000 or 8,000 men.

"What now?" the Master demanded. "We cannot reach Preston without crossing that valley. There are three fires in it. If that means English troops there also, the alarm will be given and surprise lost."

"Yes. Who would have thought that they would have been so spread out?"

"Let us just descend on this camp below us, at Linton," Jamie's brother said. "Overwhelm it, and then sweep along the riverside road to Preston. What is wrong with that?"

"This — that the leaders may not be here. Hotspur and Dunbar. We do not want to give them time and opportunity to rally their men. Always seek to destroy the leadership, I say. They *may* be back at Hailes — but I think not. That is not work for the proud Percy, of a night. After failing at the first assault, he would leave it to some captain and this detachment, and seek comfortable quarters for the night for himself and Dunbar. Where, think you? Not in some broken-down inn or miller's cot-house, when there is the Rectory of St. Baldred's Kirk of Linton nearby. Either that, or the monastery of Markle — but that is aflame. Hotspur and Dunbar will be at Preston Rectory, and we dare not leave them there unmolested to rally their

216

people, warned by our attack on Linton. Which they are bound to hear."

"Damnation, then — what to do?" the Master cried. "We could stand here and talk it to and fro all night!"

"Better talk now, and take a right course, than regrets after! But here's what I suggest. I will take our Dalkeith men, two hundred — it is enough — and ride quietly down and across this accursed side-valley, seeking to avoid the camp-fires and giving alarm. With all their own troops hereabouts, they might not think of us as Scots, in the darkness. Then, if we pass them, make on over the lesser slope beyond to the back of Preston's houses. Above the Rectory. When in position, I give you a signal — a blast on a horn. Then we both charge down, at the same time."

"Aye — but if you do *not* get across this valley unseen and unchallenged, what then?"

"Then you will hear it, and make your own charge, at once. Down there upon the camp at Linton. And when you can spare it, send a company along the riverside, to aid me at Preston."

The Master nodded. "So be it. The best we can do. You go now? Then, St. Bridgit go with you."

"And with you. Do you come with me, James?"

The brothers detached their people without difficulty and moved off at a walk, north-eastwards, down the gradual slope of the side-valley. There were three fires down in the floor of it, strung out, and they made heedfully for the larger gap between them. None spoke, but two hundred men cannot ride, however slowly, without some noise — the plod of hooves, the creak of saddlery, the clink of bits and bridles and men's armour, the snort of nostrils. There were more cattle on this slope, and these made more disturbances than the horsemen, lumbering off into the gloom in clumsy fright.

The more level ground at the foot was ridged with the strips of the township's runrig cultivation, with early ploughing already started. This was unsuitable ground for camping on — but whinnying from not far off revealed that there were horse-lines nearby on the left. Two of their own beasts acknowledged the greeting, amidst muttered anathemas from their riders.

They had to cross a burn, but it was small and caused no trouble. The track up the valley to Markle ran on the other side, and over this they moved, still at only a walk, glancing right and left warily. Jamie reined up to wait — since even two hundred

217

horses, three or four abreast, take some time to pass a given point. He was just about to ride forwards again, with the last files coming up, when they heard singing from quite close at hand, to the right, townwards. The men hearing it almost automatically began to kick their beasts into faster movement, with consequent jostling and more noise.

The singing stopped short. Jamie cursed — but took a swift decision. He raised his voice.

"Slow, there!" he called, quite loudly. "I hear voices." He turned in his saddle, towards where the singing had come from, down the track. "Hey, there!" he shouted. "A plague on it — you, there! Here, to me. Where are you?" He sought to give his voice not only authority but the typical Northumbrian burr — with what success he knew not.

There was some indistinct speaking, and then three men materialised out of the gloom, walking less than steadily. They appeared to be carrying heavy bundles, loot no doubt.

"You," Jamie exclaimed. "Where are we in this accursed place? Who are you? Where from?"

"We are Sir William Heron's men, sir," one answered, hiccuping. "What's to do?"

"Heron? Where is the Percy? The Lord Harry Percy? I have word for him. We were sent this way by some fool. Where is Hotspur, a God's name?"

"He is yonder, sir." The spokesman pointed northwards. "In the village, some place. Some house yonder."

Jamie grunted. "This night is as black as Satan's belly!" he grumbled. And without a word of thanks moved on after his disappearing last files.

No alarm broke out behind.

He was trotting up, to get to the head of his now quite extended column again, when noise did break out, ahead. There were cries, shouts and then the clash of steel. Uproar developed — including the skirls of women.

Spurring hard now, Jamie pounded over grassland, not cultivated rigs, gently rising. He found his brother and the first horsemen milling around quite a large crowd of men and some females, presumably coming back from Preston to their Markle camp, with captives. Markle being a monastery, would be short on women. Swords were drawn and there was much indiscriminate fury and noise.

All virtue in silence gone, Jamie found and raised his horn,

218

and blew a single high blast — for the Master's sake, but it also had the advantage of drawing his own men's attention to his commands amidst all the other shouting.

"Come!" he yelled, drawing sword. "Leave here. Follow me. James — all speed!"

A gallop might have been disastrous in that lack of light, and even the canter at which Jamie led was dangerous. But then the entire situation was fraught with dangers. On he drove, directly for the rear of Preston township now, with a bare quarter mile to go.

They met no more straggling English. More camp-fires appeared before them presently, having been somewhat hidden behind a fold of the pastureland. The thunder of their hooves, as well as the shouting and clash must have given some warning to the men there, but no coherent defence met them — not un-naturally, for it was only evening and many of the men would be roaming the town in search of amusement, and not a few undoubtedly drunk, the time for posting of sentries and night patrols not yet come.

Slowly, only sufficiently for him to wave and order his horse-men into a wide front instead of a column, he swept them on through the camp area, swords slashing, the dread Douglas slogan shouted, riding men down, trampling the recumbent, overturning stacked lances and pennons, scattering fires, stampeding horses. Actual fighting there was none. In only moments this camp at least was a shambles, men fleeing in all directions, opposition none.

Jamie perceived a small knoll ahead half-right, with a towered building dark on top — the church. He did not know just where the Rectory was, but it would not be far from the church, for certain. He plunged on without reducing speed.

There was the usual walled graveyard round the church, reaching down the sides of the knoll. Cottages began where the kirkyard ended. There were men moving about here, in the shadows, some mounting horses in haste. Jamie swore. He was too late. The leadership was warned, alert.

He noticed a larger building downhill to the left. Against the glow of the riverside fires of the main camp he could see that it had a less bulky roof-line than the cottages — slate not thatch. The Rectory, for sure. Spurring towards it, he saw that it had a range of subsidiary buildings, thatched, and a yard, a farmery. There were more horsemen here.

Reining his mount up to block the entrance to this yard, he shouted for the first files of men behind to join him. With a score or so of them jostling and rearing around, he urged his brother onwards, with the rest of the two hundred.

"Down into the riverside haughs!" he shouted. "Break up the camps. Ride down all you can. Cause confusion, panic. Back and forward."

Then into the Rectory yard he drove his own mount, sword pointing, his twenty piling in behind. There were half-a-dozen men there, mounted or mounting. Some stood their ground, others leapt down and bolted into the houses at sight of the superior numbers. Advancing horsemen always have the advantage over the stationary, and Jamie had no difficulty in unseating the first man he came to. The others were overwhelmed in the rush of Scots.

Jumping down, he yelled for his men to follow him in at the open door, prepared for tough fighting in the easily-held narrow lobbies within. But no-one was there to oppose him. Stumbling through, in his heavy riding-boots, he peered into this room and that. The first two were empty, although candles and lanterns lit them. In the third, a kitchen, two women and an old man huddled in alarm, servants obviously. Beyond, and up the twisting turnpike stairs, more empty rooms, more candles and fires.

Fighting his way back through the press of his own men, Jamie made for the servants in the kitchen again.

"They've gone? Bolted?" he cried. "Where?"

Wordless the old man pointed a trembling hand, in the other direction from which they had entered. Presumably they had come in at the back door and their quarry had bolted through the front.

"Who were they? Hotspur? Dunbar?"

"Lords, sir. Proud lords," the ancient quavered. "English knights . . ."

Snorting, Jamie flung out of the kitchen, along the lobby and out at another open door. Just too late. If he had been only moments earlier. It was damnable! But at least they would be on foot. The horses would be at the back, not this front door. Though they would soon find themselves new mounts.

Waving his people back through the house to their own horses, he wasted no time. Hurling themselves into the saddles, they rode on down towards the river.

Jamie had told his brother to spread confusion and alarm. It might not be all Sir James's doing, but that was certainly the situation along the west bank of Tyne that evening. Everywhere men rode, ran or scurried in every direction, amidst shouts and wails and conflicting commands. Cries of "A Douglas! A Douglas!" resounded — and Jamie's party added their breathless quota. Most of the camp-fires had been scattered, and there was little light. Heaps of booty, piled saddlery and arms, and runaway horses trailing their tether-ropes added to the chaos. It was no sort of battle, only sheer and multiple pandemonium.

Jamie was concerned to keep his own score of men together, for in such conditions a tight, disciplined group of even so few can wield an influence out of all proportion to their numbers. To and fro over the narrow half-mile of haugh they cantered, therefore, with considerable shouting but precious little actual bloodshed, content to have men flee before their solid certainty rather than do battle. And most men there did, a great many having been fleeing before ever they arrived on the scene. The majority of these undoubtedly poured along the haughland southwards, towards the Linton camp area, but fugitives hurried wherever they could, and not a few plunged into the river itself, running high as it was after the winter rains.

They kept collecting groups and individuals of Sir James's company who had become detached. Obviously it had been much more difficult to keep one hundred and eighty together as a unified force, in such circumstances, than a mere twenty. Although, when they found Sir James himself, presently, at the far northern extremity of the township, in a state of high excitement, he did not appear to be greatly concerned that only about seventy of his one hundred and eighty remained with him now. The others were about somewhere, he declared cheerfully. Why worry? It was victory, all the way!

James was less delighted, inevitably. The enemy still outnumbered them many times, and their leaders were still at large. There could be a rally at any time. They must drive back up the haugh, collecting their people as they went, and seek to join forces with the Master again.

He blew his horn, to bring in stragglers, and formed up into line abreast, but four or five deep, and set off at a disciplined trot southwards.

All the way they were herding fugitives and runaway horses before them, flushing out skulkers, passing hiders. None stood to fight. There was a bare half-mile between the two sections of the township, a narrow strip along the riverside, with encampments all the way. All were already deserted. Almost from the first they could hear the clash and shouting from the struggle ahead, where the Master was savaging the Linton area. Nearing this, they began to meet men fleeing their way, both mounted and afoot, although mainly the latter. At Jamie's command they recommenced their "A Douglas! A Douglas!" slogan, in a regular, deep-throated rhythmic chant as they rode. Few English waited for closer inspection.

They achieved no real fighting. If there had been any spontaneous resistance to the Master's sudden attack, it had disintegrated before they arrived. All was a noisy horror of dead and wounded men, screaming horses, uncontrolled fires and the debris of war rather than of battle.

They rejoined the Master of Douglas at the wooden Linton bridge over the Tyne, near the south end, where he was endeavouring to collect and reform some major portion of his force — and finding it a difficult task. Once men become dispersed, attackers equally with defenders, in a town especially and in darkness, reassembly is no simple matter, however many horns may blow. He hailed the Dalkeith company thankfully, the more so when he heard that the Preston end of the encampments was over-run and cleared.

"But we failed to get Hotspur and the leaders," Jamie panted. "Which was my main aim. We were too late."

"Never heed, man. We have them beat. That is what matters. It is victory . . ."

"It is *not* victory! It could still be total failure, defeat. We have taken them by surprise — that is all. We have scattered them meantime, yes — but we have killed few. They are still many times our numbers — and now *we* are scattered likewise! Their leaders are still free, and will recover from their surprise — experienced fighters. Hotspur is no fool. He could regain all."

"Jamie was ever a prophet of woe!" his brother assured, laughing. "We could scarce have done better than we have done, I say."

"I am trying to gather my people again," the Master said. "What more can we do? Who knows where Hotspur and Dunbar may be?"

"We must try to find them. And forthwith. Not give them

time to rally any large numbers. Keep pressing them — not standing here waiting."

"But . . . how? In this darkness. Where do we seek them, man?"

"What would *you* do if you were Hotspur, in this pass? He does not know how many may have attacked him — but he will think more than we are. He finds his Preston camp over-run. Then his Linton camp. What then? He still has a fighting-force up at Hailes Castle, facing an enemy, not camped and standing down. There is a camp at Markle too, but that is different, resting and smaller probably. If I was the Percy, I would have no doubts. I certainly would not just flee. I would leave someone to seek rally the folk scattered hereabouts, and send someone to bring down the Markle folk. Myself, I would ride with all speed to Hailes, to put myself at the head of a force still in order and in arms. Then bring it back here, to do battle when *we* think we have won and are off guard, scattered."

The others stared at him, in the flickering fires' light, silenced.

"You said that you reckoned perhaps only a quarter of the English force was left at Hailes?" Jamie went on. "But that could be over 2,000. And how many are we here, gathered here — four hundred, five hundred? We cannot face an attack from Hailes, here, with these numbers."

"No. But it would take Hotspur time to mount such an attack."

"Aye — and that is our chance. We must grasp it, and at once. The Hailes valley is very narrow, little more than a ravine. We must ride for it, get up into it, block it. Then their larger numbers will serve them nothing. They will not be able to learn *our* numbers. They will only be able to engage our front, and with their own front, equally small. To get out of the valley they will either have to flee south-westwards, up-river, or clamber up the steep sides, leaving their horses — which they will be loth to do, far from home, in enemy territory. And the river in its gorge to cross, at one side."

"God save us, Jamie — you keep a cool head, I declare!" the Master cried. "You are right — on my soul, you are right! We shall leave James here, and Kilspindie, to rally our own folk and keep the English from rallying. To deal with the Markle camp, likewise. The rest of us make for the valley to Hailes."

They did not count their men, but the Master probably had about four hundred mustered at the bridge, and with the

Dalkeith contingent this made a reasonable force to tackle the valley. They crossed the bridge and spurred south-westwards along the south bank of Tyne, soon leaving the houses behind. It quickly became very dark, as the light from the fires behind faded and they could not ride so fast as they would have liked; but at least there was a road to follow, the main Haddington road indeed.

After half-a-mile they could sense the jaws of the deep narrow valley drawing in on them, thankful that they had reached thus far without any sign of the enemy. Whatever else, they had now closed the gap, blocked the passage and isolated the Hailes group from the rest.

Although the road itself continued, it narrowed and its verges all but disappeared, with the rushing river in its steep rocky bed on the right and the whin-dotted hillside rising abruptly on the left. The column inevitably lengthened noticeably, jostling men unable to ride more than three abreast. In the circumstances, any fighting would have to be done by the leading files.

The valley, and therefore the road, twisted continually, and the leaders were ready for trouble around each corner. It was just under two miles from the Linton bridge to the castle, and about halfway they began to see a glow ahead from the campfires around Hailes. Gradually this provided some light of a sort, to aid them. It would also make them more evident to others, admittedly, but on balance was probably in their favour since they would still have the dark background.

It indeed proved so a minute or two later, when suddenly round a bend a fast-riding party was silhouetted approaching. In the moments before they themselves were perceived, Jamie and the Master had opportunity to shout their orders and be ready for the clash.

There was no clash, however, for there was sufficient reflection on their armour and drawn swords to give the newcomers warning whilst about two hundred yards still separated them. There followed a great rearing and wheeling of horses. The party proved to be no large one, and clearly recognised that the people in front were unlikely to be fellow-countrymen, and in numbers exceeding their own. Before ever the Scots could come up with them, they were turned around and heading back fast whence they had come.

The Master was beginning to shout for pursuit at all speed,

to prevent these being able to warn the rest at Hailes, when Jamie grabbed his arm.

"No — let them warn them," he jerked. "Better so. They will say a large force is coming up this valley. There will be panic, at first. Ride slowly. Calling our slogan. Sound full confident. In the dark, in this close gullet, with their other camps already overwhelmed, that will add to their fears. God willing, they'll bolt!"

The other was doubtful. "It could give them time to form up against us."

"We will not give them *that* long. They will hear our Douglas slogan. They are deep in enemy country, the smell of defeat already in the air. I say they will flee, not knowing that they still outnumber us. And if they do not, we are little the worse."

"Play-acting!" James the Gross, the Master's brother snorted. "We came to fight, not to play guizards! This is worthy of Davie Stewart!"

"*You* may have come to fight 10,000 with 1,400!" Jamie retorted. "*I* did not. I came to help rid our land of these Englishmen as a fighting force. Are we not doing so?"

"Jamie's right," the Master said. "We may have to fight — but try this!"

So they slowed to a steady trot and started up the rhythmic chanting of "A Douglas! A Douglas!", that dread cry which had been striking terror into Northern English hearts for the century since the Good Sir James had commenced his campaign of cross-Border raids in the cause of his friend the Bruce. And from some five hundred throats, in the narrow confines of the valley, it made a grim and menacing sound indeed. It had its own effect, moreover, on the chanters themselves, making their deliberate advance seem inexorable, undefeatable, each man half as puissant again. It might be guizardry and play-acting, but it was excellent for morale.

They had only another half-mile to go, so that even at a slower pace there was only two or three minutes in it. With the firelight increasing before them, and prepared for immediate action, they rounded the final bend of the road before Hailes Castle.

A notably strong and effective site had been chosen for the Hepburn stronghold. A small stream in a shallow, tree-lined ravine came down steeply to join the Tyne in its gorge here; and perched on the tip of the rock above the junction, the castle walls rose — so that it was protected on three sides. The fourth side was defended by a deep artificial dry ditch, spanned by a drawbridge, presently raised. Without ballista and heavy siege machinery, it was most evidently a hard nut to crack; at the same time completely dominating the road and wooden bridge which here crossed the lesser stream. Because of this side ravine, the main valley was a little wider here, which had given the English invaders room to concentrate and camp.

As this scene opened before the chanting Scots there was however no sign of concentration. Indeed there was little sign of the English invaders at all. The fires still blazed, arms, gear and booty littered the open area flanking the road, and some shadowy figures could be seen scurrying away up the wooded ravine on the south. Otherwise the castle-hollow seemed to be deserted.

"Praise be — they've bolted, as you said!" the Master cried, panting from his chanting. "Some up yonder gully . . ."

"Not many there. They could not take horses up there. And this is a horsed force. They will have fled up the road, for Traprain."

Cheering and shouting from the castle itself interrupted him, and men waving torches appeared on the parapet-walks and tower battlements. The clanking sound of the drawbridge chains being lowered had the Master spurring forward to greet Sir Patrick Hepburn, when Jamie again intervened.

"Now that they are fleeing we must keep them so," he urged. "Keep them running. Give them no time to recover. Nor to try to rejoin the others at Markle or round the town. A bare mile on, this valley opens and levels off. We must prevent them from rallying there. This south side opens to gentle slopes. They can ride out, and up round the skirts of Traprain Law, and so make for Lammermuir."

"They will never rally now, man."

"For a wager, Hotspur and their leaders are still there in front of us. With 2,000 men, scattered and in flight, but capable of turning the day against us. We cannot risk it."

"Oh, very well. James," the Master turned to his stout brother. "Go you speak with Hepburn. Then come on after us — bringing some of his men if you can."

They rode on, into deeper darkness now, with the fires left behind. They did not attempt to flush out fugitives on foot up the ravine; there would be comparatively few and they consti-

226

tuted no danger. They could not ride fast in the gloom, but they quickened their pace somewhat and resumed their chanting, however unevenly and breathlessly. Despite this so evident challenge, however, they were very much on the look-out for any attempt at ambush, this valley being apt therefor.

Nothing of the sort developed. They emerged into the more open country presently, to discover no stand being made there either. There were now three possibilities. The English flight could have gone straight on, or else turned left or right. Straight on up the Tyne would bring them past the Bere Ford and Stevenston to Haddington's walled town, in three miles, clearly an unlikely course. Right, northwards, meant crossing the river, still running through a difficult rocky bed, and then climbing back up the quite major ascent of Pencraik Hill, whence they could reach Markle and the Preston area again. Would they hazard that, when the way lay open on the left, southwards, to escape to safety in the hills or the Berwickshire Merse, the Borderline only some thirty miles away? From their performance hitherto this night, the chances were that they would seek to cut their losses and continue with their flight whilst they had opportunity. Generalship throughout had been poor; it was unlikely suddenly to become boldly vigorous at this stage.

So the Scots turned southwards, leaving the road, to climb the open grassy and whin-dotted slopes which lifted towards the thrusting hump-backed hill of Traprain Law. It was a dark night, without moon or stars, and with even the glow of distant fires now all but died away it was too dark to discern hoof-marks, horse-droppings or other signs of the enemy passage. They could only hope that they had calculated aright.

But up at the top, under the very crags of the Law, the hamlet of Cairndinnis lay. It appeared to be deserted, but when they shouted their Douglas identity, folk crept out from hiding, thankfully, to declare that an English patrol had savaged them earlier in the evening, whilst a much larger company, riding fast, had driven past only a short time before — without halting, God be thanked! Yes, they were riding southwards, as though making for Whittinghame and Lammermuir.

"Dunbar will be with them, and knows this country like his own hand — since his own it is!" Jamie exclaimed. "They are not stopping. In full flight still."

"Then we must keep them so doing," the Master agreed. "Show Hotspur Percy can spur as hotly backwards as forward!"

They sent back word to the various groups behind, and hurried on.

All that weary night they followed the fleeing English through the Lammermuir foothills and beyond, flagging as to speed inevitably — but then so must be the enemy. They got near enough their quarry to ensure that they did not lose them in the darkness and broken country — and to ensure that the fleeing men were well aware that they were on their heels. But anxious as they were to catch up — the Master now especially eager to add a feather to his bonnet by capturing the celebrated Hotspur and the traitor Dunbar — they never quite managed it. Dunbar would know the country even better than did Jamie Douglas; and frequently the pursuers had to waste time by casting about to pick up the trail. The enemy in fact did not push directly on into the empty Lammermuir Hills, but swung away south-eastwards round their flanks, parallel with the coast but a few miles inland, by Stenton and Spott, behind Dunbar itself, and the hillfoot villages of Innerwick and Dunglass.

At Colbrandspath, where there was a steep and deep ravine and rushing river to be crossed, they had their first real fighting of the night. The English had left a party behind here, to destroy the wooden bridge by fire and demolition. These had not had time to achieve their objective when the Scots arrived — had they been able to do so, it would greatly have aided them, for the gulf below was almost sheer and quite impassable for horses, entailing a lengthy detour. But the Percy had left a group of mounted archers with the demolition party, and though these could not see to aim their shafts at individual targets, by pouring arrows at random over at the northern bridgehead area, they could and did greatly hold up and harass the Scots. Indeed, had the main English force stood their ground on the far side, they could have halted the pursuit indefinitely. As it was, the Master had to send parties of men on foot left and right, clambering precariously down the steep and difficult banks amongst the clinging rowans and birches, to struggle across the fast but not deep stream and up the equally steep opposite side, eventually to outflank the bowmen and bridge-wreckers. After a sharp tussle, they managed to drive them off.

The substantial bridge was only partly damaged and quite passable. The main Douglas force crossed over, and set off again without delay but left behind over a score of casualties, the first of the night.

After that it was just hard slogging over the dreary high wastes of Coldinghame Moor, to the River Eye crossing at Ayton Castle — which was not held against them. Then on along the high cliff-top road by Lamberton Moor, the Borderline drawing ever closer. This was the main north–south road now, and the going consequently much easier. But men and horses were tired indeed and the pace eased and dwindled. They had come about twenty-nine miles from Hailes, and Berwick town lay only some three miles ahead. It was almost a relief to recognise that they could go little further.

One last flurry there was, almost within sight of the very gates of the fortress-town, with the grey dawn beginning to lighten the leaden plain of the sea to their left. It takes time to arouse the guards of a walled city to open the gates at night and to admit 2,000 horsemen through a narrow access-tunnel. To allow for this process, a rearguard had been left at a marshy stretch of the Borough Meadows, common pasture where the road crossed the wet ground by what was almost a causeway, a well-known defensive position for those concerned with the security of Berwick. Here, once again, the Scots could have been held up long enough for reinforcements to come out from the fortress garrison — and indeed, there was little point in them pressing the issue, since they must needs turn back anyway in a mile or so. But the very proximity of the walled city and its security was a heavy temptation for the rearguard manpower, sapping its resolution and fighting-spirit — for why should they now throw away their lives, at this late stage, in order to allow the rest of their companions to have comfortable access to safety? Accordingly, the defence at the causeway was a mere token one, a gesture, which was hardly made before the weary troopers were streaming off along the road the remaining mile to the Scots Gate of the town. The Douglases gave chase in only similar fashion, sufficient to capture the red-and-gold banner of the rearguard's leader — which proved to be that of Sir Thomas Talbot, brother of the Lord Talbot.

It made a notable trophy for the Master to take home — for Talbot was one of the premier barons of England — even though its owner himself escaped. There was no point in going further — indeed real danger, for Hotspur was still Warden of the English East March and therefore Governor of Berwick, and could order out the permanent garrison against them, fresh men and numerous, for a strong force was always maintained in this captured Scots city. They turned back, therefore, tired, stiff but satisfied. And just to demonstrate the realities of the situation to all concerned, they started up their hoarse chanting of the Douglas slogan once more. For two or three minutes they bellowed it out, towards the awakening town, before reining round and trotting off northwards on the long road home.

XI

JAMIE DOUGLAS WAS aiding his wife to tidy up the walled-garden at their small castle of Aberdour in Fife, scything the weeds which were already growing high beneath the gnarled old apple-trees, while she raked up the scythings into heaps — which the children almost as consistently scattered in their joyful fighting. Jamie was a less than enthusiastic gardener, and scything was sore on the back; he would much have preferred to leave it to Tom Durie, the steward's son, whose job it was, and gone fishing this sunny June day. But Mary enjoyed the garden and its tasks, and complained that he seldom was available to help her there, and when he was, usually found excuse to do something else. So this fine forenoon he had succumbed — on condition that she came out in the boat with him in the afternoon, to fish for flounders in the bay between Aberdour and St. Colm's Inch. They would land the bairns on the island with their nurse Janet Durie, beforehand, and win some peace from the clamour of small tongues on the sparkling waters of the firth. Then they would return to the island to cook the hoped-for flukies on stones heated on a fire amongst the rocks, to the delectation of all. This programme, skilfully angled to coax Mary Stewart who had an especial interest in Inchcolm, had been accepted. But meantime there was the back-breaking business of wielding a scythe, an instrument designed by fiends, with all the wrong dimensions, shapes and angles to ensure maximum distress to the wielder, not to mention risk to life and limb.

Much straightening of back, groaning and mopping of brow — for it was sheltered in the walled-garden and the June sun was hot — was the order of the day, then, with curses at hidden stones amongst the weeds, apple-tree trunks, ill-behaved brats and pestiferous flies, when the noise of clattering hooves, jingling accoutrements and halloes came from the direction of the courtyard at the other side of the castle.

"Ha!" said Sir James Douglas.

His wife frowned accusingly. "Ha, indeed! What now? Who comes noisily to our door at this hour, spoiling our day? Is this some ill ploy of yours . . .?"

"Not so," he asserted. "I have no notion who it is. Interrupting the good work. Perhaps I will be able to send them about their business in no time, at all." But he was discarding his scythe and rolling down his shirt-sleeves efficiently as he spoke.

"No need to be in such haste then, my goodness!" she protested — but he was already striding off for the garden-gate.

Round at the front of his stocky, square stone keep, he found a whole troop of horsemen in the colours of the royal guard. Even so, he was unprepared for the Lieutenant of the Kingdom himself to be sitting his stallion there within the cobbled court-yard, with the handsome Sir John de Ramorgnie on one side and the Archdeacon Thomas Stewart of St. Andrews on the other. It was the Duke David's first visit to Aberdour Castle. Normally he summoned people to his presence, not called on them in person.

"Jamie Douglas!" the prince cried, "A picture of rude health, and sweating like a hog! So this is your roost by the silver sands. Hay-making — or love-making?"

"Being a better husband than some, my lord Duke!" the other gave back. "But — welcome to my house." Jamie nodded distantly towards Ramorgnie but more warmly to the Archdeacon, whom he liked and who was indeed his own brother-in-law, having the same father and mother as Mary, which father was the late King. He looked very undiaconal in scarlet velvet.

"We are on our way to St. Andrews," David said. "Bishop Trail is sick. I needs must have speech with him. But meantime, I have an errand for you, Jamie."

"I feared as much!" Mary's voice spoke from behind.

"Ah, my comely aunt!" the Duke exclaimed. "On my soul, you look almost as warm as your spouse — and none the less fetching for that! I vow we have caught you at a hot work, the pair of you! Haymaking . . . or other!"

"Scythe and rake work, Nephew. More honest than some! Greetings, Tom. You keep unlikely company! A good day, Sir John."

"You spoke of an errand, my lord," Jamie said. "I am sorry to hear that the good Bishop is ill. We could do with more of his like in Scotland."

"To be sure. But the errand does not concern Trail. It is more important than that, than any one man."

"You had better come within, Davie," Mary said. "A beaker of wine and a bannock whilst you wean my husband away from his honest duties! Durie will serve your men ale . . ."

Dismounting, the leading visitors were conducted upstairs to the first-floor Hall, bright in the forenoon sun with the glittering sea acting mirror.

"You are on the road early," Jamie observed, "to have won here at this hour." The Duke of Rothesay was not noted for his early rising.

"Aye — we were at Dunfermline. Yesterday, I had a letter which made it more than ever urgent that I see Trail — which I was for doing anyway. Money, Jamie — siller. We are going to require a deal of siller. And Trail, as Primate, has the key to Holy Church's coffers in his episcopal hand. The realm's coffers being, as usual, empty!"

"I know that he has been aiding you, yes, this year and more past. You need more?"

"Much more, I fear. I am going to have to muster the realm in arms."

"Dear God! The English again?"

"Aye, the English again. But not just Hotspur and his friend Dunbar, this time. King Henry, with his whole might."

"War? Full armed invasion?"

"No less. Clearly Henry has decided on it. Mainly as a means of drawing attention away from his own troubles with his nobles, I think — but none the better for us, in that! Ever since yon affair with Hotspur in Lothian, that you were at, we have been getting word that Henry was assembling men at York. I hoped that it might be to deal with his own dissident barons, who still name him usurper. But now he has moved his army to Newcastle. And yesterday, from there, he sent my father a letter — as good as a declaration of war."

"Is it not another trick? A feint? With so much unrest in his own realm? They say that even the Marcher earls are making common cause with the Welsh against him — and when that happens, anything could happen in England."

"Maybe so. Henry Bolingbroke may be a trickster, yes. But he is also a gambler. And this time I believe he intends to risk much, possibly all, on a toss. This is no mere feint. He could lead his armies away south again, to be sure, at little cost. But not ships. My information is that he is assembling shipping from all the east side of England, at Newcastle, and loading them with arms, supplies, forage and siege-engines. That is too costly a ploy for any trick."

Jamie was silent.

"His letter does not sound like play-acting, either," Ramorgnie put in.

"Aye — the letter is a deliberate provocation. Designed to cover his invasion with some cloak of legality. He writes to my father in seemingly friendly terms, but styles him his vassal. He declares that since the days of someone he names as Locrinus son of Brutus the Kings of England have been Lords Superior of Scotland — God knows who these were! And declares that he will come to Edinburgh before the 23rd day of August, the Eve of St. Bartholomew, to receive my father's homage and fealty."

"But . . . this is sheerest folly!" Jamie exclaimed. "All must know it — the English no less than others. There is no thread of truth in any of it. How can this serve him?"

"Use your wits, man," Ramorgnie said. "Edward the First started this ancient canard — or revived it. And got the English parliament to accept and confirm his claims. As did his son Edward the Second and his grandson Edward the Third. Richard likewise. All obtained their parliaments' agreement and authority. This Henry merely follows precedent — and thereby establishes himself in the good Plantagenet tradition. A worthy successor of these more lawful monarchs. But, more important than that — he needs parliament's backing in money to pay for his armies and ships, for he has little of his own. He would not have got the moneys for putting down his own rebellious lords. So he takes the Scots for his whipping-post. That letter was written for the English parliament rather than for the Duke's royal father."

"It is no mere flourish of the pen, nevertheless," David added. "He is giving us warning not to oppose him. A swift triumph in Scotland would suit him very well. As victor he would then seem to unite the English, and turn and deal with his factious lords and the Welsh. But his victory would have to be swift, for a prolonged and costly campaign in Scotland would *harm* his cause as grievously. We must see that it is so. But for that I need a deal of siller!"

"You need more than siller, my lord!"

"To be sure. But the money will help, if our full muster is to be achieved. Most of our good Scots lords will require priming with siller to produce their greatest numbers of men. The burghs likewise. But Holy Church will help in the matter, I am assured — with my beloved Uncle Tom's good offices! God knows whether Trail's present malady will aid or hinder in the matter!"

"Bishop Trail has ever been a leal friend to your father and mother," the Archdeacon Thomas said. "And to the realm. He will not fail you now, I think."

"And his see the most wealthy in that realm!" Ramorgnie pointed out, smiling thinly.

"And *my* errand?" Jamie put in.

"I wonder that you need ask! The Douglas power in men is the greatest in the land. *And* readiest to take the field! I want you to go in haste to Threave, in Galloway, and get the Earl Archie, my good-father, to call out the whole of Douglas. The old devil is bed-ridden, they say, but he keeps the power in his own hands. The Master will lead, of course, but his father's authority is required to muster Douglas, as you well know."

"Yes. Where is the Master?"

"In the Borders, somewhere. Find him, and send him to me, Jamie. I shall be at Edinburgh Castle. And Jamie — call on your own father in the bygoing, and see what Dalkeith can raise. In men . . . and siller too."

"How long, think you, have we to muster our force?"

"Who knows? Henry says he will be in Edinburgh by St. Bartholomew's Eve. But he could invade much earlier. However, an English parliament is called, at York, for next month, July. The Feast of St. James. If we judge aright, Henry will wait until after that. It will be a packed parliament and will get him what he wants. He will prefer to wait for it, I think. So we have a month, perhaps. Even six weeks. But no time to waste."

"We cannot prevent it? This invasion? By guile, as you did yon time at Haddonstank. Or by striking first?"

"Not if Henry is determined — as I conceive him to be, this time. And to strike first, in sufficient strength — at Carlisle or

235

the Middle March say — requires that we be *mustered* first. Which is scarce likely. And we have not got the Isle of Man to use as threat this time, with Dunbar on the wrong side. We have to watch Donald of the Isles, too. This might seem to him his opportunity. No — I fear on this occasion we must stand and fight, Jamie."

"Sir James is the warrior-hero!" Ramorgnie said. "He will relish that."

"While Sir John will no doubt write us a prolocution!" Mary added tartly.

*　　*　　*

In the event, they were granted nearer eight weeks than six — and required it all. What delayed Henry Plantagenet was not clear, from Edinburgh — if indeed he ever did intend to start before mid-August. But it was then that he gave command for his great army to march and his fleet to prepare for sea. Not that the Scots could point any fingers of scorn over delays in mustering and preparation, their own performance being little more expeditious. It was hay-harvest time, to be sure, at first, and the lords and lairds, as well as vassals and farmers, claimed it vital to get the hay-crop in, to provide the necessary forage for the horses and cattle on which all depended. The same would apply to the English, of course. Then the corn-harvest began to loom ahead. The Douglases assembled fairly swiftly, although not quite in their fullest strength even yet. But others were more dilatory. They greatly missed the fine Mersemen's contingent which the Earl of Dunbar could have fielded, and which would not rise in any numbers for anybody else. Arousing full mobilisation of the North-East was always a problem when the danger was in the South, from over the Border — to the Ogilvys, Keiths, Gordons, Hays, Cummings and the like it was all too far away to constitute an evident threat, with internecine clan warfare much more pressing. And much of the South-West particularly was inhibited from major participation for fear of what the Lord of the Isles might do to their unprotected lands whilst they were away fighting the English. The word from the Hebrides, indeed, was that Donald was assembling his war galleys at Islay by the hundred — and that made almost as ominous a sound in Lowland ears as did the slogan "A Douglas!" in Northumbrian.

In the great fortress of Edinburgh Castle on its lofty rock

above the crouching grey city, so like Stirling, the groups of
men around the Duke of Rothesay gazed north-eastwards from
the battlements in some doubt and dismay. For long they had
been watching and counting and wondering. Out there on the
wide firth they could see at least thirty-two large vessels, their
sails white against the blue water, a vast fleet. They had been
beating up the Forth estuary against a light south-westerly
breeze for hours, and now the foremost ships were almost
opposite the harbour of Leith, Edinburgh's port, less than three
miles away. This huge flotilla represented menace, however fair
a sight to the uncommitted observer. But more than just menace,
it represented a grievous problem, a possible upsetting of the
Scots defensive plans. The latest reports from the Master of
Douglas put King Henry and his army of allegedly 60,000 no
further north than Lauder. The English had chosen to invade,
not up the east coast from Berwick but by the Tweed fords of
Coldstream and Carham and thereafter through the Middle
March, by Kelso and Dryburgh, Melrose and Ercildoune, and
so up Lauderdale. They appeared to be in no great hurry, proceeding at the deliberate pace of the large numbers of foot and
the clumsy destriers of the heavy chivalry, the Douglases
skirmishing warily before them, not risking any set engagement
but nibbling, harassing and seeking to delay. The Master
advised that at this rate they would not be in Edinburgh before
the following evening. Yet here was this fleet already off
Leith.

Alex Stewart, who had brought six hundred Badenoch and
Clan Chattan clansmen to the muster, with more to follow,
shook his fair head. "I do not see why you are so concerned,"
he said. "Shipping cannot be timed, like marching men, whatever. Contrary winds, flat calms, can greatly delay a fleet.
Therefore they must allow ample time. They have arrived first —
and so will wait for their King."

"If we could be sure of that we would not be concerned,
man!" David snapped, impatiently. "The question is — what is
aboard those ships? Supplies — or men? Troops. If troops,
then all could be changed. They could be landing in large
numbers any time now. Long before Henry and his array
arrives. Worse, long before *our* main strength arrives."

"We can oppose their landing," Jamie said. "Landing men
from large ships at a port is slow work, and difficult. Against
opposition, more so. We could prevent those ships from tying

237

up at the quays. Only a few could do so at a time, forby — that haven is not sufficiently large to take many. Not like Berwick or Dumbarton. This will force them to use small boats — to our advantage. We could greatly delay a landing."

"Perhaps . . ."

"That means dispersing more of our own men," Ramorgnie put in. "And we have few enough with us here, as it is."

That was true, at least. The main Scottish defensive forces had been assembled at Stirling and Lanark, and were not expected to reach Edinburgh before that evening at the soonest. The Master of Douglas had his force detached in the Borders, though now falling back on Edinburgh. And of the 2,000 or so meantime in Rothesay's immediate command, quite a large proportion were engaged in the town, superintending the reluctant evacuation of the citizens. This had been an unhappy decision David Stewart had had to take; for though Edinburgh was a walled town, it was not nearly strong enough to resist the assault of a major army; and Henry had said that he was coming there. The great castle on its rock was indeed defensible, the more so once the additional pits and barricades hurriedly being contrived were completed. It would be folly, with their present numbers, to attempt to defend the city itself. So an exodus had been ordered for the folk, with their most precious belongings, and this being unpopular with many, troops had to be used to enforce it.

"A few hundred could much hold up a landing at Leith," Jamie contended. "Better than standing here idle."

"Very well. Take a horsed force down to the port," the prince said. "Do what you can. But be ready to return here at any moment. You can see this castle and rock from Leith. A column of smoke by day, or a fire by night — two fires, say — to bring you back. You have it?"

So Jamie and Alex took some four hundred men, mainly Dalkeith horsemen and Highlanders from Badenoch, and hurried down the three miles to Leith haven, where the Water of Leith entered the firth, directly across the eight-miles-wide estuary from his own house of Aberdour. By the time that they got there, the leading ships of the enemy fleet were standing off only half-a-mile out, and a daunting sight they made. Even as they watched, small boats were being lowered from one or two, no doubt to come and inspect at closer quarters the landing facilities and state of defence. To discourage all such, Jamie had bonfires heaped up and lit all along the waterfront, to at least warn of a hot reception.

The haven of Leith lined both sides of the river-mouth with quays and jetties; but these were mainly for small craft and fishing-boats and no more than half-a-dozen of the large English ships would be able to tie up at one time. There were a number of fishing craft and coastal vessels already in the harbour and these Jamie ordered to be moved so that a tight wedge of the former blocked the harbour mouth, and the latter were disposed to occupy the deeper berths which the large enemy ships would require.

This activity would be fairly obvious from the sea, and the English rowing-boats did not approach too closely. Alex had a few archers with him — the Highlanders were more proficient with bows than were the Lowlanders, since they used them for stalking deer. These he caused to wing a few arrows with blazing tow out towards the boats — which, although they fell hopelessly short, served to show that any landing would be opposed by bowmen.

The small boats duly kept their distance.

All the rest of the day Jamie's force, reinforced by such of Leith's manpower as had not moved out, showed themselves determinedly riding or marching to and fro with great activity, not only at the port itself but along the shoreside links east and west, lighting more fires, even digging trenches in the sand and erecting sham barriers on the dunes, to look like counter-archery defences. The entire English fleet, now thirty-four vessels, came to cluster at anchor in the roads; but though there was much passage of small rowing-boats between them, no move was made at a landing meantime.

No summons showed from Edinburgh Castle commanding a return.

As the late-summer dusk settled on land and sea, there was no respite for the busy defenders. The English might well attempt their landing under cover of night, either in force on the harbour or, more likely, dispersed along the coast. On the other hand, as Alex pointed out, they might not, considering a descent in the dark upon an unknown, warned and defended shore more hazardous even than by day. Jamie took no chances. Continually replenished fires seemed to be the best indication that the defence was alert and eager, and these were increased in numbers all along the shoreline for at least a couple of miles.

Fuel was becoming a major problem, and everything which would burn was pressed into service — drift-wood, old boat-timbers, tree-branches, straw, whin-bushes, even house furnishings, unpopular as was their requisition. The Gaelic-speaking Highlanders were good at this — and impervious to the complaints and threats of the outraged citizenry.

No attack came, but Jamie would permit no relaxation. The enemy might well be waiting for the dawn, when the defenders could be expected to be weary and at their least acute. Weary they were. When no early morning developments took place, Jamie did allow some standing down and sleep. They would now have sufficient warning of any attempt. It looked as though the foe were, in fact, prepared to wait until their land host arrived — in which case the probability was that the fleet did indeed bring only supplies, not troops, and all their own defensive façade was unnecessary.

It was in mid-afternoon that a tall smoke-column could be seen rising above Edinburgh Castle rock on the southern horizon, summoning the defensive force to return — to the alarm of the remaining Leithers. Jamie was sorry, but had no option. He made a final replenishment of the fires, advised the townsfolk to move out, but unobtrusively, and then withdrew his own people as secretly as possible so that their going should not be obvious to the ships.

They arrived back at the fortress to find all in a state of excitement. The castle was now packed with men and horses, the Master of Douglas and his force having arrived, with the word that King Henry's forward troops were only a few miles off. Jamie's half-brothers were with the Master; and his father, frail now but on his feet again, had come also, with his wife and womenfolk, since Dalkeith was directly in the path of the advancing army, which had streamed over the west Lammermuir pass of Soutra from upper Lauderdale. The Lady Isabel Stewart and her husband from Edmonstone had also been brought, for security.

David Stewart was in a quandary. There were no tidings of the main Scots muster from Stirling and Lanark, although he had sent urgent messengers to make contact. He had not intended the Douglas force all to crowd into the castle precincts like this, in especial their horses; for though the fortress covered a large area of the rock-summit, there was no room, nor forage, for hundreds upon hundreds of horses. The Douglases had been intended to join the main army, coming from the west, under Lindsay, Earl of Crawford, and so to constitute a major threat to the English flank. But they had been harassing the enemy advance day and night for three days, and were exhausted. They must be given time to rest. In the end, it was decided to send away the horses, under a small guard, to a safe distance westwards. Whether the riders joined them there later would depend on circumstances.

David's designed strategy was to get the English army cooped up in Edinburgh town — which was now almost wholly empty of its townsfolk — immobilise it as far as was possible in siege warfare, and then have it attacked by night by the main Scottish forces, on at least two flanks, whereupon the castle defenders would sally out and hope to complete a rout. Whether or not this was feasible depended on a number of factors; but nothing could be attempted until the reinforcements did arrive somewhere nearby — hence the prince's agitation. Lindsay was a veteran soldier and should be well aware of the situation.

Meantime, however, to delay matters, he resorted to a device. Under his personal banner and his own Rothesay Herald, he sent a challenge to King Henry, whom his scouts sent news had in fact halted at Dalkeith for the night, some seven miles to the south. In true if somewhat outmoded chivalric fashion, he sent his cartel and requested a face-to-face duel between himself and Henry, to settle their differences, carefully referring to the Plantagenet, not as King but as his 'adversary of England'. And if this was unacceptable, he suggested a knightly fight between selected noble contestants of 100, 200 or 300 a side. It was not expected that Henry would agree to this — few of his family had been noted for their chivalric qualities — but it might serve to delay, by producing an exchange of notes and so give time for Crawford to arrive.

It was dark before the herald got back from Dalkeith. He brought a letter from Henry thanking the Duke of Rothesay for his message but pointing out that he could not, as monarch and Lord Paramount, accept challenges from his own vassals however high-born. As for knightly combat, he was here to receive due submissions of fealty not to engage in tourneys and the like. He would present himself before Edinburgh Castle next forenoon, and expect to receive all necessary tokens of leal duty. He remained his esteemed cousin David's loving friend, protector and liege lord, Henry R.

Next morning they watched the endless columns of the English might stream down over the low escarpments of Edmonstone, Gilmerton and Liberton towards Edinburgh's Burgh Muir. Then one of David's own messengers arrived hot-foot from the west, to announce that the Scottish main army was at last approaching into Lothian. When he had left, it was nearing the Calder area some fifteen miles to the west, but in no great haste. He had urged all speed, but the Duke of Albany had refused to be hurried.

"Albany!" the prince exclaimed. "He is there? What in God's name has he to do with it?"

"He is in command, my lord Duke. He has superseded the Earl of Crawford and the Earl of Moray in the command."

"But — fiend seize him, *I* appointed Lindsay to command! My Uncle Robert has no authority to do anything of the sort. He is no soldier. Lindsay still must command — and you will go back and tell him so!"

"My lord," the messenger quavered, "how can I do that? The Duke Robert will not heed me. He is a proud man and more like to slay me!"

"I shall give you a writing. I am Lieutenant of this realm, and will not have my orders set aside by any soever. Lindsay must resume command and carry out the plan I told him of. I will not have my uncle interfering."

The prince ordered Ramorgnie to write a mandate for him to sign. The Douglases, with Alex Stewart, drew aside, long-faced.

"This is damnable!" the Master declared. "What is the meaning of it? Albany is not a fighting-man, no commander. Why do this?"

"It may be that he wishes to make a gesture to the nation," Alex suggested. "Smarting at having been put down as Governor, in favour of David, he would show that he is still a force to be reckoned with. Come hastening to aid the realm in this pass. He may only *seem* to take command, in name — since he could scarcely serve under Crawford. But leave the true direction of the army to Crawford and Moray."

"I think not," Jamie said. "Albany never acts without careful thought. He does not make gestures. He hates his nephew and will pull him down if he can. I fear that he will seek to use this trouble to do so. He will ignore David's written orders, I swear."

242

"You mean, not carry out David's plan against the English? You would not make him turn traitor?"

"Not traitor, no — for he hates the English also. But not use the army as David wishes. Something has brought him out from Doune Castle at this time, to take a hand. I cannot think that it bodes well for us of David's company."

That foreboding was reinforced a short time afterwards when, soon after the messenger had departed once more for the Calder area, a new arrival reached Edinburgh Castle — none other than David Lindsay, Earl of Crawford himself. Never a patient or gentle man, he came in a towering rage, announcing that he had never been so insulted and abused in his life, that he would not stay another hour in Robert Stewart's company, that the man was impossible, arrogant, presumptuous. He had taken over command of the entire Scots force as of right, and had even appointed his own oafish offspring Murdoch Stewart as second-in-command. That weakly puppy Moray had elected to stay on under this precious pair. But he, the Lindsay, was damned if he would!

The prince tried hard to make the irate Crawford go back and resume his command, with his own express authority, but to no avail. He was then considering going himself — although he felt that his place was here, to confront Henry in person — when the matter was settled for them. The English advance cavalry arrived in force in front of the castle, the last Scots troops in the city scurrying into safety before them, and all entry to or exit from the fortress was barred. For better or for worse, the situation was crystallised.

Crawford could tell them little of Albany's intentions. He had come to them not at Stirling but at Linlithgow, on their way here, and had insisted on all marching southwards to join the Lanark muster instead of coming on direct to Edinburgh, thus causing much delay. Montgomerie of Eaglesham was commanding the Lanark and South-West contingent, a good man who would do his best; but what could he achieve against Albany's steely will? The total muster of the combined force was about 20,000. It was Crawford's belief that Albany had little intention of fighting, but rather of seeking to use the Scots army as a bargaining piece.

"Bargaining?" David exclaimed. "What has *he* to bargain with?"

Crawford shrugged. "I cannot see into Robert Stewart's dark

mind. But this I do know — that he believes that Henry has come now principally to lay hands on the Mammet."

"The Mammet! God's eyes — that mountebank! Mount his great invasion for that?"

"Your royal father does not call him a mountebank. And even if Henry does, he could wish to remove him, as a figure-head for his dissident lords to rally round, a threat against his throne. So Albany believes. He said as much. *I* believe he would use the Mammet to bargain with."

"But — he it was who cherished the man! Entertained him in his house. Brought him to my father. To hand him over now to Henry would mean his execution — nothing surer."

"Think you that would trouble your uncle? It was not for love that he cherished him, I vow! I wondered why, at the time. This may be the answer."

"The man is with my father at Turnberry."

"Perhaps that was why Albany delayed the army? To give him time to send to Ayrshire and take this Richard out of the King's keeping? He could do it, could he not?"

"Yes — oh, yes. My father keeps but a small guard."

"Then that may be Robert's strategy. That *he* may seem to deliver the realm, not you. And without bloodshed it may be, offering the Mammet and a clear return to the Border, and holding our army as threat . . ."

Discussion was halted by the personal arrival of Henry Bolingbroke. He came in style up to the castle forecourt in a colourful company, mounted on magnificent destriers, all gleaming armour, tossing plumes, heraldic surcoats and ban-ners, with mounted musicians playing a stirring march and a forest of slender lances at his back. Just outwith bow-shot of the drawbridge and gatehouse, this splendid cavalcade halted, and trumpeters blew a prolonged fanfare, whilst the bareheaded, fair-haired, gilten-armoured figure sat his white charger beneath the fluttering Leopard standard of Plantagenet England.

A tabarded herald, with two pursuivants, rode a little further forward, and when the trumpets fell silent, raised his voice.

"In the name of the high and mighty Prince Henry, by the grace of God King of England, France, and Ireland, Prince of Wales, Duke of Normandy and Aquitaine, Lord Paramount of Scotland — greetings! The Lord Henry, fourth of his name, requires whosoever represents his vassal, Robert, King of Scots, in this hold, to come speak with him, in peace and duty."

David Stewart and his party had moved down to the gate-house-tower, but now, on its parapet-walk, deliberately turned his back on the visitors, and laughed aloud. No other response was made to the high-sounding summons.

After an uncertain pause, the herald tried again, repeating the same wording, save that he changed requires into commands, and added the phrase, ". . . under penalty of His Grace Henry's severest displeasure."

David had had a brief word with his cousin Alex, and now two of his Clan Chattan pipers started to blow on their instruments, and out of the preliminary wails and groans developed a lively skittish jig tune, tripping, skirling, toe-tapping, which rose and continued as the musicians strutted, all but skipped, to and fro along the parapet-walk.

After a little of it, the herald turned and moved back to his master.

Still the pipers blew and jigged — and perforce the King of England must stand and wait, or else leave the scene, since by no means could voices carry above the disrespectfully cheerful ranting. Trumpets might possibly have out-blasted the pipes, but assuredly, requiring so much more puff, they could not have continued for so long, and would have had to yield ingloriously eventually. It was a difficult situation for Henry, but after his first black frowning he made the best of it, turning in his saddle and chatting smilingly to some of his near company.

At length David signed for the pipers to stop, and assumed the initiative.

"Henry, Duke of Lancaster and Earl of Hereford, usurper to the English throne," he called clearly, "I, David, Prince and Lieutenant of Scotland and Duke of Rothesay, declare that you have grievously injured and insulted my father's ancient realm of Scotland by entering it uninvited and by armed invasion, contrary to all treaties and compacts. Indeed contrary to all honest behaviour between neighbouring states in Christendom. You have refused to meet me, or mine, in knightly encounter or combat, and so further besmirched your own escutcheon. In the name of the King of Scots, I command that you leave this city and realm forthwith and retire across your own borders. Whereafter, if you have any due cause or reason for debate, we may discuss it at some chosen point, as honest men should. Or take the consequences."

245

"What consequences, sirrah?" That brief question brought a shout of laughter from the English ranks.

"Threefold consequences, my lord Duke. First, lest the main forces of my father the King, presently assembling to the west, fall upon you in great numbers. Second, lest I send signal to our strength waiting in Galloway, to descend upon and sack your towns of Carlisle, Lancaster, Newcastle and Durham. And third, lest we raise the standard of your rightful liege lord, King Richard of England, presently in our care, and march south in full might, summoning all leal Englishmen, lords and commons, to his support. The Welsh likewise."

"Hollow threats!" Henry called back. "None of which you can achieve. Besides, I have not come in war. Had I done so, you would have discovered it ere this, I promise you! I have come to receive the fealties due to me as Lord Paramount, as is my undoubted right. Make such due fealty — I shall accept yours, in your father's name, since I understand him to be a sick man — and I shall return to England, in amity and good-will."

"Amity and goodwill!" David cried. "Do you require 60,000 men to show your amity? You do not know what the words mean . . ."

"You think not? Why then have I come all this way, sparing your people? There has been no burning, no sacking, no ravishing. I have used all in my path kindly. As the Abbots of Kelso, Dryburgh and Melrose. I have no wish to fight the Scots. I have the greatest regard for your lady-mother the Queen Annabella, of whom all speak well. I have Scots blood in my own veins, Comyn blood. I come to offer my hand in friendship."

"In friendship we might accept your hand. But none, in this independent realm, will kiss it. Or hold it in fealty."

"We shall see. It was not you that I came to speak with. But a certain magnate of your land, anxious to give him opportunity of establishing his innocence or proving my guilt. For he has grievously libelled me to the so-called King of France. But he has not dared to answer me, or face me . . ."

"If you refer to my uncle Albany, my lord Duke, you must seek him elsewhere. *I* now rule this realm, in my father's name, and by due nomination of parliament."

"And little the better for the realm, I swear!" Abruptly Henry Plantagenet had had enough. He turned to his herald, with an impatient gesture of his hand, and wheeled his destrier around.

The trumpets blared out their high flourish before those deplorable bagpipes could start up again, and the English ranks parted left and right to allow their King to ride off.

Prolonged cheering arose from all Edinburgh Castle's battlements and towers.

"So much for talk," Jamie observed, to Alex. "Now we shall see what deeds may achieve."

"I have never been concerned in a siege," the other said.

"I have — but never as a defender."

"This hold would look to me impregnable?"

"To direct assault, perhaps. But prolonged siege is another matter. We have much too many men cooped up here to feed. Of water there is plenty, for excellent wells pierce the rock. But food and forage . . ."

"How long do you give us?"

"God knows. It scarcely rests with us, now. So much depends on what Albany does. And in how much haste is Henry Plantagenet."

*　　*　　*

Albany, in the event, did nothing — or if he did anything, no hint of it became evident to the besieged in Edinburgh Castle; nor, it appeared, to the besiegers either, for no sign of alarm or concern was to be seen amongst them. The deeds which were to succeed Henry's words were also slow in developing. All next day the English were occupied in bringing up the heavy and cumbersome siege-machinery from the ships at Leith — mangonels, ballistae, sows, rams, scaling-towers and the like, massive equipment shipped in pieces which had to be drawn up from the port by great teams of oxen at a snail's pace, and then assembled. All was entirely evident to the watchers up on the castle-rock, spread below them as on a map. No assault was mounted that day, and all night the besieged could hear the hammering of carpenters and smiths as they put together the engines by the light of torches and bonfires.

Even so it was mid-day before the first of the vast lumbering devices was moved up into position on the forecourt which spread like a fairly narrow apron before the gatehouse-towers. The huge rock was precipitous on all sides save a segment to due east, where a sort of ramp slanted down, the commencement of the long spine of ridge on which the city was built and which sloped for almost a mile down to the Abbey of the Holy

Rood at the foot of the crags of Arthur's Seat. Only on this ramp-like terrace, levelled to form the forecourt, could anyone approach the fortress; and here the engines were brought. The first two were mangonels, great slings for the throwing of heavy stones to batter the defensive masonry and towers, mounted on massive wooden scaffolding. The English pushed and manoeuvred these unwieldy monsters up to just outwith bow-shot, and began trundling up their supplies of stones and small boulders. These averaged about twice the size of a man's head.

The besieged were not entirely defenceless against these. The castle had four lesser mangonels and some ballistae of its own, though these had not the range or power of the enemy's. The Master of Douglas — who, as keeper of the castle was responsible — waited for the English to fire their first ranging shots — which went wide and did no damage. Then he loosed off all four of his own engines, hidden hitherto behind flags and banners. Two missiles fell short, one overshot, but the fourth smashed into the base of one of the enemy mangonels, scattering the men grouped there — to loud cheers from the castle.

In the circumstances, the lighter Scots weapons were more quickly reloaded and adjusted as to aim, and another salvo was hurled at the enemy. Two of these shots missed altogether, but the other two both hit the same target, putting it at least temporarily out of action. It was good shooting — but then the defenders had had ample time to practise and range their machines.

There followed hasty English efforts to withdraw their difficult contrivances out of range of the Scots, and more damage was sustained during the slow process, and casualties caused, before the things were dragged backwards sufficiently far.

A good start had been made, and first blood to the defenders. But none allowed it to go to their heads. The larger enemy mangonels could still operate from further off; and the element of surprise was now lost.

It was some time before the first English shot came from the new position, about one hundred and fifty yards back and at the very edge of the forecourt area. This missile fell considerably short, but the impact and the hole it made in the cobblestones of the approach to the drawbridge, showed that its force was far from spent. That lesson was reinforced with the next shot, which crashed into the walling north of the gatehouse, doing no real damage but proving that they were certainly not out of range.

After that the defenders just had to stand and take the bombardment. Fortunately for them only the one enemy engine was now in working order, and ballistae were of no avail at this range. Moreover the mangonel, operating from fairly near extreme range, had less force in its impact than might have been the case. But even so, considerable damage was done to the gatehouse-towers and parapets and the contiguous walling; and some men were hit, mainly by flying chips and splinters from their own masonry. The raised drawbridge itself was protected by the iron grating of the portcullis, fortunately. But by evening, the outer east frontage of the fortress was beginning to have a distinctly battered appearance.

No sign nor signal came from the Duke of Albany on Calder Moor.

The Scots feared an assault under cover of darkness, when the battering-rams and sows and scaling-towers might be brought up into position fairly secure from the attentions of defensive bowmen and ballistae. To seek to counter this, bonfires were lit and kept blazing all along the battlements. But this meant that the target area was well illuminated for the English mangonel, and the bombardment continued. Their own engines kept up flinging in the intermittent shot, to discourage closer approach.

They could hear the clanking, creaking and thudding of heavy equipment being moved up, and sensed the continual stir just beyond vision.

It was Alex Stewart who, just after midnight, suggested the idea of a sally, put to Jamie. After discussing its feasibility, they went together to the prince.

"We have the men," Alex declared. "The English will scarcely expect it. A swift stroke out, and then back. Put their preparations in disarray. It could be good for our people's spirit. Better than inactivity."

"It could be costly in men's lives."

"I think not. There, where they are working and assembling, is narrow. Where the town street joins the forecourt. They will be much congested, unable to bring up large numbers. If we give them little warning, we might overwhelm those there, do much damage before they could recover, and then retire."

"Damage? To the engines, you mean?"

"Fire," Jamie put in. "Take many torches, kindling, pitch.

Make fires under the legs of yonder mangonel. Others, too. Hold the English back until they are well alight, if we can."

"By the mass — a ploy! How many do you need?"

"Not many, too many would be but a hindrance. Say two hundred. Highlandmen and Douglases."

"As I see it, the danger is here," Alex said. "The noise made by the portcullis and drawbridge chains, giving the English warning."

"We could make other loud noise. To drown it."

"That likewise could warn that there was something to do . . ."

"Grease," Jamie said. "Melted fat. Poured on the chains and hinges."

"That should help, yes. You will lead the venture, Jamie?"

"Both of us," Alex declared. "One to see to the burning, one to command the guard. Let us be doing, I say . . ."

It did not take long to prepare the sally, and there was no lack of volunteers. The greasing of the drawbridge and portcullis machinery took longer, the chain-drums being in an awkward position. The fighting-men fretted lest the enemy should make their move first.

At length all was ready, with two hundred men, armed with swords and axes and some lances, and carrying torches, turpentine-pinewood and pitch-soaked rags, massed at the gate-house pend. The signal was given for the raising of the portcullis and the lowering of the bridge. The former creaked and scraped metallically as it came up, and the latter clanked and rumbled as it came down, its chains far from soundless. Nevertheless, the noise was a lot less than normal, and probably would not be noticeable at any distance, especially if the enemy were busily engaged on their own noise-making activities. The Scots prayed so, at any rate.

Even before the bridge was fully lowered, Jamie and Alex were out on its timbers, men thronging close at their backs. In chain-mail armour and laden as they were, they could not actually run; but at almost a trot the close-packed force hurried out onto the forecourt cobbles.

They had almost two hundred and fifty yards to cover. Every yard of the way they could go undetected, the better their chances. All but holding his breath, Jamie cursed every scrape of boot on cobblestone, every clink of steel, even the puffings and pantings of their followers.

Half-way, and no sign of alarm ahead. Dark figures could now be distinguished moving around the tall silhouettes of the siege-engines, outlined against the glow of the fires. Hammering and sawing resounded. But no shouts.

"*Dia* — we will do it!" Alex jerked. "We have them, whatever!" He was right. The two hundred were within a score of yards or so of the working men before they were noticed. Astonished Englishmen dropped tools, ropes-and-pulleys, baulks of timber. Clearly they were repairing the damaged mangonel. Some rushed to snatch up weapons. But it was too late for any immediate defence. Most of the men around the great engines realised it and fled.

"All drop torches and wood!" Jamie shouted, need for silence over. "Alex — on with you! My fifty — here. Flint and tinder. Stack the wood. Quickly!"

Stewart and the majority of the force pressed on, as arranged. Beyond the forecourt entrance, the Castlegait narrowed between tall buildings, then opened out to the wider space of the Lawnmarket. That would be where the forward English troops would be assembled, waiting, where they would not hinder the work on the engines. Pursuing the fleeing men down the narrow hundred yards or so of the Castlegait, Alex halted his people within the far mouth of it, stoppering it like the neck of a bottle, one hundred and fifty men packed tightly, ten deep, lances like a jagged frieze before the front ranks.

Beyond, all was now noise and confusion, as the carpenters, wrights and smiths burst in on the long ranks of resting soldiery, in panic, shouting that the Scots were upon them. The files of armed men stretched far down the Lawnmarket and into the High Street beyond, past the great High Church of St. Giles, thousands of waiting men, ready to advance, but meantime relaxed, idling, many asleep on the causeway. They were scarcely to be blamed if their reaction was slow and unco-ordinated. The Lawnmarket and High Street were considerably wider than the Castlegait, but were only city streets for all that, and a city on a spine of ridge — not the best marshalling-place for troops. Moreover it was dark, and the leaders were not meantime spaced out amongst their commands but assembled, actually in St. Giles Church, for final orders, and awaiting word that the repairs to the siege-engines were completed. No swift counter-attack on the Castlegait party developed.

Meanwhile, Jamie and his people were busy. It did not take

long to light the torches and use them as the nuclei of bonfires which they heaped around the massive timbers of the mangonels, ballistae and scaling-towers. But it seemed to take an unconscionable time for the heavy structures really to catch alight. There were more items to damage than they had realised, assembled there, and their fuel supply had to be rationed out. All the time, Jamie was expecting Alex and his men to come streaming back, urging hasty retiral, before the fires could get a grip.

In the event, there was ample time. Indeed, presently Jamie sent men down the Castlegait to discover what had happened to their friends, with the word that the fires were now burning fiercely and the engines' supporting frames, smeared with pitch and wrapped around with the rags, were themselves blazing strongly.

Alex was glad enough to retire, for though no full-scale assault on his position had transpired, English bowmen had been summoned to harass his blocking party. It was dark, and the archery was more or less blind, indiscriminate; but even so it was unpleasant and, despite the steel plate armour and chain-mail, they were suffering casualties. So a staged withdrawal was ordered.

They reached the fires area to find all blazing merrily, flames leaping high around each of the siege-engines, their timbers adding satisfactorily to the conflagration. How soon there would be the inevitable counter-attack they could not tell; but whenever the enemy came, it would be too late now to save their equipment. Well content, Jamie commanded a return to the castle.

They had to carry back half-a-dozen wounded men from the archery, fortunately none fatal. For all that, their going was very different from their coming, open, cheerful, unhurried, with even reassuring shouts to the waiting men on the battlements. They were welcomed back like conquering paladins.

It took the enemy some time to quench those pitch-induced fires. No other and more aggressive activity developed that night.

Nor indeed next day. Daylight showed that the damaged engines had been dragged away, no doubt for more basic repair in some less exposed spot. No assault by armed men with scaling-ladders would have been practical, without enormous losses; and Henry was obviously no hot-head. It was to be assumed that, at least until he could remake his siege-machinery, it would be a case of simple investment, containment, in the interests of starving out the defence.

Surprisingly, this proved to be a wrong assessment of the situation — and to be demonstrated in most unexpected fashion. In mid-afternoon, the watchers on the castle's topmost towers, their eyes tending to be turned westwards, looking for the hoped-for appearance of the Scots main army, were diverted in their attention to another direction altogether, the south-east. There, long and substantial columns of men were beginning to appear beyond the city walls, marching *southwards*. At first it was assumed that this was some sizeable force being sent out possibly to try and outflank Albany's host, although moving in an odd direction to do so. But as time went on and the column grew longer and denser and showed no signs of stopping, it became evident that some sort of major withdrawal was in progress.

The Scots leaders could see it all now from the ordinary battlements, and great was the wonder, discussion and specula-tion. None ventured to suggest that the English were actually leaving; but that they were reducing their numbers in Edinburgh very substantially was not to be questioned. When, in late afternoon, however, the standards and banners of a large leadership company could be made out, in horsed array, climb-ing the long slow hill beyond Liberton, there could be no other interpretation. Henry Plantagenet was moving out.

There was wild elation in the Scots camp — but still more mystification than delight. The most general estimation was that Albany was at last moving, and into some strategic position to the south-west, which the English felt to be a threat to them and which they preferred not to face cooped up in city streets. Jamie Douglas, for one, did not hold this view, declaring that a long open withdrawal like this, in column of route, would not be the way any experienced commander would react. He would send out scouting parties, then swift flanking forces of light cavalry, left and right, before setting his main infantry columns amove, and certainly not marshal all his leadership in one bannered throng. This was a line-of-march movement—whether withdrawal or not he would not hazard a guess.

Then, further surprise, a group of ordinary citizens were seen to be hurrying up the forecourt from the Castlegait. They began to shout long before they reached the gatehouse. The English were gone, all gone, they yelled. They had pulled out, for good.

Marching for the Border, at speed. The King and all his people. Edinburgh was saved. They had not waited even to sack and burn it before leaving. It was God's great deliverance . . .

Whether it was that or not, it was one of God's servants, the Abbot of Holy Rood no less, who presently brought them the explanation, trotting up in person on his white palfrey. Henry and his chief lieutenants had, of course, been lodging in the comfort of the Abbey beneath Arthur's Seat, and their reluctant host had not failed to learn the news which had set the English by the ears. That afternoon an exhausted courier had arrived from the South with the tidings that Owen Glendower, the true Prince of Wales, had crossed into England with a large army, taking advantage of the King's embroilment in Scotland; and instead of opposing the Welshmen as was their duty, the English Marcher earls had joined forces with them, declaring Henry usurper. All England was in a turmoil. Henry had no option but to head for home at his fastest, with all his strength.

The rejoicings in Edinburgh Castle and town that night were wild and prolonged. But David Stewart was not the only one to have bouts of thought which seemed less than joyful. Robert of Albany remained, even if Henry Plantagenet did not. He had been prepared to take over Scotland's army, contrary to the Lieutenant of the Realm's orders, and had held it idle, inactive, when it was gravely needed. There was still no sign nor word from him. What was his intention now? Was there to be outright war between the King's son and the King's brother? Civil war, in Scotland as well as in England?

For responsible men, that 26th of August 1400 was scarcely the time for carefree revelry.

XII

REVELRY, CAREFREE OR otherwise, was, however, the order of the day, or twelve days, four months later, at Stirling — on the Duke of Rothesay's express orders. There was no attempt, this year, to repeat or rival the ambitious and elaborate festivities of the previous Yuletide, when the century turned; but the prince required that gaiety, feasting, mirth and celebration should be unconfined, amongst high and low. David Stewart of course approved of revelry by nature, a born reveller. But on this occasion it was to be more than natural ebullience. He, and others, were in fact much concerned for that intangible but supremely important matter, the spirit and morale of the Scottish people.

It had been a difficult and depressing back-end of the year that had started so auspiciously, despite the all but miraculous delivery from the invading English in August. The enmity between the Dukes of Rothesay and Albany had become a thing palpable and dire to all men, bearing within it the ominous seeds of widespread conflict, possible war. There was no question as to which was the more popular. The people preferred the young and dashing prince to his stiff and sour uncle. But amongst their masters, the nobility and ruling class, there was a fairly strong conviction that *Robert* Stewart was the man wise men should support. This was not concerned with popularity or even equity, but with sheer expediency, advantage, practical politics. Robert was strong, utterly determined, experienced, ruthless. David was brilliant, yes — but the Scots had always been chary of brilliance. Moreover habit, custom, had something to do with it. Robert had been the true ruler of the land for long years, and though they had scarcely been years of happy rule, the lordly and lairdly caste had on the whole been well looked after — or allowed a free hand to look after themselves, which was almost better. Not so with David, who had awkward ideas about the alleged rights of burghs and traders and craftsmen and the like. He could be ruthless too, of course, and was notably good at hanging malefactors, irrespective of their breeding; but he seemed to fail to recognise where ruthlessness was best applied, and tended to alienate the powerful.

So the nation was divided. The siege of Edinburgh Castle in August had made that crystal clear to all. That Albany should have been able to assume control of Scotland's assembled army and prevent it from going to the aid of the beleaguered prince and Lieutenant was eloquent sign as to where the true power lay when it came to the test.

And further to all that, the situation was by no means happy as regards the English. Henry had retired — but he had not been beaten, by either the Scots or the Welsh; only humiliated and angered. He had indeed managed to put down the Welsh and Marcher earls' eruption meantime, and Owen Glendower and his people had been pushed back into Wales. At the end of November, Henry had called for a six-weeks truce — in order to treat, he said. That this was an ominous request, none could deny. Truces hitherto had been for a period of years, when negotiated at royal level. So short a period as six weeks could only mean that Henry required a mere breathing space. And when envoys of the two nations duly met thereafter on the Border, it was made clear from the start that the Plantagenet had forgone not one whit of his demands. The kernel of all his proposals was that Scotland should and must accept him as Lord Paramount and pay him due fealty. This done, all would be well, and the Scots would find him a generous and forgiving liege-lord. The Bishop of Glasgow, whom David had reluctantly sent to represent him, declared that there was nothing to treat about, in that case, and marched off. But the shadow remained. Henry was resolute, implacable, and would undoubtedly be back — and Scotland had already revealed its inability to present a united front. The six-weeks truce was nearly over.

There were other, less political, causes of anxiety. Queen Annabella, beloved by all, was now seriously ill and thought unlikely to recover. None could fail to recognise that the effect of her death on her unhappy husband would be drastic indeed, to the realm's further hurt. Also she had had some restraining

256

effect on her son's extravagances, and that withdrawn would be no light matter. Almost as serious was the growing weakness, amounting almost to senility, of the Primate, Walter Trail, Bishop of St. Andrews, whose firm and moderate hand had guided the Church for so long and aided and supported the Crown — and there was no obvious and sound successor, although many contenders. Finally, the old Earl of Douglas had died on Christmas Eve. Archie the Grim had hardly been beloved; but he was strong, reliable, shrewd and of course immensely powerful. The Master, now 4th Earl, was not of the same calibre, possibly a better man morally than his father, but moody, lacking the confidence in himself which being head of the house of Douglas demanded. These three indeed, Queen, Primate and Earl, had been David Stewart's great support, stay and moderating influence in his Lieutenantship. Who was adequately to take their place?

To add to this catalogue of woe, there was the pestilence. Plague had been raging in England for many months now, although it died down somewhat in winter. Presumably some of the English soldiers had brought the infection to Scotland. It was not a serious outbreak as yet, confined mainly to Edinburgh, Leith and Lothian. Nevertheless, it cast its own menacing shadow on a land unused to such visitations.

So David decreed Yuletide jollity, good cheer and festivities, not only for the Court but for all the land — and said that he would pay for it, if out of an all but empty Treasury. It may not have been the surest, soundest way to meet the nation's difficulties, but it was typically David Stewart's.

Jamie Douglas had been summoned to Stirling Castle, along with the rest, although he would much have preferred to celebrate Yule quietly at his own home at Aberdour. At least he was able to bring Mary with him. There were two notable absentees from the assembled company — the new Earl of Douglas and Sir John de Ramorgnie. The former, to be sure, could claim to be in mourning — although he had never got on well with his irascible father. Naturally, the Duke of Albany was not present either.

There was no snow, but the weather was on the whole wet, cold and miserable, restricting the outdoor activities David planned — hunting, hawking, skating, curling, hurly-hacket and the like. Those interested did get some wildfowling, with hawks, on the vast marshes of the Flanders Moss, but it was a chilly and puddling business and the hawks had the best of it. It was on their early return from one of these damp expeditions, and before the feast and entertainment scheduled for every evening, that Jamie sought out the prince in his private quarters — having ascertained that he was not in fact at present engaged with one or other of the ladies currently interesting him. The Duchess of Rothesay was, as frequently the case, elsewhere.

He found David, his wet clothing off, stretched before a roaring fire, in a furred bed-robe, wine-beaker in hand and in less than his usual spirits. Indeed, despite all the arranged merry-making, the Duke had been subject to quite frequent bouts of preoccupation, if scarcely depression, for some time. He looked up at his visitor narrow-eyed and scarcely welcoming.

"Jamie Douglas — I have seldom known you as harbinger of good tidings," he jerked, "when you seek me out thus. I can do without your forebodings, if that is what you are at. I have sufficient of my own!"

"No doubt, my lord. Yet the word I bring could be important to you, and to this realm."

"I feared as much!" The other sighed. "It concerns my accursed uncle, I'll be bound?"

"Yes. At the hawking, I was riding with a Graham, young Patrick Graham of Kilmadock, in Menteith. His house is near to Doune Castle. He told me that the Duke, your uncle, has his own visitors this Yuletide."

"Aye, no doubt. And he told you that Archibald Douglas, my good-brother and your new chief, was one of them?"

"You knew, then?"

"Oh, I am none so ill-informed, Jamie — even on what goes on at Castle Doune. I know that the Douglas arrived there three days ago — after excusing himself from coming here on account of his father's death. Scarcely brotherly, would you say? What is he at?"

"As to that, I know not. He mislikes your handling of his sister, my lord . . ."

"His sister is a sour and unfriendly bitch!" the prince said briefly.

"M'mm. That may be so. But as she *is* sister to Douglas, if naught else, she might be better cherished . . ."

"Jamie — when I require your sage counsel on how I should deal with my wife, I shall ask for it. Have you anything more valuable to tell me?"

258

"Aye — but you may be aware of it, since you knew of the other. Sir John de Ramorgnie is also at Doune."

"Ramorgnie!" This time David Stewart sat up. "You say so? Are you sure, man?"

"Graham appeared sure enough. When I questioned him, he said that he assumed that he was there as courier from yourself. I doubted that."

"And you were right, by God!" The prince opened his mouth to speak further, and then thought better of it.

Jamie eyed him keenly. "I thought it strange that he should be there, rather than here. He has been . . . very close to you."

"And you do not like him — and trouble not to hide the fact!"

"I do not trust him — have never trusted him. And grieved that you seemed to do so, my lord. He is a clever man — but dangerous. And he used to be close to my lord of Albany. What is he doing at Doune?"

"Why ask me, man? He may visit my uncle, if he so desires."

"Or your uncle desires! He could have been your uncle's man, all the time he was with you."

The other drummed silent fingers on his settle. "Scarcely that, I think. Or he proposed to show his devotion in a strange way!" He paused. "After the business at Edinburgh, Jamie, when Robert held back my army from coming to our aid, John de Ramorgnie came to me with a plan. A proposition. He said that my uncle had surely acted traitor, and should be tried for it. But since it would be difficult to arraign and convict him before a parliament, he suggested that he should be disposed of, quietly! He, Ramorgnie, said that he would seek to do it for me!"

"Dear God — assassination?"

"He did not call it that. He is a lawyer, to be sure! He said that it would be a judicial act, only done discreetly. And he offered to do it for me."

Jamie stared. "You mean . . .?"

"No, I do not! That is not what he is at Doune for. Christ's Blood — what do you take me for? I told him that I would have none of it. That although I much misliked my uncle, I would not have murder done, or anything such. I forbade him to consider anything of the sort."

"And now he is at Doune, in your uncle's house. Do you think that he intends to disobey your command?"

"I wonder? That perhaps. Or even . . .?"

"Worse? What could be worse, of a mercy?"

"Much, perhaps. For me! It occurs to me that that offer of his, to slay my uncle, is fell dangerous knowledge. Dangerous for Ramorgnie — and therefore for me. If it came to my uncle's ears, Ramorgnie would not long continue to draw breath! Robert is none so nice in these matters, I think. It was secretly said, to be sure. And I have told no-one but now you. But if Ramorgnie feared that, having refused his offer, I might one day tell my uncle of it, his life would be worth but little. So, it could be that he has gone to Doune on his own behalf — perhaps to save his skin at the expense of mine!"

"You mean betray you, somehow? Explain it away in lies . . .?"

"I mean that a man who could offer to slay one royal duke might conceivably offer to slay another! Suppose, Jamie, that Ramorgnie went to Robert and told him that *I* had proposed that he should assassinate him for me? And *he* had refused. It strikes me that if he then offered Robert to get rid of me, for him, my loving uncle might possibly consider the matter!"

Jamie gazed at him, speechless.

The prince shrugged. "It may not be so, to be sure. I may be doing Ramorgnie injustice. But this going to Doune instead of coming here for Yule, requires a deal of explaining. I believed him in the North, at Kildrummy, with Isobel of Mar."

"The Countess? Alex Stewart's friend?"

"Alex is not unique in his appreciation of the lady's charms, Jamie — mature as they are! John de Ramorgnie finds her to his taste — and she does not noticeably rebuff him. She is more of his own age, after all, than Alex Stewart's."

"Alex is deeply engaged with her, nevertheless, I think. This of Ramorgnie would hurt him."

"Ramorgnie — and others, man! Isobel Mar is a lusty woman. And Malcolm Drummond her husband little satisfies her. Cousin Alex will have to accept that, like other folk. But — that is another matter. It is not Ramorgnie's bedfellow I am concerned with, but with whom he is closeted now!"

"At least you will be on the watch for him. How can we find out if what you fear is truth?"

"Lord knows! Robert can keep things mighty close. But I shall seek to discover it, never fear. And shall keep a sharp eye on Sir John. As do you, Jamie, if you can. Tell no-one else of this — not even my good aunt, your Mary. Now — off with you. Send in my man. I must dress for this night's delights . . .!"

At the banquet-table that evening, Jamie sat preoccupied beside his wife and her brother the Archdeacon, paying but little attention either to the viands or the entertainment — or even to his companions, if truth be told. Mary taxed him with it, at length.

"I have had enough of this false gaiety," he told her. "It sticks in my throat. The realm is in danger, dire danger, and all we do is feast and gape at spectacles. The Roman Nero did as much!"

"What would you have?" Mary asked. "I would rather be at home with the bairns, yes. But David has sense in this, too. It would serve us nothing to sit wringing our hands in woe! Better to seek keep the people's spirits up this dark winter, is it not?"

"All this must be paid for. And David is going to require every siller piece he can lay hands on, presently. The English are going to be back, sooner or later. Henry will not accept that reverse. We cannot look for another convenient Welsh rising. The realm should be looking to its arms, girding itself, not feasting and play-acting."

"We can scarce be standing to arms in mid-winter, Jamie," the Archdeacon pointed out. "The lords must be kept content, if David is to gain what he wants from this parliament he has called for February. The burghs likewise. This Yuletide money is well enough spent, I'd say."

"And since it is *your* money, I suspect — or at least Holy Church's — who are we to say otherwise?" his sister remarked. "Jamie is ever gloomy until it is time for action — and then he becomes a very paladin! Unlike most, who are quite the other way."

"What you mean is that I look more than one step ahead of my nose!" her husband asserted. "If this indeed is at the Church's cost, then the money would be better spent paying for the troops and arms we are going to need."

"That is debateable," Thomas Stewart said. "Spent now, thus, it may aid David's cause, keep the lords happy, maintain the people's spirit as Mary says, their confidence in their ruler. Later, when the time comes for paying troops, or paying the lords to lend their men-at-arms, it may not be available. Or not from the present source."

"So you say spend now, in case it is not there to spend later? If that is your advice, David is the man to approve it!"

"Something of the sort. See you, my master, Walter Trail,

cannot last much longer. Even now he is scarce in his right mind most of the time. As Archdeacon, I hold the purse-strings, under him, of the richest see in Scotland. And so, with his favour, may aid David today. But tomorrow, who knows? A new bishop could appoint a new archdeacon, favour a new policy. And all know that Robert is determined to have his own man into St. Andrews — that creature, Dennistoun."

"Surely the appointment is the King's?" Mary said. "With the acceptance of the Holy See?"

"No. The appointment is with the Dean and Chapter of the diocese. Admittedly they usually accede to the royal nomination — but need not. And this will be a very special occasion, with Robert striving his utmost. For there is no clear successor. Moreover, since the primacy by custom goes with the appointment, the College of Bishops is concerned. There will be much competition, much making of compacts. The Earl of Douglas, or the King himself, is succeeded by his eldest son, if he has one; the Bishop of St. Andrews is otherwise."

"Could *you* not be bishop, Tom?" Mary asked. "You have all in your hands. The Chapter knows and likes you well. You are the King's brother, though illegitimate — Robert's likewise. He might be hindered from working against you. The King would nominate you gladly, I swear — and David rejoice."

"No, lass — no. I have said it before. I am not of the stuff of bishops, primates. Indeed I am no churchman, in truth. I was put into this position by our father, not by any choice of mine. I do well enough on diaconal duties, look after the Church revenues, lands, buildings and the like — and need not be too careful for my sanctity! But I am no pastor, no shepherd of souls. And I have just sufficient conscience to keep it so. I cannot accept nomination, and have told David so."

"Thomas is right," Jamie said. "Would that the Church had more like him, honest men!"

"That is just it!" Mary exclaimed. "He would make a better bishop than most who will be put forward, as well as saving the realm a deal of trouble. But, no — there has to be some quibble about conscience! I know what it is, Tom — it is those women that you keep at St. Andrews! Or at your manse at Boarhills. Are they so important to you? And do not other bishops have their women? I could name a few!"

"No doubt, Mary. But I am not the man to be Primate and Bishop of St. Andrews — and that is the end of it. If I may stay on there as Archdeacon, with the new man, I shall. And aid David all I can. But that is all. I have myself to live with, see you." He smiled to her. "Now, of a mercy, let us enjoy these dancers I have paid for there, expensive as they are despite the little clothing the females appear to be able to afford! I like yon plump one — eh, Jamie? An archdiaconal choice, if scarcely a bishop's . . . !"

XIII

PERHAPS DAVID STEWART'S policy of bread and circuses was more effective than Jamie Douglas expected; for the February parliament at Scone was a major success for the prince, with a clear majority of those attending voting for most of his measures and supporting his designs. If this, by the same token, might have been seen as a set-back for the Duke of Albany's cause, that astute individual was far too wily an operator to let it appear so save to the deeper thinkers. He attended the sessions off and on, manipulated where he could behind the scenes, but, with an uncanny ability to test the way opinion was forming, never allowed himself to appear openly on the losing side in any cause. That he was much displeased and frustrated could not be doubted; but he preserved his chill imperturbability, and indeed himself frequently voted, in the end, for measures which it was suspected he had previously done his best to wreck. Ramorgnie also played a careful part, seeking to be helpful in the correct framing and legal wording of the new statutes, not allowing himself to be seen much in Albany's company, and accepting the prince's new coldness towards him with urbane lack of offence. Nevertheless, David, who was having him watched closely, knew that he frequently visited Albany's quarters secretly at night. Moreover, the new Earl of Douglas was much in the former Governor's company — which especially worried Jamie.

The parliament however achieved great things — at least on paper — and should have done much to enhance the Duke of Rothesays's reputation with the ordinary people, for he was quite clearly personally responsible for many overdue reforms in government and the administration of justice. Jamie, and

Alex Stewart likewise, who was attending as *de facto* Lord of Badenoch, expressed considerable surprise at the depth and range of the pleasure-loving prince's concern for and interest in the plight of the common folk, the trade and well-being of the towns and burghs, and the humdrum but essential general administration of the realm's affairs. This was the sort of thing normally left to underlings — and therefore apt to be neglected, mismanaged and a prey to corruption. Admittedly, David did not actually involve himself in the practical working out of these matters; but he was *concerned* in a way which few others of his kind had been, and he encouraged others to be more deeply engaged. This was exemplified in the measures passed, pushed, through this February parliament, often against the inertia if not opposition of the powerful landed interests. Despite all his whoring, drinking and personal extravagance, David Stewart was more of a reformer than any of his forebears since the Bruce himself. He had the backing of the Church, of course, which counted for much; and the lower ranks of the lairdly class, as well as the burghs' representatives. But he was making many enemies amongst the nobility.

Like other reformers however, the prince was not immune to the great brake and handicap on all improvement — lack of money. The existing system, however corrupt and inefficient, was entrenched, its ramifications widespread, much more easily legislated against than altered and amended. Reform of the sheriffdoms, the game laws, illegal seizures for debt, freedom on bail for lofty persons, the correcting of false weights and measures, the standardisation of the currency, the doing away with private tolls on roads, bridges and fords, repairs to harbours and works, the removal of unlawful charges at markets and the like, all demanded revenues to establish. The collection of such revenues, customs duties, cess, export dues and other taxes had long been farmed out to a vast army of individuals from whom no-one expected to produce more than a small percentage for the Treasury, the rest going into their own and their lordly patrons' pockets. No-one, that is, until the Duke of Rothesay. With his reforms to pay for, and an army to collect, train and equip, in the face of English threats, he demanded a true accounting — and did not get it. So after the parliament was over, he began a personal campaign against the customs-farmers.

Jamie was much involved in this, heading a flying column

which roamed the country inspecting, enquiring, threatening, demanding payments, taking them where necessary and possible. It was unpleasant work, uncovering much wickedness, greed and vice, and inevitably bringing down upon himself resentment, hatred and accusations of fraud and corruption on his own part. But he collected a lot of money for the prince's cause, and felt that what he was doing was worthwhile. It was unusual to find even one-half of the customs dues extracted from the payers being forwarded to the Treasury. And in cases innumerable the full dues themselves had been partly remitted to the payers in return for various privileges and favours. Illegal and exorbitant extortions, too, were commonplace; and threats and intimidations, all in the King's name, the quite normal corollary. Jamie, not of course the only one employed on this task, learned much that he had not hitherto realised as to human cupidity, deceit and man's inhumanity to man. Indeed, although it may have been only his suspicious nature, he came to wonder whether even all his fellow-inspectors were as honest and incorruptible as he was himself. When he discovered that not a few of the prince's friends, relatives and supporters in high places were to some extent involved in the system, his disillusionment could go little further. The fact that some churchmen, as quite frequently the only persons who could read and write in their districts, acted as customers and were not always faultless in the matter, not only upset Jamie but caused some rift in David's relationship with their superiors.

At least the plague seemed to be on the wane.

So the spring of 1401 passed. The word from England was of constant preparation for war. The Welsh were still seething, and a proportion of the English baronage was by no means reconciled to Henry. But he appeared to have the situation fairly well in hand and be acting with discretion, forcing nothing. This situation David judged as ominous for Scotland.

Then the prince gained secret information from London that Sir Adam de Forrester of Corstorphine, a Lothian magnate, was concerned in some strange activity. He had sought, and obtained, permission to leave the country on a visit to kinsfolk in England, and received a safe-conduct from King Henry. But according to David's informant he had been visiting Henry himself and seeking to negotiate, on behalf of the Duke of Albany, the exchange of the Mammet Richard for certain unspecified advantages. He was still in England.

This news much disturbed the prince. It showed that his uncle was actively plotting against him, and prepared to deal with Henry behind his back. What bargain he sought was not declared; but it could be assumed to be something substantial, Robert Stewart being who he was, and Henry Plantagenet's desire to put down the possible rallying-figure of his dissident lords well-known. David suspected that it would be some English agreement to support Albany in ousting himself from the rule in Scotland, possibly by armed force, more probably by more devious means. It was not something with which he could challenge Albany openly; that inscrutable individual would merely deny all coldly, and proof would be impossible.

David was therefore very much on his guard — or as far as that was possible for a man of his outgoing and carefree nature. He was concerned to keep the Mammet under closer watch and guard, likewise. But this was difficult, for the King was now much attached to his alleged fellow-monarch and unfortunate, and kept him by his side, most of the time at Turnberry in Ayrshire. David would have tried to persuade or manoeuvre his father into bringing the man to Stirling, the most secure castle in the kingdom, but Queen Annabella was too ill to move from Turnberry and the King would by no means leave her. The prince sent an added guard, and warned his father — but John Stewart was so other-worldly and feckless, so trusting, refusing to believe sufficiently ill of Albany or anyone else, that such precautions might be of little avail.

An uneasy summer settled on Scotland.

Then Annabella died, the realm grieved, and the unhappy monarch became quite inconsolable, almost unhinged. As well as his wife and only true friend, she had been his prop and stay and adviser. Without her he was not only heart-broken, desolate, but lost, out of his mind. He shut himself up at Turnberry and would see no-one save the Mammet and his younger son James, now aged seven, apparently harbouring a grudge against David — which was not like him. He blamed his elder son for heedlessness in not having done more for his mother, and in not even reaching her death-bed in time.

David himself took the Queen's death, not unexpected as it was, harder than might have been anticipated. She had been, probably, the greatest influence in his life, and even though the results perhaps were not superficially very apparent, her place was unfillable. Unfortunately for himself, and a great many

267

others in the circumstances, his reaction was to drown his sorrow in wine. He had always been a heavy drinker, even as a youth, but until now few had ever seen him actually drunk. That autumn he drank in such excess as to be drunk much of the time, his notorious riotous living the worse. No doubt it was not only his mother's death that was responsible, or even the estrangement with his father, but the long period of strain, the chill hatred of his uncle, the ever-present threat of assassination and the lonely burden of rule. His women perhaps helped him; clearly his wife did not.

Then, only a month after the Queen, her friend and confessor, Walter Trail died also — so that three of David's principal supporters had gone within a few months, with the old Earl of Douglas. Immediately the manoeuvring started, or came out into the open, to replace him as Bishop of St. Andrews and Primate of Holy Church in Scotland — with David in no fit state to use his wits to best effect in the matter. Albany came out strongly and at once with his nominee, Walter de Dennistoun, Parson of Kincardine O'Neil, an unscrupulous time-server wholly unfitted for the position, but shrewd in his own way, cunning, who could be relied upon to manipulate the vast revenues of the see for Albany's benefit. The College of Bishops put forward Gilbert de Greenlaw, Bishop of Aberdeen, who was already Chancellor, an able churchman if on the worldly side. But he had been appointed both Bishop and Chancellor when Albany was Governor, and so owed his rise to that man. David had no particular friends amongst the clergy, and in his preoccupied state could think of nothing better than to insist on the Archdeacon Thomas, his uncle, being nominated. Thomas Stewart declined, but David imperiously commanding it, the Chapter of St. Andrews Cathedral duly elected him to the see. Then a hitherto unsuspected obstinate streak was evidenced in the King's illegitimate brother. He flatly refused to take up the appointment, and be consecrated. David, furious, would not budge — and in the subsequent confusion and mismanagement, Albany got Greenlaw to withdraw and Dennistoun became Bishop almost by default. It was a sorry business, of credit to none.

The price fell to be paid for that folly.

The King was back in his royal castle of Stirling — but it was not his son and heir who had persuaded him to return there, but his brother Albany. The Duke Robert, acutely, had recognised that the written word, carefully chosen, might have more effect upon his scholarly brother than any personal approach, and had sent a succession of letters to Turnberry, their gist the mismanagement of the realm, the shameful behaviour of the prince, the disarray of Holy Church, the dangers of war posed by the rejection of the hand of friendship held out by Henry of England, a hand still extended, and the monarch's ultimate responsibility in all these matters. So the King had reluctantly allowed himself to be coaxed back to Stirling in the interests of his people, bringing the Mammet and young James with him. David, bemused, was on the look-out for attempts on the person of the Mammet; he was quite unprepared for what did in fact transpire.

He had arrived back from a November day's hunting, and a buxom lady was aiding him, in his private quarters, to recover from the exertions of the chase, when Jamie Douglas put in one of his inconvenient appearances.

"My lord Duke," he said, briefly, bluntly, ignoring the lady, "your pardon, but I bring a summons for you to attend upon your royal father in the Great Hall. Forthwith."

"Damn you for a pest!" the other got out thickly, over a plump white female shoulder. "Summons! Forthwith! That is not how anyone may speak to David Stewart!"

"Nevertheless, my lord, that is the message I was given."

"By whom, man?"

"By your brother, the Lord James, Earl of Carrick. Sent from your father."

"M'mm. Tell him I shall come so soon as I may." He found a hand free to gesture the messenger away.

"My lord — there is this you should know. In the Hall are come many of your unfriends, with the Duke of Albany. Also his brother, the Lord Walter of Brechin, whom we seldom see. Likewise the Earl of Douglas. And Ramorgnie. And the new Bishop of St. Andrews."

"Ha — the buzzards gather!" The prince sat up, interest engaged. "Off, Jeannie — off! Here is something I must see, to be sure. God knows, I prefer my unfriends where I *can* see them, before my eyes rather than behind my back!"

"I would walk warily, nevertheless," Jamie warned. "The Duke Robert it was who brought your father here. Not to your advantage, I think. If he has brought these others today, also, he will have his reasons."

"Stop preaching, Jamie, of a mercy! You should have been a priest, on my soul! I'd have made *you* Bishop of St. Andrews! Think you that you are the only one who can see an inch before his nose?"

Bowing, the Douglas withdrew.

Even so it was some time before David Stewart put in an appearance in the Great Hall — which was notably full of folk, lords and lairds, clerics and courtiers and pages, many of them but infrequently seen at the prince's Court. Albany and his brother Walter sat at the dais-table, the latter already drunk — but then he was usually drunk and incapably so, the youngest and only other surviving legitimate brother of the monarch, a poor character and unpleasant. The boy-prince James, dark-eyed, sensitive-featured, wary, lurked near the dais-door, on watch for his brother. He slipped away when he observed his entry, presumably to inform their father. Archibald, Earl of Douglas, stood by, frowning.

David's entry on the scene was carefully calculated to offend his elder uncle, at least. He came strolling in, only partially dressed, his rich clothing thrown on anyhow, one arm around the shoulders of the plump and now blushing lady, hand actually inside her notably low and loose-necked bodice. He was laughing and jollying her, and though he nodded genially here and there, he paid no attention to the illustrious company up on the dais. He paused to chat to various of his friends, still leaning on the lady — who was in fact one of the very few women present, and uneasily aware of it.

Jamie, from a corner, watched doubtfully.

Slowly, casually, David made his way through the throng to the dais, his gait just a little unsteady, using his companion as support. They mounted the platform with some small difficulty, and moved over to the well-doing fire of birch-logs — for the dais area had its own fireplace — the prince only glancing at the table-sitters in passing.

"My good uncles," he observed, easily, "or, leastways, uncles, good bad or indifferent! A notable sight! Make your bow, lass."

The confused girl bobbed towards the older men nervously — and in so doing all but upset the prince's unsteady stance.

"Stand still, m'dear. A pox on it — stand still, woman, I say!" David requested, but affably enough. "Would you have me on my back, *here*? Again! Before all!"

"Where we'd see the best o' you, by the Mass!" the sprawling

Lord Walter of Brechin hiccuped. To add, "My lord Governor. Or Lieutenant, or whatever you call yourself — God save us!" He had some difficulty in enunciating all that.

"There speaks jealousy, Uncle! *You* are past it, man, I swear! Too fat. Is he not, Jeannie? Even you'd make naught of old Uncle Wattie, hot as you are . . ."

"Peace!" the cold voice of the Duke of Albany cut in, like a whiplash. "Peace, I say. Young man — your father." The Duke rose, all sitters rose — save Walter Stewart, who could not.

David turned to look behind him, as a temporary silence fell on the crowded chamber. The King, stooping wearily, features ravaged, thinner than ever, had aged grievously. Limping, he was led in by his younger son — who looked hurriedly, anxiously at his older brother. David bowed to his father, and nodded to the boy, still managing to keep his hand deep within the bulging bosom. But it was to Albany that he turned and spoke, with a mocking smile.

"Ah, yes, my lord Duke — peace!" he said. "Who indeed more apt to cry peace than my Uncle Robert — who has not the meaning of the word in him, on my soul! And would have this bedevilled realm of Scotland not to know it, either! God save us — peace from *you*, man!" It was a sign of the prince's state of inebriation that he allowed himself thus to react unwontedly.

"Silence! You'll speak me respectfully, sir. Or suffer for it."

"Ha — respect! For you? This is rich, i' faith! And you would threaten, my lord! Me? Rothesay? Beware how you do that, by Christ's Rood! Have you forgot, Uncle? You are no longer Governor, no longer master of this realm. *I* bear the rule now. Heed it, I say."

"Master, you say? I think not. Have *you* forgot His Grace the King?"

David's laughter rose almost to a hoot. "God's eyes — this from you, Uncle! Spare us, for very shame. I swear it was largely to spare my royal sire from your slights and afflictions that I assumed the governorship. Is that not so, my lord King and noble progenitor?" He gestured an unsteady flourish towards his father.

"Aye, Davie," the King said, low-voiced, troubled. But he looked at his brother rather than at his son.

Quiet had fallen on the Hall during this exchange. The clash between the royal dukes had of course been known to all

271

Scotland for years. It looked as though, now, it might be coming to its inevitable head.

Albany spoke, sternly but levelly, no hint of emotion in his rasping voice. "I will pay no heed to your foolish words, sir. But since you have come here on matters concerning the well-being of this realm, I suggest that you put that young woman from you and behave more as befits your place and station."

"I am here, Uncle, because as Lieutenant of the Realm I choose to come. For no other reason. I came at my father's request, but of my own decision. And as for this lady, she is at least honest in her behaviour and function — which is more than can be said for all this company! I brought her — and she stays."

"You'd have done better to have brought your wife, Davie," the King said mildly but vexedly. "Aye, you would."

"My wife is . . . otherwise, Sire." David withdrew his hand, however, from its warm resting-place, the young woman sniggered and would have edged away, but he held her by the arm firmly, even yet.

Albany pointed an accusing hand. "Your father has summoned you here, Nephew — and for sufficient reason. Overdue, I say. You stand accused, with much to answer for. I would advise you to comport yourself accordingly."

"Accused? Me? Here? Who dares?"

"I do. And many another. You are charged with the shameful misgovernance of this realm, Nephew. With wastage of the kingdom's substance. With the alienation of Crown lands and revenues. With subversion of justice . . ."

"Charged, is it!" the younger man interrupted. "How charged, sirrah? I was appointed Lieutenant by the King in Council, confirmed by parliament. If I, the Lieutenant, am to be charged, it can only be by the said King in Council. Is this the Privy Council of Scotland?" He gestured around. He appeared to have sobered quickly.

"A warning, Davie," his father mumbled unhappily. "A warning just. No more, lad."

"You would prefer to answer these charges, in detail, before the assembled Council, Nephew?" Albany asked thinly.

The prince frowned. "These are no charges. They are but vague accusations, unfounded. Representing but the spleen of an old man, jealous! One who indeed knows what misgovernance, subversion and the rest mean!"

"You would have chapter and verse for them, then? Such can be produced readily enough . . ."

"You lie, as ever! These are but wild denunciations. Stone-throwing. I cast them back in your teeth! You, who trampled on the country for ten sore years. You would never dare face me before Council and parliament — you who have too few friends in either. You know full well that the folk of Scotland much prefer me to yourself."

Jamie winced in his corner. This was not the David Stewart he knew and relied upon.

The older man was not to be deflected for a moment from his purpose. "You are summoned here, Nephew, in order that the King's will and decision be made known to you . . ."

"Before all these? Can my father not express his will and wishes to me save by *your* lips? And in his own chamber? Not before a gawping crowd." David swung on the King, who gnawed his lip and shook his head, but said nothing.

"It is the King's royal will and decision," Albany went on, as though there had been no interruption, "that you should be warned and restrained, given due notice to amend your ways. The governorship is not taken from you — but you are to be restrained in certain respects. You will accept the guidance, in pursuance of your duties, of myself, and the lords of Brechin, Douglas, Moray, Crawford, St. Andrews and Aberdeen, as you should have done all along. These acting in the King's express name. You will order your daily life decently and discreetly. Should you fail to do so, and not mend your way, I shall, with His Grace's and the Council's authority, resume the governorship. You understand?"

"My . . . God!" David whispered, into the hush which now gripped the great room, staring. "This is beyond all belief! And all bearing!" He looked at his father. "You, Sire — you heard? Spoken in your royal presence! To your son, to the heir to your throne. You heard?"

Swallowing painfully, audibly, the monarch shook his white head. "Aye, Davie, I heard," he got out slowly, sighing. "It must be. You have brought it on yourself, I fear — the sorrow of it. See you, the rule of this realm is not a game to be played, a sport for braw laddies. God forgive me, who say it — for my failure is greater than yours, lad. Aye, the greater. The fault is largely mine, I do confess before all. But . . . God's will be done."

273

"*God's* will!" his son burst out. "Is that what your brother's intrigues and schemings are named, now? The Devil's will, rather! But . . . I'll not have it. There are more wills than Albany's in this realm — even if *you* have none! Aye, and more than words to count. There are such things as swords in Scotland, I say!"

In the complete silence which followed that statement, the prince's glance left his agitated father's face, to slowly circle that vast chamber. Few men there, of any note, met his searching gaze.

"My lord of Crawford," he said, at length, to his Aunt Jean's husband, "how see you this matter?"

"But dimly, and with little pleasure," that gruff individual replied. "But I prefer *your* kind of misgovernance to the sort that went before!" Crawford did not greatly love David, but he hated Albany.

"Aye. And you, Cousin Thomas?"

Thomas, Earl of Moray, was the son of David's Aunt Marjory, and no very stalwart character. He coughed, looked down, and mumbled. "Some improvement there must be, David."

"Indeed!" The prince's scornful glance passed over Lord Murdoch Stewart, now calling himself Earl of Fife; also Albany's son-in-law the Earl of Ross. Likewise the new Bishop of St. Andrews and the Chancellor, Bishop Greenlaw of Aberdeen. It came to rest on Archibald, lately Master now Earl of Douglas.

"And you?" he enquired. "My lord and good-brother. How says Douglas?"

That stolid and moody young man did not move a muscle. Not so much as an eyelid flickered. Silent, impassive, he stood, whilst everywhere in the hall breaths were held and men awaited decision, the fall of the scales. For the Douglas, though not the man his father had been, was still the most powerful and influential individual in the kingdom, head of the most puissant and warlike family in Scotland, which differed from the Stewarts in being united. By position and the vast manpower he could wield, he was the realm's war-leader, however lacking in expertise. As all knew, he was angry with David over the way that he had treated his wife, Douglas's sister; but he was known not to love Albany either, although recently he had been seen much in his company. Whose side he took in this present power-struggle could all but decide the issue, for many would follow his lead.

As the tense moments passed, it dawned upon all, not least David Stewart, that his brother-in-law was not merely being more than usually slow of speech. He was not going to answer at all. Straight ahead of him he gazed now, wordless.

A long sigh escaped from the assembled company. Walter of Brechin barked an abrupt laugh. Albany changed neither stance nor expression.

The prince drew himself up, head high. He did not trouble to look at the lesser men present. Their support or otherwise would not decide the day. Drawing a long quivering breath, he swung back to face his accuser, and took a couple of steps up to the table. Without taking his eyes from Albany's aquiline features, he groped until his hand contacted a goblet half-filled with wine, set down by someone. Raising this to his lips, he gulped down the contents in a single draught, before them all. Then, holding it there, he spoke.

"My father's words I have heard," he declared, strongly now. "He says that the rule of this realm is no game. That I accept. As its Lieutenant I shall see that none play it — I promise you all! Warning has been given — and taken. I add mine. Let none seek to govern save the Governor! When King, Council and the Estates of Parliament, duly assembled, command me to lay down that office, then I shall do so. Not before. His Grace says 'God's will be done!' To that I say Amen — but let us not confuse Almighty God with my Uncle Albany! I charge you all to say, rather — God save the King! And, by the Holy Rood — to remember who will be King hereafter!"

With a sudden explosion of force, violent as it was unexpected, he hurled the heavy silver goblet, empty, down the littered length of the dais-table. Scattering and upsetting viands, flagons and the like in its course, it crashed to the floor beside the Duke of Albany.

In the resounding clatter, David, Prince of Scotland, flung around, and jumping from the dais went striding down the Hall without a backward glance, making for the outer door to the main courtyard. Right and left men parted to give him room. After a little hesitation, the unfortunate young woman went hurrying after him, biting her lip.

In the uproar that succeeded, King Robert, empty open hand raised tremblingly after his elder son, dropped it, moaning incoherent words. He took an uncertain step forward, to pluck at Albany's velvet sleeve — and was ignored. The boy James, features working, took his father's arm again, and gesturing towards the dais-door, led him away.

Jamie Douglas felt moved to hasten after the prince, but restrained himself. David would not want his sermonising company just now. It was a bad business — a notable exit, but a deal more than that was required to right this grievous situation. In the end, David's power emanated from the King — and the King had evidently withdrawn his favour, however sorrowfully. Just why, at this stage, was not clear. It could scarcely be all on account of Annabella — although the loss of the Queen's advice and strength was undoubtedly important. And Albany had clearly been able to get at his brother and in some measure fill the gap. Jamie found himself almost hating his new chief, Archibald Douglas. Who would have thought that, in the end, he would have thrown in his lot with Albany? For, even if he had not actually done so, his denial of the Douglas support to David came to the same thing. That David had treated his sister shamefully was true; but it was surely no sufficient reason to risk overturning the government of the realm.

Until the end, the prince had not behaved well or adequately, seeming almost to have lost his grip. Drink had been responsible, no doubt — but drink had never previously affected his capabilities. More than that was wrong.

Whatever happened now, David's position was gravely weakened. Albany now was obviously working, and openly, to bring him down and supersede him; and if Albany seemed to have the support of the monarch, then many would see the end as inevitable, and act accordingly. If one of them had had to die, why could it not have been their feckless, spineless weathercock of a monarch instead of his noble and reliable wife? John Stewart himself undoubtedly would have preferred it that way — had declared as much. And David, mounting the throne, would have been unassailable, supreme, with all the authority he required, able to deal with Albany once and for all. If, if . . .!

Desiring speech with none save his Mary, Jamie slipped away from the Hall. It was Aberdour for him.

XIV

IT WAS AT Aberdour Castle, on a forenoon of early spring, that David Stewart came, from Linlithgow, to pick up Jamie, after crossing Forth by Queen Margaret's Ferry.

"I am bound for St. Andrews," he announced. "In God's good mercy the man Dennistoun has died, before he had time to replace my Uncle Thomas as Archdeacon — a great comfort! I intend to collect what treasure I can from the see's deep coffers, before my other uncle gets his hands on it. Also to try to ensure that the Canons and Chapter will not accept another of Robert's minions. Come with me, Jamie. Mary too, if she will, to see her brother."

"Dennistoun dead? Already?"

"Fear you not — I had nothing to do with it! A higher power, shall we say? He ate too much, I swear!"

Mary had ploys of her own in hand, and excused herself.

Jamie was concerned that the prince had come so little escorted, with a mere half-dozen of the guard at his heels; and he provided another four of his own men to accompany them. David declared that he did not want to draw attention to himself or his errand, on this occasion, and had slipped out of Linlithgow at first light discreetly. The smaller the party the less notice would be taken of it — and in Fife it might be wise to go unobtrusively. If Dennistoun's people got word that the Lieutenant was on his way, they might well take steps to hide away what he sought.

So they rode north-eastwards, by unfrequented ways, by Balmule and Kinglassie and the eastern flanks of the Lomonds, carefully avoiding the Fife seat of Falkland Castle, and so into the long Eden valley which led through the centre of Fife to St. Andrews, a journey totalling about twenty-eight miles.

As they went, David held forth on the new situation which arose from the death of Dennistoun. Another Bishop would have to be appointed, and to avoid all the previous trouble he was purposing to nominate Henry Wardlaw, Precentor of Glasgow Cathedral, nephew of the late Cardinal Wardlaw, a sound man who had shown no interest in the appointment hitherto. He was well liked by the senior clergy, and the College of Bishops would almost certainly support him as Primate. A secondary reason for this St. Andrews visit was to convince the Prior, Canons and Chapter to elect him, and quickly. Otherwise Albany would be fielding a new candidate, probably Greenlaw again.

To Jamie's query as to whether Henry Wardlaw would accept, the prince made his customary gesture of dismissal.

In the late afternoon, with the sinking sun at their backs and the towers and spires of the ecclesiastical metropolis already in sight before them against the blue plain of the sea, they were riding through woodland in the Strathtyrum area when, rounding a bend in the road, they suddenly were confronted by a large body of mounted men barring the way.

Jamie's hand dropped to his sword-hilt in immediate reaction, as they reined up, but Sir John de Ramorgnie came forward, doffing his bonnet and waving.

"That viper!" the Douglas jerked. "I do not like this. What is he doing here?"

"He lives somewhere hereabouts, I think? His barony of Ramorgnie is in the Howe of Fife, is it not?"

"A dozen miles and more to the west. But . . . see you who is with him. Lindsay of Rossie — another of your unfriends! And why all these men? This smells ill to me . . ."

"Perhaps so — but put back your sword, nevertheless, man. There are over a hundred of them, I'd say. Too many even for you, Jamie! We shall see what they want . . ."

Ignoring that, Jamie wheeled his horse around, and spurred back whence they had come. Round the bend he found more horsemen streaming out from the woodland to bar their retreat in that direction.

Without pause, turning again, he dashed back. "Into the trees!" he yelled. "Quickly. Through the wood. They are behind us, as well."

But it was too late. David was already riding forward to meet Ramorgnie and Lindsay — the same cousin of Crawford's

278

whose sister the prince had played with and declined to marry years before.

"Well met, my lord Duke!" Ramorgnie called. "We greet you. We shall escort you into St. Andrews. Well met, I say."

"Met, certainly, John — whether well or not! Why are you here? And how did you know that I came to St. Andrews?"

"A traveller journeying to Falkland mentioned that your lordship had left Linlithgow for St. Andrews," the other returned easily. "And what more natural, with Dennistoun dead and the succession to consider anew?"

"Your traveller must have foundered his horse to get to Falkland in time with this important news!" the prince observed. "And you, Sir William — you are a long way from Rossie. Or Doune Castle, where you are apt to be!"

"I was at Falkland," that man said briefly, with no attempt at the civilities.

"Ah, then I take it that my good Uncle Albany is likewise there? And that this kind reception is of his making?"

Ramorgnie shrugged. "It is our pleasure to act escort, my lord Duke."

"Here is no escort but an armed ambush!" Jamie said bluntly, at David's back. "There are as many men blocking the road behind us as in front."

"Then let us on to St. Andrews with our escort," David said. "And discuss these matters of bishops and ambushes over a flagon of wine at a priestly board — for I am hungry."

"With pleasure," Ramorgnie said. "It is not far . . ."

It was only a couple of miles in fact, and the prince's party rode there tightly surrounded by their guard, David and Ramorgnie chatting with every appearance of ease, Jamie and Lindsay riding side by side with nothing to say to each other and plenty of mutual scowling. Through the streets of the city they clattered, so much broader and better paved, the houses finer, than those of Stirling or Edinburgh or Dundee, to the great episcopal castle on its coastal promontory.

Dismounting in the courtyard, David was ushered quite ceremoniously into the Sea Tower, the Bishop's private quarters. But once he was inside, there was nothing ceremonious about Jamie's treatment. He was grabbed by Lindsay's men, disarmed, and hustled urgently to one of the lesser lean-to buildings of the courtyard, protesting but unheeded. There he was pushed along a passage and thrust into a vaulted cell or storeroom, lit only by a narrow slit-window, the heavy door slammed on him, and the key turned.

Alone, with miscellaneous lumber, he was left to cogitate, to the sound of the waves breaking below his window.

* * *

He had plenty of time for gloomy rumination, for there were no developments, no-one came near him, neither food nor drink were brought. What was happening to David he could only guess at; but since these people treated himself in this unknightly fashion, a recognised adherent if not friend of the prince's, it looked ominous. They would never have dared this unless they had Albany's fullest backing. It looked, therefore, as though that man had decided on an all-out trial of strength — in which case he must be very sure of the outcome, for Robert Stewart was no rash adventurer. Which was not an encouraging thought.

Darkness came early to that ill-lit cell — although not before Jamie had satisfied himself that there was no possible exit save by the securely locked and solid door. Thereafter, as philosophically as he might, he lay down on the stone-flagged floor in a corner, and sought the release of sleep, at least.

He was awakened some unspecified time later by the door being unlocked and a shadowy figure with a lantern entering, and closing the door quietly behind him. Prepared immediately to leap on the newcomer, the prisoner was restrained by the stealthy manner of his visitor, which surely did not indicate a normal gaoler.

"Jamie?" the caller whispered, holding the lantern high. "Are you awake?"

"Thomas? I am here, yes." It was the voice of his brother-in-law, the Archdeacon. "Here's a bad business."

"Aye. Keep your voice down. The porter's lodge is just across the courtyard and they have a guard set." Stewart moved over to the slit-window, and stuffed into its narrow, draughty aperture a cloak he was carrying. "That is better — and the light will not shine out. I was at my manse at Boarhills, when a servant brought me word of this. I fear we are going to have great trouble."

"No doubt. Your brother, Duke Albany, making sure that St. Andrews and its treasure remains in *his* grip?"

"That, yes. But much more, I think. These minions of his

would not have dared lay hands on David if there was not much more to it. They must be sure that he, the Lieutenant and Governor — for he is still that — will not be in a position to repay them for it hereafter. Which means that *Robert* is sure. How, and why, I know not."

"David is held prisoner? Held, as I am?"

"Yes. Locked up under close guard. I could not get to him, as I have done to you. Lindsay and that Ramorgnie are very sure of themselves — insolent. They have taken over this castle. They say I shall not be Archdeacon much longer. They are holding David until my brother comes, tomorrow."

"And then?"

"God knows. But I have no doubt Robert has prepared this well. He does not act on impulse."

They were silent for a little.

"What can we do?" Jamie asked.

"I do not know. I came to you, to ask that. *You* are the man of action, Jamie — not I."

"There is no hope of rescuing David?"

"Not from here. I tell you, he is guarded close."

"*I* must get out of here, then. Raise the country to his aid."

"It will not be easy. Robert is greatly feared."

"The King, your brother? Weak as he is, this cannot be to his liking."

"I do not know. But I greatly fear that Robert would not be daring this if he had not got some assurance from John, some agreement. John is lost without Annabella, a poor thing, clay in Robert's clever hands. Put no reliance on him, Jamie."

"He would not abandon his own firstborn? To this, this monster!"

"He will not see him as a monster, man. Only as the sure strong hand he relied upon for years. Robert was ever the strongest of our family."

"Then I will go to Douglas. Archibald does not love David, but he would never agree to this laying hands on him, the Lieutenant and heir to the throne. The Douglas power is greater than anything that Albany can wield. I will go to my father, and the Earl of Douglas. And Crawford, Angus and the rest."

The other looked doubtful. "If David had not offended Dunbar, and Moray . . ."

"Can you get me out of here, Thomas?"

"From this cell, perhaps, yes. From the castle itself, less easy. It is after midnight, and I will not be expected to leave again this night. The gatehouse is manned, the bridge up . . ."

"Is there no postern?"

"This is an episcopal palace, Jamie, not a baron's hold. But . . . there is the Sea-gate. It is used only by the servitors, for cleaning the privies and the like. Taking the night soil out, to throw in the sea. It is below the Sea Tower."

"That will content me well enough. I shall act the servitor, gladly. It will not be watched, likely? Can you get me there, unseen?"

"At this hour, I would say so. Through the basement vaults . . ."

"Good. Let us be gone, then. And can you win me some food? I have eaten nothing since I left Aberdour before noon. Aye, and a sword and dirk, if you can. They took mine."

So the Archdeacon opened the cell-door as quietly as he could, peered out, with his lantern, along the vaulted corridor, found no-one there, and led Jamie forth, locking the door again behind them. He took him by sundry dark passages with doors off, where no doubt much of Holy Church's wealth was stored, up and down winding turnpike stairs and through damp cellars. Presently through narrow slit-windows they could hear the sigh of the waves again.

Thomas Stewart came to a door with an iron yett as outer gate, a key in its lock and a strong draw-bar securing it. That all was in constant use, however, was clear, all greased. The yett opened with only a small creak, the draw-bar slid smoothly into its deep slot in the masonry, and the lock clicked only quietly. Opening the door, the cold sea air blew in their faces. Closing it again, the Archdeacon said,

"Wait here until I see what I can find for you. If another comes, do not wait. Out with you. If I do not come back within a short time, the same. I could be stopped. It is but the rocks of the beach outside — but watch where you tread!"

"If you have to choose between a sword and victuals, Thomas — take the sword!" Jamie told him.

His brother-in-law was back sooner than might have been anticipated, for it seemed that the Bishop's kitchens were quite close. He brought an old sword, clumsy but effective enough, a dirk and a satchel with bannock and a flagon of ale.

"What will you do, Jamie?" he asked.

282

"Go hide somewhere in the town until the gates open at sun-up. Then slip out and wait outside, for Albany's coming. They may search the town for me. Wait until I can learn what Albany does with David. I can do little until I know. I will come into the town again, later, to learn the gossip . . ."

"*I* might be able to tell you, better than tavern gossip. If I am allowed my freedom."

"Aye. Think you that you will suffer for releasing me thus, Thomas?"

"They will not love me for it! But I *am* the King's brother — or, more important perhaps, Albany's! Also, lacking a bishop, this is in some measure *my* house. And you are my good-brother. They will not wish to offend Holy Church more than they must. I do not think that they will lay violent hands on me."

"No. My sorrow to have brought this upon you."

"I brought it upon myself. And David is my nephew, mind. Let *one* of his uncles be as loyal as yourself!"

"To be sure. Shall I look for you, then, tomorrow? In the town?"

"Come to the Cathedral, before Vespers. None will look for you there. The Lepers' Chapel — St. Lazarus. Folk avoid it. If I do not come, then you will know that I am held. You must make your own way, then." He shrugged. "I am no true churchman — but God go with you, with us both, Jamie."

"Yes. I thank you. And if you see David, tell him that I will seek to raise Douglas to his aid."

Jamie opened the door and slipped out into the chill night air and on to the slippery rocks of the beach.

It was much too late to expect any house or tavern to open its doors for him. So, when making his way with difficulty, in the dark, over the ribs and reefs of the shore, he came to the harbour, it occurred to him that one of the vessels there might offer him as good shelter as any, and be unlikely to be searched as might the churches, should his escape be discovered before morning. There were many craft tied up at the quays, for the Church did much foreign trade, especially in the wools and hides from her innumerable farms and granges. Fishing-boats, not being decked-in, provided little cover or shelter; but the second of the larger vessels he tiptoed aboard was a wool-ship, part-loaded, and he was able to bed down, under the poop, among oily-smelling fleeces, with a fair degree of comfort. Rats hopped and squeaked all about him, their eyes gleaming red, but did him no harm. He ate his viands, leaving none for the rats, and resumed his night's slumber, having done much worse in many a campaign.

Up with the dawn, still no sign of life about the harbour area, he found the Harbour Port to the town still shut, barring access. Deciding that, in the circumstances, he could probably work his way round the walls without having to enter the town at all, he set off on a south-about course, so as not to pass the castle again. It was awkward going, and smelly — for it was clear that however fine a place St. Andrews was, its folk found that the easiest way to get rid of garbage and refuse was to hurl it over the town-walls, and not only where the tide might eventually clear it away. It was a long time since the city had had to use its walls for more military purposes.

Jamie had worked his way almost round to the South Port when the bells began to chime. He heard the first with some alarm, fearing that it might have something to do with himself, a warning that a fugitive was at large. But when innumerable others joined in, presently all dominated by the great booming of the Cathedral carillon, he recognised that it was just St. Andrews' way of greeting each new day. It was a dull grey morning, with no sign of sunrise, but presumably that was the hour. He hurried to get past the South Port before the gates opened, for no-one waited there yet to gain entry and the last thing he wanted was to make himself conspicuous.

Away from the coast now, he kept further back from the walls. The West Port was the main entrance to the city, the way Albany would almost certainly come. His plan was to hide up somewhere on the western approaches, to watch for his arrival. He might learn *something*. He would have liked to slip into the town first, to purchase food and drink for the day, but reluctantly decided against, as not worth the risk. It occurred to him that probably the best place for him to go was the selfsame spot in the woodlands of Strathtyrum where Ramorgnie had ambushed them the day before, no doubt chosen with care. Thither he made his way, as the country folk began to move in towards the town for the day's market. He drew some odd glances, for although he always dressed modestly, there was no hiding the fact that he was of the gentry, unhorsed yet wearing thigh-length riding-boots of fine doeskin, however unshaven and unwashed. But his dark Douglas glower, or perhaps his prominent sword, discouraged enquiries or spoken remarks.

In under two miles he found the place he was looking for, the tight bend in the Cupar road in the Strathtyrum woodland. Here he constructed himself a hide amongst the dead bracken and scrub birch, and settled himself to wait.

Soon he slept.

The first time he was awakened, it was by a monkish party passing, on palfreys, their leader a heavy and rubicund churchman carried in a fine horse-litter, four singing-boys chanting before him to lighten the journey's tedium. This was about an hour before noon. The second time, it was a much larger and faster-moving company, all jingling harness and clanking armour, led behind two streaming banners. The first was not unexpected, the yellow-blue-white of Stewart of Albany. It was the other, hidden at first behind, which shook Jamie — the red crowned heart under the blue chief of Douglas, undifferenced. Behind these, riding beside the Duke Robert and in front of a large group of gallants and at least one hundred men-at-arms, was Archibald, Earl of Douglas.

Angry and depressed, Jamie watched this authoritative column disappear down the road to St. Andrews. The presence of Douglas there meant that he must drastically change his outlook, abandon many of his hopes for the situation. The new Earl would not be riding with Albany to St. Andrews unless he was in the plot, agreeing to David's apprehension. So nothing was to be hoped for from Douglas arms — at least, the main Douglas arms. There were others, of course — his own father and brothers, the Earl of Angus, the Lairds of Drumlanrig and Cavers and so on. But how far would these be prepared to act against their chief? The position was suddenly very much darker.

There was nothing more to wait for now, and after a while he started to walk back to the town, hunger hastening his steps. The West Port was wide open, and unwatched. He had no difficulty in entering. The streets were full, for a market, and he mingled with the crowds unhindered. At an alehouse he re-provisioned his satchel, and then made his way to the Cathedral.

That great fane, the finest in Scotland since Elgin had been burned by Alex's father, the Wolf of Badenoch, was by no means empty, with merchants haggling in the main nave, chanting going on in one of the side-chapels, fish being sold in the south porch, this being Lent, market-women resting, with their bundles and gear, before starting for home, candle-hawkers crying their wares. One or two people were even praying. But there was nobody in the small lepers' chapel dedicated to St. Lazarus, with its squint-window giving narrow view of the main high altar, as far as these accursed of God were permitted to approach. Here Jamie settled himself, after having explored all possible exits.

He flogged his mind as to how he might affect the situation in David's interests. The fact that Albany had dared this against the kingdom's lawful ruler must mean either that the King had given consent again, or could safely be ignored. In which case there seemed little point in seeking *his* intervention. With no Primate, and the Chancellor in Albany's pocket, plus Douglas aiding, there was really no-one with sufficient authority to counter Robert Stewart. In some kingdoms, in England indeed, someone would see to it that the feckless monarch was put away, or quietly assassinated — whereupon the prince would automatically become King David the Third, with all authority vested in his person. But this was not a thing to be contemplated in Scotland, where the monarchy, although less powerful and autocratic than in England and elsewhere, was more sacrosanct, more honoured of the people, *Ard Righ*, High King of Scots, not King of Scotland, a major difference, a more patriarchal figure. What source of aid was left, then? The fact that Sir William Lindsay was involved, the Earl of Crawford's illegitimate brother, did not augur well in that direction. Moray was a broken reed. No doubt some of the lesser lords and many of the bishops would be sympathetic; but would they, *could* they, provide sufficient pressure on Albany, or armed men, to counter the combined strength of Douglas and Stewart? He knew the answer to that without asking. Just as he knew that few would commit their men or their powers into the hands of a small knight such as himself, however well disposed towards the prince. He saw no way out of the predicament.

He was little further forward, therefore, when the Archdeacon Thomas arrived at the chapel, in mid-afternoon, earlier than he had said.

"They have gone," he announced. "Robert stayed only long enough to eat and bate his horses. He has taken David back to Falkland, a close prisoner."

"The Lieutenant. With what authority, other than some hundreds of armed men!"

"The King's authority, he says."

286

"But . . . what has changed since November, at Stirling Castle? David has been more careful since then. Done nothing amiss. The King has had no reason to allow Albany to go further than he did then."

"There was the matter of Sir John Wemyss."

"Wemyss imprisoned Walter Lindsay in his castle of Reres, unlawfully. It was the Lieutenant's *duty* to free him and to punish Wemyss. If the King's Lieutenant cannot do such a duty without incurring the King's censure, what rule is there in Scotland?"

"Wemyss is neighbour to Ramorgnie, in Fife. No doubt a supporter of Robert's. This has but been used as an excuse. There may be other such excuses — but that was the only one that I heard mentioned. But what matters it? The facts are there. Robert has taken David into custody, allegedly with the royal authority. No doubt he has been waiting to do so for long, waiting for opportunity. David was foolish to come to St. Andrews so ill-escorted. He should never have travelled abroad without a strong force at his back. That, or else himself taken the very steps Robert has done — taken Robert himself into custody. That would have been the wiser course."

"Aye — even Ramorgnie suggested that. And worse! David had sufficient excuse: Albany's failure to come to his aid at Edinburgh, and word that he was in negotiation with King Henry, secretly, with Forrester of Corstorphine — sufficient to hold Albany on a charge of treason. But he would not. He said that it would provoke war, civil war, and give Henry the opportunity he wanted. David has had to rule from a position of great weakness. With his father so feeble, useless . . ."

"Aye. My royal brother may be saintly disposed — but saints can on occasion do more mischief than other men!"

"What to do now, then?"

"The good God knows! Did you see who was with Robert? Douglas! If he has decided to support Robert in this, I cannot see that there is much than any can do."

Jamie nodded unhappily. "That is the crowning blow!" He jerked a mirthless laugh. "Crowning, indeed! If only . . . if only . . ."

"You mean, if only the King would die? Yes, we can all think of that. But — he is the Lord's Anointed. And though frail, in fair enough health, I think. And but sixty-five. David could wait for many years yet, for the throne!"

"Is Albany assuming the rule? The governorship? As he said. He cannot do that lawfully without the authority of parliament, where David's cause will be upheld . . ."

"In law, no. But in fact, he can rule now. And so order matters that a parliament is delayed until he is so entrenched that he will be harder to dislodge than last time. Robert is no fool. We must face the fact."

"How did he treat David, today? He is never anything but harsh and cold. But . . ."

"I do not know. I was not allowed to see David again. I had a word or two with Robert, but to little purpose. Our brotherly ties are of the weakest. He has little love for me — indeed, I doubt if he has love for any. A strange, sour, friendless man — but able, determined."

"And without scruple. David, in his power, may fare but uncomfortably. He has taken him to Falkland, you say? For what purpose?"

"I know not. They have all gone. They gave him a ragged cloak and mounted him on the sorriest nag in the stables. To make for Falkland."

"Aye. Then I had better follow, learn what I can. I shall need a horse. What has happened to my men?"

"They are all at the castle still, David's likewise. Your horses also. Robert took only David. The castle is mine again. So, come you . . ."

Back at the castle — and strange to be able to walk therein openly again — it was decided that there was no point in riding to Falkland that night. They could not get there before dark, and there would be little to learn, so soon, anyway. Better to wait, eat well, have a good night's rest, and ride in the morning.

Despite impatience, that was Jamie's programme.

* * *

Falkland, the main seat of the earldom of Fife, lay some twenty miles west of St. Andrews, a little grey town clustering round the large castle, lying in the shadow of the East Lomond Hill. It was not the sort of place that a party of mounted men could ride into without attracting a deal of attention, and all being seen from the castle. So, next day, about noon, nearing its vicinity, Jamie sent his own men and the half-dozen of the royal guard, back to Aberdour, another fifteen miles, retaining only the one groom to guard their two horses, in a wood half-a-mile from the town. Then he went forward alone to investigate.

There was no fair going on here unfortunately, and Jamie went very warily. But he perceived that no banner was flown from the castle keep, as might have been expected, with its master in residence. And when he asked some of the townsfolk whether Albany was there, he was told that the Duke had left that morning, where none knew, but it was presumed back to his main seat of Doune in Menteith. Carefully seeking to discover who had gone with the Duke, without seeming to press too keenly, he gathered that the Earl of Douglas and Sir John de Ramorgnie had accompanied him, and seemingly his entire entourage; but there was no mention of the Duke of Rothesay. None volunteered the name, and Jamie refrained from bringing it up. He did ask who remained in charge at the castle, however, and was told the constable, John Wright, and the steward, John Selkirk.

Jamie had heard of the man Wright, a harsh and boorish character, highly unpopular in Fife, known for his heavy hand and brutality in his master's service.

At an alehouse opposite the castle gatehouse, he made more discreet enquiry. Men-at-arms from the castle used this place, and he was able to learn that a captive, identity unknown but a young man, had been brought in with the Duke's party the previous afternoon, riding a baggage-horse and covered in a rough russet cloak. He had not gone with the Duke and the rest this morning, so was still a prisoner in the castle. Despite his humdrum appearance he must be somebody of importance for the Duke to have gone to St. Andrews in person to fetch him. Albany, it seemed, had now gone only to Culross, in Fothrif, where some sort of meeting of great ones was summoned.

Very thoughtful indeed, Jamie made his way back to his horse and groom.

Later, at his own fireside at Aberdour, he recounted all to Mary, who listened grave-faced.

"Robert must be very sure of himself to do this," she said eventually. "It is not really like him, to act so directly, so openly. He prefers intrigue, using others. This is more like my late half-brother Alec! What is to be done, Jamie?"

"I have racked my wits to think of something," he told her. "You think the King will know of this imprisonment? By agreeing to it?"

"I fear that he must. Robert would never dare to lay rough

289

hands on the heir to the throne, and hold him captive, and in his own castle, otherwise. He will have played on John, told him lies and half-truths. Saying that it is for David's own good . . ."

"If we went and saw the King? You, and possibly Thomas and myself. Told him the truth?"

"I doubt if it would serve much purpose. Having gone so far, Robert will not be likely to draw back now, save on the strongest of royal commands. Which are not likely to be forthcoming, from John. Especially if he can sway this Council at Culross to support him — Robert, I mean."

"The devil of it, that Douglas should be on his side! This is the final blow. I can still go to my father, and Angus, with Cavers and Drumlanrig and the others. But, against their chief, I would not wager that they would do much."

"Would David Lindsay help — Crawford?"

"Help, perhaps — but no more than that. He will not take any lead, I think. With his half-brother in Albany's pocket and the Lindsays disgruntled over the Lady Euphemia business."

"And the Church is leaderless and divided. Oh, that Annabella and the good Bishop Trail were still alive! Even Archie the Grim. That they should all have died at the one time! It is as though God's hand is against David."

They sat staring into the fire for a while, unhappily. Then Jamie shrugged. "Tomorrow, at least, I shall go see my father. He has a wise head — although too cautious now, with age. He is still a member of the Council, although he but seldom attends. He does not like Albany. Perhaps he will think of something that we can do. Then I will try Angus, at Tantallon."

She looked up. "Jamie — has it not occurred to you that *you* are now in danger? All know how close you are to David. All know that you are a man of action. Robert has always disliked you — as you him. Ramorgnie likewise. You have escaped from them once. They will take you again, if they can. And perhaps treat you less gently."

"They may try. But I am warned now, at least. They will not take me so easily again. What would you have me do? Sit still, here? Attempt nothing for David? Flee somewhere safer . . . ?"

"Just be careful, lad," she said. "Just ever be taking care . . . !"

XV

IN HIS FATHER'S overheated chamber at Dalkeith, Jamie wagged his head in exasperation. The Lord of Dalkeith was old now, admittedly — in his seventieth year. But he still had sound wits, and was moreover still a powerful figure in the realm, probably its richest noble, experienced in government.

"You cannot just sit there and say God's will be done!" his illegitimate but favourite son protested. "If you make Albany's will God's will, then you make the good God a murderer! For nothing is surer than that Albany committed murder."

"Hush, lad. That is no way to talk. I do not say that Albany's will is God's — but only that God may even use such as Albany to work *His* will. David needs a lesson, it may be. He has been foolish, headstrong. A term in captivity may do him no harm, bring him to a better appreciation of his duties, so that when he is King, he may rule the more wisely. All his days he has had his own wilful way."

"So you would do nothing? Accept any wickedness on Albany's part, however unlawful, as possibly serving God's purpose? Is this how you, a Privy Councillor, are prepared to rule the realm?"

"Not so. But in ruling a realm, as in all else, what cannot be mended is best accepted, Jamie. And betterment worked for, thereafter."

"I prefer to work for the betterment first!"

"Tell me how, lad? As I see it, there is only one key which will unlock David's prison-door, and that is the King's. For no-one else will Albany yield — if even then. And Falkland is a strong castle and will be well guarded, you may be sure. You will not bring David out of there, even with a host at your back."

"Then we must go to the King."

"And what will you say to him? How persuade him? How prevail against Albany's stronger will? Think you he would heed *you*, Jamie. Or even see you?"

"He might see his own brother and sister — Mary and the Archdeacon Thomas."

"See, perhaps. But *heed*? Use your wits, lad. If the King has so turned against his own son that he allows his brother to lock him up in a castle, will he be likely to heed lesser men's pleadings?"

"If we could show him that Albany was a monster, an evil man seeking only power for himself . . ."

"He would take a deal of convincing of that, at this stage. But . . ."

"If we told him that he, Albany, wanted to hand over the Mammet to Henry? In return for aid against David. Would that not sway the King?"

"If he believed it! But see you, Jamie — there is one matter which might sway our weak and foolish monarch against his brother. And that is fear. Fear not for himself — for I believe that he might well wish to die — but for his little son. Young James is now John Stewart's all, the apple of his eye. His link with his dead queen. Was he to see a threat to James in this, all might yet be changed."

"And could there be?"

"It could be represented so. And with some justice perhaps. If David were to die, there is only young James between Albany and the throne, when the King goes."

"Aye. And you think . . .?"

"I say only could be. But Albany is perhaps ambitious for more than just power. He had the power before. He has always resented John's primogeniture, when *he* would have made the strong and able king. John must know this very well. Here is the only chance I see . . ."

"Aye, it could be. It could very well be so. You think the King would rise to that lure?"

"If it was skilfully presented to him, he might."

"You will come? And so present it? The King is at Turnberry again. With young James and the Mammet . . ."

"No, no. Not me, lad. I am past traipsing the country — an auld done man. You must make do your own self. With your wife and her brother Thomas. I will send your brother James with you to represent me, if you wish. He is not so bright as

292

you are, but he is a good lad. And he can take a troop of Douglas horse — for I jalouse that there's some who might seek to interfere with you, Jamie. You'll have to watch out for yourself, lad, in this business."

"Mary said as much." Jamie was fond enough of his half-brother, his father's heir, but had no particular desire for his company on a difficult ploy like this. But the hundred men-at-arms was a welcome suggestion and James would captain them suitably.

He was impatient, of course, to be off to Ayrshire to put the matter to the test, but had to restrain himself. Apart from the assembling of the men-at-arms, it was important that he gain the support of such magnates as he could. A day or two would make little difference, he told himself.

Next day, then, he rode to Tantallon, in East Lothian. He found the young Earl of Angus most evidently happy in his marriage, and well content with life, immersed in the management of his lands and people — and in consequence not disposed for adventures. He was concerned to hear Jamie's tidings, outraged at Albany's behaviour and anxious for the future of Scotland implicit in all this; but saw no personal involvement, nothing that he might usefully do. He offered the use of some fifty of his men — that was as far as he would go. Jamie accepted these with what grace he could, and moved on.

There was nothing more to be done in Lothian, since Douglas and Dunbar divided all between them, all lesser lairds being in vassalage to one or the other, or at least indisposed to take a contrary line. Crawford, it seemed, was at his Angus castle of Edzell, which was a long way to go. But, after Douglas, he was the next most important noble in the land, as well as being David's uncle by marriage. Jamie would go there, via Aberdour and St. Andrews, and arrange for Mary and Thomas to accompany him to Turnberry. At least he could ride secure with a bodyguard of a hundred and fifty men.

The Lindsay chief was of more practical help than was Angus; but even he lacked real enthusiasm. It was Albany's reputation for caution, strangely enough, that was the main handicap. In view of this, the fact that he now dared to act so drastically, convinced Crawford, like others, that he was entirely confident, assured of success, unbeatable — which inhibited opposition. Crawford saw nothing to be gained by approaching the King — who must have given his consent. He said, however, that he would demand a meeting of the Privy Council, and do what he could to ensure that that body took strong steps to have David released, and insist upon the calling of a parliament. A parliament would be David's best hope, undoubtedly. On Jamie's expressed determination to see the monarch, he shrugged. He could not stop him — but it was a waste of time; and he, Crawford, would by no means accompany him.

So it was a small party of four, three of them bastards, who eventually set off westwards for Ayrshire, however strongly escorted. They suffered no interference *en route*.

* * *

They had some difficulty in gaining entry to Turnberry Castle, for although the King personally was much more accessible than many of his nobles, those concerned with his government were ever on watch for attempts to kidnap him and use him as hostage for their own ends. The present royal guard, needless to say, was of Albany's appointment; but even they could not permanently deny the monarch's half-brother and half-sister audience.

Eventually they won their way into a private apartment, where young James, Earl of Carrick, received them. He was a serious, dark-eyed, watchful child, old for his years, with good and regular features and a surprisingly direct gaze, however modest in manner — so notably different from his brother David at a similar age. He bowed gravely.

"Aunt Mary. Uncle Thomas. Sir James. I greet you." He looked at Young Dalkeith. "You, sir — I regret that I do not know your name?"

Jamie introduced his half-brother. Mary went to kiss her nephew.

"Have you travelled far?" the boy enquired politely. "You will require refreshment."

"Thank you. Your father, the King — he is well?" Thomas asked. "We have come far to speak with him."

"I shall tell him. But . . . His Grace is much troubled. Scarce himself. It is . . . it is about Davie?" The grave young voice trembled a little.

"Yes, James — it is about Davie," Mary said, as gently as she might. "Things go very ill with Davie. Does your father know it all? Is he fully aware of what is done?"

"He knows that my brother has been taken into custody. It does not please him, but he believes it necessary."

"Does he understand how close is the custody? How rigorous and harsh for the heir to the throne, the realm's Lieutenant?"

"He knows him to be in Uncle Robert's keeping at Falkland."

"He agreed to that?"

"Yes. Uncle Robert said that it was necessary. For Davie's own good . . ." That was tremulous again. James was known to all but hero-worship his brilliant elder brother.

"And the King accepts Robert's word as against his own son, my lord?" That was Jamie Douglas.

The boy bit his lip. "I, I fear so," he whispered. He turned away. "Come — to the Lesser Hall, for your refreshment. And I will go tell His Grace."

It was some considerable time, and the visitors were finishing a meal of cold meats and wine in the Lesser Hall, before the King came to them, leaning on the Mammet on one side, his other hand held by the boy-prince. He looked the utter wreck of a man, bent, drawn, his lower lip trembling all the while, his great eyes rheumy. As the callers rose and bowed, he shook his white head.

"If you have come about Davie, Tom — aye, and you Mary — I canna do aught," he said. "He'll have to bide at Falkland meantime. He's a good lad, but foolish, headstrong. He'll need to learn his lesson before he can rule this realm again. There's no two ways to that."

Mary it was who spoke. "Perhaps, Sire. But — greetings! We offer our leal duty, and wish you well."

The others mumbled agreement.

The King shook his head, then seemed to recollect the Mammet Richard. "His Grace of England," he said.

They all bowed again.

"Thomas — if you have come about St. Andrews, we could still have you Bishop, I'd say. Robert wouldna stand in your way, I think."

"I have no wish to be Bishop of St. Andrews, Sire. I am not of the stuff of primates! We are here on a much graver matter — the life of the Prince and High Steward of Scotland. Whom you have allowed to be shut in a prison cell."

"I told you — he'll have to bide there awhile, Thomas. Until he's learned his lesson. He's been fell foolish."

"What has he done since yon day at Stirling when you warned him? What especial folly to deserve this? He has been careful, discreet . . ."

"No, no. Robert knows better than that. He has had him watched, see you. He has but been hiding his follies. Robbing the Customs, mishandling those who will not give him the moneys he wants, whoring and drinking. I canna have my Lieutenant and heir so behaving. When, when he's like to be more than heir soon enough!"

"Sire — I swear that you have been misinformed," Jamie exclaimed. "I am the Duke David's man — Douglas of Aberdour. I have aided him in his campaign against the wicked misappropriation of customs dues. There has been shameful thievery for years — but not by him. The Duke has been most honest in this, I promise Your Grace. He has been stamping down a notorious evil which, which . . ." He swallowed. "The Duke of Albany's information on this is not correct. I have been concerned in it, and know."

"Shall I prefer *your* opinion on this, sir, to that of my own brother?"

"Sire, I also am your brother, if on the wrong side of the blanket!" Thomas said. "And I would remind you that Robert hates David, resents his position and covets his power. Robert is without scruple and does not hesitate to lie to gain his ends. And worse. You prefer to trust him, rather than your own son?"

John Stewart gnawed his lip. "Who *can* I believe?" he quavered. "Not Davie, who has deceived me times without number. I can trust none, I tell you — none! Save James, here. Aye, and King Richard."

"Sire, you can trust me, your half-sister," Mary said strongly. "I have never lied to you. Nor ever would. I tell you that Robert is concerned only to bring David down. He cannot do that without your aid. He appears, by his lies and plotting, to have gained that aid. David is no saint — but he is a deal better man than Robert."

"David is weak, Robert is strong, lass. And the realm, any realm, requires a strong hand to rule it. I, God pity me, who have *no* strength, know that! I have tried, the saints know how I have tried, to teach Davie how to rule — I, who myself can by no means rule. But he has never heeded me. It is not only Robert, Mary. It is for Davie's own good. For the time grows short. I shall not live much longer — Heaven be praised! And when I am gone, Davie will be King — and none then will be able to control him. Somehow he must learn his lesson before then. This way, I pray, he may at last learn, and quickly."

296

"Learn to be a king — from a prison cell?"

"Aye, lacking better. A monk's cell would have been more seemly — but he would never have agreed to it. He had to be removed from temptation, away from all women and wine, communing only with himself and God — vigil, fasting, repentance, learning to know himself. I pray that he comes out of that cell in Falkland a man fitter to be King of Scots. For he has wits, courage, ability, lacking only responsibility. He may be learning it now, at last." That was a long speech for John Stewart, and he was panting at the end of it.

His visitors stared at him and at each other, speechless, scarcely able to believe their ears. That the King was in earnest was not to be doubted. Yet it was all but incredible that he should believe this, out-of-touch with the world and sheltered from reality as he was.

Thomas found words at last. "Is this . . . Robert's ploy?" he asked thickly. "Did he put it thus to you?"

"Not so," the King said wearily. "Robert was concerned only with restraining Davie from more folly. It was I myself, after much prayer, who saw how much good might come out of seeming harshness."

Jamie muttered under his breath, and his brother nudged his arm, brows raised.

Mary spoke. "Sire, the harshness you speak of could be more grievous than you think."

"Why say you so, Mary?"

She glanced at her husband.

Jamie cleared his throat. "Your Grace, I bring a message from my father. Which my brother here will substantiate. You may think more highly of the advice of my lord of Dalkeith, long a member of your Privy Council, than of my own. He asks, in all duty, whether you have considered that your sons, *both* of your sons, could be in danger? Great danger. Even of their lives?"

The monarch peered short-sightedly. "Are you out of your mind, sir? And the Lord of Dalkeith likewise?"

"My father, at least, Sire, is a notably level-headed man. Your Grace has known him long. He asks — have you considered that there are but two steps between the Duke of Albany and your throne, when you, h'm, vacate it — the Princes David and James, your sons. And the Duke of Albany is a man who seeks power above all things."

The King held out a hand that trembled violently. "No!" he exclaimed. "No! How dare you, sir! You, such as *you*, accuse my brother! To me — the King!"

"With respect, Sire — not me. It is my *father's* message," Jamie insisted, woodenly. "Although I agree with it. The Duke Robert already has the Duke David in his power. One step all but taken. It would be less difficult to take the Earl of Carrick, here, a mere child. Then, Sire, if aught should occur to *your* injury, your brother is in a position to reach for the throne himself. None to gainsay him."

"This is beyond belief! I *will* not listen to you, sir. Or your father." The King was clutching his young son closer to him, however. He turned to the Mammet. "Richard — have you ever heard such, such wicked imputation?"

That strange man spoke low-voiced. "I would remind you, my friend, that my throne was wrested from me. And by a kinsman!"

Unhappily the older man eyed him. "Dear God Almighty!" he said.

"Sire," Thomas put in, anxious to exploit even this opening. "It is a real danger. You must see it. But even if Robert has no such intention, it is surely most damaging to David's reputation and authority to be shut up in a cell in Robert's castle? He is the *Lieutenant*! It cannot but injure his name as ruler. Even here in your house, it would be less hurtful. But in Robert's own hold — the man who would supplant him as Governor, if naught else . . ."

"It must be where Davie could not suborn the guards, or he would be out. And I do not see any guards but Robert's proof against him!"

"*Must* he be locked in a cell?" Mary asked. "Tom is right. Apart from the danger, it cannot but harm his authority afterwards — for him to have been imprisoned while he was still Governor. Who will respect his powers after that? Unless, of course, you do not intend that he has any? That you are removing him from the governorship entirely?"

"No, not that. Robert will act Governor again meantime. But thereafter in due course, Davie will rule again."

"If he survives!" Jamie murmured.

Mary laid her hand on his arm. "How long do you intend that he be confined, Sire?" she asked.

The King gestured vaguely. "Who knows? Not for long. A month. Two months. Until he has learned his lesson."

"And you will not heed us, Sire?" Thomas demanded. "Pay no heed to all we have said? Ignore the danger . . . ?"

"I will consider it. Aye, I will take thought. And pray. Pray to God to guide an erring servant."

"But . . . before too long? David meantime *may* be in danger."

"Do not harass me, Thomas. I will not be harassed! I have said that I will consider the matter. God knows, I have sufficient on my mind." The monarch began to turn away.

Greatly daring, Jamie spoke again. "Your Grace, I hesitate to cast more upon your royal mind. But before he was arrested by Sir John de Ramorgnie, the Duke of Rothesay told me that he had sure information that the Duke of Albany was negotiating with King Henry of England, for the return to him of, of King Richard, here, Sir Adam de Forrester of Corstorphine acting as messenger. To exchange King Richard for certain advantages. I conceive it my duty to tell you."

The Mammet had drawn a quick and audible breath, and grasped the King's arm.

"Merciful Lord Christ!" John Stewart gasped. "No — it cannot be! I do not believe it. Robert would not do such an evil thing."

"The prince had it on most reliable information from London, Sire. Forrester gained safe-conducts to visit kinsmen elsewhere in England. But he made his way to Henry's Court. The word there is that he came to offer the return of King Richard."

"That I will *not* permit!" the monarch cried, with a deal more decision than he had shown in regard to his son. "Never fear, Richard, my friend. I will not have it."

Thomas Stewart drove the point home. "Nor would David, Your Grace. But Robert, our *strong* brother, will do anything he thinks to his own advantage — if he has the power."

John Stewart muttered something unintelligible, and turning, hurried from the hall, his attendants following.

The visitors waited for three days at Turnberry, hoping for definite word from the King that he would command the release of David. All that they gained eventually was that he would write to Robert, urging that his elder son be transferred to Stirling Castle. He would also declare that under no circumstances was King Richard to be the subject of negotiations, and would remain in his own royal care and keeping.

With this they had to be content, as they turned their horses' heads eastwards again.

XVI

It was Tom Durie, the steward's son at Aberdour, who brought the first word of the appalling news. He had been attending a cattle-fair at Freuchie, near Falkland, and he said that the whisper there was that the Duke of Rothesay was dead. Dead in Falkland Castle.

Neither Jamie nor Mary believed it, of course. It was assuredly the foolish gossip of ignorant folk. But Durie declared that some of the men of Falkland that he had spoken with at Freuchie were of the better sort, responsible. They even gave the cause of death — starvation.

Nothing would do but that Jamie must go and try to find out the facts despite Mary's warnings of danger. It might be that the prince was only ill, and the tale had been exaggerated. But even so, they must find out, and seek to aid him. So, dressed in his oldest clothes and riding his poorest nag, Jamie set out for Falkland.

At the little grey town under the hill, he scarcely required to make secret or even discreet enquiries, for the whole place buzzed with the stories. There were various versions, but all agreed that the prince had been given no food of any kind by his gaolers since coming to Falkland eighteen days before. Some had it that he had been consistently maltreated by John Selkirk and John Wright, Albany's minions, from the start, as well as starved. Others declared that he had been given nothing to drink either, and had run mad. Others explained that he had managed to survive thus long because his cell had been beneath the castle granary, and grains of corn trickling down between the floor-boards had fallen to him. There was even a story that one of the women in the castle, a nursing mother, had been so distressed by the prisoner's state that she went to his aid by squeezing milk from her breast, by means of a straw poked through a crack in the masonry from the next cellar, for the prince to suck — although this sounded more ingenious than practical to Jamie Douglas. But all agreed that David Stewart was dead — and had in fact been taken to Lindores Abbey that very morning for burial. And it seemed to be substantiated sufficiently that a corpse of some sort *had* been removed from the castle during the forenoon, in a horse-litter.

Jamie grimly decided to go on to Lindores, only seven miles to the north, and the Fife family burial-place. If the corpse had indeed been taken there, it was significant — for of course ordinary folk who died at Falkland would be buried in the local kirkyard.

In a sort of numb horror of fear, Jamie rode over the hill, past Rossie, Sir William Lindsay's barony, the little town of Auchtermuchty, and Pitcairlie. But he was not so numb as to fail to take avoiding action when, still a couple of miles from the Abbey, he perceived a fast-riding company coming towards him from that direction, on the road for Cupar, the sheriff's town. He drew off the track into whin and scrub, and dismounted.

The horsemen, about a dozen strong, drummed past him at speed — but not so fast that he could not identify the man at the head, Sir John de Ramorgnie.

He rode on more desolate than ever.

The Abbey of Lindores was a handsome and extensive Benedictine establishment, founded by David the First, but largely maintained by successive Earls of Fife. In due gratitude, the Abbots maintained in their turn the highly practical and useful sanctuary arrangement, known as the Law of Clan MacDuff, whereby felons within the ninth degree of kin to the Earls of Fife, man-slayers included, could claim sanctuary at the MacDuff Cross nearby, and secure all remission by payment of a fixed and modest compensation to the victim's heirs. Many had found this convenient provision to their advantage.

Jamie was in some doubts as to whether to discard his disguise and go openly to the Abbot, as Sir James Douglas of Aberdour, requesting information; or to retain it, and seek some humbler informant. He decided on the latter course, arguing that the Abbot, whom he knew only by repute, was bound to be more or less in the pocket of Albany, as Earl of Fife, and might well have been warned against enquirers. In the circumstances it seemed wiser to try more subtle methods.

Lindores, down on the Tayside plain, had the usual hospice for travellers, and here Jamie presented himself, seeking the plain but substantial fare offered by Holy Church to all comers. From the black-robed serving-brother there he gleaned little, save that there had indeed been a funeral of a sort that day, although the body was not yet actually buried but lying coffined in the Abbey chapter-house — presumably some great one, for there was a guard of armed men. But later, out in the orchard, he discovered a more talkative monk, digging beneath the trees, who, when Jamie jocularly asked if he was excavating a grave for the newly-arrived corpse, looked disapproving, almost shocked.

"Not so," he said severely. "That's a fool question, man. This isna hallowed ground. Yon puir soul deserves better than a bit leek-patch to lie in!"

"I but jested, friend."

"You shouldna jest about suchlike matters." The other had a broad Fife accent. "Yon one had had ill and unChristian handling, to bring him here. At least we'll gie him good Christian burial."

"M'mm. You mean that the body had been mishandled on its way here? I heard that it had come from Falkland or Freuchie or some such place?"

"Na, na. The mishandling was afore that. Whilst the puir mannie was alive." The monk lowered his voice. "Man, I helped lift him frae the litter he came in, and put him in the bit kist he's in now. And the shroud he was happit in came unwound someways, and an arm pokit out — an unchancy thing! And every finger was gnawed down to the white bone, see you — gnawed clean awa'! Now — what for would a man do the likes o' that, tell me?"

Jamie drew a long quivering breath. "God knows!" he got out. "Unless he was starving. Desperate for food. And drink. Mad with hunger and thirst."

"Aye, mebbeso. Mishandled, I said, did I no'? UnChristian, whoever did it. God will judge them, aye."

"Do you know whose this is? The body?"

"Nane hae said the name. And the body and face has aye been covered. But . . . it's no' some common loon. Else why set a guard on the chapter-house door, with nane to enter?"

"Who set the guard?"

"Him they ca' the Proculator, or suchlike name. One o' the King's officers."

"The Prolocutor-General is Sir John de Ramorgnie. One of Albany's men, rather than the King's."

"Aye, mebbeso. But what's the differ? It's a high matter, but an ill one. No' for such as oursel's to speir into. But God's judgement will fa' on whoever did this thing, high or no' — mark my words. *Dominus regnavit*!"

"I hope that you are right, friend," Jamie said heavily, and turned away.

He left Lindores sick at heart, to ride southwards for Aberdour.

* * *

"Jamie, Jamie!" Mary cried urgently. "Listen to me. You now are in direst danger. We all are. If they can slay horribly the heir to the throne, think you that they will hesitate to slay you, his friend and servant? You have escaped from their clutches once. Robert knows well that you are his enemy. Ramorgnie hates you — has never hidden the fact. You know too much for your own good. You cannot stay here. We must get away."

"Where, lass — where?"

"I do not know. But away from here. Away from Fife. Away from wherever Robert's men may lay hands on you."

"That, I fear, is anywhere south of the Highland Line, my dear."

"Then let us go north. Go to Alex Stewart in Badenoch. We could be safe with him. Anywhere, so long as Robert cannot reach us."

"But . . . I cannot just turn myself into a hunted fugitive, Mary," he protested.

"Better that than a corpse, like David! You must see it, Jamie. Robert will stop at nothing, now. He will learn that you have been to see the King. Knowing what you do, he will esteem you a danger. A man who can starve to death his own nephew, will kill such as you as he would a fly! And you have no powerful protector, now, in the Earl of Douglas. He is on Robert's side."

"We could go to Dalkeith, I suppose — my father's house."

"And have to go guarded by many men every time you

303

ventured out? It would be only a matter of time until they got you."

"If we knew what were Albany's plans, now? Whether he but aims to have the rule? Or the throne itself?"

"The rule first, then the crown, I'd say. I would not give much for young James's life, poor laddie! Nor his father's — although John would give up the ghost gladly enough."

"He will not act precipitately — Albany. He never does. Always hides behind others. He will find some excuse for this terrible deed, claim that he knew nothing of it. Condole with the King, lull his suspicions. And then, in due course, strike again."

"Perhaps. But I do not see how *you* are served . . .?"

"If that is how it goes, he may not wish more trouble meantime. If I also was to be slain, now, David's known friend and servant, then it would look very black. He might not wish that. He might well leave me alone, meantime."

"Do not cozen yourself, Jamie. Robert has gone too far now for half-measures and caution. Poor David was the turning-point. He need not fear the King, and James is only a child. Whom needs he go warily for, now, with Douglas supporting him? I say his days of caution and the hidden hand are over."

"David should be avenged," he said.

Exasperatedly she shook her head. "Not by you, Jamie Douglas! Will you never learn? You sought for years to avenge the Earl James Douglas, against Robert. To what end? He is far too strong, too secure, for such as you to reach. If David could not master him, how could you do so? Forget vengeance, Jamie — or leave it to God. David's end is terrible, beyond all contemplation. And I was fond of him. But you cannot bring him back, and you cannot reach Robert, now less than ever. You must consider yourself. And me. The children. We must not stay here where Robert can reach *us*."

"Archie Douglas, the Earl, does not hate *me*. However much he misliked David. Indeed, I believe he thinks well of me. If I put myself under Earl Archie's protection . . .?"

"Do not believe it. Archie Douglas is not like his father, Archie the Grim. He is not much better than a weakling, I think. As clay in Robert's hands. If Robert wanted you, Douglas would not save you — that I swear. No — the only man who can protect us now is Alex Stewart, a hundred and more miles behind the Highland Line. We must go there,

Jamie, and quickly, before it is too late. Leave our home, meantime. Change our life. There is nothing else for it."

Unhappily they eyed each other.

He sighed. "It may be that you are right . . ."

*   *   *

Two evenings later, the 1st of April, they slipped out of Aberdour Castle with the dusk, leaving old Durie the steward in charge, Jamie and Mary, the two children, now eleven and nine years old, their former nurse Janet Durie and her brother Tom, and six of the barony's men as escort, to ride eastwards. The youngsters were greatly excited by this night-time journey, but none of the others found it to their taste. The county of Fife was too full of potential enemies to risk travel by day.

All night they rode, by infrequent ways, due eastwards towards the East Neuk of Fife, avoiding the coastal towns and fishing-havens, the children asleep most of the time in front of their parents. Fortunately the weather was dry, although there was a chill easterly wind, and conditions might have been a deal worse. They suffered no interference, saw few signs of life, were barked at by sundry wakeful dogs, that was all.

They came to the village of Boarhills, not far inland from Fife Ness, soon after dawn — it seemed to be Jamie's fate to lurk secretly about this coast at daybreak. Here was Thomas Stewart's archdiaconal manse. Roused, he was astonished to see them, but agreed strongly that their flight was necessary and wise. He was as shocked as they were over David's death, although he had heard no details. The rumour had indeed reached St. Andrews that the prince had been starved to death; and whilst that might be inaccurate, he acceded that death was unlikely to have been from sudden illness or by accident, in the circumstances. Jamie's account of what he had learned at Lindores appalled him.

In practical matters Mary's brother was a great help — seeming not in the least embarrassed by the presence of the lady who was currently sharing his bed with him. Jamie had not forgotten the ship in which he had taken refuge at St. Andrews harbour, and reckoning that sea transport was the safest method of eluding Albany's possible clutches, wondered if Holy Church could help. Thomas said to leave it to him. One way or another the Church controlled much of what went on at St. Andrews haven, and it would be a strange thing if he

305

could not find a skipper to sail at short notice and put them ashore somewhere on the Angus or Aberdeenshire coast, from which it would be comparatively simple to reach Badenoch. Jamie suggested the North Angus port of Montrose, not very far from Edzell, where the Earl of Crawford was apt to have his domicile. He would aid them on their way.

So Thomas left them, presently, to go to St. Andrews, four miles distant, while the fugitives rested. He was back in mid-afternoon, with all in train. A coasting vessel going to Aberdeen would take them, with the next morning's tide. They would not even have to risk going to St. Andrews; the *Good Cheer* would come to the nearby harbour of Crail for them, this evening. They could go aboard after dark, and sail with the early tide. If this south-easterly breeze held they could be at Montrose, only thirty-five sea miles to the north, by the following evening.

None found fault with that programme.

That night they said goodbye to Thomas Stewart at the fishing haven of Crail, round the other side of thrusting Fife Ness. The *Good Cheer* was already tied up at the quayside, a medium-sized, sturdy-looking craft, unlovely and smelling of hides but adequate for their purpose. They bade farewell to their escort, too, save for Tom Durie who would go with them to act general aide and factotum — for there was no accommodation for horses on the ship, and it was hoped that, anyway, a mounted escort would not be necessary where they were going. The children were happier than ever, secretly boarding a ship by night. Their elders were less appreciative of smelly and cramped quarters, but grateful enough nevertheless.

They sailed at first light, beating precisely up the glittering path of the rising sun.

It was only a fair day's sail, across the Tay estuary and up the Angus coast, to Montrose, although it would have been a ride of more than a hundred miles by land; and with a south-easterly breeze backing south, they made it in excellent time, although latterly the sea became distinctly jabbly, with a strengthening wind crossing a long ocean swell. Fortunately, living at Aberdour, they were all used to boats and sailing, and the motion upset none of them. With the Highland mountains, still snow-streaked, beckoning them on, they put into the large harbour at the mouth of the great and almost landlocked Montrose basin where the South Esk reached the sea, in late afternoon.

This was Lindsay country, and when Jamie announced that he was making for the Earl of Crawford's castle of Edzell, in the Mounth foothills, he met with no difficulties from the burghers of Montrose. Hiring a guide and horses, they set out within an hour or so, westwards up the Esk valley. There was no need for secrecy here.

It was some sixteen miles to Edzell, and they put up for the night at the inn at Dun, five miles on their way, well satisfied with progress.

They came to Edzell next midday, in the mouth of Glen Esk, with the great Highland hills drawing close now, a lovely country of woodlands and green braes under the white-patched brown giants of the heather mountains. They were fairly sure of their reception here, for not only did the Earl David approve of Jamie, in his gruff way, as a fellow-warrior, but he was wed to the Lady Katherine Stewart, another of Robert the Second's daughters, and therefore half-sister to Mary. As sisters they had never been close, for Katherine was considerably older; but the fact that she, like her husband, heartily disliked her brother Albany, helped.

They were indeed kindly received, and when the circumstances were explained, pressed to stay indefinitely. Their host and hostess had not heard of David's death, and were much startled and distressed, the Earl vowing that Robert Stewart would pay dearly for such a deed. It was tempting to stay there at Edzell; but Jamie recognised that he would not feel really safe before he had put a broad barrier of the Highland mountains between them and the Albany-dominated Lowlands. They agreed to stay for a day or two however, before commencing the long journey across the uplands to Badenoch, another hundred difficult miles at least. Meanwhile the Earl would send messengers ahead to Sir Alexander Stewart at Lochindorb, to acquaint him of their coming; and when they went, they would go with a good Lindsay escort through that wild land. With this they were well enough content.

Edzell Castle was a pleasant place to linger, within its green enclave, its attendant township nearby. It was by no means the Earl's major seat; but he had been Lindsay of Glenesk before he succeeded to the chiefship of his line, and this had always been his home. He found it preferable to his many and larger houses in the south, particularly as he found little to tempt him towards Court attendance these days. The travellers, feeling distinctly less like fugitives now, indeed remained there longer than they had intended, whilst Jamie discussed endlessly with the Earl methods by which Albany might be made to pay for his crimes. It was decided that, in the first instance, Crawford should combine with the Lord of Dalkeith in demanding either a parliamentary or Privy Council investigation of the prince's death, with a view to arraigning Albany and his henchmen on a trial for murder and high treason, this to be set in motion forthwith. If that failed to produce adequate results, a meeting of the Estates of Parliament should be called for — which would be necessary anyway for the appointment of a new Lieutenant or Governor. Moreover, the King should be urged vigorously to place the young James, now heir to the throne and Prince of Scotland, in some sure place of safety, if necessary overseas, perhaps even in France.

It was on the fifth day of their stay at Edzell, with an escort assembled and plans made to start off the following morning, that the Earl's messengers returned from the North — and Alex Stewart himself with them. He greeted the travellers with warm sympathy and affection. When he had heard of their present predicament, he had dropped all and come hot-foot. He mourned his Cousin David, damned his Uncle Albany, feared for Scotland, and welcomed his friends to the Highlands. They might be driven from their own home, but they would find another meantime at Lochindorb, where they should stay for as long as they cared — the longer the better. His mother sent warmest greetings, and was preparing the North-West Tower for them. Badenoch was theirs, and nothing that anyone south of the Highland Line could do or say need concern them. There *he* ruled, and no writ ran contrary to his own.

With that welcome and assurance next morning they made their farewells at Edzell, and turned their backs on even the sight of Lowland Scotland — for how long they could not tell.

XVII

JAMIE DOUGLAS COULD scarcely credit it, but the next few
months of 1402 were amongst the happiest of all his life.
He felt somehow that it should not be so, exiled from his
home, his prince and friend unavenged, all he had worked for
in the melting-pot and the realm abused, under threat of
invasion and in a state of chaos. Moreover, it seemed the more
improbable circumstance that he should feel so well content,
so much one of the family almost, in this castle of Lochindorb
amongst the heather moors of Braemoray, where once he had
been a prisoner and indeed feared for his very life. But this was
the situation, with not only himself thoroughly and comfortably
settled, but his wife and children also, all enjoying a Highland
summer on the roof of Scotland in excellent and friendly
company — and seeing a deal more of their husband and
father than was their wont at Aberdour. Mariota de Athyn,
Alex's mother, was kindness itself, a magnificent woman still,
only in her early fifties, who frankly informed Mary that it was
as well that she was there, or she herself might be inclined to
lose her silly old head over dark Jamie Douglas — but who
nevertheless quickly became Mary's bosom companion. Alex
was his unfailing, friendly, courteous self. And Sir James, his
youngest brother, had developed into quite a personable young
man — whilst the other three tough and somewhat oafish sons
of the Wolf were little in evidence at Lochindorb, all having
fled the osprey's nest and now roosting in other Badenoch
castles. The only daughter of the unofficial union had now also
gone, married to the youthful Earl of Sutherland. Mariota, like
her eldest son, was clearly delighted at the influx of young folk
into the loch-girt stronghold.

With hunting, hawking, fishing, visiting clan chiefs and accompanying Alex on his judicial duties — for he was still acting Deputy Justiciar of the North, none other having come north to supersede him — the time went in pleasantly. Alex was clearly both respected and popular — as indeed had been his father, the Wolf, up here, despite their astonishingly differing characters. In the South he might be only the bastard son of the late and unlamented Earl of Buchan, not even lawful Lord of Badenoch and Lochaber; but in the North he was accepted as a power in the land, the figure around which the otherwise feuding clans would rally, with his own proud patronymic of *Mac Alastair Mhic an Righ*, Son of Alexander, son of the King. He spoke Gaelic like a native — as indeed he was — and dressed normally in tartans. But he could play the King's grandson when so he wished, with marvellous authority and dignity, much more so than any of his innumerable cousins, save for the late David himself. Somewhere there was a hint of steel behind the gently assured and thoughtful manner. Jamie rejoiced to have him as friend — but would not have liked to have him as enemy.

Despite their distance and comparative detachment from southern affairs, the visitors were surprised to find how well-informed they were at Lochindorb. Holy Church was largely responsible for this, for, unlike his father, Alex made a point of keeping on good terms with the churchmen, and there was a constant coming and going between North and South of monkish couriers, wandering friars and diocesan officials, the clerics recognising no division in the realm as did secular folk. Alex had an understanding that, in return for his concern and protection as Justiciar, the Church kept him up-to-date with news. He also had his own sources of information in the Moray sea ports, where news from Aberdeen was quickly relayed.

By these means they learned that the death of his son, although it had undoubtedly further shattered the composure of the unhappy monarch, at least seemed to have aroused in him a spark of spirit. He was said to be refusing Albany audience, and had put Turnberry Castle almost into a state of siege. He had given authority for the Privy Council to command a judicial enquiry into David's fate, and this was to be held at Holy Rood Abbey on the 16th of May, Albany, Douglas, Ramorgnie and Lindsay all cited to compear. He had, totally unexpectedly, taken the matter of the bishopric of St. Andrews into his own hands, had turned down Albany's candidate, Bishop Greenlaw of Aberdeen, the Chancellor, and appointed Henry Wardlaw, his former chaplain, Precentor of Glasgow and nephew of the late Cardinal-Bishop of Glasgow, to the see — to the delight of most churchmen, who did not want Greenlaw, already powerful enough, to have authority over them as Primate. Wardlaw was a quiet studious man, no ambitious cleric, and undoubtedly the College of Bishops would happily appoint him Primate in due course. A further item of interest was that Douglas seemed to have taken over the matter of the defence of the realm, Albany being no soldier. He was instigating a series of raids over the Border, with the object of keeping the Northern English ill-at-ease and unprepared to leave their home areas to join King Henry's muster, in case of attack. The first of these raids had already taken place, under Sir John Haliburton of Dirleton, penetration having been made as far south as Bamburgh, much devastation done and considerable booty taken, with some prisoners captured for ransom. There was no lack of volunteers for further such adventures.

"You wish that you were there, Jamie?" Alex asked. "You are good at that, are you not?"

He shook his head. "Raiding, reiving, I have never loved. To sally against an armed enemy, yes, pitting wits against his, defeating him if may be. But descending upon an undefended countryside and laying all waste, burning and harrying — that is not to my taste."

"Yet it is an established Border custom, is it not? At which the Douglases have ever been foremost?"

"Perhaps. But that commends it nothing to me. Any more than your Highland clan feuding appeals to you."

"If the clans did not feud, I fear that they might turn their steel on other targets less able to defend themselves! This is something I aimed to speak to you about, Jamie. For most of the year the Highlander has insufficient to do. The pastoral life scarcely demands enough of a man. Tending flocks and herds on the high pastures is boys' work, not men's. There is little tilling of the soil, as in the Lowlands. Most work is done by the women. Men cannot be hunting and fishing all the time. Once the peats are dug, the wood cut, the sheep clipped and the hides tanned, the women can do the rest. Save perhaps distil the spirits! Which leaves much time for other activities!"

311

Alex shook his head. "It is my fear that some day someone will learn how to unite the clans, halt the feuding, and turn them against the South. That would be an ill day for Scotland."

"You surprise me," Jamie said. "I believed that you misliked the South and loved your Highlandmen?"

"To some extent that is true. I mislike the arrogant Southron belief that all north of the Highland Line are barbarians, savages. There is a deal that we could teach the South, yes. I resent the notion that we are scarcely part of the realm of Scotland because we speak a different language. It is the *ancient* language of Scotland. We are the true Scots, having the pure blood, not mixed with Saxon or Norman. I mean, my mother's people. She was a Mackay. My father, being a Stewart, was as Norman as the rest!"

"The Douglases are a true Celtic race," Jamie asserted. "Lords of Douglasdale when the Stewarts were still French land-stewards."

"Yes. But do most Douglases love their Highland cousins? Or despise them? That is the test."

The other was silent.

"I say that there is but one realm of Scotland, Highland and Lowland, under the one High King of Scots — who draws his title and line from the Highlands, mark you. *Ard Righ*. The division, the gulf between us, is bad. And dangerous. If the Highlanders, aroused by resentment, united to attack the South, it could be a disaster. For the Highlanders would win, in the first instance. They are the fiercest fighters, by far."

"And you fear this, Alex?"

"I do. Have done, ever since my brothers made their great raid on the South after the burning of Elgin. Partly to gain *my* release from my Uncle Robert's castle, the same in which David died. That showed me what might be, Jamie. They carried all before them, defeated the best the South could throw against them. You know that."

"But is there the least fear of it, today?"

"There could be. Donald. Donald of the Isles could do it — and might. He is no fool. He can see the possibilities, the threat. He is the descendant and representative of the ancient Celtic and Norse Kings of the Isles, who once governed much of the Highlands. He is also lawful grandson of Robert the Second, great-great-grandson of the Bruce. As indeed am I — but he is legitimate. He greatly resents Robert Stewart, who has stolen

312

his Ross earldom from him. He *could* send out the fiery cross, to unite the clans and march against the South."

The other stared. "But . . . *would* he? Might he?"

"There are rumours that he considers the matter. With David dead, he sees Albany as undisputed master of Scotland — and does not like the sight!"

"Nor do others. I had no notion that you feared this, Alex."

"I have done, for long. I spoke of it to David. But David's death makes it all a deal more urgent. More likely."

"A stroke against Albany I would not greatly grieve over. But a Highland attack on the South, civil war — that is different."

"Yes. Robert would be the last one to suffer, if I know my uncle! The clans could never be controlled, once they were victorious, south of the Line. It would be massacre. Your Border raiding would pale before it. Centuries of debts to pay off. The land would be submerged in blood. I know my people. And whatever the final result, the cause of the unity of the realm would be set back for generations."

"This, this is something quite new to me. I swear none in the South think aught of it, perceive any threat. Is there anything that can be done?"

"I do not know. It is one reason why I welcomed you the more, Jamie — I admit it. You are a fighter, and with sound wits. I value your advice and aid, as well as your company!"

"Then you think this is urgent? For now, not for some future time?"

"It could be any time. Donald keeps calling councils of his Islesmen, at Islay. And consulting the mainland chiefs — especially those in what he still considers to be his earldom of Ross. Albany's goodson, the so-called Earl of Ross, is never there to check them, a Lowlander and a weakling. And Donald keeps sending messengers to Drummond, at Kildrummy. What for, I do not know. But . . ."

"Drummond? Sir Malcolm, of Cargil and Stobhall? The late Queen's brother? The Countess of Mar's husband?"

"The same. She is my friend. That is how I know of this. It troubles me, as it does her. If Drummond was to unite with Donald in this matter, it could be direly dangerous. Drummond has great power in the South-East Highlands — his own large clan of Drummond, and some sway over the great Mar earldom

He is linked in kinship to half of Atholl and Breadalbane. With Donald in the west and Drummond in the east, all the Highlands could be taken in . . ."

"But why, Alex? Why should Drummond make common cause with the Islesman?"

"For the same reason as might you! Fear, and hatred, of Albany. You are not the only one to be concerned over David's death, Jamie, to see the writing on the wall. Albany will have this kingdom, if he can; has gone a far way to getting it. He must be stopped, if possible. Many will see that. But — it must not be at the cost of savage war between Highlands and Lowlands, I say. Not delivery at Donald's hands."

"I see that, yes. But this of Drummond. I cannot see him in Donald's camp. He is no longer young, a man who takes little part in affairs of the realm now, however powerful. A strange man, yes — but scarcely one to resort to arms. What has he in common with the Lord of the Isles — save this hatred of Albany?"

"They are kin. Drummond's aunt was Queen to David the Second, his sister Queen to King Robert. Donald is linked to both. And each man has a grudge, through their wives. Donald's wife is daughter of the last Earl of Ross, and is deprived of her inheritance by Albany's machinations. Drummond is deprived of the unentailed lands of Douglas, which *his* wife, your Earl James's sister, should have heired. They *may* not be in alliance — but it is very possible. If I knew what these messengers were about. Donald's messengers are apt to mean trouble. He is certainly planning some adventure in force — all reports say that. I believe he may strike when the South is engaged with the English. That has always been the Islesmen's strategy. That is why I do not like these sallies of Douglas over the Border. They are bound to provoke retaliation from Henry. If we have full war with England — then, I say, look out for Donald! And possibly Drummond. And who knows what others . . ."

Uneasily they left it at that.

*   *   *

It was three weeks later, and well into the second half of May, with no significant news reaching them meantime, that another visitor arrived at Lochindorb — Thomas Stewart. He came, not as any sort of fugitive or refugee, but to see how his sister fared, breaking his journey to the Chanonry of Ross in the Black Isle, on an errand for the new Primate-elect to the Bishop of Ross. He had come by sea to the port of Findhorn on the Moray coast, and from there had found his way up the river of that name, and the Dorback Burn, with a friar as guide provided by the Abbot of Kinloss.

The Douglases rejoiced to see him, the Lady Mariota to welcome what she might almost look upon as a hitherto unknown brother-in-law, and Alex as an uncle.

At the dais-table in the hall that night, after the meal and with the lesser folk withdrawn, all sought the Archdeacon's news, which so far he had only hinted at. Although the visitors were happy enough with their present life in the North, their desire and need for news of the South was not to be denied.

"What of the trial, Thomas?" Jamie demanded. "The judicial enquiry of the Privy Council, or whatever it was to be called? Was it over when you left?"

"It was over before it started!" his brother-in-law declared. "What else did you expect? It was never other than a mummery — Robert saw to that."

"But . . . were they not questioned? Something of the truth brought out?"

"The truth? What is the truth, Jamie? The truth, the realm is assured, is now ascertained, made clear to all and for all time. David, Prince of Scotland, by God's will, died of a sickness, a flux of the bowels, no doubt due to his wayward living. Although well looked after at his uncle's castle of Falkland by kindly servitors, he sickened, waned and died — an act of God, for which none were to be blamed. The Duke of Rothesay departed this life by Divine Providence, and nothing else. All witnesses called testified to it."

"But . . . but . . . this is crazy-mad! Of course Albany and Ramorgnie would so claim. But what of the rest of the Privy Council? What of Crawford? My father? They would not accept such shameful travesty?"

"They had little choice. The Council could not all sit in judgement. So they appointed a panel. And no doubt Robert knew how to get at the panel. The witnesses were carefully chosen . . ."

"What of David's fingers? Gnawed at. How did they explain that?"

"They did not require to. It was not mentioned."

"Witnesses at Lindores Abbey could have testified to it."

315

"No witnesses from Lindores were called, David being dead two days before his body was brought there."

"Dear God — I should have stayed. *I* would have testified to another tune. I should never have fled here . . ."

"Your testimony would have been only hearsay, inadmissible. But think you that you would have been ever have been allowed to testify, man? You would have been disposed of, long before that. Robert, whatever else, knows what he is at."

"I thank God that we did flee," Mary said. "Otherwise I would have been a widow by now, I swear!"

"And the rest of the Council did nothing?"

"What could they do? They had appointed a panel, and the panel found thus. They could disagree, privily, at the next Council-meeting. But one or two individuals could not disown the lawfully appointed panel and its findings, however much they might dissent."

"I never expected otherwise," Mary said. "It is not by such methods that Robert will be brought to book — if ever he is."

Her brother nodded. "It was a shrewd move to have the Earl of Douglas arraigned with Robert and the others — shrewd on Robert's part. Few would wish to challenge both Stewart *and* Douglas power. Your chief, I have no doubt, had nothing to do with David being starved to death — and so he helped to exonerate the others."

"So nothing is to be done? David's murder goes unpunished? The King and the realm accept this play-acting as truth, and none suffer for vilely slaying the heir to the throne?"

None answered those rhetorical questions. But Thomas Stewart dryly made the position crystal-clear. "The Council finished not only by declaring all innocent, but by announcing that all subjects of the King without exception were forbidden to detract, by word or deed, from the fair fame of the Duke of Albany and the Earl of Douglas. God Save the King!"

Out of the grim silence that greeted that, the Archdeacon went on. "But at least the King is warned. I have word from the new Bishop Wardlaw that John intends to place his new heir, James, in *his* care and keeping, at St. Andrews Castle, where I also can help keep watch over him. That far he has seen the light."

"And will young James be safe at St. Andrews?" Mary asked.

"Safer than anywhere else, I would think. Robert will not

wish too greatly to antagonise Holy Church, at this stage. Particularly while this trouble with England simmers."

"Yes," Alex put in. "This of England? What is the latest, there? We heard of Haliburton's raid — naught since."

"It is a great folly. Douglas is determined to keep on with these raids, possibly lead one himself. He says, to prevent Henry from invading Scotland. But it seems to me more like to *provoke* the Plantagenet into so doing. They say that Robert himself is in doubt about it. But he needs Douglas and so will not restrain him, even if he could, for Douglas is Chief Warden of the Marches."

"It is folly, yes," Alex agreed. "Is this Douglas a fool?"

"I think he feels that it is expected of him — as Douglas. A reputation to keep up. Always they have been great warriors. The first Earl led many raids. Earl James won Otterburn. Archie the Grim likewise. The present Earl's illegitimate brother, Will of Nithsdale, a notable hero. Even Jamie here, something of another. This Earl is not of the same quality, but would have men believe that he is. And he has his family feud with the Percy. And now also with Dunbar, who is aiding Hotspur."

"His feuds could cost Scotland dear! Dearer than he knows."

"There is word that Henry has sent instructions to his March Wardens and sheriffs, and all Border lords, to muster their fullest strength. And keep their men in armed readiness. He is dealing with Owen Glendower again, meantime. But after that . . ."

"Glendower?" Jamie asked. "Have the Welsh risen again?"

"Yes. Had you not heard? All the Welsh Marches are aflame once more, seeking to throw off the English yoke. Owen claims that he alone is Prince of Wales."

"Thank God for Owen Glendower!" Alex said. "If Donald knows of this — and I shall make sure that he does — then it may delay him. He will wish to move south at the same time as Henry moves north, for greatest effect. This may give us time . . ."

"Donald? You mean the Islesman?" Thomas asked. "What is this . . .?"

His nephew explained his fears.

Thomas stayed a few days with them at Lochindorb, apparently in little hurry to move on to the Black Isle. When he did decide to go, Alex said that he would escort him down into the Laigh of Moray, and then turn south and visit Kildrummy

Castle in Mar. He wished to discover, if he could, just what Sir Malcolm Drummond was up to. He suggested that Jamie should accompany them.

The night before they left, Mariota de Athyn came to the North Tower, where the Douglases were ensconced, to speak with Jamie. Recognising that privacy was desired, Mary excused herself and went to the children.

The woman who had been the Wolf of Badenoch's mistress and best influence, came straight to the point, being of a direct nature.

"I am concerned about Alex and the Countess of Mar," she said. "You know of the association, Jamie?"

"Yes," he said, warily.

"I am in no state of grace to offer blame," she sighed. "But Alex is the best of my clutch, a son to be proud of — and with large responsibilities. I can see this entanglement harming him. Isobel Douglas is much older than is he, and married to a powerful man. She is a lusty and indiscreet woman. So am I, no doubt! But I do not control a great earldom, and am not wed to the King's good-brother."

"No."

"I have reason to be anxious, Jamie. This woman has her claws in Alex. It is not some passing fancy — it has been going on now for three years."

"You are sure that the claws are not Alex's? He is no child, no youngling, to lead by the nose. A man of much strength . . ."

"All that, yes. But still, in some ways, innocent. Unversed in the ways of the world, and of women. Reared here amongst the mountains. No courtier. Perhaps I am in some measure to blame. But he is no match for Isobel of Mar."

"You may be right. But . . . he will do what he wants to do."

"You have much influence with him, Jamie. He admires you greatly. If you would watch him, seek to guide him . . . ?"

"In such matters one man cannot guide another. You should know that. I would, belike, do more harm than good were I to interfere."

"Not interfere, Jamie, just watch. A word here and there, discreetly. That is all I am asking, as a friend."

"If I see opportunity," he said, doubtfully. "I do not like this of the Countess, myself. I have naught against her, my former master's sister. But she is scarcely right for Alex."

"No. And the business with Malcolm Drummond is dangerous. He is a strange man. Alex conceives him to be a poor husband to Isobel Douglas, declares her a deprived and wronged woman. I say that one can look after herself! But I think that she uses that to hold Alex."

"Drummond could be all that . . ."

"Yes. But they have been married for long, twenty years. Late to be rescuing her! And this of Donald of the Isles. She uses that also, if you ask me. An excuse for messages, letters. He too, perhaps . . ."

"I'd swear that Alex is honestly concerned. Over the possibility of the Drummond and Donald planning an uprising."

"Yes. But he is well aware that it offers him opportunity also. As now. It troubles me. Alex may run into serious danger, interfering with Drummond. He is too powerful to antagonise so."

"But if the realm is endangered?"

"The realm has managed well enough without Alex Stewart hitherto!"

"A Highland invasion of the South would have to be stopped, if possible."

"No doubt. But not necessarily by Alex. Nor by Jamie Douglas, for that matter! Let Robert of Albany see to his own defences."

"Neither of us would lift a hand to save Albany. It is the bloodshed, rapine and pains of civil war which we would wish to save, the clans unleashed on an undefended land."

"A land that never fails to slight us. Despises the clans and calls us savages?"

"Even so . . ."

"I know. Forgive me, Jamie. But you will try to guide Alex? In the matter of this woman? Do what you can?"

"I will try, yes . . ."

*　　　*　　　*

They came to Kildrummy in the Garioch of Mar four evenings later, to a casually warm welcome from the Countess Isobel, her husband again not at home — and Jamie with a shrewd notion that his friend knew that he would not be. *An Drumanach Mor* had his great estates in Perthshire to manage, of course, not to mention the Countess's southern lands. Jamie also had the impression, perhaps inevitably, that though Isobel Douglas greeted himself civilly enough, she would have preferred his absence. That Alex had asked him to come, in the circumstances, might have held some significance.

Kildrummy was a large fortress of a place on the Upper Don, and Jamie had long thought it strange that so lively and strong-minded a woman as the Countess should coop herself up in this remote upland valley when she, as well as her husband, had so many south-country properties. But here, of course, she was undisputed queen, and over a vast territory.

In the silver-gilt evening of early June, they sat on the parapet-walk of the castle's Snow Tower, and gazed out over the fair and farflung countryside, so green, so different from the true Highlands to north and west, despite the range upon range of blue Aberdeenshire hills which rimmed the horizon, it seemed, to infinity. As far as they could see, it was all Mar — and a deal further still.

"A noble heritage," Alex said. "The realm's most ancient earldom, a lordship lost in time, before even earls and mormaors were."

"To be sure. But a *lordship*, not a ladyship!" the Countess answered. "It requires a man's hand, a man's strong hand."

Surprised, they looked at her.

"You have a husband," Alex said, almost roughly for him.

"Malcolm Drummond and I were wed almost as children," she replied. "He is not the man I would have chosen for husband. Nor the man to manage my earldom. I have never made him Earl of Mar, in my right, as I could have done. Some say should. He is not of the quality for that."

Jamie coughed, embarrassed. "Sir Malcolm is namely as a proud lord. Has fought boldly. I have never heard his qualities questioned."

"Ah, but then you are not a woman, Sir James!" That was tart.

"But he has *some* say in the earldom, has he not, Isobel?" Alex demanded. "He has raised men from it, ere this?"

"To be sure. He looks after my rents. He is good at that! Some of my vassals look to him, rather than to me."

"If he sought to raise men from the earldom, today — how many would follow him?"

"If I said yes, four thousand."

"And if *not*?"

"One thousand, perhaps, Or less."

"M'mmm. Even a thousand, horsed men of Mar, could

greatly aid a Highland invasion of the South. In especial, with another thousand *Drummond* horsed men-at-arms. Cavalry Donald lacks."

"But . . . have you reason to believe that Sir Malcolm will join the Lord of the Isles?" Jamie looked at the Countess rather than at his friend. "Has this fear aught to support it? Other than, than . . ."

"Other than a woman's malice towards a failed husband?" she finished for him. "I believe so, Sir James. Constant messengers arrive from the Isles. He has never had such exchange before, with Donald. And he is concerned with matters of arms and men, as I have not known him before. He does not confide in me, in this. He is unusually secretive."

"It could mean much, or little," Jamie insisted. "He does not love the Duke of Albany. He may therefore be looking but to his own defences — as many another must be doing in Scotland today."

"And this of Donald? What of the Islesman?"

"They are kin, after a fashion."

"Have been all these years. And never required such coming and going. And this secrecy. We have gone our own ways, for long. But do not seek to hide too much from each other." There was a certain significance in the look she gave Alex as she said that.

He coughed, "If we could lay hands on one of these messengers," he said, "or get one of your vassals whom Sir Malcolm is close to. Get them to talk . . ."

"Less than easy, I should think. But try, by all means. You act Lieutenant and Justiciar of the North — perhaps you have methods to make folk speak?" She paused. "How long will Robert Stewart leave you in that position, Alex?"

He shrugged. "He tried to unseat my father in that, and could not. I think he will be no more successful with me. No doubt he has already appointed some other. His son Murdoch again, perhaps? But that is little to the point, north of the Highland Line. The danger to my position, I'd say, does not come from Albany but from Donald of the Isles. He could overturn all."

They sat until the last light faded from the sky to the northwest, and a coolness stirred them. Isobel Douglas rose.

"I shall retire to my virtuous couch, my friends," she said. "I may even sleep — who knows? Your chambers await you.

Inform me if I may do aught further for your comfort. My room is in this tower."

They bowed, wordless.

There was a long silence after she left them.

"You are very quiet, Jamie," Alex said, at length. "You do not greatly approve of our hostess, I think?"

"Not so. I find her a fine woman — fair, strong, able. Aye, that and more."

"But . . . ?"

"It is you that I am concerned for, Alex — not her. You are . . . fond of her?"

"Yes."

"You know best. But . . . is it wise?"

"Wise? Is it wisdom you seek, in a woman?"

"No. But unwisdom can always be dangerous. The price to pay for it."

"You mean that she is forty-two years old — fifteen more than am I? And wed to *An Drumanach Mor*, chief of his name and a powerful lord. A countess in her own right — too high for the Wolf of Badenoch's bastard? All this I know, Jamie. But I am fond of her, nevertheless."

"Aye, no doubt. But where will that bring you? Save into disrepute and possible danger. If you tamper with his wife, Drummond is not going to like it — even though he does neglect her. And if you further interfere with his plans, it could cost you dear. The dearer."

"Are you concerned for my soul? Or my safety? Or this realm of ours?"

The other was silent.

"I am sorry, Jamie. We will not come to blows over this. Your concern for me I cherish. But in this matter I must follow my own path."

"Yes. As you will." He touched the other's shoulder. "I am for my bed."

"Good night, then, Jamie. Tomorrow we shall go see some of the Drummond's friends. Discover what we may."

Although Jamie lay awake in his room for long that night, he did not hear Alex Stewart come into the next chamber.

*   *   *

In the next few days they called upon three or four fairly prominent vassals of Mar, indicated to them by the Countess as being supporters of her husband, beginning with Forbes of Glencuie, known as Chamberlain of Mar, who acted steward to the earldom. They did not visit only these, of course, which might have been too obvious; so they had to make many calls, combining it all with hawking and hunting and the like. They learned comparatively little, save that something was definitely afoot, concerned with the mustering, arming and training of men, the reasons therefor always given as merely the uncertainties and dangers of the times consequent upon the death of the Duke of Rothesay, anarchy in the realm and the English threat. Few of those interviewed were actually subtle or devious characters, and the enquirers came to the conclusion that, in the main, they were not being deliberately misled. The Chamberlain was rather different, admittedly, a wary man, obsequious as far as his mistress was concerned, but less than open towards her guests, and clearly knowing more than he admitted. But at no time did they get the least hint of a link with Donald of the Isles; and without making their suspicions altogether too plain, they dared not themselves introduce the name of that faraway western potentate.

On the sixth day of their stay, they returned from a boar-hunt in the Ladder Hills to discover Sir Malcolm himself back at Kildrummy. He was a rather fine-looking man, now in his middle sixties, stockily built, with a leonine head of greying hair and the curious habit of looking slightly over the heads of those he spoke to. He greeted Alex Stewart only coolly civil, but was quite affable towards Jamie, whom he had known slightly since the latter's boyhood when he was the Earl of Douglas's page and esquire, and of whose activities he seemed generally to approve. But the arrival of *An Drumanach Mor* nevertheless put something of a damper on the visit.

They saw little of him that first evening, for after the meal he disappeared. That night was the first in which, so far as he could judge, Jamie's companion spent all the time in his own bed-chamber.

Next morning, Sir Malcolm appeared to be in good fettle and declared that he was going to visit his new castle of Kindrochit, in Brae Mar, some twenty-three miles to the south, and suggested that the visitors might like to accompany him. They could scarcely refuse, even had they wished to — although the Countess Isobel rather pointedly announced that she would stay at home.

As they rode into the forenoon sun, through the green rolling hills of Cromar, it was noticeable that it was Drummond who was now the questioner. In a conversational but quietly persistent way, he wanted to know what they were seeking in Mar; how they saw the situation consequent upon David Stewart's death; what they thought of the Duke of Albany; whether the realm would accept the verdict of the parliamentary enquiry; whether they believed English invasion to be imminent or merely a useful threat; whether Alex was likely to remain Justiciar. And so on.

They answered him with some degree of caution — although he asked nothing which was an actual embarrassment. Until he said,

"And what part do you see our Highlands as playing on this changing scene, Stewart? Great or small? None of our concern? Or much our concern?"

"Much," Alex answered, after a moment, briefly.

"So say I," the other nodded. "For too long the North has turned its back on the South, and the South scorned the North. We can do better than that."

"To be sure. But . . . it depends what you mean by betterment? Better for whom?"

"Better for the Highlands. Better for our people. It is time."

"Perhaps. But not at the rest of the realm's cost."

"That need not be."

"My lord, you have had long experience of fighting and war, I know. But it has not been Highland war, I think? You have fought in England and on the Border. Have you ever seen how the clans fight? Not just feud, but war. In a defenceless land. I have. The Islesmen, now? Have you seen what they can do to a country? My Lochaber, see you. Slaughter of women and children, fire, rapine, destruction, death to everything that lives, man and beast. I have seen this time and again. Would you see it unleashed upon the South, where there are the many more people?"

Drummond frowned. "No. But that could not happen. Under good and sufficient leadership."

"What would you name good and sufficient leadership? The Lord of the Isles himself? Clanranald? Maclean of Duart? I have seen Alastair Carrach, Donald's own brother, leading just such warfare. Maclean likewise."

324

The other snorted. "Your father, Sir Alexander, would have seen little so wrong with that, I warrant!"

Alex drew himself up in his saddle. "I am not my father, sir," he said stiffly. "Nor was he so ill a man as some would make out." And he reined back a little from Drummond's side — Jamie of course doing the same.

They rode on, after that, for some considerable distance, unspeaking.

They came to Kindrochit, in the upper valley of the great Dee, where the Clunie Water dropped to the river, where there was a ferry. Here a fine new castle was arising on the massive foundations of an earlier stronghold of Malcolm Canmore's, the tall outer curtain-walls already completed. Drummond explained that it was necessary to control the caterans who were forever raiding down from the mountains, here where two great droving routes across the Mounth met, down Glen Clunie and Glen Shee to Atholl and over the Fir Mounth to the Cairn o' Mount passes to Angus. He did not actually state that the caterans involved were apt to be those of Badenoch, and quite frequently led by one or other of Alex's deplorable brothers, but that was clearly implied, and no doubt the reason for this excursion. That the Justiciar should keep his own kin in order, as well as others, was the lesson to be inferred — and then law-abiding men would not have to build expensive castles in out-of-the-way places to maintain the King's peace.

Alex swallowed all this with admirable self-control and seeming imperturbability — although Jamie knew that he seethed beneath the calm surface.

An Drumanach Mor was clearly no turner of the other cheek.

The long ride back to Kildrummy was more notable for its silences than for pleasant converse.

That night, Alex Stewart announced to his hostess that they would have to be on their way back to Braemoray next morning. Being a realist, the Countess did not urge them to stay. Jamie at least was well content.

They arrived back at Lochindorb to find two items of news awaiting them. One was from one of Alex's regular sources of information in the South, to say that there had been a disastrous Scots raid over the Border, led by young Sir Patrick Hepburn of Hailes, which had not only been driven back with heavy casualties from Northumberland but had been followed up by a large English force under Hotspur Percy and Dunbar and utterly decimated at Nisbet Moor in the West Merse. Many prominent Scots knights had been slain and many more captured.

The second item was a letter for Jamie from the Earl of Douglas no less, sent by a special messenger who was waiting to take back an answer. In it, after the usual honorifics and preamble, he wrote, in the same stilted and awkward manner in which he spoke:

> . . . They tell me that you blame me in some measure for David Stewart's death. I had no hand in that, I promise you. I but believed him to be held at Falkland for a time. If there was ill done, it was not with my knowledge. I do not deceive you. They say also that you have gone to Badenoch in fear for your life. You need have no fear. You are ever my good friend. The Douglas power will protect you against any soever. This on my honour. I wish that you come back. I need you. As does the realm. It is to be war with England. Not raiding but full war. We have suffered a grievous defeat under Hepburn. Now George Dunbar and the Percy lay waste the East and Middle Marches. Henry Paget musters his fullest forces at York, to invade our land. It is necessary to strike first. Before he returns from the Welsh Marches to lead it. I am assembling a great host. We muster at Dunbar. All Douglas to be there. Moray, Graham, Haliburton, Maxwell, Gordon, Montgomerie, Swinton. Even Murdoch Stewart of Fife. But I lack experienced leaders in war. Few have fought in true warfare as have you. I need your present aid. Your brothers come. Come you, Jamie.
>
> I remain your friend,
>
> DOUGLAS
>
> Signed and sealed at Dunbar on Saint Swithin's Eve.

Long Jamie considered that letter and its implications before he showed it to Mary and then to Alex.

"I must go," he told them. "I cannot hold back. It may be foolish, but I am a Douglas, and this is my duty."

"This Earl may be your chief, and declares himself your friend," Mary said. "But what has he ever done for you? Would he have saved you from Robert?"

"He might. I did not give him opportunity. We do not know . . ."

326

"*Could* he save you from Robert, even now? How do you know that this is not a trap?"

"I think not. He stakes his honour on my protection. In writing. And it is not only Douglas. The realm needs me. We invade England in force. My brothers to be there. Would you have me to hold back when all others go?"

She shook her head at that, helplessly.

"My friend," Alex intervened. "It may be that you could serve the realm better here. In the North. This venture may well be what Donald has waited for. All the main forces of the South engaged over the Border. If he was to strike then, he would be all but unopposed. Save by me!"

Jamie frowned. "I see that, yes. But . . . it may not be. *You* fear it, but there is no certainty that the Islesmen will come. Or Drummond aid them. I cannot wait here, kicking my heels, when naught may happen. Besides, yours is a Highland matter. *I* am no leader of Highlanders. The clans have their own leaders."

"As you will," Alex said. "But I would have been glad of your support. When will you go?"

"So soon as I may. It is a long journey."

"We shall surely find a ship for you. From one of the Moray ports. That will land you in Lothian. Leith or even Dunbar itself. Save you much trouble and the dangers of crossing Uncle Robert's territories. Even with your Earl's messenger as escort!"

"Yes. I am sorry, Alex. It is something that I must do. You understand?"

XVIII

JAMIE LANDED AT Leith, not Dunbar, some ten days later, and hired a horse to take him the nine miles to Dalkeith. There his father rejoiced to see him, claiming that he had missed him sorely, and was glad to equip him with the armour, horses, body-servants and all that he required for a campaign. His two legitimate half-brothers, Sir James and Sir William, and his younger full brother Johnnie, had already gone to Dunbar, leading the Dalkeith contingent of some four hundred horsed men-at-arms for the national army.

The old lord was, however, considerably depressed about the state of Scotland, talking gloomily about wishing that he was well away and in his grave, with no desire to see what he feared was coming upon the kingdom. Jamie, who was fairly full of foreboding himself, found himself reassuring his sire that things were not so bad, that they would warstle through, that Albany would over-reach himself and meet his due deserts one day — and so on.

Old Sir James was much concerned about the safety of young James Stewart. He was now, at last, in the care of the new Primate, at St. Andrews Castle, ostensibly being tutored, the King having been sorely loth to be parted from the boy. But, though Bishop Wardlaw was a good man and reliable, if Albany was determined to take the child, the episcopal castle was insufficiently strong to withstand him, any more than the anathemas of Holy Church. Robert Stewart would pay as much attention to these as his brother Alec the Wolf had done. The child should be got out of the country, to safety — to France possibly, with the Pope, or the Low Countries. Otherwise, sooner or later, Albany was going to be king. And when that happened, all honest men beware! He, Dalkeith, had written to King Robert, but had received no reply.

Jamie admitted that, in this, his father's fears were no doubt justified — but did not see what was to be done about it.

Next day he rode the score of miles to Dunbar.

Despite himself and his forebodings, he could not quell a lift of the heart when he trotted down on to the coastal plain from the Lammermuir foothills. He had not seen such a colourful and spirited martial assembly in the fourteen years since 1388 and the great adventure which had ended in Otterburn, the murder of the Earl James Douglas and his own knighting. The entire plain around the little red town and its harbour and castle, outlined against the blue sea, was alive with men. In great ranks and squares and formations the tents and pavilions were pitched, each of the last in the colours of its lord, baron or knight, with his banner fluttering above. The horse-lines appeared to stretch for miles, the stands of arms were like a forest, the smoke of cooking-fires rose blue over all, and everywhere steel glinted in the sun. Men by their thousands were marshalled there, the might of a realm in arms. Whatever the cause, it was a stirring sight.

Picking out the various blazons as he approached, Jamie distinguished Seton, Haliburton, Sinclair, Montgomerie, Swinton, Scott, Leslie, Erskine, Graham and others that he did not recognise — as well as Stewart and Douglas, Moray and Lindsay. The Earl of Douglas had managed to assemble a notable and representative host, then — an excellent augury. Scotland was not done yet.

The Douglas banners were the most easily discerned, for there were many more of them than any others. They seemed to have almost a tented city to themselves, and Jamie made therefor.

Almost the first persons he saw, to recognise, were his two friends Will of Drumlanrig and Archibald of Cavers, who had been knighted with him after Otterburn. They were as joyous to see him as they were surprised, and soon had the entire Douglas camp in an uproar of welcome. Jamie was astonished to discover that, instead of being all but forgotten and possibly criticised for bolting off to the Highlands, his good name and fame were enhanced. He was the man who had given up all for the dead prince, the man who had escaped from St. Andrews Castle, the individual who defied the Governor, the hero of

Foulhope Haugh, Arkaig and Prestonkirk. Even his brothers added to this paean of praise — which was certainly not their custom. Quite overwhelmed by it all, Jamie had to recognise that it meant something when even the Earl Archibald came hot-foot, summoned from elsewhere, and greeted him almost effusively for that moody man.

"So you came, Jamie — you came!" he cried. "Good! Good! I rejoice to see you."

"I came because you besought me, my lord. And in the realm's need. Although I cannot see my service as so important . . ."

"But yes, my friend. We need you. We are scarce rich in seasoned fighters. We have many stout lords and knights, excellent in any tulzie, notable raiders, well versed in arms; but experienced in war — that is different. You have proved yourself on many fields. We could not spare you, hiding way in those ungodly Hielands, with the kingdom in danger, Jamie."

"I hid in the Highlands for my *life*'s sake, I'd mind you! Not from choice. Your friends, the Duke of Albany, Ramorgnie and Lindsay of Rossie had me imprisoned in St. Andrews Castle, with the Duke David. Had I not won out, as *he* did not, would I have been alive to come to you today?"

"M'mm. That was an ill business. Mismanaged. Naught to do with me, man . . ."

"I saw you ride into St. Andrews with the Duke of Albany, my lord. You rode out again, with those others, taking the Duke David to Falkland. Had I not escaped during the night, would I not also have been taken captive to Falkland? And fared any better than my master?"

There was a stirring amongst the assembled Douglases.

The Earl looked, and sounded, uncomfortable. "Not so, Jamie. I would have looked to your safety. But you had gone, none knew where. I could not help you when none could tell me where you might be. David was but to be warded, for his own good. *You* were in no danger, I swear."

"David was warded to his grave! You will forgive me, my lord, if I doubt your friends' goodwill and honest purpose."

"Damnation, man — these are not my friends!" the other cried. "You will find none of them here, in my host. Ramorgnie and Lindsay are ill limmers, Fifers with naught to do with me. Albany, acting Governor, called on me to aid him carry out the King's command. What happened after was none of my doing, or with my knowledge. You have my word for that. You are secure with me, Jamie, I promise you."

"Very well, my lord — I accept that. I would not have come else." Jamie glanced round the circle of faces, however, to ensure that there were sufficient witnesses. "Enough of that. Now I am here, what would you have of me?"

"Aye. In this venture I would have you ever close — to advise me, as you have done well, ere this. I do not give you a command — there are plenty for that. What I need is your wits and counsel."

"I cannot refuse you that — such as they are. But — what is intended? This venture? Just what do you attempt?"

"We wait a few more days, for more men, for further arms and supplies, above all, for more horses. I am having great numbers to come from Galloway. Then we march."

"Aye, but march where?"

"Into England — where else? Through Northumberland, to Newcastle, perhaps to Durham. English Henry is mustering all the North to arms. At present he himself is engaged in bringing Owen Glendower and the Welsh to heel. Then he will turn on Scotland — he has promised it. We must strike first. Ensure that the Northumbrians and Percy, with the traitor George Dunbar, will be so concerned for their own lands and homes that they will not rally to Henry, forestall invasion of our realm. We have been raiding, to this end. But that was not enough. This great host will do it in proper fashion. We will make Henry think again!"

"And what says the Duke of Albany to this? He does not ride with you, I think? He, who exchanges letters with Henry Plantagenet secretly!"

"He is getting old. But he has sent his son, Murdoch of Fife. He approves never fear. But . . . why look so doubtful, man?"

"Because I fear that this could turn into but one more Border raid, larger, deeper, but otherwise the same — more cattle gathered, more villages sacked, more homes burned, more corn trampled, more women raped. Of such I have had my fill."

"Not so. That is not how it is to be. This is invasion. Our counter-invasion. Is that the word? In the name of the King of Scots. Led by four earls — Angus, Moray and Fife, as well as myself. And the lords of Maxwell, Seton, Eaglesham, Dundaff, Buccleuch, Swinton and many more. With the whole house of Douglas. Here is no raid, Jamie, but a great host on the march."

He nodded, but less than fully convinced.

"Come, then — wine, refreshment. You will eat in my own tent, tonight . . ."

*   *   *

They were five more days at Dunbar before a move was made, waiting for a large contingent of Gallovideans under Fergus MacDowell, with a huge herd of Galloway ponies, sturdy, broad-hooved garrons — the Earl Douglas being also Lord of Galloway. With this addition they made a host of just over 11,000 — and what was vitally important for this sort of campaign, all horsed.

Before they set off, news reached the camp — which not all found so significant as Jamie Douglas. Alexander Leslie, Earl of Ross had died, although still a young man, leaving only a little girl as heiress, by Albany's daughter. His father-in-law had acted promptly, declaring the child, Euphemia, Countess of Ross, and taking her into his wardship. This meant, of course, that the Governor would now personally control and administer that great northern earldom, to add to the others of Fife, Menteith and Strathearn — which could not but further infuriate Donald of the Isles, who claimed part of it in his own right, part in his wife's. Alex Stewart would be the more anxious. Uneasily, Jamie put the matter to the back of his mind. There was nothing that he could do about it.

The great array rode off next morning in fine style, under a waving forest of banners, company by company, extending mile upon mile along the road southwards, the baggage-trains and spare horses increasing the column to almost five miles. Although in theory Jamie's position was at Douglas's side, he did not in fact ride with the earls and lords up at the front, but with his brothers at the head of the Dalkeith contingent — fairly near the front of the column as that was, the Douglases of course coming first. An advance-guard scouted ahead.

They followed the coast, by Skateraw and Thornton, negotiating the deep ravines of Bilsdean and Pease Dean, scenes of many a fight and ambush, the major strategic hurdles between Berwick and Edinburgh. Thereafter, at Colbrandspath, they climbed high on to Coldingham Moor. Throughout it all, Dunbar's and his vassals' country, the folk eyed them sullenly; for *their* lord was on the other side, in England, and Douglas usurping his lands.

Evening found them a few miles north of Berwick, and they turned inland, by Mordington, on the eastern edge of the Merse, where the Lord of Dalkeith's younger brother, Sir William, was master, and there camped for the night, being made much of by that cheerful character. Berwick, although an important Scots seaport, was still in English hands — had been for many years — and, one of the most strongly-fortified towns in two kingdoms, was best left alone on this occasion, since none wished to start this gallant expedition with a prolonged siege. Hotspur Percy, as East March Warden, was also Governor of Berwick, but tended to appoint deputies, the present incumbent being none other than George, Master of Dunbar, cousin both to the Earl of Moray and the Lord Seton, here present. It was all rather embarrassing. Master George would be well aware of their approach, and had no doubt sent urgent messages south to his father and Percy. But he would not be in any position to challenge their passage. So he could be left quietly in Berwick.

They crossed Tweed next day at the fords near Fishwick, taking four hours to get all over. Now they were in England, and subtly all men's attitude and behaviour changed quite distinctly. They were in the land of the Auld Enemy. Everyone here was a potential foe. More specifically, all was fair game for the strong — and *they* were the strong today — cattle, horses, property, valuables, women. All had been warned that this was no pillaging raid; but with a column miles long, there could be little surveillance of the majority.

They went by Shoreswood and Duddo to the fertile valley of the Till; and it was the sight of tall smoke-clouds behind them in the Crookham area, in mid-afternoon, that sent Jamie spurring up to the Earl of Douglas at the head of the array.

"My lord," he exclaimed, interrupting Angus and Moray, "look yonder!" And he pointed rearward.

"Ha — smokes!" the other observed. "We have a fire or two. Our own folk no doubt. I suppose it was to be expected. A pity — but no matter. Our presence must be known to Percy, so the smoke will only warn the country-folk — no bad thing."

"I am not concerned with whom it warns — save yourself, my lord! Those fires, so soon, are a sorry augury. They mean that your command is insufficiently firm. You are being disobeyed already. Those who lit those fires, against orders, will do more than that."

The Earl frowned. "Jamie, you make too much of it, The men

333

are high-spirited. We must let them have their heads a little. The English burn, slay and harry whenever they cross the Border — always have done. This first day we must not be too strict. There are generations of debts to pay off."

Jamie could frown as blackly as his chief. "Not today!" he jerked. "We are not here for debt-paying. We are here to counter invasion. Think you those who have set those houses, farms, villages, afire will have done *only* that? They will have entered those houses first, taken all that they wanted, of goods, cattle, women. Will they leave these lying, for others to take? I say that even now many may be riding back over Tweed with their booty. And others seeing it, will do likewise."

"They would not dare . . . !"

"You think not? I have seen it time and again. You must stop this, or you will see your army melt away before your eyes."

"How can I stop it, man? We are stretched for miles . . ."

"Stop it as the Earl James did. Tell all that you will hang any guilty of looting or burning. And do so. You will not require to do it twice! That, and do not all your lords ride ever together here at the front of your host. They would be of better service spread throughout."

"Sirrah — you are insolent!" Moray barked.

"Aye, Jamie — I sought your presence with us because I valued your counsel in battle. Not to order our line of march!"

"Very well, my lord. Have I your permission to retire to the tail of your army, less illustrious than its head, and seek to ensure that it follows your noble lead?"

"Sir James — I'll thank you to watch your words! But, yes — do that. Take what men you need, and stop any looting and burning. If you can!"

So Jamie went back, gathered two of his brothers and half of the Dalkeith men-at-arms, and rode to the rear of the column.

There it was as he had feared. No sort of order was being maintained. Men were scattered over a wide area, in bands, doing what they would, often their own lairds abetting. Many were already streaming back northwards, with laden pack-horses, stolen or even commandeered from the army's horse-lines. How many had already departed, none could tell — although any halted assured that they would come back, once their booty was safely deposited across Tweed. Fires were to be seen on all hands, thatched roofs, farmsteads, haystacks; cattle were being rounded up, beasts that were not worth taking or able for the journey, hamstrung, left lying. Human bodies lay here and there, likewise — although clearly most of the local people had fled — and not all of them men who had put up a struggle to save their homes and property.

Jamie and his men, under a Douglas banner, drew their swords and went into harsh and vigorous action, laying about them, shouting, commanding not arguing, beating down protests. They moved to and fro, backwards and forwards across that fair vale, herding the marauders back to the line of march and onwards, leaving bewildered cattle and abandoned goods and valuables everywhere around. Jamie was determined, thorough, remorseless, shouting the authority of the Earl of Douglas until he was hoarse, caring not on whose toes he trampled. And presently they turned the tide of anarchy, loot and lust, and stopped the rot.

For the rest of the afternoon and early evening, the Douglases policed the miles of the column, and found that it was not only at the extreme rear that men were turning aside. At last, weary and angry, they came up with the great camping area near Milfield.

Jamie did not go near his Earl's tent that night, to report, but stayed amongst his own kin, in no very congenial frame of mind. It was there that the Earl Archibald had to come seeking him, in time.

"So there you are, my friend," he said, awkwardly. "How did you fare? With the looters and burners?"

"We stopped them looting and burning, my lord," he was answered stiffly.

"Yes. To be sure. Jamie — I regret that I had to speak to you as I did. But . . . you are cursedly outspoken, man! Before these proud lords. They are not bairns, to be told their duty by, by . . ."

"By bastard lairdlings? But nor are they fighting-men, my lord — and this is fighting-men's work. This is no tourney or lordly parade, but war. I had not thought that, in war, I must needs measure my words to match court manners!"

"No. But there is discretion, Jamie. I could not have one of my Douglas lairds seem lacking in due restraint and respect, in my very presence."

"I did not know that it was discretion, restraint and respect that you required of me, my lord, when you besought me to

335

come south. Nor was it any of these that we required this afternoon, towards the rear of your army!"

The Earl cleared his throat. "No doubt. But . . . you halted the trouble?"

"For this day, yes. But how many men and horses you had lost before we stopped it, who knows?"

"Some had gone?"

"We saw not a few disappearing. This will have to be stopped, or you might as well turn for home, now!"

"I shall speak to all leaders and under-officers."

"Speaking will not serve. Announce that you will hang the first men seen looting and burning, tomorrow. Only so will you stop the rot."

"I cannot hang our own folk, Jamie. Besides, their own lairds would never permit it."

"Then command that their lairds do the hanging."

Douglas shook his head. "That is not the way. I shall not command my host through fear of hanging."

"Your father would not have been so nice, my lord."

"Perhaps not. But I seldom agreed with my father. See you, this I will do. I shall tell the lords to ride not with me but all down the column. Have them to ensure obedience. Myself ride up and down, on occasion. That should serve."

"It should *help*," he said. And then, "Your permission to ride in the rear again?"

"If you will. Take your whole Dalkeith company, if so you wish." He glanced around him. "Or, h'm, your brother's. There will be no need for hangings, I swear. Besides, soon now we shall be into the Percy's home country. Hotspur is bound to oppose us. We shall have fighting, or at least skirmishing. Men will be too busy for looting."

"Perhaps . . ."

The next day was better, undoubtedly; but still there were breaches of discipline, individual sorties, burnings and decampings for home with booty. With an unpaid army consisting of hundreds of independent units with little sense of cohesion, and a tradition for Border reiving, it was inevitable. And when the host was strung out over many miles, with inexperienced and carelessly over-confident leaders in the main, passing through rich territories, nothing short of the most drastic measures could be effective. Jamie Douglas and the Dalkeith contingent became the most unpopular part of the army.

No sign of real opposition developed. Small parties of unknown horsemen were frequently glimpsed on skylines well out on the flanks, sometimes even far to the rear, and the advance-guard reported minor skirmishing companies falling back steadily before them but never waiting to give battle. The countryside was warned and most of the villages and manors they passed had been deserted — which provided added temptation for looters. But of the Percy and Dunbar there was no sign. Rumour had it that they were at Newcastle assembling their forces — or Henry's forces. Newcastle, therefore, was the Scots' objective. It seemed improbable, however, that the English would sit tamely in that walled city, waiting to be besieged.

Moving a force of 10,000 men, even a horsed force, presents many problems in logistics, sheer numbers complicating and delaying every move. In consequence they made much less mileage per day than a smaller force might have done, averaging no more than twenty miles. Which again left too much time and opportunity for rapine and indiscipline.

Jamie grew the more concerned. Somehow he felt more responsible for this expedition than any other he had been on. Which was foolish, just because the Earl had sought his aid as some sort of adviser. Especially after he was proving by no means eager to take that advice.

The day following, when they reached Morpeth in the Wansbeck valley, they were only fifteen miles from Newcastle. But Jamie reckoned that they must have lost 1,000 men — and without a blow struck, or at least, exchanged.

That night the Earl of Douglas held a council-of-war in his pavilion, going so far as to seat Jamie at his right shoulder. All the lords, lairds and leaders were there, with the tent-sides open so that all might take part. He told them that on the morrow they might well come face to face with Hotspur — which was after all what they had come to do. They would give of their best, naturally, and the day would be theirs. But there might be some hard fighting, for the Percy was no sluggard. They would meet him in fair fight, and show the Northumbrians what it meant to threaten the Scots. If he came out of Newcastle to meet them, well and good. If not, they must needs go in and pick him out. Either way they would ensure that the English North would be in no condition thereafter to aid King Henry in his invasion plans.

Considerable cheers greeted this spirited statement — in which Jamie Douglas forbore to join.

The Earl went on to say that Angus would command the right wing, Moray the left, he himself leading the centre, thereafter allocating to the lesser lords and knights their places in one or other grouping, and indicating sundry supporting duties. He intimated that should he by any chance fall, the Earl of Angus would take over command. He insisted that the Earl of Dunbar was to be captured alive, if at all possible, and brought to him personally, for execution as a traitor. And so on. He asked if all was clear.

There were sundry questions, as to procedure, precedence, positions of honour, numbers of men commanded, and the like; but no lack of enthusiasm.

Jamie listened, scarcely believing what he heard. Time and again he almost intervened, but restrained himself, telling himself that his duty was to advise his chief personally, and certainly not to show him up before all the others. But it was hard to keep silence when folly was being cheerfully expounded all around.

At length, however, Douglas actually turned to him. "Sir James," he said, "you are much experienced in warfare. Have you any matter to add, which has not been touched upon?"

He swallowed. "My lord," he jerked, "my lords all, I . . . I am concerned for certain matters, yes. Matters which seem somewhat to have escaped your notice. This is war, not chivalric tourney. Hotspur is no fool. You do not know that he *is* in Newcastle town. But if he is, think you that he will sally out to meet you, at your challenge? And throw away the strength of one of the strongest walled cities in England?"

"I said, Jamie, that if he does not, we must go in and pick him out. It will take longer . . ."

"My lord — have you ever besieged a strong fortress like Newcastle? I have. Newcastle itself, and Percy inside. If they are prepared for us, and the gates shut — as they will be, for our presence here must be well known — there is no way of gaining entry, save by using heavy siege-machinery, rams, sows, trebuchets, mangonels — of which we have none. And even so, a long and bloody business. If Hotspur Percy chooses to shut his gates in our faces, there is nothing that we can do — save shout at him, and come away."

There was a long moment's silence, then murmurs, less than accepting and friendly.

"Hotspur is a noted warrior," Douglas said. "Why should he behave so?"

"Why not? I would, in his place. If he does bide in Newcastle. You have entered and harried his lands. Why come out and fight you on *your* terms? Better stay there, secure, until he can attack you on *his* terms. Or wait, as is more likely, until he is reinforced from Henry's army on the Welsh Marches. Messengers are probably summoning such now."

"What would you have us do, then, man?"

"Forget Newcastle. Swing westwards up the Tyne valley. Ride to and fro all over Northumberland, over into Cumberland even, on the widest front. Show that the land is at our mercy. Not pillaging or looting but leaving all afraid for their homes. Is that not what you came to do? Not to assail fortress-cities. Moreover, that way you may coax Hotspur out of Newcastle. If he is indeed therein — which I doubt."

There was a spate of talk and discussion.

"To turn away from Newcastle now would seem as though we were afraid," Moray called.

"Then send a small party to sit before it. Make a demonstration. Help coax them out. The rest up Tyne . . ."

"We have come to fight, not traipse the country like packmen," the Lord Maxwell declared.

"Aye! Aye!"

"I believed that we came to counter the wills of the North Country English to invade Scotland, my lord."

"We shall not do that other than by fighting, I swear!"

"Nor will you do it sitting around Newcastle, waiting."

More controversy.

To halt it, Douglas went on, "And if Hotspur and Dunbar are not in Newcastle, Sir James?"

"Then we must find them, and quickly. Send out many swift scouting parties, whilst we range Northumberland, else we may be caught unawares. If they have a large force assembled, they will not be hard to find."

"Very well. We shall see what the morrow brings forth." The Earl rose. "To your tents then, my lords. We ride at sun-up . . ."

On the heights of the Town Moor above Newcastle to the north, the Scots army was halted, gazing down to the walled city in the valley of the broad and silvery Tyne. Even from here they could see that the gates were shut — at least the New Gate and the West Gate, those within sight. No doubt thousands of eyes were watching them from the walls and towers and close-packed houses. No Percy banner flew from the topmost turret of the tall castle near the New Gate, which gave the town its name — but that was not to say that Hotspur was not present. It might merely mean that he did not wish it to be known.

It had been obvious to Jamie from the beginning that his advice was not going to be taken. The entire force had come on to Newcastle, and there was no move to turn away westwards. Now, all the talk amongst the leaders was of which gate they should assail, whether a summons to surrender was necessary, or a challenge to single combat likely to be accepted. When the Earl of Douglas himself declared that if there was to be single combat with Hotspur, then *he* had an unassailable right in the matter, because of the ancient Douglas–Percy feud, Jamie recognised that the case was hopeless.

"You are going to assault the city, my lord?" he asked then, levelly.

"Aye, Jamie — we cannot turn away now. Our people would not have it."

"And if Percy is not there?"

"We shall see."

"At least, send out patrols far and wide. To find him. Otherwise we could be trapped here."

"This great host would take a deal of trapping, I think. But, see here — since you are so anxious, take *you* a swift company and go find Hotspur for us. If you can. Take so many as you wish, your own Dalkeith people."

Jamie knew that it was just to be rid of him and his objections. But he accepted the suggestion nevertheless, glad to get away from a venture in which he had lost all faith.

"To be sure," he said. "I do not need four hundred. Half that would be sufficient, and two hundred fewer will make little difference to your force here. Elsewhere they might serve you notably well."

"Where will you go?"

"Up Tynedale to Hexhamshire first. If they are not there, then south to the valley of the Derwent. If Percy has a large force to muster and forage, he will need space and much fodder to do it in. He will be in one or other of these great vales, I think."

The Earl frowned, tapping his saddle-bow. "If he is in Tynedale, with a large force? Not far away . . . ?"

"I shall endeavour to send you warning, my lord. Although I would prefer that you came yourself, and wasted no time on this walled town."

"Newcastle is the greatest city of the North, Jamie. Next to York, the greatest north of Trent. If it falls to the Scots, it will do more to damage English spirit than much riding to and fro in Northumberland."

On that note they parted.

XIX

JAMIE AND HIS hard-riding two hundred Douglases, a tough, self-contained and fast-moving company just the right size for the task, too strong to assail save with a much larger force but not so big as to be unwieldy or unable to live off the land without time-wasting foraging, found no trace of any large muster of men in Tynedale, although they rode its length, well up into the hills beyond Hexham. Small groups of English horsemen they did see, but these kept their wary distance. In the main this fertile land appeared to be almost cleared of its menfolk and horsemen — no doubt gone to join their lord elsewhere. Or, rather, their lord's son and heir, for the old Earl of Northumberland was still alive, although little seen. Jamie sent a courier to his own Earl, informing him.

So they turned southwards, as he had said, by Allendale and the high commons of the Pennine foothills, threading upland valleys, seeking to reach the roughly parallel vale of the Derwent unheralded. It made for slower going, against the grain of the land; but it had the advantage of them making the many river-crossings where they were young and shallow, rather than by the major fords further down which might well be guarded. The second night after leaving Newcastle, they were at Sinderhope, after covering some fifty miles.

Next morning, coming down into the Derwent valley, they began to find, not assembled men but the traces of them. At first, however unmistakable, they were modest in scope — trampled grass, horse-droppings, the black circles of recent camp-fires, gathered firewood left unburned, dotted here and there. But as they progressed down the widening valley, these signs grew and multiplied on every hand, until they came to

342

what had been a very large encampment in the broad meadows below Blanchland — had been, for it was now deserted quite. But the trail of a great host led onwards, eastwards, down the vale towards Durham. It was impossible to say how many its numbers, even as to thousands; but the indications were that here was an army at least as large as that of the Scots.

This naturally gave Jamie and his brothers furiously to think. There could be little doubt that this was Hotspur's array. None other was likely to be mustered north of York. But why had he chosen to muster here, so far to west and south? There was no need for such secrecy; the Percy and his ally the Prince-Bishop of Durham, were supreme lords of all hereabouts, and could assemble where they would. And up in these high valleys could be convenient for few indeed. Why, then? One answer could be that this was in fact a rendezvous, that here the Northumbrian and Durham muster had waited for others, coming from the west and south-west, across the Pennines — for instance, across England from the Welsh Marches. Reinforcements from Henry, indeed. It could well be. And in that case, the reinforcements had now arrived, since the host had moved on. And what would Henry send from afar, at short notice? Not slow-moving infantry, which might take many days to the journey — but fast light cavalry, possibly mounted archers, the troops they had most to fear.

Although they had found what they came for, anything but relievedly they rode on in the wake of the English force, slowly.

By mid-afternoon Jamie had the first vital information he required. The host in front had left the eastwards-going vale and struck north-eastwards through the rolling Durham moors, by Ebchester and Chopwell, a line which would bring it to Newcastle. He immediately sent off two sets of urgent messengers, by different routes, who, riding fast, would get well ahead of the English and warn Earl Douglas. He reckoned that, here, they were some twenty-one miles from Newcastle, so that there should be time. He and his party continued to dog the enemy force. By the state of the horse-droppings they calculated that they were now only about three hours behind it.

With nightfall they pressed on at a better pace, assured that they were unlikely to stumble upon a great camp unawares; and any small outpost or patrol they could deal with. Actually they soon saw the glow of innumerable camp-fires ahead of them, somewhere in the High Spen area, and they were able to move forward until they could take up a good position in woodland above a great hollow, site of the encampment, where they could see without being seen. Here they settled to rest, taking it in turn to watch and patrol.

In the morning, they watched the all-too-familiar routine of a large army waking, eating and breaking camp — and noted that it took the English just as long as it did the Scots. But they noted much more — number, armament, colours, banners. They reckoned that there were fully 14,000 men involved, all horsed, with many knights and much half-armour, most men equipped with lance and sword, axe or mace, but an ominously large number with bows, mounted archers. Troop by troop, company after company, they watched them mount and ride off northwards.

"They make a goodly show, Jamie," his brother Will declared. "But no better than our own host. Nor so greatly more in numbers."

"Perhaps. But they can draw added numbers from the land, as we cannot, since it is their land. A fine force like this will attract many. Nor will they be hampered with booty. And they are strong in archers. Of which we have none."

"You are ever gloomy, Jamie — a prophet of woe."

"No. I do not prophesy woe. I only say that if we do not underestimate our enemy, we are the more likely to beat him."

Now their task was simple and straightforward — to ride round the slower-moving English force and get to Newcastle with all speed, to rejoin Douglas with their fullest information. They had only some fifteen miles to do it in. Percy could easily cover that in one day, even with all his host — but was unlikely to do so. He would go warily, as he neared his enemy. And would not wish to reach the possible battle area with his men weary, towards evening. So he would camp short of Newcastle, south of Tyne, to make his dispositions. They had time, then.

Without any hold-up or trouble, however tired their horses, going west-abouts and fording Tyne at Horsley Wood, without further sight of the foe, they came to Newcastle in the late afternoon. And there found only their own messengers sent from the Derwent valley awaiting them. The Scots army had left for home that morning.

Jamie heard this news with mixed feelings. He was surprised, but relieved also — since he was anything but confident that the Scots were in any state to meet the English in pitched battle.

This now looked less probable. On the other hand, it all seemed a notably feeble and abortive end to their great expedition, with little attained. It might still be possible, of course, to achieve some worthwhile result. His messengers told him that they had arrived here the previous evening, to find the Scots already packing up, to go. They had, it seemed, tired of sitting round Newcastle's walls, unable to make any impression on the city, hooted at by the defenders and shot at by bowmen if they ventured too close. The massive gates remained shut, and there was no other entrance, without heavy siege-engines to batter holes in the walling. Two days of this had been enough. Now they were withdrawing slowly northwards. The news that Percy had been located and was on his way had been received with acclaim, but had not altered the programme. They would continue to move north and draw the English after them, until some suitable position was reached where they would turn and fight, with their backs to Scotland.

Jamie had to admit that this might be the best course.

Horses and men desperately weary, they rested that night amongst the debris of the great camp on Newcastle's Town Moor.

An early start revealed no signs of the advancing English before they set off. But they had not gone ten miles on their way northwards before it was not the English behind but the Scots in front who were worrying Jamie Douglas. For, away ahead, columns and palls of dark smoke were once again rising to stain the forenoon sky, many smokes and covering a wide area of the front. The situation was self-evident. The Scots army was not going home empty-handed.

"Fools!" Jamie burst out. "Purblind, headstrong fools!" And he dug in his spurs angrily.

It was beyond Morpeth that they began to see the traces, on the ground as distinct from in the sky — burned farms, granges, villages, manors, mills, smouldering heaps of grain and hay, trampled corn, littered furnishings, dead bodies. And everywhere tracks of cattle on the move. This was clearly the work of the night before.

Hurrying on, they came up eventually with the main Scots force about seven miles north of Morpeth in the Longhorsley area — and before reaching it they had to work their way through enormous herds of cattle, thousands strong, driven by cheerful and drink-taken men-at-arms. It was, however, a grievously reduced main force, not much more than half the

345

total strength and even this slow-moving indeed, weighed down with plunder.

Earl Douglas, although he greeted Jamie and the others warmly enough, was slightly on the defensive. "So, my friends, you have accomplished your task, and done it well," he commended. "We are all grateful, I swear. And, as you see, we have followed your advice and wasted little time on Newcastle. Now we retire by slow stages towards the Border, seeking the best place to turn and face Hotspur."

Jamie had for some time been schooling himself to ensure that his too-frank tongue was properly under control. "Yes, my lord," he said.

The other shot a quick glance at him. "You do not again disapprove?" he jerked.

"Not with your policy, my lord — no."

"What, then?"

"It is the policy you are permitting others to pursue. Half your host is off raiding, looting, pillaging. It is now less an army than a horde of caterans and reivers!"

"We cannot hold them in all the time, man. Now we are facing for home, we must give them their heads a little."

"And when the Percy catches up?"

"We shall call them in again, never fear. And they fight the better for having gear at stake, perhaps."

"Or prefer to ensure their gear, and not fight at all!"

"Never that. You miscall our people, I say."

"My lord, a party with a sizeable herd, nearing the Border, will think twice of turning back to fight before it has bestowed its beasts in some safe beef-tub. And few men fight their best weighed down with plunder. Moreover, once a force has got out-of-hand it is ever the less reliable."

"God, Jamie — you are a sour, thrawn devil!" the Earl cried. "Enough of this. We have had peace from gloom and blame while you were away. It has not taken you long to be back at it! I will speak with you again when you are in better temper!" And he rode off.

Jamie's brothers grinned at him. "You never yield, do you?" Johnnie said.

"Not while there is still a chance to halt sheer folly. Folly that could cost us all dear. Lord save the army of an incompetent commander!"

The Scots host was now reduced to moving at the pace of a

cattle-drove, which in turn allowed ever more time for acquisitive-minded groups and companies to hive off and see what they could appropriate and damage. They would certainly allow the English to catch up with them long before they reached the Border, if that was Hotspur's intention.

That night they camped on the flanks of Shirlaw Pike, only some fifteen miles north of Morpeth, deafened by the bellowing of hungry and alarmed cattle, the night lit above them by the glow of fires innumerable. The Earl of Douglas did not come near the Dalkeith company.

They made no better progress next day, with the host now spread over a front almost as wide as it was long — and as such practically uncontrollable. No word from the rearguard, however, intimated the close approach of the enemy, although Jamie, for one, kept riding back to check. The Percy seemed to be in little greater hurry to come to grips as they were. Jamie feared that he was delaying for still further reinforcements. Nightfall found them still a few miles south of Wooler.

The Earl still did not come to Jamie, and Jamie was too proud to approach the other — especially as Murdoch Stewart, Earl of Fife, who never ceased to display his illwill and contempt for Jamie, was now ever closest to the Douglas's side.

It was near the following midday that an urgent rider came at a canter down the long straggling line-of-march. "Enemy in front!" he yelled, as he rode. "Enemy in front! Close up. Douglas says, close up." That was all his message as he drummed past.

Cursing, Jamie forgot his pride, and with his brothers spurred forward, like many another.

They found the head of the column — although it was no longer a column — halted in some agitation on the moorland heights west of Wooler. This time there was no cold shoulder from the Earl Archibald as they rode up.

"Jamie," he cried. "Here's strange tidings. They tell me that the English are in force ahead, in great force. Filling the entire wide vale of Till, from Doddington across to Milfield. The way we came. God knows how they got there . . .!"

"Hotspur? Is it he?"

"They say his banner flies, yes. And many another."

"Then it seems, my lord, that he has been less dilatory than have we. Worked his way round our flank whilst we herded cattle, and so won in front of us."

"Yes, yes — we can all guess that! He seeks to halt us. We will give him battle, gladly. It is what I intended. But scarcely that he should be in *front* of us."

"In front or behind matters little, my lord. So long as *we* choose the battleground, not he."

"Aye. To be sure. I had hoped to prospect a place, once we heard that he was near. But now . . .? Who knows this country well?"

A few Border voices were raised.

"Where is our best place to go? Where should we make our stand? Where Percy has not the Till and Glen rivers to aid him."

Various suggestions were made, some good enough, others less so, some quite impracticable.

The Earl looked directly at Jamie, although he did not say anything.

"My lord," that man said levelly. "Your host is direly scattered. It must have time to be brought back and reassembled. Time. That limits your choice. Hotspur will know that we are here, you may be sure. And he is stronger in numbers. He will wait for you to ride down into his trap."

"Well, man — well?"

"Bear with me. A little time spent now could be a deal more valuable than much time later. We must move from here. This open moor is no place to face the Percy. Forward we cannot go, down into the Vale of Till, into the re-entrant of those rivers — a trap if ever there was one, why Hotspur has turned there. Backwards we may not go either, without trampling through our own rear and all the cattle-herds. Besides, it is moorland for miles. The Percy knows his country, knows what he is at. Therefore, we must move left or right. Right, we have to cross Till, left to cross Glen. We shall not cross Till easily. Therefore it must be the smaller river. We must turn left, into the hills."

"And then? Can we stand there? In the hills?"

"If we choose our hills well. It will mean that Hotspur will have to leave his positions on the rivers and follow us. To *his* disadvantage."

"Yes. Well, then. But we will have to cross the Glen River. If he was to catch us at that, we would be lost."

"There are fords at Coupland and Canno and Kilham. Others too, maybe, but these I know. Kilham furthest west. And before that, the Glen winds through a narrow ravine — from which it gets its name, for it is the Bowmont Water before that. A small company could hold that ravine, while the others cross higher. Then, at least, we have nothing to fear from the rivers."

"I know the place," Scott of Buccleuch called. "Between Canno Mill and Reedsford. It is called Canno Glen."

"Very well. And once we are across. Is there a place to hold and fight, beyond it?"

"Aye," said Jamie. There are two hills there, nearby — I misremember the names. You can see them, from here. Beyond them, and this side of yonder green scarp, Flodden Edge, is a high but open valley. In it is Howtel Peel. Whoever built it chose well. It is a place to withstand an assault, protected by marshes."

"Housedon Hill and Homildon Hill," Scott amplified, obviously an expert reiver. "The Howtel valley between them and West Flodden."

"We are not interested in withstanding assaults, man," the Earl of Fife growled. "Our task is to bring Percy low, not to withstand him."

"The Howtel valley will serve for that also, my lord," answered Jamie, "if you are still of that mind after withstanding his assault!"

"So be it," Douglas cried. "We move westwards. All to your places, my lords. Enough of talk. Let us be doing."

* * *

It was, to be sure, natural, perhaps inevitable, that Jamie and the Dalkeith contingent should be ordered to hold the Canno Glen position while the great strung-out host crossed the fords further up. He had recommended its defensive advantages, and the four hundred or so of his company was just about the right number to entrust with the task.

They hurried ahead, skirting the village of Kirknewton, reaching the Glen River beyond, and proceeding upstream. In a mile they were opposite Canno Mill and into the jaws of the defile between Kilham Hill and Housedon Hill, a deep, twisting, wooded pass enclosing the rushing river, here almost a torrent, with a track on both sides. It was ideal for their purpose, but they were on the wrong side. The English, if they came, would be on the north. So they had to go on until they emerged from the ravine, and at the wide, shallow reach beyond, were able to splash across at the farmery and mill of Reedsford. Leaving a couple of men here to guide the main body, and sending a small party further up to take and hold the major ford at Kilham, they turned back into Canno Glen.

It was, indeed, as good as made for an ambush, with no length of view anywhere, steep rocky slopes and a sheer drop to the foaming river. But it was not really an ambush that they were here for, only to ensure that no English won through this gap to disturb the Scots army at the delicate business of fording the river. Fighting was not the object. Leaving the horses hidden at the west end, Jamie placed his men to best advantage above the narrow track, where they could gather and eventually roll down rocks upon the enemy. Through the trees they could occasionally glimpse their own folk winding round the base of Kilham Hill in a seemingly unending stream.

They had to wait for some considerable time, and were beginning to wonder whether their vigil was in fact necessary, before they heard the deep drumming of hooves which bespoke many horses hard ridden. The Dalkeith Douglases, their rocks and boulders already loosened, tensed, ready.

Normally in this sort of warfare, they would have allowed some files of the horsemen to pass before hurling their stones, to obtain maximum effect, break the enemy column in two and so destroy command. But on this occasion that was not what was wanted. Jamie himself was at the extreme west end of the line, so that, by the time that the first of the English riders, steel-capped and jacked, led by two knights in half-armour, came into his vision, the rest of his people had been restraining themselves for agonising moments — for 400 men can stretch for a considerable distance along a hillside. No actual signal was required. When, with the leading English directly below them, Jamie and his immediate neighbours pushed their boulders into hurtling motion, in only moments the entire ravine resounded to yells and screams and crashes. All along the line the rain of rocks commenced.

It was, of course, utter disaster for those below, There was no means by which they could avoid the bombardment, or attempt to hit back, nor yet turn back on the narrow choked roadway. On their left the ground dropped sheer into the torrent. Most were swept over the edge into this in the first volleys, not all by the stones themselves but by their own colleagues desperately seeking to take avoiding action, or by terrified horses out of control. Succeeding rocks found fewer targets merely because the gaps in the column were suddenly so wide. But even the survivors were in a hopeless situation. Some turned back, and found the track completely blocked by their own struggling and fallen folk and animals. Some spurred furiously forward — and there could be left for others to deal with, and could do little harm. Many leapt down from their now completely useless mounts — and found themselves little better off.

It was a complete and bloody shambles, savage, inglorious for all, but highly effective. Jamie had been ready to order a general descent, with sword and dirk, upon the survivors, after the third volley of rocks. But this he saw to be unnecessary, and despatched only a few men to deal with the scurrying unfortunates, instead sending along the line the command to collect more stones, boulders and logs. Then he himself went at the run eastwards, making for the far end of his line.

His brother Johnnie was in charge there. Gleefully he announced complete triumph. How long the enemy column had been they could not tell, for there was no distant vision in this close country; but all behind the stone fusillade had turned and fled, in direst confusion.

"They will be back," Jamie assured. "Probing. I shall stay here meantime. I left James in charge at the other end, Will in the centre. These English will go back and report. When they come again, it will be warily."

He made arrangements for this east end of the line to be prepared to swing round at right angles, up and down the hill, at short notice. The next enemy move might well be on foot and in depth.

Actually they again had to wait quite some time for developments — which made it look as though the main English command was still some considerable way off. Jamie was not really familiar with the area, but he remembered enough to be fairly sure that to move westwards out of the Vale of Till hereabouts it would be necessary to climb out either by this pass or by a wider and shallower depression to the north, between the village of Milfield and the escarpment of Flodden Edge. From Milfield to Howtel Peel that way must be at least four miles. If Hotspur was actually doing that — and this prolonged interval might imply it — then he could conceivably reach the Howtel valley before the main mass of the Scots did. Jamie sent a messenger off hot-foot to warn Earl Douglas of the possibility.

When the enemy did reappear, however, it was horsemen cautiously feeling their way along the road again, eyeing each yard and bush and shadow, moving at a walking-pace — obviously scouts for a larger party. Jamie signed to his people to keep down, to let them pass. Where the debris of the earlier slaughter began, they went more warily still, staring uphill, ready for immediate flight. Unfortunately, at this stage somebody further along the Scots line skirled a laugh — and that was enough. The riders wheeled their mounts around and spurred off at speed.

Jamie cursed. Not only was that the end of all hope of a second surprise attack, but it meant that they must change their position and tactics. Those scouts would go back to their leaders and report that the road was still held. And the leaders would then order either a general retiral to the main body, or an attempt to outflank the force in the ravine. This, on the hillside terrain here could only be done on foot by infiltrating men through the steep woodland and undergrowth above; which meant that he must swing his line right round to face a new and inclined front.

This took some time to achieve, resulting at length in an L-shaped front being established, two hundred men still lining the ravine track and another two hundred strung out up the hill amongst the trees at the east end. They were barely in position before the first tentative probings began, figures flitting from tree-trunk to bush to hollow, darting, creeping, at various points of the steep braeside. The Scots made little attempt to hide their presence, only their numbers — for Jamie did not really seek battle, merely to deny this pass to the foe and so protect the fording-places for the Scots army. There were one or two minor hand-to-hand skirmishes, but no major fighting. Presently, after an interval, it became clear that these scouts also had withdrawn, no doubt to report once more. It was to be hoped that the enemy verdict would be that the woodland was strongly held and no passage practicable, above or below.

Be that as it may, no attack in force developed along either front.

After something over an hour's waiting, Jamie decided that it was long enough. Surely the Scots must be well across the fords by this time. All the cattle might not be — but he was not greatly concerned with them and their herders. He sent out orders to move back westwards to the horses.

They did find cattle-droves still crossing at Reedsford Mill, but the drovers assured them that all except stragglers of the main force had been across for some time, on their way to this Howtel.

So they turned north again. But it was quickly clear that it was not the Howtel valley that was their army's immediate destination, but the hill above it to the east — Homildon Hill, according to one of Jamie's party. Up there, on the quite steep upper slopes of the hill, the Scots force was building up, rank upon rank, an extraordinary sight, thousands of men and horses darkening the green braes.

Jamie stared. "Dear God!" he exclaimed. "Look there! What does it mean? What do they up there?"

"They are assembling there. Halted," his brother James said.

"But why?"

"A good viewpoint?"

"*All* need not climb to see the view!"

"A strong defensive position . . . ?"

But Jamie was already reining round, to face the hill. "Wait here," he shouted. "There is already a sufficiency up yonder."

Spurring up and up through the press of men and beasts, he came at length to the lofty ridge some hundreds of feet higher, where there were the green embankments of a one-time British camp. It was beyond this, a little way down the farther side, that the banners of the lords were clustered. To them he pushed his way, warning himself to watch his tongue.

The Earl Douglas saw him coming, and raised a hand. "Jamie," he called, in seemingly good spirits. "I hear that you held your pass to good effect. First blood in this tourney!"

"No tourney, my lord. But — we held the pass. I looked for you at Howtel." And he pointed downhill, northwards.

"Aye. But your messenger said that Hotspur might reach there before us. Besides, this is a better defensive position, by far."

"I beg leave to differ, my lord. And my message was only warning that the English might move that way, and to be ready." He gestured downwards. "The Howtel position is still un-occupied, as all can see."

"We are better here," Murdoch of Fife rapped. "Hotspur will assail us here to his sore hurt."

"And when he is sufficiently discouraged and weary, we shall sweep down and defeat him utterly," Douglas added. "Even you, Jamie, must approve such strategy."

"Possibly — were it not for *that*!" Jamie swung half-right in his saddle and jabbed a pointing finger upwards.

Immediately to the west of this Homildon rose the higher summit and ridge of Housedon Hill. Indeed, the one was but a spur of the other. There was a steep dip between Homildon's crest and the grassy side of the other, a shallow col.

"Would you have us up there, then? Better than here?"

"I would have you down there, around Howtel Peel. As we said. It is still clear. See you, my lords — whoever built that tower knew what he was at. It stands on firm ground, with ample space — yet is protected to north and south by wide marsh, waters drained off these hills. There is a mound to the west, to offer flanking support. Any cavalry attack must come by quite narrow causeways, entrants, easy to hold."

"And how should we attack, from there?" Moray demanded. "Since we are here to fight, not to hide in bogs!"

"Let the Percy expend his strength — as you say to do up here. Then sally out from the Peel area, and the mound, both. On foot over the marsh, cavalry by the causeways. Sufficient fighting then, my lord."

"What advantage have we down there that we do not have up here? We have height. A charge downhill, to sweep them away."

Again Jamie turned, to point upwards. "That hill . . ." he began — but was interrupted by shouts all around, as other hands pointed.

Round a low ridge to the north, two miles or more away, this side of the scarp of Flodden Edge, steel gleamed in the afternoon sunshine, much steel. More and more glittered and flashed even as they watched.

"Too late," the Lord Maxwell exclaimed. "I would think to agree with Sir James — but now it is too late."

"Not so," Jamie cried. "You could still be at Howtel before them. Let us go down."

"No!" Earl Douglas decided. "We are very well here. It would be folly to change now, in disorder. Here we have all under our eyes . . ."

"Except the far side of that Housedon Hill, man! They could come up there, hidden. And be *above* us!"

"What of it? There is this gap between. They cannot reach us without climbing this steep."

"Not with swords and lances. But what of arrows?"

"Eh . . .?"

"I told you, my lord. The Percy is aided by a host of mounted archers. From the West. If he places them on that hill . . ."

"It is too far. Out of range."

"On the ridge, yes. But if he sent them part-way down that slope. How far then, say you?"

"Four hundred yards? More?"

"Less. And English yew long-bows will drive a shaft five hundred yards and more, with a falling shot." He paused. "So, I say, let us down to Howtel while there is time."

"If . . . if . . . if!" Murdoch Stewart jerked. "*If* Percy comes up behind the hill. *If* he sends archers there. *If* he places them half-way down the hill. *If* we stand and let them shoot at us! I say this doomster would have us fleeing from shadows, by God!"

"I say Jamie is right," the Earl of Angus said. "The English could fill the valley below us. Then we are trapped up here."

"It is too late to move now, George," Douglas declared. "The host is drawn up here in good order. To change now would mean confusion. Jamie is too fearful. We shall stand our ground."

"Then let me climb that hill with my Dalkeith people. And seek to hold it," Jamie requested.

"Very well. No harm in that . . ."

So he rode back down the south side of Homildon, through the crowded ranks again, to his own folk. Quickly he told his brothers of the situation, and they wasted no time in starting up that long climb of the higher hill. It was fairly steep from this side, and they had to set the horses zigzagging up, slithering and sliding. A burn-channel now aided, now hindered them. The summit ridge ran north and south for almost a quarter-of-a-mile. At length they reached it.

At the very crest Jamie, in front, reined back violently. Not five hundred yards away down the far and gentler slope, the first of a great host was climbing.

Urgently he waved back his company, and reined round his own beast.

He was almost bound to have been seen — which might delay the enemy a little perhaps, make them more wary. Time for themselves to get away — for there was nothing that they could do about this except flee. There were thousands mounting the hill, and no delaying tactics by his four hundred would avail anything.

So back downhill they went, as fast as they dared on the steep terrain, not directly down the face as they had come but to the col between the two hills. As he went Jamie could not but note how vulnerable the Scots position was, across the gap, to long-range archery.

On their own hill again, his company could by no means push their way through the crowded ranks already drawn up there, so Jamie had to leave them, to force his own way upwards. By the time he could reach the leadership group, his information was out-of-date, for the first ranks of the English were now plain for all to see on the ridge of Housedon Hill.

"My lords," he shouted, as he came near. "We must get off this hill. Without delay. There are thousands coming up — and Hotspur would be the veriest fool not to send his archers. We have little time left. Down with us!"

"Look there, man!" Douglas said, briefly.

There was a much lower spur of hill immediately to the north-east, Kype Hill, jutting into the Howtel valley; and over the green swell of this a mass of enemy horse was now swarming. Before the Scots could possibly reach the valley floor they would be outflanked by these.

Jamie swore. "Nothing for it but to turn back, then. Down the south side, whence we came. Back across the Glen Water. Hold the river line. This hill could be a death-trap."

"I will not turn back," Douglas declared. "Flee in the face of the Percy. And from a strong position. Besides, there is the cattle. Thousands of beasts between us and the river. We would have to push our full array right through them."

"Better that than be trapped here."

"No. Here we stand. Forget your fears, man!"

Groaning, Jamie turned away. He could say and do no more. Not for these, anyway. He would go back to his own people from Dalkeith. His duty now was to them, surely. Not that there was much that he could do for them, or for any, since he could by no means desert the army now.

As he pushed his way down the south side of Homildon once more, none had any eyes for him. All were gazing up at the ridge of Housedon, black now with massed men and horses. Even as they looked the horses were being led away, down the far east side, to make room for more men on the summit. Clearly no foolish attempt was going to be made to assault the lower hill with cavalry. It was indeed to be the archers, then.

Reaching his brothers, he barked out his grim tidings.

"What now, then?" Johnnie demanded. "Do we just die where we stand?"

"Not if I may help it. We are in one of the worst positions, here. At least let us move round this accursed hill, if we can. To the west side. It will be surrounded. But there the bowmen up yonder will not reach us. We may be attacked from below, but that is better than being shot from above."

"We cannot just go hide there, Jamie!" Will protested.

"Hide? What do you propose that we do anywhere else?"

"Are we not going to make sallies, at least?"

"Against massed archers? That is worthy of the Earl Archibald! Let the English make the sallies, meantime. Come — get our own folk round to the west."

By going slightly downhill again, and round, they were able to move their compact squadron reasonably quickly. Others, of course, saw and sought to do likewise. But long before the bulk of those seeking to do so could move away, the arrows from the summit of Housedon began to fall amongst them. These were only sighting shots, of course, fired high to curve over and down, testing the range. They did not do much damage, even though they could hardly fail to find a mark, so tightly was the hill packed with men and horses; for they were not only losing their impetus but, being dropped shots, tended to fall on the heads and shoulders of the Scots, which were in the main protected by steel morions and jacks. It was principally the unprotected horses which suffered. Nevertheless there was much shouting, jeering and even screaming, to indicate that hostilities had at last commenced.

The Dalkeith contingent found that the English cavalry had now practically encircled Homildon Hill to the west. But they were not attempting to come up the slope as yet, the nearest some six hundred yards below.

"They but contain us," Jamie said. "Few bowmen down there, I jalouse. Percy will have sent all his archers up the hill — as I would have done. A plague on it — we could still break out of this col, if we had the will!"

"Ourselves, mean you — or all the host?" James asked.

"The host. We could do likewise, I believe, in wedge formation. Down the steep and through them. Nothing would stop us. And out to the west, the Cheviot foothills. Reassemble there. But the Earl will not."

"Perhaps, when he has had enough of arrows . . .!"

357

Johnnie was right, of course. Jamie, no more than his brothers, could bear to sit his horse idly there in comparative safety whilst the bulk of the army was facing the major threat. Admittedly more and more men were pressing round to this side of the hill; but even so, sheer numbers meant that the greater part must inevitably face the menace of Housedon Hill. So, leaving one of the Dalkeith under-stewards, Mattie Douglas, in charge meantime, the four brothers set off uphill again.

They found conditions direly changed. The enemy had moved the first companies of bowmen almost half-way down the west face of Housedon, safe in the knowledge that the Scots would have no archers of their own, as Jamie had said they would, and were in process of moving most of the rest. Already the difference in range and angle was grimly evident. Casualties were mounting steadily. It was not only the harder hitting-power of the shafts but the fact that they now could be aimed directly, so that instead of dropping on helmets and breast-plates they could come straight at the unprotected parts. And it was impossible to miss, man or beast. The men-at-arms, of course, suffered the most, being less well-protected by steel; but even the lords and knights were not in full armour — since it was impossible to ride far and fast so garbed. As the newcomers rode up men were dying under the lethal, swishing hail with yells and moans, horses falling in lashing, screaming agony, the press of men and beasts surging this way and that, pushing, trampling, stumbling. And none could hit back.

Hotspur's tactics were entirely clear now. He had the invaders where he wanted them. His main force surrounded the hill-foot area in a belt of steel, waiting, whilst the archers pinned them down. There was nothing particularly brilliant about it; indeed it was the obvious thing to do, given the folly of the Scots for ever putting themselves in such a position.

Jamie and his brothers had swift intimation of the desperation of the situation, had they required it. For, riding through the tight press towards the Earl of Douglas's stance under the massed banners, Johnnie was hit by an arrow. It struck his cuirass, was deflected by the steel, and drove in slanting upwards at the joint with the gorget, piercing the leather beneath and into the shoulder. He toppled from the saddle of his rearing, frightened mount.

Most men were dismounted now, as making less prominent marks, and hurriedly the Douglas brothers did likewise.

Assuring himself that Johnnie was not dangerously injured, Jamie left the others to deal with him, and pushed on through the angry seething crowd. He found a heated argument going on beneath the banners, all the leaders seeming to be shouting at once.

It appeared that Sir John Swinton of that Ilk, in the Merse, kin to Douglas, was advocating action, declaring that he for one was no longer prepared to stand there and be shot down as target-practice for English bowmen. They must mount a charge, he said, down this east face of the hill and up the slope of Housedon, and sweep away those accursed archers. It would be costly, he agreed — but the only way they could be saved from outright disaster. Although most of the others were disagreeing, some were supporting him vehemently, notably and strangely one, Adam, Lord of Gordon and Strathbogie. The Swinton and Gordon lands adjoined in the Merse, indeed the two families were of the same root, but they had been at feud for generations. Yet Gordon was now vociferously agreeing with his enemy that this desperate assault was necessary. And not only that, but that he was prepared to lead it. All this under the tide of arrows.

Jamie's arrival at least provided a distraction.

"Ha — Jamie!" the Earl Douglas cried. "We suffer much loss. Do you hear what is proposed? My lords of Swinton and Gordon are for a direct assault on those archers. I say that they would lose half their men. How say you?"

"Better than losing the same men standing here idle!" Swinton barked.

"It would be useless," Jamie said. "You would never reach the archers."

"Some would," Gordon asserted. "They would never bring us all down. And once amongst them we would scatter them like chaff. Bowmen are useless at close quarters fighting. They will never stand for steel."

There was more vigorous debate, as men died around them. With their long shields and better armour, of course, the lordly ones were much the less vulnerable.

Jamie gained approximate quiet by banging his dirk-hilt on his own shield, slung from his shoulder, with its colourful heraldic device for identity.

"I tell you, none would get to the archers," he insisted. "This hillside is steep and whin-grown. You could not ride down it, horsed, at speed. Every bowman would be aiming at you. And not only these, part-way down, but those above also. Climbing *their* hill beyond, you could not rush them either. The ground is bad for horses. At such short range it would be massacre."

"But, by God and His saints, we cannot just stand here, waiting to be shot down!" Swinton exclaimed.

"No, I agree. We should move, yes. But down this other side of the hill. North by west, in a series of wedge-formations. It is less steep. The English main host is there, yes — but it is spread round the entire base of the hill, none so thick at any point. At speed, in tight formation, we could charge right through. Then on, beyond, into the Cheviot foothills. There to reform."

"It is too late for that," Earl Douglas declared.

"No. They think they have us trapped up here. If we did it swiftly, we could surprise them, and through."

"And if we did *not* win through, we are lost, finished. No — that is not the way. We would risk total defeat."

"And this way . . . ?"

"I say we can clear away those archers," Swinton interrupted. "And then we are secure, up here. I will do it, with my own Mersemen."

"I said *I* would lead!" Gordon shouted.

"We cannot both lead — and I am senior. The older. And knight."

"God's sake — *older!* Will someone here knight *me*, then? So that I may show this aged Swinton how to fight?" the Gordon cried.

There was a great shouting, even some laughter, despite the occasion. But Swinton's voice rose above all.

"A pest — but I will knight you myself!" he declared. "So that you may at least die a knight, Gordon!" He drew his sword. "Kneel, you!"

The Gordon hesitated. Then, throwing back his head, he laughed deep-throated. Both men looked at the Earl of Douglas.

It was a curious tense situation in more ways than the obvious. In the field, it was the accepted custom for any knightings to be bestowed by the commander in person. Douglas had made no such gestures. Swinton's tossed out suggestion was in fact something of a challenge to Douglas almost as much as to Gordon. Implied was that the commander was not the man to bestow the honour — for proud men were very concerned as to the calibre of those who gave them the accolade.

Implicit further was that he was but a poor general to have got them into this fix.

Archibald Douglas must have been aware of at least some of this. But he gave no sign save a frown — and he was apt to wear a moody frown anyway. It was within Swinton's right, of course, looked at from another viewpoint. Any knight can in theory create another knight — and only a knight can do so.

"Very well!" There amongst the hissing arrows and cries and shouting, with a flourish Adam Gordon whipped off his plumed helmet and sank on one knee. "On this field, beggars may not be choosers! But — haste you, Swinton, or I shall be skewered as well as dubbed!"

The other slapped down the sword on the steel-clad shoulder with a clang. "By this token I dub thee knight!" he rapped out. "Arise, Sir Adam! Be thou good and true knight until thy life's end. Which 'fore God, is like to be but shortly!"

Laughing, the other rose. "Come, then — let Gordon and Swinton deal with these insolent bowmen. And I swear that I reach them first!" He held out his hand.

Snorting, the older man took it. "Better than waiting here to be slain like deer!" he said. And together they turned to push their way through the crush, calling for their horses.

"This is madness!" Jamie declared. "You should stop it, my lord."

Douglas shook his head, tight-lipped. Swinton had married the first Earl of Douglas's young widow, and retained with her certain lands which succeeding Douglases coveted.

There was now a surge of the Scots leaders south-eastwards, the better to view this attempt — which meant, to be sure, that they were forfeiting something of their beneficial position on the hill, at the receipt of directly-aimed arrows instead of merely dropping fire. However, their shields and superior armour would still aid them. And there was no backwardness among the rank-and-file in giving place and occupying their former stance.

Actually, of course, once the Swinton–Gordon company of under two hundred was mounted and marshalled, the rest of the Scots array could forget about arrows for the time being — or at least their own vulnerability to them; for, from that moment all the archery was concentrated upon the mounted squadron. Even before Gordon's horn-blast sounded the advance, half-a-dozen men and horses had fallen. Men not involved advisedly drew back to give them ample space, as well as clearing a passage for them.

They went at a heartening trot at first, and in good formation, Swinton and Gordon banners streaming side-by-side at the head. But this could not be kept up as the hillside steepened and the whin-bushes and fallen boulders proliferated. All the time, the concentrated rain of arrows poured upon them, the range ever shortening. Saddles were being emptied continuously, amidst yells and screams — although more were emptied by the mounts' collapse than by the riders', for, whether it was policy or merely that the horses provided the larger and less protected targets, these suffered much the greater number of hits. Furiously yelling their slogans, the leaders sought to urge all to greater speed, despite the terrain, and it became hard to tell whether crashing horses and pitching riders were casualties of the bowmen or the hillside.

It is safe to say that not one-half of the Mersemen reached the col between the hills.

All the time reinforcements of archers had been running down from their ridge to join their fellows, bringing fresh supplies of arrows — for they were expending vast quantities of the shafts. These additions produced an intensified and accelerated rate of fire, and it was a positive storm of bolts which swept the horsemen, their ranks now scattered and terribly gapped, as they began to breast the opposite braeside, and now at only some two hundred and fifty yards range.

It was quite hopeless, of course. Nothing could withstand that vicious hail. By the time Sir John Swinton fell, not seventy of the two hundred remained. By half-way up the slope, when Gordon's horse was shot under him, not forty survived. Waving his sword and roaring defiance the new knight lurched on on foot. When, eventually, he crashed to the ground, a bare hundred yards from the first bowmen, three arrows projecting from his person, only a dozen men straggled behind him, none now mounted. None turned to flee. All fell in a swathe, as from a single lash, facing the enemy.

A great corporate groan rose from the watching Scots — to be drowned in yells of triumph and derision from the English.

The archers lifted their aim once more, to the major target.

That gallant débâcle had a profound effect on the Scots — much more than the numbers involved might seem to warrant. Men saw it as underlining the hopelessness of their position.

Flight began to be considered. Scowls were directed towards the leadership. Men commenced to push and struggle away from those south and east flanks of Homildon Hill, further from the bowmen, caring little for orders.

More significant still, perhaps, was the effect on the Earl of Douglas himself — or it may have been as it were, the effect of the effect. After such long uncertainty and temporising, he seemed to come to a conclusion. He turned suddenly to his trumpeter and ordered a summoning blast.

"To me! To me!" he shouted, thereafter. "All leaders to me." They had lowered the banners now, as too obviously pinpointing targets.

When most of his lords and knights had gathered round, he spoke.

"We cannot wait longer here," he declared. "Swinton and Gordon have died bravely. But they have shown us the way. We shall not waste their sacrifice. There were too few of them. And mounted was not best. But their notion was right. We shall *all* go. Afoot. Down and across that col, and up at the archers. Some will die, undoubtedly. But some are dying now. There are many of us. We shall up and overwhelm them. And when we have taken that higher hill from them, and are no longer over-looked thus, we can bring our horses over. Enough of standing waiting."

There was a ragged cheer, the reaction of frustrated, impatient men, desperate for action.

Jamie did not cheer. "My lord," he began, "if it was folly for Swinton and Gordon, it is more so for you! I say that . . ."

"Sir James," the Earl interrupted, strongly now, "enough! The decision is mine. If you do not like it, bide you here and guard the horses."

There was a grim laugh at that.

Jamie's face set. "Is that your command, my lord?"

"Yes. To be sure. Someone must do so, lest Percy's cavalry come up this hill while we are at it." Douglas turned away. "Come then, my friends — let us all deal with these accursed bowmen . . ."

Hot anger in the head but leaden cold at heart, Jamie watched and listened as the Scots nobles and gentry made their hurried dispositions. After the long inaction and abdication of leadership, they were anxious to prove their courage, prowess and determination. They themselves would form the forefront of the assault — with their finer armour and shields they were the better equipped for it, anyway. Behind them the serried ranks of the men would march, in their thousands. They would march indeed, not race nor run nor scurry, until they were within a hundred yards or so of the enemy; then they would charge, and drive those archers before them like chaff. With their numbers, they could not fail.

With an added pang, Jamie found that his brothers James and Will had brought him the wounded Johnnie, to leave in his care; they themselves were hurrying off to join the other lairds.

"Come back, you fools!" he shouted after them. "You are going to your deaths! To no purpose."

But they did not so much as glance behind them.

"Are they all crazy-mad?" he demanded of Johnnie. "God pity us all — this day Scotland goes down in senseless ruin! And the Douglas leads the way!"

Johnnie muttered something incoherent.

Recollecting, Jamie turned. "Your wound? How grievous? Is it sore pain?"

His brother was very white, reeling on his feet. "Shoulder," he got out, from tight lips. "I am . . . well enough."

"They got the arrow out? Broke it off?"

"Yes."

"See you — sit, Johnnie . . ."

A trumpet-blast heralded the Scots advance. Banners raised again, and beginning to chant their various slogans, the marshalled lines moved downhill, pacing deliberately behind the illustrious front rank — although to be sure men were falling before they even began. Helplessly Jamie watched, praying that somehow he should be wrong in his judgement and prophesy.

He was not. What he was watching was steady, unremitting bloody slaughter, on a vast scale. How many archers were now facing them they did not know, but it obviously ran into thousands. Aiming and shooting with swift competence and monotonous regularity, each sent a succession of deadly shafts into the advancing mass. They could not miss with a single shot — the target was solid.

The nobles and knights fared only a little better than the men-at-arms and mosstroopers. Their half-armour did not cover their lower quarters, and arrows were able to pierce joints and openings in helmets and cuirasses. So they were falling long before they reached the floor of the col, and the banner-bearers with them. Jamie saw Livingstone of Callander drop and Ramsay of Dalhousie, while still on their own hillside; and others whom he could not recognise at the distance. He saw Douglas himself go down, with an arrow projecting from his gorget, and then rise again and stagger on. Behind men were pitching and crashing all the time, the slogans and yells now tending to be lost in a horrible cacophony of screams and groans.

Jamie's own groan rose to join the others as he saw his brother Will lurch, reel and drop on all fours, to be lost under the advance of the others. Crossing the col with half the knightly forefront gone now, the Earl of Douglas again dropped — and again he struggled to his feet, limping now as well as staggering. His standard-bearer had been replaced three times already.

The Earl of Angus fell as they began to breast the opposite rise. Maxwell followed him in no more than a couple of paces. Then Sinclair. Everywhere the ground was littered with the Scots dead and dying.

Gulping down his emotion, Jamie dragged his gaze away from the shambles to look back and down. The host of English cavalry below still awaited developments. From down there, of course, they would not be able to see what went on up between the hills — and since sizeable numbers of the Scots rank-and-file, including the Dalkeith contingent, had elected not to join the suicidal assault, it might not seem from below as though the situation had much changed. At any rate, no advance was attempted up the hill meantime — although it was only a question of time before word must reach Hotspur, or whoever was in command down there, of the Scots move, and vigorous reaction would follow.

When the unhappy watcher faced front again, loathing himself for his own safety and entire lack of activity in face of all this horror and desperation, he was just in time to see the Earl Archibald reeling backwards into the arms of those immediately behind, a shaft actually protruding from under the upraised visor of his Douglas-plumed helmet. That must be the end of him, surely. But no — part lurching forward on his own, part propelled and supported from behind, he struggled on, the arrow, half-broken off but still obtruding from his helmet like some additional crest. Clearly the archers were making an especial target of him. There was nothing wrong with Archibald Douglas's personal courage, only with his wits and generalship.

Jamie beat his fist on his breastplate in an access of fury, bafflement and helplessness. The urge to do the obvious was now all but overwhelming — to gather together as many as he might of the Scots left on the hilltop, with his Dalkeith men, mount, and hurl themselves down to the rescue of the hard-pressed ranks below. So simple an action — if men would follow him. But useless, he knew — quite useless. It would merely mean many more dead, to salve his conscience. Half the archers would but transfer their aim to his company for a little. The Swinton disaster had demonstrated the hopelessness of anything such. His own witless folly would not help any.

Even as he stared, biting his lip, he saw the reeling Douglas go down once more — and this time he did not arise. Earl Murdoch of Fife, Albany's son, appeared to be the only noble-man left on his feet, and even he was hirpling on, using his sword as a crutch. Only two or three knights remained, including the Douglas brothers of Drumlanrig and Cavers. There was now no sign of Jamie's own brother James.

Still there were perhaps three hundred uphill yards to go before the first of the massed bowmen.

It seemed to dawn upon the thinned ranks of the survivors, then, that they could by no means make it. Further struggle was quite pointless. The recognition appeared to sweep across the ragged front as though by some signal. In only moments the forward momentum, sorely flagging as it was by now, came not so much to a halt as changed into dispersal. Without pause men turned left or right or round about. Suddenly what was left of the assault was a flight, a rout. What remained of the leadership stumbled on until it fell.

Jamie Douglas's agonised watching and waiting was at an end. He knew what he had to do now — action at least and at long last. Raising Johnnie up, he shouted,

"To me! To me, Douglas! To horse! To horse!"

The men left above on the hilltop were, of course, desperately awaiting a lead. Swiftly the word spread, and there was a rush to do his bidding. Jamie grabbed a spare horse — and there were literally thousands of these — and somehow hoisted and heaved his wounded brother up into the saddle.

"Can you hold on?" he gasped, and at Johnnie's nod, found a mount for himself. To the men now surging all around them, he pointed downhill, westwards, towards where he had left the Dalkeith company.

He was spurring to ride thither himself, leading Johnnie's horse, when he perceived many men hoisting wounded on to their horses, to carry before them at their saddle-bows. Frowning, he hesitated, then shouted.

"No! Leave them. Leave them, I say. Only wounded who can ride. It is hard. But what we do, we cannot do burdened by wounded. Only those who can ride, I say. Bring spare horses, rather . . ."

If men cursed him, then, he had to accept it as part of *his* burden.

As he rode down to his Dalkeith people, he saw that there was now movement in the mass of the English cavalry below the hill. They were beginning to stream south by west — or some considerable proportion of them. That meant, he feared, that they had been informed of the débâcle up on the higher ground, and were moving round to cut off the escape of survivors and stragglers. Which but made his task all the more urgent, although not necessarily more difficult.

Swiftly he calculated that there might be five hundred men behind him. That, with his Dalkeith contingent, would give him almost 1,000. Fewer would have been more easy to handle. But no point in splitting up meantime.

Placing himself at the head of the Dalkeith men — whose thankfulness to see him was evident — he yelled his instructions.

"Follow me. Round the hill. Save what we can of the others. Battle lost. Then, down and through. In wedges. Come!"

Whether these orders reached far back amongst the nine hundred or so was doubtful; but the following on, meantime, was obvious. They set off fast round the swell of the hill, at about the six hundred-feet contour.

It was not long before they were into the first of the fleeing survivors from the disaster, none mounted of course. The spare horses were grabbed gratefully.

On they swept, round to the south end of the col, or just below it. As Jamie had calculated, the bowmen had dispensed with their archery at last, broken their serried ranks and had in the main descended upon the killing-ground, swords in hand, to capture lords and knights for ransom, hunt down stragglers, kill off wounded, and collect their spent arrows — of which they must now be in very short supply. They were accordingly in poor state to cope with the unexpected Scots mounted force.

Chaos ensued — at least, chaos on the part of the English. For the archers left behind higher on Housedon Hill could not now shoot down into the mêlée without risk of skewering their own colleagues. Jamie did not have as firm control over his miscellaneous crew as he would have liked, but sufficient to retain the initiative meantime.

They could have saved a great many men undoubtedly — had they had time. And they did save more than they had horses for, and had to send others running up Homildon again to collect beasts still roaming riderless up there. But Jamie was oppressed by the thought of the English cavalry host streaming below, making for this re-entrant and less steep approach. They would be here in a matter of only brief minutes. And then all would be lost. He had no doubts as to his task, duty and priorities.

There was no time for search or quartering the field, no time for seeking out and rescuing highly-placed wounded, no time for any consistent slaughter of the enemy archers, however tempting the opportunity. Jamie wanted desperately to look for his brothers, but could not do that either. He would have extricated the bodies of the Earl Douglas and other lords if he would — not for their own sakes so much as for the fact that a defeat was considered to be less damaging if most of the leadership escaped. But amongst the thousands of slain and wounded, he discerned only the Lord Sinclair of Roslin and Ramsay of Dalhousie, and both were dead. They did collect Will of Drumlanrig, dazed but only slightly wounded supporting his brother of Cavers, more so; but there was no time for more. Hating himself, yet resolute, Jamie blew his horn, to break off the engagement.

"To me!" he cried. "To me! Muster!" He pointed southwards, whence they had come. "Leave all. Come!"

There were murmurs, even amongst those close to him, at that harsh command. But he was insistent.

Already their time was short. There were fewer murmurs when they faced south behind the lip of the col. There, coming up the hill to them, in the groove of the re-entrant, was the broad front of the English cavalry, banners at the head, and not four hundred yards away.

Shaken, men stared.

Jamie wasted no more precious moments. "Back to our former position!" he shouted, pointing westwards once more, and led his enlarged and distinctly unwieldy company round the contour of the hill again, at right-angles away from the enemy advance.

Part of the English array broke off to swing and follow them.

At approximately the position where the Dalkeith men had waited formerly, he drew up. At the foot of the hill below them the English main body was still streaming southwards, before turning up the re-entrant, squadron upon squadron. If there had been little time before, there was less now that they were being pursued.

"Wedges," he ordered. "Form wedges. Three of them. Quickly. Will — take one. About four hundred men. Wattie — you too. Hurry! We go down in three wedges. Together. God willing, right through! Halt for nothing."

It had to be a very rough-and-ready business, only really a gesture at arrowhead-formation. It was to be hoped that they could improve on it as they went down. Into three approximate triangles they split up, uneven in numbers as in shape, wounded in the centre, leaders at the apex, under-officers at the rear flanks. Jamie, with his Dalkeith people, had that furthest to the north. He waited as long as he dared — which was only for a few moments — before raising horn to lips again. Then, with barely one hundred and fifty yards between their last wedge and the oncoming English from the battle approach area, he slashed his sword forward and down, and drove his horse onwards. In some sort of fashion, in an attempt at unison, the other two formations did the same.

Riding knee-to-knee, save for the lone individual at the tip of each apex, as close and tight-packed as horses at speed over uneven ground could move, they thundered directly downhill, three phalanxes in line abreast, yelling — and since all three were led by Douglases, it was "A Douglas! A Douglas!" that they shouted, a chant which until this day had brought fear and quaking to every North of England heart.

Below, the English reaction was, not unnaturally, confused. None of their senior leadership was present — for this, after all, was fully half-way down their lengthy column. They were meantime in line-of-march, not in the right formation to withstand such an attack in flank. And they would have been congratulating themselves that victory was already theirs. All of which would help the Scots. Only, there were many more of

369

them than in the wedges. And they were not burdened by wounded.

With less than six hundred yards to cover, at a scrambling canter, there was only about one minute between start and impact — which gave little opportunity either for the enemy to change front and regroup, or for the Scots to improve their formation. So that the crash, when it came, was less than a copybook example of arrowhead-charge and defence. Nor was the attack completely synchronised. Inevitably, Jamie's wedge, first off the mark and best led, hit the English line ahead of the others. This was no serious matter in the circumstances, but it did have the effect of buckling the enemy front somewhat and so lessening the impact of the others.

Impact, impetus, was the essence of this tactic, rather than fighting or swordery. Indeed it might be argued that weapons were all but immaterial — or at least that, in theory, it could still be effective with all the attackers unarmed. Jamie, in the lead, went in swinging his sword in a figure-of-eight pattern, left and right; but whether it made contact with any of the foe was not important. What was vital was that the encounter should be violent, the momentum overwhelming and, above all, continuing. To lose impetus would be fatal. In this, the steep hill down was much in the Scots' favour. Also the fact that men, stationary or nearly so, are almost bound to flinch before the final impact of a head-long charge — and if, by superhuman willpower they do not, their horses can be guaranteed to do so.

All depended upon these two factors, therefore — willpower and horses — on both sides, but with the balance strongly in favour of the attackers.

Jamie was aware of wild-eyed animals rearing and swerving and backing before him as he smashed in, sword swinging, breathlessly gasping his own surname. The lances which could have skewered them wavered, veered or were tossed aside. One snapped off short against his shield, all but unseating him with the jolt. Recovering himself partly by major effort and partly by the enormous pressure behind, he was almost immediately into further trouble as his mount pecked and stumbled over an English horse fallen directly in its path. Flung over its arching neck, he clung on desperately, somehow managing to retain his sword. If his beast had gone down, nothing could have saved him from being trampled by his own followers. But the animal recovered itself, and a strong arm at his side, or a little behind, helped him to regain his saddle once more. He plunged on.

Even had he sought to reduce speed he could not have done so, with such weight of driving, snorting horseflesh behind him. The enemy was not now in any recognisable ranks, and he had little idea as to what width was the barrier of men he had to plough through. But since they had been in column-of-march and not forming a front, it could not be so very wide.

Borne on, he found that the further back the English the less inclined they were to stand and face it out — a very natural reaction, no doubt. If he had achieved little with his sword hitherto, he was offered no targets sufficiently near now. A swift glance behind, however, showed that the riders at the flanks of his V were able to do better, were more in actual contact with the enemy, slashing and thrusting continuously.

The vast majority of the Scots, including the wounded, in the tight-packed centre, scarcely saw their foes.

Suddenly Jamie was through, with only scurrying fugitives before him — and was scarcely able to believe it. Behind him his wedge emerged all but intact, their few casualties almost wholly caused by horses stumbling and falling over obstacles.

Pounding on without pause, he gazed to the left. There, so far, was only a confused mass of milling men and beasts, with the other two wedges not to be distinguished as such. His impulse was to swing round to their aid — but he stifled it. That was not the priority, and could be dangerous. The enemy who had been pursuing them round the hill were now in turn streaming down. They could rally their colleagues down here. To maintain velocity and the initiative was still his objective — and this could still be lost.

So they thundered on westwards towards the welter of foot-hills which rose to the Cheviots, the first barely half-a-mile away. But every few moments Jamie was glancing over his left shoulder. Thankfully he saw the wedge next to his own, Will of Drumlanrig's, emerge from the mêlée, still in some sort of order. The third was not yet extricated.

The urge to turn back, to go to the help of the group under Wattie Douglas, the largest but almost certainly the least effective of the formations, was stronger than ever. But it would be folly — and Jamie reminded himself that there had been more than enough folly for one day. He pressed on.

Shouts caused him to turn his head again. All along the rear of the confused and gapped English line riders were emerging, breaking through in ones and twos and groups. The third wedge had broken up, then, but some of its people were winning out.

Presently they could see many men streaming after them across the Howtel valley-floor, just south of the marshland. Undoubtedly these were their own folk, not English in pursuit. Not yet.

On the skirts of the first of the foothills, Jamie breathlessly blew his horn, and signed all to draw rein. Everywhere men thankfully pulled up. The second wedge came pounding up. Jamie at last could look to his brother. Johnnie was slumped in his saddle, held upright by the muscular arm of one of the Dalkeith men. Many another was in like case, including Archie of Cavers. Men of the third formation were now coming up, many of them also wounded. They made a grim company of perhaps eight hundred, survivors of eight thousand and more. Wattie Douglas was one of the last to join them, helmetless and bleeding.

Jamie raised a hoarse voice. "My friends," he called, "you did that passing well. I say you did that well. *We* live to fight again! This has been a sorry day. But . . . let us thank God for what we can."

There was a murmur through the ranks — although somewhere a man was gabbling hysterically, no doubt part-concussed.

"We are not out of trouble yet," he went on. "We are a long way from home, and many of us are hurt. The English, once they have recovered from their surprise, will be after us. We are in no state to do battle. Therefore, it seems, we must continue to ride — however sore a trial."

None commented.

"*My* sorest trial was, and is, leaving behind our wounded on yonder hill," he jerked stiffly, harshly. "I left two brothers there. But . . . we could do no other. We could by no means have won through that line burdened by grievously wounded men. We all know it. If anything was to be saved, it had to be this way."

Again the silence of unwilling assent.

"By the same token, we cannot go back there. Naught that we can do. They are more than ten times our number. It . . . it is a most grievous matter. To ride off, for home, and leave our friends in this fell place, hurt, dead or prisoner. But this is war. Many will escape the field, no doubt. Is there any here who can tell me any other course?"

No voice was raised, save that of Will Douglas of Drumlanrig. "Jamie — they are massing now. In the centre. I think they are coming after us."

"Aye. So be it. Time we were amove. We shall head north by west. Branxton lies west of Flodden Edge, I know, and Cornhill beyond Branxton. Tweed cannot be more than six miles. God with us, we can ford it at Wark or Coldstream. These English will not follow us beyond, I think — not this day . . ."

So they rode away from the Vale of Till and the sorriest defeat Scottish arms had suffered in over a century. They were followed, but warily, and by a company apparently not seeking to bring them to battle again, only to see them off English soil. In less than an hour, broad Tweed was gleaming before them, at Learmouth. Avoiding Cornhill village, they forded the river at Wark, their numbers sufficient to prevent any attack from the castle garrison there, their pursuers remaining almost a mile behind.

On Scots soil at last, Jamie turned and looked back. "We may go more gently now, Johnnie," he said. "And soon you may rest. Six more miles to Swinton. Is it bad?"

"Not so bad that I cannot make Swinton. Bearing but ill tidings."

"Ill, yes." He bit his lip. "Johnnie — did I do rightly, back there? Did I make the right choice, at Homildon?"

"Any right done this day, *you* did!" his brother said thickly. "James and Will would say the same. Now — let us on, for God's good sake!"

XX

IT WAS SOME days before Jamie stood before his father in the castle of Dalkeith, for he had had much to see to. He had waited on in the Merse, between Swinton and the Border, in case the English did decide to make a retaliatory raid, and to collect stragglers. He had bestowed the wounded in the nearby Abbeys of Kelso, Dryburgh and Melrose, where the monks were skilled in the healing arts. And, on his slow way northwards thereafter — for his brother Johnnie was in no state for riding fast or far — he had gone to inform Margaret, Countess of Douglas, the King's eldest daughter, at Dunbar Castle, of her husband's fate, but had found the princess gone elsewhere, with the news already preceding him. And so he had brought his brother home to Dalkeith at length, and now stood in the lord thereof's book-lined study, aware, as he had never been before, of being less than welcome there.

For the ill news had preceded him here also, and the old lord's fine features were cold, cold.

"So you have come!" he said stiffly, tightly, although there was just a hint of a quaver behind the strained voice. "I doubted whether you would dare. Aye, I doubted it."

"Why should I not, Father? To tell you of all, ill as it is? And to bring Johnnie home."

"Aye — to bring *Johnnie* home!" the other exclaimed. "Johnnie — your bastard brother! Him you saved. But what of James, my heir? And Will? My lawful sons! What of them? They were your brothers, too, were they not?"

"Yes. Yes, to be sure. But they . . . they went their own way. Johnnie was wounded . . ."

"They were wounded also, were they not? You left them there, on the field. Fallen. And you fled. Bringing back with you only the other bastard like yourself! And now come to tell me of the deed!"

Jamie drew a deep breath. "My lord — I believed that you would wish to hear how your sons fell. Bravely, if foolishly. But then, all was folly, at Homildon . . ."

"But *you* were wise — and turned tail!"

The young man opened his mouth, and shut it again, almost with a click. He turned, and strode to the window, to stare out, not trusting himself to speak.

"Tell me then, boy," the old man cried hoarsely. "Tell me what you have come to tell. Since you deemed it worth the coming."

Jamie turned back. "My lord — you are sore at heart, at your loss. But so am I, at mine. For I love my brothers. As I love you." That took some getting out, for this was not a man who talked of love and affection easily. "You have always shown love to *me*. Do not hurt yourself, and me, the more, by deeming me false. That I was not, I promise you. I may have made a mistake, many mistakes. But I was not false, nor craven. You know me, surely? I did not flee. I cut my way out. And saved near nine hundred. I did not *flee* from Homildon."

"Yet you came home safe. And left your brothers on the field. You, the most experienced, the warrior. And left your chief, the Earl of your name. You are not denying that?"

"Deny, no. The chief of our name is a fool. He mismanaged all, from the start. I was there to counsel him — he had sent for me, for that. Yet he would heed me nothing . . ."

"And because he was a fool and would not heed you, you deserted him? And your brothers?"

"No! How can I make you understand? The Earl's last command to me was to bide there on the hill-top. To see to the horses, left behind, and the residue of the force. That was folly, likewise — but it *was* his command. Not that I would not have disobeyed it, had there been cause. But he was leading the rest to disaster. Hopeless, inevitable disaster. Charging massed archers, with a valley between and a higher hill beyond. The veriest child should have known the outcome. I told him, but he would nowise heed. I sought to keep James and Will from following him — but they did not so much as answer me. The Earl ordered me to bide where I was, to see to the rearward and

375

the residue. Then dismounted, marched down with his main array, to fall under the arrows of thousands of bowmen. Should I, then, have followed on, to fall likewise, with the residue? None could ever have reached those archers on the hill."

"God knows, boy! But, as I heard it, you did go down. Later. When it was too late. Saved Drumlanrig and Cavers. But fled when the cavalry came up?"

"There is some truth in that, yes. I did not ride down, into the arrows, but round the hill. To come in from the far side. To seek save what I might. The bowmen had stopped shooting, were slaying and plundering. But the English cavalry were on their way up — we had seen them coming. We had only a little time. I had but some six hundred men then — against thousands. Many wounded — Johnnie amongst them. If we were to cut our way out, at all, it had to be done in good order, in tight wedges. We dared not be caught, scattered, beforehand. So that we did — and must needs leave the rest. Did I mistake?"

"You could have saved your brothers. And the Earl."

"I did not see where they lay. There were *thousands* dead and dying in that col! In the moments we had, would you have had me seek and search only for them? Leaving all others? Would my name have smelled the sweeter, then?"

His father ran a hand through his scanty hair. "I do not know. But this I do know — your name now stinks in the noses of honest men. And others! Notably the Governor's. For as well as your brothers, and Douglas, you left behind his precious son Murdoch Stewart, his heir. You returned, but Murdoch of Fife did not. For that he will not forgive you — and he mislikes you sufficiently already."

"I would have saved the Earl of Fife if I had seen him there before us. As any other. Would you have had me seek him out specially?"

"Not me, lad. But *Albany* would. And Albany rules this land, and with a heavy hand. I am told that decree is out for your arrest already, as craven and traitor! A son of mine . . .!"

"Dear God — traitor! Me, traitor? Any English slain at Homildon, *I* slew! Craven, because I cut my way through the enemy cavalry instead of falling helpless under their arrows without striking back? Is that Albany's judgement?"

"You left his son on the field. As you left your chief. There is no getting past that, boy. What think you the whole house of Douglas will call you now?"

"Surely not . . . ? Not Douglas! I saved many Douglases . . ."

"Not the right ones, it may be!"

"I will go tell them. Go round Douglas. Tell the truth . . ."

"That you will not, Jamie. Do you not understand? You are an outlaw. Decree out for your apprehension. By the Governor's personal warrant. Every man's hand is by law turned against you. None may aid you, an outlaw, under penalty of that same law. Douglas *might* have risked supporting you against Albany — but will not now. Albany has wanted you brought down, for long. Now he has you. You cannot bide here. Anyone sheltering an outlaw acts against the realm. Treason. And you have no Duke David to protect you now."

Shaken, Jamie stared at his father. "He can do that? On no more than ignorant hearsay?"

"To be sure he can. And will. You will have to go back whence you came — and swiftly. Back to the Hielands. Hide yourself with your friend Alexander Stewart. As before . . ."

"I would go there, anyway. Mary is there, and the children."

"Aye. But this time, not to come back! Not until your outlawry is lifted. Which could be years. Do you understand? Albany does not forgive."

They looked at each other in silence.

"James and Will?" Jamie said, at length. "Have you heard anything of them? Any sure tidings?"

"Yes. They are prisoners at Alnwick Castle. Both wounded but not grievously, thank God. Hotspur sent word. They are his prisoners. For ransom. As also is the Earl Archibald. He has lost an eye, and is otherwise wounded, but will live. The Percy demands large ransom. I have to collect it. He prices Douglas high!"

"The siller, gear, is the least of it."

"True. But it has its importance. We cannot overlook it, boy. As you have ever been apt to do. Lacking it, we should be a deal lesser men than we are! Mind it. And, Jamie — while we are on this of gear and property, I require something of you. I am sorry, lad — but it has to be. And you have brought it on yourself. I have a paper here for you to sign."

"A paper? Are you charging my brothers' ransom to *me*, because I did not bring them home?"

"Not that, no. I shall pay their ransom. This is otherwise." He rose stiffly, and went to a table, where he sought and found a paper. "This is a letter. From you, Jamie. Resigning to your

377

brother Johnnie all your lands, properties and titles whatsoever In the baronies of Aberdour, Stoneypath and Baldwinsgill. Given to you by myself at sundry times."

"What? *Resign?*" the younger man gasped. "Aberdour? My home! You cannot mean this . . .?"

"That I do, lad. It is necessary, see you. There is no other way."

"This . . . this I did not think of you, my lord!"

"Fool, boy — do you not see? An outlaw's whole property is forfeit. To the Crown. Albany will have it, nothing surer. This way, it will be in Johnnie's name, not yours. Safe. Who knows, one day you may get it back. But meantime, Albany will not get his hands on it."

"And Mary and our bairns are homeless! Penniless . . .!"

"You are that, anyway, so long as you are outlaw. Use your wits, Jamie. It is for the best."

Biting his lip, son stared at father. "I pay a price for coming south to give the Earl of Douglas counsel!" he said.

"The price is rather for your headstrong fight against the Duke of Albany, I think."

"A man you yourself despise and hate!"

"But have the wits not to cross unnecessarily! He is too strong for you, Jamie — too strong for me also. It is a wise man who knows his own strength and weakness. Now — sign you this..."

Heavy-hearted and heavy-handed, Jamie Douglas signed away his home, lairdships and status. Though they could not take away from him his knighthood, at least . . .

* * *

Jamie had proved, before this, that it was impossible to approach Lochindorb Castle in its Braemoray hills unannounced, with news relayed thither, from far and near, by means undisclosed but little short of wonderful to southern minds. On this occasion, now fully a month after Homildon, weary and dejected, with only a single groom as companion, he topped the long ridge of Creag an Righ to see the silvery gleam of the loch ahead, it was to see also three horsed figures riding up through the heather towards him, and all beginning to wave at sight of him. His heart warmed as it had not done for many a day, as he spurred to meet them.

They met in a welter of incoherences, throwing themselves from their mounts to embrace and exclaim, to laugh and hug

378

and cling, Mary and their two children and the travel-stained fugitive reunited at last. The groom discreetly held back and looked away.

It was some time before any sense was spoken — although Mary had the name of being an eminently sensible young woman. But eventually the emotional tide ebbed a little, and they could look at each other in more rational fashion.

"You are thin, Jamie," she charged. "My dear, my dear, you look but poorly."

"And you, my love, look more beautiful than ever, I swear! And these two, grown, on my soul! Larger, taller. Or do my eyes deceive me?"

"It must be your eyes, I think," the practical David said. "For we cannot have grown much in but three months, see you."

"Three months? Only that since I left? Save us — it seems a lifetime!"

"Has it been so bad, Jamie?" Mary asked, holding him to her. "Was it all a great evil? I am so thankful to know you safe and see you back to us, that I can think of little else."

"It was bad. All of it, from start to finish. How much have you heard?"

"But little. Only that there was a great defeat. In England. That the Douglas fell, and Angus with him. Indeed the flower of Scotland lost . . ."

"But that *I* came out with a whole skin! Left the field, and home in safety! All Scotland rings with that word, today!"

Troubled, she looked at him searchingly. "We heard only that you had escaped — thank God! Amongst the few. No more."

"Albany would be sore disappointed! He expects better than that from his whisperers, I warrant!"

"What do you mean, Jamie?"

"I mean, my dear, that the land is loud with your husband's infamy and treachery! Or the Lowlands are — where Albany's word reaches. I am the man who deserted the others, ran off the stricken field, leaving better men to their fate. Rode for home in haste, leaving his chief, even his own brothers, to the English spleen."

"None who know you would believe a word of that!"

"No? Then many know me less well than I had thought. My own father, it seems. *He* blames me. For bringing home only

379

another bastard and leaving his heir, and Will, on Homildon Hill."

At the bitterness in his voice Mary drew a deep breath and glanced at the children. Noting her look, he changed his tone, nodding.

"To be sure. I am tired, hungry. They say that an empty belly gives but a poor report. Let us down to that kindly Stewart table, then."

As they remounted and set off, he asked, "Alex and his mother — how are they?"

"Sir Alex has been fighting the Islesmen," the boy informed. "There have been battles and burnings. But he won. You would have been better here."

"So-o-o! Donald did strike, then?"

"Yes," Mary confirmed. "Not himself. He sent Alastair Carrach again."

"And Drummond? Did Drummond join him? What of Drummond?"

Mary hesitated. "I shall tell you later. It is a long story."

At her tone, he glanced at her quickly. Again her eyes went to the children.

"Aye," he said. "Time enough for that. What is important is that all is well with you here?"

"Yes. All is well, now that you are back. It has been an anxious time. Still may be. But — so long as you are here, the rest we can thole. Alex is still chasing Islesmen back to their Isles. Mariota will welcome you . . ."

They came to the shore of Lochindorb and were ferried over to the castle-island. It seemed a secure haven indeed to the man who had travelled furtively two hundred miles to reach it.

Later, with the children safely out of hearing, they sat in Mariota's own chamber before an aromatic birch-log fire, at ease in body at least.

"This of the Islesmen?" he enquired. "It was all as Alex feared?"

"Yes. The death of the Earl of Ross, and Albany's assumption of the heiress's wardship ensured it," Mariota said. "A great fleet of galleys landed in Moidart, where MacDonald is kin to Clanranald. They crossed the land swiftly. Inverness they burned. They turned south for Forres and Elgin, harrying, slaying. There Alex caught up with them, with a Highland host, in the main Clan Chattan, and defeated them — but not before

380

Alastair had burned much of Elgin and the canons' houses. He chases them still."

"Aye. That is Alex! And Drummond? Did Drummond not rise, after all?"

There was a pause. "Drummond could not rise. Because Drummond was dead!"

"Dead!" He stared. "What is this?"

"Drummond was slain. And I fear that Alex will get the blame for it."

"Save us — not that! That is not Alex's style."

"No. But still he is like to be blamed. We do not know all of it. Or much. Alex has not been back here since it happened. When he heard of Alastair Carrach's landing, he sent a small force under three of his brothers to watch Drummond, whilst he gathered the main force to halt the Islesmen. Drummond was taken, in some fashion, whilst riding in Brae-Mar. Captured and held in some lonely house in the mountains. And there given neither food nor drink. He died . . . of starvation!"

"Merciful God! Starvation — Drummond! The same death as David!"

"The same death as David," the woman repeated, level-voiced. "And not by chance, I fear. You will see, therefore, why Alex may well be blamed."

"But . . . but . . . who did it?"

The mother of five sons shook her handsome head. "We do not know. None have been back to Lochindorb since. We cannot tell who, or why. Save that it was not Alex's work. That I know well."

Jamie looked from Mariota to Mary and back. "This is beyond all! I can well see what his enemies will make of it. And the Countess . . .?"

"We have no word of that accursed woman! Who knows what her part will be? Or was?"

That was not like Mariota de Athyn, a generous and friendly soul. Her hearers could understand, however. For even though it was not Alex, it looked as though one or other of her sons had done this terrible deed. And she had always hated Alex's entanglement with Isobel of Mar.

"She would have no part in this, any more than Alex," Jamie asserted hurriedly. "What of Drummond's people? Have they risen? In wrath?"

"Not that we have heard."

381

"You would have heard if they had, I think! The Drummonds are a potent clan. Alex will have to counter this, clear his name. And he is in the West? Would that I had never left his side."

"Amen to that!" Mary said. "What went wrong, Jamie? With *your* venture?"

"All was wrong, from the start. The Earl Archibald is no commander, no soldier at all. Nor those near him. He could not, or would not, control his men. Brave enough, yes — but more than that is required of a general."

"But he knew all that, did he not? And sent for you to advise him?"

"Sent for me, yes — but did not heed me." Unhappily, Jamie went on to describe for them something of the follies of that ill-conceived campaign, and its aftermath.

"Mother of God!" Mary cried. "But at least there was no blame for you in all this?"

"But I *am* being blamed. Do you not see? I am the survivor, the one who got away. Ran away! The man of experience, who saved himself."

Unhappily she considered him. "Jamie — this is not like you. To care what others say."

"I care what my father says . . ."

"A man can only do what he deems right, at the time," Mariota declared. "What he thinks of later is nothing to the point."

"You could say that of the Earl of Douglas also! He chose the wrong course, whilst no doubt deeming it right. Perhaps *I* chose wrongly? I chose to save something, a remainder, eight hundred and seventy men. It may be that the better part would have been to go and fall with the others?"

"*I* thank the good God you so chose!" his wife said fervently. "And you are safe here, at least — where Robert's writ does not run . . ."

"God Almighty!" he burst out. "Can you not see? Even you! It is not safety I seek, but, but . . ." With a great effort he controlled himself. "I am sorry, lass. Forgive me. I am weary, scarce myself. Some sleep, and I shall be a better man. Give me a little time . . ."

"Time indeed, Jamie — all the time you need, my dear. And the love, affection, peace you need also. I think that *you* were wounded in this sorry battle, as sore as any! These you shall have, in good measure, I vow!"

"Yes — but the safety too," Mariota insisted. "You may not seek it, my friend, but you shall have it, in this house and country. That *I* vow!"

He looked from one to the other. "Forgive me," he said again. "I do not deserve it, but I see that I am rich indeed. When, in my self-pity, I esteemed myself poor, penniless, a beggar indeed . . ."

Mary laughed, if with a catch in it. "Scarcely a beggar, Jamie? Sir James Douglas of Aberdour, Stoneypath and Baldwinsgill!"

"No longer of Aberdour, Stoneypath and Baldwinsgill, lass. My father prevailed on me to sign all these away. To Johnnie. *He* is laird of all, now. Lest Albany take them, as the property of an outlaw — as my father says he most certainly would. Albany now rules all unchallenged, with not even the power of Douglas to restrain him. The rewards of unwearied evil-doing! My noble sire has a great respect for property, and would not see it forfeited for my . . . failures. So all is now Johnnie's."

"Aberdour? Our home . . .!"

"Our home, lass, I fear is now wherever your outlawed husband can find shelter for his wife and bairns! I have, all along supported the wrong — or leastways, the *losing* side — in this your royal brother's Scotland. And now you and our children must pay the penalty. The truer riches you provide for me are to my much advantage. But, for yourself, I fear they offer but doubtful exchange for a roof, bed and victual! You wed the wrong man, my dear."

"I think otherwise. Besides, your father will give you back your lands when all this trouble is past, will he not?"

"There is no certainty of that. And he is old, and may not live so long. His heir, once ransomed, may feel less than grateful to his bastard brother who left him lying on Homildon Hill."

"I care not. We shall do very well, I swear. Turn Hieland, and make a new life for ourselves . . ."

"Yes, start anew," Mariota agreed strongly. "Put the past behind you. As, I fear, Alex will have to do also. He will not be able to remain acting Justiciar, I think. That was possible so long as the Highland chiefs supported him. But now, with *An Drumanach Mor*'s death hanging over him, the Clan Donald his enemies, and Albany controlling the earldom of Ross, it would be difficult indeed. Besides, knowing Alex, he will wish to have no part in it until his name is cleared. So . . . you both must make a fresh start. And if you do it together, hold to each other, I have no doubts for either. You will make a pair hard to beat

Jamie — Douglas and Stewart. With, between you, what is best in both. I am no spaewife, but I foresee great things for you if you hold together. Fear you nothing and none, lad, Albany, Donald or other. You have all that is required to beat them." She rose, and came to kiss him frankly on the lips. "Now — to your bed. And tomorrow start afresh, Sir James and Lady Douglas!"